1 7

# Learn Love in a Week

Andrew Clover is a Writer/Actor/Dad (a WAD). He's got a wife and three kids and his life changed five years ago when his 'Dad Rules' column in the *Sunday Times* became a big hit. But apart from that, he's absolutely nothing like the hero of this story. Got that? Good. Now read the book . . .

# Learn Love in a Week

## ANDREW CLOVER

CENTURY

Published by Century 2013

2 4 6 8 10 9 7 5 3 1

First published in Great Britain in 2013 by Century,
Random House, 20 Vauxhall Bridge Road,
London SW1V 2SA

www.randomhouse.co.uk

Addresses for companies within The Random House Group Limited can
be found at: www.randomhouse.co.uk/offices.htm

The Random House Group Limited Reg. No. 954009

A CIP catalogue record for this book
is available from the British Library

ISBN 9781780891187

The Random House Group Limited supports The Forest Stewardship
Council (FSC®), the leading international forest certification organisation.
Our books carrying the FSC label are printed on FSC® certified paper.
FSC is the only forest certification scheme endorsed by the leading
environmental organisations, including Greenpeace.
Our paper procurement policy can be found at:
www.rbooks.co.uk/environment

Printed and bound by CPI Group (UK) Ltd, Croydon, CR0 4YY

# Sunday

## Polly

I first saw Arthur at college.

He swooped past the library on a bike, and he looked happy and so handsome that my heart skipped. 'Who's that?' I said. 'That's Arthur Midgley,' said Em.

I next saw him at a party in a field. It was dawn. I was by the bonfire, waiting on a lift home, when Arthur appeared and we talked. He was tall and he had a hat and a passionate look in his eye. 'You are without doubt,' he said suddenly, 'the most beautiful woman I've ever seen.' I was astonished. I felt like doors were being opened. Clothes were being ripped off. But my lift arrived, so I said: 'I'll . . . see you soon!'

I didn't see him for four more years.

It was in London. I was twenty-four. I was sitting outside Bar Italia, and he just sat down beside me and we talked. I'd just started at JTS, he was at the RSC, everything felt fun and romantic and right. As he walked off I admired his big friendly frame and I thought: Arthur Midgley, I want to know *everything* about you.

And now, ten years on, we have three children, and . . . *I do*.

He leaves earplugs by the bed. He leaves his big tent-sized boxer shorts on the radiator. He's moody. He has a friend called Malcolm. He doesn't earn much money. He seems to have a phobia about emptying bins. And he supports Arsenal.

Now . . .

Obviously you can't *chuck* a man, just because he supports Arsenal. But recently I got the news that every wife dreads: my husband felt inspired, he announced, to write a novel. It's called *Looking For Lost Magic*. It's a teen novel about a sixteen year old who's the reincarnation of King Arthur. Em said: 'Sounds like the sort of thing teenage boys like to read.' 'Teenage boys don't like to read,' I said. 'They like to wank.' She said: 'Is that fair?'

The whole relationship isn't fair! That's the point!

OK. Give him his due . . . He looks after the kids from 3.30, every day bar Friday. But I pay the mortgage. I pay the electricity, I pay the home insurance, I pay the car insurance, I arrange the holidays. What does he do? Erm . . . He walks the dog, and it's he who, when necessary, showers her bottom. Anything pet-related he does (apart from vet's bills and pet insurance). That aside, he does nothing. OK, he's big and good-looking, though not actually as strong as he looks. He's the IKEA wardrobe of husbands. He looks good in the pictures, but if you ask him to hold anything, his back pops out.

He is still, however, the father of my three children, and obviously I love him very much. But then this happens . . .

**Em**

It's a Sunday evening in late-May. We're at a party in the garden at Polly's mum's.

I'm probably drinking faster than I should. No one is paying any attention to me at this party, which is partly because I am next to Polly. (Polly thinks she's getting pear-shaped; she's still 5' 10" and almost supernaturally beautiful.) And I've had a nightmare of a weekend with Dan, which I'm *trying* not to think about.

But Polly says: 'How was the trip with Dan?'

Right away, I'm feeling panicky. 'I can't discuss anything that involves Dan,' I say. 'Or there is a very real chance I may lose it, and the next thing you know I'll be taking hostages at the bus stop.'

Polly smirks.

'Tell me,' she says. 'Do you love him?'

'Really,' I say, 'I cannot discuss it now.' I'm not trying to be dramatic. I'm the editor of *Lifestyle*, the features section of the *London Times*. I'm supposed to be at the office tomorrow morning, filled with ideas for five editions packed with advice and features. It's Sunday night. I've got nothing. I need ideas. Quick.

'How's Arthur?' I ask Polly.

She rolls her eyes.

'His friend Malcolm,' she says, 'is trying to persuade him to do that online course – *Learn Love in a Week*.'

'I've not heard of that,' I say.

'It's a massive trend, apparently,' she says. 'Loads of people are doing it.'

Obviously my ears prick up like a hare's, at the mention of a massive trend.

'What do you have to do?'

'Each day you read advice, then you have to do an exercise, then a challenge. Apparently it's changing people's lives.'

'Who runs the course?' I say.

'Nobody knows,' she says. 'I think it's someone in California. Apparently they're determined to stay anonymous.'

I like the idea of that even more.

'Why are you grinning?' asks Polly.

'If they want to stay anonymous,' I say, 'then they won't sue me if I nick the idea for *Lifestyle*.'

And I get straight into action.

## Polly

I wish I hadn't mentioned it.

I've managed to keep Em off the subject of work for five minutes. She's now furiously typing into her phone. As usual she's showing off far too much cleavage, and the tops of her tits are wibbling.

'Are you signing up for the course?' I enquire.

'No!' she says, looking aghast. 'I'm getting someone to write about it. What do you think of Alain de Botton?'

'You could try Arthur,' I say.

She finishes her message, then looks up. 'Lovely Arthur,' she says, a bit mistily. Weirdly, Em rather fancies Arthur. She fancies anything that's mine. 'Would you say you love him at the moment?'

'We've been together ten years,' I say. 'My exact feelings are somewhat buried.'

'Why don't you dig down and find them?'

'That'll be like striking oil,' I say. 'I'll let loose a great spume of Resentment, then a few million gallons of sheer Rage, then a little jet of Lust for bad men.'

'So this is a good question,' says Em, turning up her irresistible journalist charm to full effect. She leans her breasts towards me and flashes her minxy eyes. 'What do you resent most about coming home to him?'

'He's grumpy,' I say. 'He's messy. He contributes nothing. Apart from that, he's a dream.'

Em smiles. 'I thought he was writing a book,' she says.

'He *is* writing a book,' I affirm. 'His last one earned him eight grand. He also does stand-up comedy, occasionally. He sometimes does cartoons. In fact, if there's a job that's erratic and poorly paid, he probably does it. He recently earned eighty pounds by walking round Battersea Park dressed as a Snapple bottle. Some kids threw him in a pond, where he was attacked by a swan. "Why didn't you get away?" I said. "It's not easy to get away," he said, "when you're in a big inflatable costume, and the swan's already pecked your lid!"'

**Em**

I laugh at this.

See . . . this is why I like Arthur. He's very funny. OK, I can see he's not for everyone. He's very clever and, like a lot of bright people, he's completely without cunning. He blunders through life being honest, which obviously upsets people. But he gives excellent advice. I always call him when I need a male POV. He's also six foot three and gorgeous. I tried to get off with him when we were students. Everyone did. At college, he was our Brad Pitt, he was our Hugh Grant: he was the one everyone wanted.

'*I'd* like to write a book,' says Polly. 'I'd really love to be designing gardens. But we have children and a gigantic overdraft so I have to work. Which means I subsidise Arthur, by working in a boring office where men in bad suits talk about "hitting the ground running".'

'Arthur is very talented,' I tell her. 'I'm sure his luck will change.'

'I can't take it!' she protests.

I give Polly a sympathetic look, while I reach for another drink. They're bloody good, these drinks. I think I've had six now.

'Come on, darling,' I say. 'You must see that Arthur is a sexy hunk of a man, that any woman would want.'

Polly's lip starts twitching. 'Well, right now,' she says, 'they can have him. But they'll need a truck to remove his big pants.'

We both laugh.

And it's *at this very moment* that her mum comes over with James Hammond.

Polly's mum is parading James round like he's a trophy. Fair enough. He looks like Dominic West. He's swarthy and masculine and just slightly simian. I have met him before actually. We did a big feature on him when he won Businessman of the Year. We had a cover of James and Tatyana Hammond. He was dressed up in normal businessman clothes – black leather lace-up shoes, blue pinstripe suit – but he looked naughty and unshaven, and he was leaning against a seaplane. The shout-line read: 'James Hammond – Why Business is the New Rock 'n' Roll'.

## Polly

I see James and immediately I feel deeply uneasy. He is the last man I dated, before Arthur. He is my Road Not Taken.

I met him ten years ago, in a Bond Street gallery . . .

It was lunchtime. (I was young. I did stuff like visit galleries at lunchtime.) I love how you can step in off the street and stand in front of a painting that's worth hundreds of thousands of pounds. I love how, for a moment, you're staring at the world through the eyes of a great artist. And I was there, enjoying that, when the man beside me stepped forward to examine the brushwork. Meanwhile I examined how his dark blue suit clung to his broad back. I examined his buttocks, which were unusually pert. The buttocks moved left. I moved left.

Now we were both standing before David Inshaw's 'The Cricket Game.' There's not much to it, as a painting. There're cricketers of course, and also some trees, and some banks of soft green grass. But the whole scene is glowing with this heavenly yellow light. I've never seen a painting I so longed to be in. I actually sighed. And the man said: 'Why is that so pleasing?' And I said: 'It just looks so warm and magical, you can't imagine anything bad could happen there.' 'Yup,' said the man. 'I couldn't improve on that.' 'To be honest,' I said, 'I'd lose the cricketers. If I see a glorious scene, I don't instantly think: What this scene needs is a load of men standing round doing nothing. If I wanted that, I'd visit the House of Lords.' I thought that was rather funny, but the man didn't laugh. He just turned and looked at me, very directly. We shared a moment which was half uncomfortable, half electric. I noticed his square jaw, his expensive aftershave. 'Do you want to get a coffee?' said James Hammond.

We had one date.

He picked me up at my flat, and he took me to Nobu. I don't remember what we talked about. I do remember that, the next day, he invited me to a party that was going to happen that weekend, in Bologna.

I refused. Why did I refuse? (Why? *Why?!*)

I said no because I had a date with Arthur, which was not in Bologna. It was at the Battersea Arts Centre. (I've got vague memories of a squeezebox, and some mime.) And at the end of that evening, I went back to Arthur's flat. I was young: his flat seemed arty. It had books scattered everywhere (Kerouac, Coleridge, Neruda). It had a big bed with a lamp made from a bottle, and, on that bed, I kissed Arthur. I also lifted up his shirt. I saw his muscular stomach. I pulled down his jeans. He broke off. I said: 'What?' He said: 'I . . . I . . .' I've never felt so impatient. I said: '*What*??!!' He said: 'I have no . . . condoms.' 'Just . . . Just . . . come here,' I said. And I pulled him towards me.

By next morning, I was pregnant.

Which is why, ever since then, I've been condemned to stay with a messy failed actor, while my Road Not Taken has slowly turned into James Hammond – entrepreneur, hotelier, *Lifestyle*'s Businessman of the Year.

## Em

James is staring at Polly. It's like he's trying to take in everything. He wants to Hoover up each detail. I'm feeling quite a strong desire to place myself between them. Hello! I want to say. I'm here too!

## Polly

I admit it.

I've thought about him so much in the last few years, and I realise that the James Hammond in my mind is not quite the same as the one before me. He still looks like a boxer – the muscular torso, the thrilling sense of raw power. But he's got on a pink shirt and an orange tie. He looks more foppish than I remember. He also looks softer, kinder. I recall reading about the charities he's subsidised.

'It's amazing I should see you now,' says James. 'I've finally bought it.'

'What?' I say.

'Remember the Inshaw?'

'*You bought that painting*?!' I say. I'm trying not to sound too impressed, but my voice does go squeaky.

'No,' he says. 'I do have several Inshaws actually, but, no, not that one. I bought the place he painted – the fields and green hills. It's in Wiltshire.'

'Really?!' I say. I'm now staring at Hammond with an almost cretinous sense of wonder. 'And . . .' I say. 'What's it like?'

'Spectacular,' he says. 'To be honest, I think Inshaw cocked up.'

'Inshaw cocked up?!'

'Yeah! If he'd only moved his easel back a bit, he could have got something really special into the picture.'

'What?'

'Bodsham Abbey. It's a huge monastery constructed in the early thirteenth century. It's probably the most beautiful place on the planet.'

'Really?!' I say. 'You think so?'

'I know so,' says James. 'That's why I bought it.'

'Really??!!' I say. 'You bought a mediaeval monastery?'

'Yeah,' says James, and, for a moment, he smirks with pride like a boy who's got a new bike.

'But,' I say, 'where are the monks?'

'They moved out five hundred years ago. The place was a ruin, which I've done up.'

'Oh,' I say. I'm marvelling at this man's insouciance. He rebuilt a mediaeval manor. We spent four years pondering a loft extension. 'What are you going to do with it?'

'Turn it into a hotel,' he says. 'The guests will sleep in the Abbot's House, unless they want their own cottage. The grounds contain almshouses and stables and about thirty acres enclosed within a high stone wall. And if you look over the wall, you see the green hills Inshaw painted.'

**Em**

While James is talking, Polly is staring at him dreamily.

'Don't!' She says

'What?' says James.

I explain it to him. 'Property,' I say, 'is the new porn.'

**Polly**

That's nonsense actually. Property is *far* more exciting than *anything* involving men. If you had a mediaeval house beside a soft green hill dotted with oak trees, you could rely on that for ever. A man could never give that degree of comfort. Even if you got George Clooney, the day would come when he would ask you to pull his finger while he farted. But obviously that's how I feel. I live in a three-bed suburban semi decorated with smears and princess stickers. While James is talking, it's not *him* that I want, it's his hotel. I want to go there. I want a glimpse into his life. I've followed his career the way teenagers follow pop stars. His life is a ball to which I could never dream of being invited.

But then he says: 'We're having a launch party on Friday to give the hotel its formal opening. Why don't you come?'

I can't believe it. He actually wants me to come. For a moment I'm not a thirty-five-year-old woman with fat knees and tattered dreams. I'm twenty-four again, and everything is possible.

'Let me think about that,' I say. That's all I ever say. Why can't I be spontaneous, ever?

He takes me in some more. I think that's what makes him

so sexy. He just seems so interested. 'Polly Pankhurst,' he says, 'what are you doing in your life?'

I spend most of my days hunting behind the sofa for shoes. Shall I say that?

'I'm rebranding Head and Shoulders,' I say. 'It's not for dandruff. It's for baldness. It's a *thrilling* campaign, and it's absorbed me for two years now.'

This isn't good. I'm sounding sour as old milk.

'What do you want to do?' he says. I've noticed this about the super-rich. They're always very in touch with what they *want*.

'Well,' I say. 'I'd *like* to design gardens.'

'Really?' he says eagerly.

'I've actually just done a Garden Design course. I *loved* it.' (I read that, if you want to be attractive, talk about what you love. And it's true – unless, like Arthur, you love Arsenal.)

'I need a designer for Bodsham,' says James. 'There's a ten-acre meadow, that we've done nothing with. Come to the launch, you can advise.'

'Well, I'd *love* to do that!' I say.

'I'd pay your normal fee, of course,' says James.

'My fee?'

'For consulting on the meadow.'

'Oh, yes,' I say, trying to sound professional. What is my fee? Five hundred? Three hundred? We owe that much for the campsite. They've asked me for it three times. 'How much do people normally charge?'

'Eight hundred?' says Hammond. 'Would that be enough?'

For that money you could have me too. I don't say that. I just say: 'Yes.'

'Wonderful,' he says. 'So you can come?'

'Erm,' I say. Friday is supposed to be my childcare day. I'm about to say I'll need to check if Arthur will be happy to look after the kids. (Obviously Arthur would never be happy; I need to check he's doing it.)

And then Hammond says: 'It'd be great if you could come. Tatyana's just left. I'd love some good company.'

Oh. My. God.

As I look, slightly startled, into James's manly face, I realise how ordinary my life has become. Normally when people talk to me, they propose playdates, they propose amendments to the text of the copy. I'm pretty sure he's just proposed sex.

Albeit in front of my mum.

She has turned away discreetly and is examining the canapés. Although Mum has a craving for sexual attention which I find positively needy, she always pretends to be innocent.

'That's such a kind offer,' I say. 'Let me think what I'm doing.'

But then Em says: 'Oh, you've *got* to go. We'll go down together.'

'Are *you* going?!' I ask her.

'Of course I'm coming,' she says, giving James the full breast/eyelash treatment. 'I think Bodsham Abbey is about to become *Lifestyle*'s favourite hotel.'

And then *my mum* says: 'Oh, you simply *must* go, Polly!' which really takes me by surprise. My mum was once an MP. She is an obsessive, relentless networker, but even I am surprised by the way she's prodding me towards the monkey man like a piece of meat. '*Why* don't you go?' she says.

'Well . . .' I begin. What am I going to say? 'Cos I have a husband? 'Cos I have *kids*? I don't want to say anything. I want this rich, gorgeous man to fancy me, just a moment longer.

'I'll help you out,' says Mum, in her sweet fake voice.

This is more surprising still. During my childhood, Mum was a committed feminist. It was a matter of dogma for her that she should not devote all her attention to her children. Or really any of it. Has my mum *really* just offered to do childcare?

But I don't want to discuss childcare in front of James.

I don't know what to say. I resolve it by pulling a card out of my breast pocket. 'James,' I say, 'could you ask one of your helpers to call me tomorrow? I'll have my diary.'

At this point James and I look at each other a beat too long. It feels like an admission.

He says: 'I will.'

Throughout this whole exchange no less than four women have been circling behind him like wasps after jam, but Hammond has concentrated on me. It's been almost steely, the way he's given me his total attention. But now the youngest buzzes forward. She's an offensively beautiful waif, who looks about sixteen.

'*Dad*!' she says. 'We've *really* got to go!'

James gives an apologetic smile. 'I'll call you,' he says, and he goes.

And as he does, the fun of the party seems to go too. The champagne is now flat. The pastries are now soggy. And I'm once again a suburban mum, who really should be home for bathtimes.

**Em**

As soon as Polly's gone, I take a drink to the bottom of the garden, and I start reading . . .

*Learn Love in a Week* – *the online course that will change your life*

**Day One**: I like to ask couples: 'What is the secret to staying in love?' The most common answer is: 'Well . . . it does take a lot of work!' This is not inspiring to the middle-aged romantic. That's what I need, we think, more work! Nobody says what the work involves, but the dark hint is that it may involve Couples Therapy – a prospect which strikes fear into the heart of the modern man. The man knows that, if he goes to Couples Therapy, he will be like Muhammad Ali being beaten round the face by George Foreman. And he knows that after a few hours of that, there's a danger he will start to talk. And then his lady will *never* forgive him.

Most couples don't need more work, I say. They need more play.

**Today's exercise**: write for ten minutes, as fast as you can, beginning with the words 'I love . . .' Be specific, be *playful*. Thus you will unearth your buried desires, and you'll start to make them happen.

**Today's challenge**: do something for fun.

Actually I do rather like that. I definitely want to do pieces on this. Alain de Botton's not got back to me. So I call Arthur.

It takes him bloody ages to pick up.

'Arthur darling,' I say.

'Hello, Em!' he says.

'I've got a work thing I'd love to ask you about. You know *Learn Love in a Week*?'

'Yup,' he says. 'My friend Malcolm wants me to do it. You've got to do exercises apparently.'

'Have you done today's?'

'I've done exercise,' he declares. 'We danced to "Chiquitita" eight times.'

'Chiquitita?'

'Our favourite ABBA song. It's got an oompah bit in the middle, where we all go mental. Malory . . .'

At this point I cut him off. People with children are always under the illusion that their lives are interesting. I find that must be contested at all times.

'Instead of writing,' I suggest, 'why don't you do the exercise on the phone? It's basically all about love.'

'Right.'

'Do you love Polly?'

'Yes,' he says, straight away.

'And . . .' I say. 'Could you expatiate? *What* do you love about her?'

'I love her arms,' he says. 'I love her smirky top lip. I love the little cigar box where she keeps her stamps. I love the leather armchair she found in a junk shop. I love her enthusiasms – the way she loves bean pods, and soups. I love her voice. I love the smell of her neck. I love her.'

'And,' I say, 'do you tell her you love her?'

'No.'

'Why?'

'She'd take advantage. "I love you," I'd say. "Great," she'd say. "So can you mow the lawn? And then can you go to the upstairs cupboard? Could you please throw out the box of Arsenal programmes, half of your stinky suits, and every garment bought

[ 17 ]

by your mum? Then . . . for the next month, could you please take care of everything? I shall be away, drinking wine."'

'And does Polly say she loves you?'

'If she's leaving on a big business trip, she might text from the airport. Otherwise no.'

I feel a bit sorry for Arthur suddenly. I asked Polly if she loved him, and she said her feelings were buried like oil. I asked Arthur what he loved, and he gave me a list.

'Sounds a bit sad, doesn't it?' he says. 'What am I supposed to do about it?'

'You're supposed to play something.'

He sighs. 'I've spent the whole day playing.'

'What have you played?'

'I've played with Barbies, as per usual. Sarah (that's the blonde one with the chewed hand) got married to Aladdin (the Disney doll with one leg). There was a lengthy service (conducted by Gruffalo). Then there was a ball, in which we all danced, in a succession of costumes. That's where "Chiquitita" came in.'

'Sounds like you need to play something you like playing.'

'Sounds like I need to drink a large quantity of beer,' he says. 'But I can't do that till I've got them in the bath.'

## Arthur

It takes me bloody ages to get them in the bath. Then it takes ages more to get them out. They sit there like infant trades unionists, refusing to budge. I finally get them out, after bringing them milk, Cheerios, and Marmite soldiers. And that was after lengthy negotiation. At one point Ivy said she wasn't moving unless she got a puppy.

I'm now downstairs.

I can't be bothered to clear up quite yet. I generally prepare for Polly's arrival by cleaning as if I'm one of Cleopatra's slaves who's cleaning to save his life. I think that's what she wants. But today she's at a party. And Em told me I'm supposed to play something.

I sit down at the kitchen table, which is still covered with paper and pens. (There was a lengthy art session, in which we all drew the dolls' wedding gifts.) I figure I could draw something for my own amusement. But what? What amuses me?

Ooh. I know . . .

I'm rereading the biography of Alma Mahler – wife of Gustav, the great composer. The Mahlers live in Vienna, in 1900, a fantastic time. Freud is inventing psychoanalysis. Schopenhauer is inventing a new kind of radical music which will be atonal, and shit. And, one night, on a thronging staircase at a party, Alma meets the other great Gustav – Gustav Klimt, the painter. Klimt presses Alma against a wall. He stares into her eyes. 'There is only one thing for it,' he says. 'Complete physical union.'

I love that.

And I'm going to do a cartoon of Klimt, uttering his immortal line. I've tried to draw him before, but I've never quite captured it. Drawing him again – that would qualify as play. I'll do it now.

I open a Hoegaarden beer. I draw the basic Klimt . . .

I'm quite pleased with him, but this Klimt looks rather mild. He looks like a sex pest, as depicted in a Mr Man book. Mr Clammy. So then I do another one, making him much more impressive and artistic . . .

Again . . . I'm quite pleased. Actually, I could do a Klimt t-shirt. But this Klimt looks fierce, I decide, rather than passionate. So then I try to do another one who's more sensitive and creative, but he just comes out a bit gay . . .

That looks like an out-of-work actor auditioning as Klimt. This Klimt would smell of hair dye and frustrated ambition. If he's an actor, he must be a great one. I try to imagine Klimt as played by Johnny Depp. But he just comes out a bit small . . .

Perhaps I'm being too tentative. Klimt lived in a different age. He produced mighty passionate work: he wouldn't have to feel guilty he'd left a cloth in the sink. I draw another Klimt, making him magnificent and powerful.

But this Klimt just looks like Hitler.

It's not surprising, I suddenly realise, that Polly doesn't say she loves me. I can't even imagine a man who a woman would find attractive.

By now it's nearly 10. I've drunk a heroic amount of Hoegaarden beer, and the table is covered with tiny Gustav Klimts who are all urgently shouting the same message at me. It's a cacophony of Germanic voices. Some are intense and breathy, some are loud and hysterical. They all give the same instruction: *'There is only one thing for it: complete physical union.'*

At this point Polly arrives.

She stands in the kitchen doorway looking gorgeous and slightly drunk. She's in that state of inebriation when you feel quietly pleased with yourself, like you've just won ten arguments and you'd be just *delighted* to have another. I smile. I approach her. I put my hands around her waist. Then I try the line: 'There is only one thing for it,' I say, 'complete physical union.'

'No way,' she says archly. 'You stink of beer, and we need to talk about Friday.'

I flinch at that.

I'd love to discuss Klimt, or what makes men attractive. But as far as Polly's concerned, the subject of men can wait. But scheduling – that can't. The schedule waits for no man. What I can't take about marriage is all the bloody admin.

I take a deep breath and start clearing up my pens.

## Polly

I've just come home. Already he's huffing and puffing. *Already* he's slightly grumpy.

I know what it is I hate most about coming home . . .

There is a fruit bowl by the fridge in which he piles all the things he wants me to deal with. It has bills, buttons, bike lights, dental floss, phone chargers, letters from the school, Barbie dolls that are missing half their limbs, and some mouldy pears. That fruit bowl is an image of my life. It is buried under a confusion of admin. It contains things it should not. And I have asked Arthur to deal with it about twelve times. He hasn't.

I notice there's something new on top of it. It's a letter from France. That'll be the campsite, asking again for their deposit.

'What are you doing on Friday?' I ask.

'Writing,' he says.

'The thing is,' I say, 'I've just met James Hammond.'

'James Hammond?' he says. 'That City boy who wanted to shag you?'

'He's not a City boy!' I say. 'He's a businessman. He owns about sixty high-end hotels.'

'Right,' says Arthur, and tips an empty beer bottle to his mouth.

'And he's launching one this Friday,' I say. 'He said I should come.'

'So he can shag you?'

'So I can advise him on the garden.'

Now Arthur looks astonished.

'Is that . . . a commission?' he says.

'Well, I don't think he's promising to do my design. But he'd pay me to go and advise.'

'How much would he pay?'

'Eight hundred quid!'

'Eight hundred?!!' says Arthur. He's grinning delightedly. We're both smiling.

'I wanted to say . . . for that money, you could have me as well!'

'For that money, he could have *me* as well! He could clamber on and he could thrust for victory.'

[ 23 ]

'I don't think he'd pay for that,' I say happily. 'But I would.'

Arthur smiles. I look into his eyes. Suddenly I feel something I've not felt for a while: I feel light and happy and just slightly horny.

'So,' I say. 'Are you happy to look after the kids?'

'Of course!'

I feel so overjoyed that, for once, he has made this easy. And I press my lips to his, and I snog him.

## Arthur

I'm so not into that.

We've been together ten years now. I have the libido of the Giant Panda. I know what sex leads to. It leads to a small person who likes to post toast in the DVD player. Plus, she's blocking my one good nostril, so I can't breathe. I'm not *against* French kissing, but I'm not prepared to drown.

I pull away.

'Are you OK?' she says.

'I've done these Klimt cartoons,' I say. I've covered the entire table with them. Why won't she even look at them? It bugs me. Why must we always discuss projects and plans, and not jokes?

She glances. 'Great!' she says quickly. This is worse. Now I've had to plead like a puppy for her attention, and I've still not got it. She kisses me again.

This time she takes it more slowly. She places her hands on the sensitive skin at the back of my ears, and she presses her soft lips to mine.

This time the kiss has a different effect.

This time I'm getting that bzzzz feeling in my rude area. I'm feeling a stirring in my loins. I feel the unfamiliar sensation of Excalibur preparing itself for combat.

Oh my goodness!

And now we're doing something we haven't done in months. We're snogging like teenagers at a party! I'm tasting the wine in her mouth. I shut my eyes, and in my mind I'm kissing the beautiful girl I first saw by a bonfire. I love her. I want her. I want her naked now.

'Darling,' I say. 'Let's go to bed.'

'OK,' she says. 'But first let's tidy!'

'OK!' I say.

'And I'll quickly check my e-mails!'

'OK!' I say.

She goes. I canter to the sink. And as I arrive, I think . . .

*How the heck did that happen?!* A moment ago, I was about to have sex. Now I'm cleaning!

I take stock.

The mess is bad. It's very bad. There are plates piled by the sink. At the bottom of the stairs, there's a pile of laundry which has been sitting there for a month. Is it going up? Is it going down? Who knows? It's like a sort of refugee camp for socks.

I think: This could take bloody hours!

Then I think: Tonight Excalibur will return to the Lady of the Lake! Feeling lusty, I thrust toys in the toy box. I scrape egg from saucepans. I even remove the wet onion that's clinging to the kitchen plughole.

By 10.48, I've finished the cleaning. I'm coming up the stairs, and once again I'm feeling good. I'm thinking about Polly's bottom. She thinks it's fat. It is. But I don't care. Some of the happiest times of my life have been spent pressing against it. And I'm going to do that any moment now. She's probably in the bath. She's probably soaping that bottom right now.

I come into the bedroom.

She's sitting up in bed with her laptop. As I go over, she shuts it guiltily.

Obviously, that gets my attention. I open the screen and look.

She wasn't looking at porn. She was looking at Primelocation.

I should have guessed that. In the last year, Polly has got *obsessed* with moving to the countryside. Finding the right place: that is her great quest. Initially her search was just online. She sized up the different counties like they were lovers. First it was Lincolnshire. Lincolnshire was plain, but cheap. Lincolnshire, she thought, I could *have* you. Then it was Kent she wanted. Kent was curvy. Kent was fertile. She wanted Whitstable, but she'd settle for Ashford. She made Kent hers. She explored Canterbury. She explored every damp corner of her Kent. She threw away weekend after weekend on the quest. Then she had a bad moment in Maidstone. She hated Kent. Kent was stuck up. Now it's Suffolk she wants. She yearns for fields and open skies. She doesn't care about Ipswich.

'I've found a great place near Colchester,' she says.

I stare at her. I do love her, very much. But if she says a single word about the great place near Colchester, I may do something untoward.

I sit beside her.

I take the computer from her lap.

I kiss her.

But then the dog starts barking.

**Polly**

There's someone at the front door.

'Who could that be?' says Arthur, pulling away.

'It's got to be Malcolm,' I say.

Let's be honest. Who else could it be?

Malcolm is a forty-two-year-old Irish builder. He is the only person in London who still calls in uninvited. He once turned up, uninvited, with his mum, who is eighty and has Alzheimer's. That was a long hour.

'Why don't you go down and ask him to return tomorrow?' I say. 'He can fix the dishwasher.'

**Arthur**

I run down. I open the front door.

Malcolm has ginger hair, paint-spattered clothing, and the soft friendly grin of Stan Laurel.

'Big Man!' he says cheerfully. 'Is this a good time?'

'Erm,' I say. 'It's nearly eleven on a Sunday night.'

Malcolm keeps smiling. 'So . . . is that a good time?'

I want to say: Malcolm, there's no one in Modern Britain who welcomes a random visitor, unless they're mad, or they're very old, or they're awaiting a victim.

I say nothing.

'What's up?' I say.

'The Springfield Park Community Festival is this Saturday,' announces Malcolm. 'And I, my friend, am in charge of the waterborne procession.'

I don't know what to make of that. 'Congratulations,' I say.

'Thank you,' says Malcolm proudly.

He turns to his old red van which is parked on the street

behind him. It has two metal canoes on the roof, plus some kind of huge papier-mâché heads.

'I've got two animal heads that are going to be in the procession,' he says. 'Would your kids like to paint them?'

'They'd love to.'

'Will I bring them into the house?'

'NO!' I say, a little too loudly. Malcolm keeps smiling though. 'Tell you what,' I say, 'why don't you come back at three-twenty-five tomorrow? We'll pick up the kids from school. We'll do the painting. And maybe you could look at the dishwasher?'

'It's a perfect plan!' says Malcolm. He hugs me. I get a whiff of white spirit mixed with skunk. 'I'll see you tomorrow. Good night, Big Man, sleep well!'

'Good night!' I say. And I beam happily at Malcolm till the door is shut. Then I double lock it.

Then I *sprint* upstairs.

I'm terrified Polly will now be going to sleep. She comes from an extraordinarily driven family. All the Pankhursts are religious about sleep. They like to get to bed early. They like to wake up early. They like to get busy busy busy, doing jobs they hate.

When I reach the bedroom, the lights are out.

*Oh, shit.*

This looks bad.

But maybe she's just lying in the darkness waiting for me. I strip. I get into bed. I shuffle over the little hump in the mattress that marks my territory from hers.

I hug her. She takes my hand.

Oh, no. Oh, no. I understand what that means . . .

I have now gone off sex, she's saying. Do *not* attempt it. And in case I don't get the message, she holds my hand captive.

Oh, *bollocks*.

I hug her. This is *love* I'm trying to show her, not just lust. I reckon two minutes should do it.

One hippopotamus. Two hippopotamus. Three hip . . . OK. That's two minutes. Let's prepare for combat.

But for that I'm going to need my right hand. Can I free it?

Ha-ha, I can!

My hand wriggles from her grip, and it creeps away like it's escaping from a witch. Then it tickles the back, and then it sneaks, with silent intent, towards the right breast. That right breast is the base camp. I know that, if I can just get there, I can wear her down.

She shrugs. She turns. She moves her arm.

The way to the breast is blocked!

Now I'm stumped. And suddenly I am also starting to feel a bit cross. (*She started this!*) I'm also feeling a bit sad. My seduction technique hasn't really changed since I've been a teenager. Basically I'm still just hanging around, hoping to get lucky.

She just snored.

Oh, God in heaven!

I roll away from her, and I'm hit by the fetid stench of disappointment.

The trouble is though . . . Excalibur is still there. He's standing eagerly to attention like a little cub scout. For a moment I do think I could . . . rub his toggle a little. I don't of course. I'm a gentleman. But I do shut my eyes, and suddenly my head floods with luscious images. I think of Polly looking beautiful by the bonfire. I think of the night I spent kissing Greta Kay in her hotel room.

I feel sickened suddenly.

I can't think about Greta Kay. It rouses too many feelings of What If, and If Only.

As I shuffle back to my side of the bed, I don't feel like Klimt. I feel like a dog returning to his basket.

Only one thing for it

complete physical union

# Monday

*Learn Love in a Week* – *the online course that will change your life*

**Day Two**: a bestselling love book argues *Men Are From Mars, Women Are From Venus*. This is too vague to be useful. I'd say: Women Are Like Bees, Men Are Like Snails. Come with me on this . . . Women are bees. They're social. They love buzzing round making suggestions: 'Let's fly to the countryside to sniff flowerzzzz!' When they sting they are deadly: 'You're just like your *dad*!' Every woman is a queen: returning home, she expects it to be perfect. She hovers over the unemptied bin. She notices the spilled juice. She enters the living room, where she's *furious* to see her snail man who's left a slimy trail up the carpet. 'We need to talk!' she says. Terrified, the man retreats into his shell . . .

**Today's challenge for the snaily men**: don't think you're going to communicate any of this by the classic male system of dropping a hint then having a sulk. Choose one thing from your list and tell it boldly to your woman.

**Today's exercise for the snaily men**: don't hide away. Say what you mean. Write the words 'I want . . .' then write fast for ten minutes (the record is 784 words). 'I want to drink more beer. I want to visit Arsene Wenger and I want to give him a hug. I want . . .'

**Today's exercise for the bee women**: don't say what you mean. Just for one day.

**Today's challenge for the bee women:** convince your partner you've lost your sting: he'll come out of his shell, and he'll reach his eager loving eyes towards you. Enjoy this! The snail's lovemaking is moist and cumbersome; it's also long and passionate!

**Arthur**

The first moments of the day are such a creative time . . .

I'm half dreaming and I'm half awake, so I can *imagine* everything I'm going to write today. On Friday when I left the novel, we were just about to see Guinevere for the first time. And now I can *picture* her. She's standing in a stream in a hessian dress. It's wet. It's clinging to her queenly chest. And . . .

**Polly**

8 a.m. I've been up an hour.

I've done laundry. I've e-mailed the campsite. I've signed the kids up for two After School Clubs. I now return to the bedroom. *Arthur is still sleeping.* And I must say . . . I do find myself sizing up his vast slumbering form, the way a toddler sizes up those Postman Pat toys you find outside post offices. I am thinking: 'How can I get this thing to work?' I'm tempted to prod. But I know if I prod it'll be like rousing a sleeping bull. He'll instantly start snorting and farting and talking about his third act.

So I just yank open the curtains.

That wakes him. He sits up fast and removes his sleep goggles.

'Good morning, darling!' I say cheerfully. 'So sorry, I've got to leave in ten minutes.'

He's pulling out his earplugs. He's not really with it yet.

'What are you doing this morning?' I ask.

'Polishing,' he announces.

I've got to confess . . . there is something about the word 'polishing' that makes me want to slap him. But he seems remarkably good-humoured. 'I'm at the bit where Lancelot meets Guinevere,' he says, 'and he falls in love.'

'Why does Lancelot fall in love?' I enquire.

'Erm,' he says. 'Because Guinevere is clever and witty and she's got great breasts.'

Arthur has a schoolboyish enthusiasm for breasts, which I find difficult. 'Do men,' I enquire, 'always think with their dicks?'

'We definitely give them a vote,' he says happily.

His laptop is next to the bed. He sits up and reaches for it. How do I broach this nicely?

'Darling,' I say, 'no one earns money from teenage novels.'

'It's true,' he admits. 'J.K. Rowling is now so skint, she's selling herself online. For a hundred quid, she'll take you up Diagon Alley. For two hundred, you see the Leaky Cauldron.'

'Why don't you try writing for newspapers?' I say. 'I could ask Em to let you write for her.'

'But . . . why?' he says. He really doesn't get it.

'If you want to sell your book,' I say kindly, 'you'll need to raise your profile.'

'Or I could just make the book really good.'

He's such an idealist. He thinks you succeed by talent alone. It's bankrupting us. 'Please write for Em,' I say suddenly.

'Why?'

Oh, God. I feel like I'm buried in debt and worry, and he doesn't even get it. He forces me to take on all the responsibility and he's not even grateful. I just want him to understand, but I can't explain now. I've got to go. And I say, rather too loudly: *'Because you're not earning any money!'*

## Arthur

Fucking hell.

The day's only been going three minutes. So far she's . . . (1) woken me, (2) shouted I'm not earning any money, and (3) she's tried to pin me into a new career. I've got to get away from her. I'm supposed to be writing today; already she's *completely upsetting* my composure. I leap from bed like a startled rabbit, and head downstairs at speed.

She follows though.

'It might actually do you some good,' she says, 'to write about real life. People don't want to read about fantasy and time travel.'

'Yup. That's why *Dr Who* is the least-watched show on television,' I say. It's the thing I resent most: when she tries to advise me on my professional life.

'I'm just saying what I feel,' says Polly. Yes, and I wish you wouldn't. 'I personally would only find *Dr Who* interesting if he got a girlfriend, or he made an offer on a nice barn conversion.'

'Dr Who is a Time Lord,' I explain. 'He doesn't have girlfriends.'

She drops the subject – wisely. She knows it's foolish taking me on over Time Lords.

'Why don't you just try writing something for Em?' she says.

'I told you,' I say, 'today I'm polishing my book.'

But Polly isn't taking no for an answer. 'There's no deadline for that,' she says.

'Polly,' I say, 'I know you think my writing isn't real work.'

'It's marvellous work,' she says. 'Luminescent. It just doesn't earn any money.'

Oh, God. She's said it outright. 'It will!' I say. I'm starting to get angry now.

'But it won't earn money in the next three days,' she says.

'Meanwhile our overdraft is standing at – three thousand four hundred pounds, and every time I try to get out money I'm refused and it makes me feel a bit sick. We can't pay the deposit on the campsite, and they've asked for it three times.'

'I'm sure I can get some money,' I say.

'How exactly?' she says. I hate it when she wants to discuss exact details.

'Well, I'm . . . I'm doing a school visit tomorrow.'

'Really?' she says. 'What's that?'

'It's been arranged by my last publishers,' I explain. 'I'm doing a show called The Seven Secrets of Storytelling, then some workshops on improvisation. They're paying three hundred quid a go.'

'And will the school give you cash straight away?' she says. 'Because that's what we owe the campsite for the deposit.'

'*Three hundred quid*!' I say. 'Just for a deposit?'

'Yes!' she says. 'We have to pay thirty per cent now, or we lose the spot.'

It seems a hell of a lot. 'Do we even *need* a campsite?' I say. 'When I was a teenager, you know, I'd sleep on the beach, or on a roundabout, and . . .'

'Darling!' she says, very loudly. It is always a bad sign, when she says 'Darling'. She only ever utters endearments to buy herself the advantage before she attacks. She says it again. 'Darling,' she says again. Oh, shit.

**Polly**

I give it to him straight.

'Ideally,' I say, 'we'd've taken a stone-fronted villa in Ithaca for the summer . . . We compromised on a week in a French campsite. I accepted that. *I won't accept a bloody roundabout!'*

That gets him. He scurries away like a cat that's been kicked.

'OK, fine!' he says. 'I wasn't saying . . . I'm just . . . saying *I could* bring in money. I actually feel I'm just finding my voice. I just need a *bit* of peace, and some belief.'

I've walked off to get my coat, so I only half caught that. But I'm pretty damn sure he just said he was finding his voice. He's been looking for it for ten years. If a voice hasn't been found in ten years, I'd venture it's time to cease looking. In the meantime, some of us have got to get to work.

'I can't talk now,' I say, as I return with my bag. 'Look . . . the children are all hungry. Can you go and do breakfast?'

He doesn't say anything to that. He stands there deep breathing.

That really annoys me. I would love to spend a morning at home. I could make them poached eggs, and I could walk them to school, and I could chat with the other mums. He gets to do all that, and he's not even grateful.

'They are your children,' I say. 'You might enjoy seeing them.'

'Oh, I love seeing the children,' he says. 'But then they talk. And they simply refuse to talk logically, or one at a time, and my head fills like a radio jammed between channels.'

'Darling,' I say, giving him a quick kiss goodbye. 'You'll manage.'

He just looks at me.

## Arthur

I'm one of those people who discovered, while reading *The Curious Incident of the Dog in the Night-time,* that they're a bit autistic. Well . . . It's not that I'm insensitive to emotions. Quite the opposite, in fact. If my wife is upset, I feel it like sand on the eyeball. But I feel constantly *overwhelmed* by information. The feeling's particularly acute first thing in the morning. Morning autism – can you get that?

I open the kitchen door. I immediately feel like a soldier who's under bombardment.

'Dad!' says Malory (seven). She's standing on a chair, wearing a flamenco dress. 'I need Cheerios!'

'My Barbie has lost her head,' says Ivy (four). 'And it has rolled under the table!'

'I have done the *first* half of my Egyptian homework,' announces Robin (nine). 'Do you want me to read it to you?'

Yup. That is what I need right now. A lecture about Ancient Egyptian clothing, read by a nine year old. I think Robin is gay. OK, he may not be gay, but he's certainly very interested in clothes. And he's remarkably clean, his favourite activity is dancing, and every Tuesday he goes to Mrs Betterton's Choreography Class. He likes football, but what interests him are the strips, which he calls 'costumes'. 'I don't know why West Ham wear purple and blue,' he said yesterday. 'That doesn't go!'

'*Furthermore*,' says Robin – that's a gay word. I've never met another nine year old who says 'furthermore' – 'we've *still* not talked about my dance. I think I should do it to "Chiquitita" and I'm going to have to get everyone to rehearse at lunchtime.'

Dance? What dance? This is what it's like being with children: you constantly feel you're joining the conversation late.

'*Dad*!' shouts Malory. She's a classic second child. An angry diva. 'I need Cheerios!'

'DAD!!' Ivy *screams*. She's the youngest: she puts all her energy into making damn sure she's heard. 'Barbie's head is on the floor and Mrs Thompson is trying to EAT IT!'

I look. Mrs Thompson (the dog, a ten-year-old schnauzer) has no interest in the Barbie head, and nor would she unless it were filled with sausage. She's scrabbling her paws in her bowl, demanding biscuits.

'Dad!' says Malory again. 'DAD!'

'*Please*!' I say very loud. 'Just **shut up** one minute. You're all talking at once and it's making me confused!'

But things get more complicated still. Someone else joins the battlefield – my wife. Field Marshal Polly Pankhurst. '*You* shut up,' she says, 'I hate it when you shout at everyone!' And I hate it when she overrules me in front of the children. '*Please* keep calm today,' she continues. 'And can you, *please*, today, empty out that fruit bowl?'

She grabs her wallet.

''Bye, everyone!' she says, and she heads off to work.

**Em**

Every week starts the same way: at 9 a.m. all the Section Heads gather in the meeting room. Then Sarah Shelton arrives, our esteemed editor. Then one by one the Section Heads run through their ideas. Then everyone else, as politely as possible, says why they're shit. It's like being back at college at the world's most competitive tutorial, except you never break for holidays, and your essays get printed in a paper.

This is how to cope . . .

1. You prepare killer ideas, and, preferably, some very famous people to write them.
2. You surround yourself with allies to help you remain calm. If – say – you're outlining your feature on *Why Childcare Spells the End of Equality*, and Mike Linson, Head of Sport,

says: 'Didn't we do that last year?' it's not appropriate to say: 'Didn't we do football every day last week?'

3. It's also key to have an excellent beverage.

This morning, I'm feeling perfectly prepared. It's still only 8.56. I have got Alain de Botton prepped and ready, and I'm sitting next to Dan. He's the editor for *Vroom*, which covers cars and gadgets. It's the Boys Toys section, so it suits Dan perfectly. He is my Boy Toy. He's thirty-two. He's extremely handsome and trendy. He has skinny jeans and tufty Hoxton hair. I'd been aware of him since he joined *Vroom* three years ago. Everyone knows about Dan. He's slightly famous. His dad was a genuine pop star, and Dan once went out with Kate Moss. Dan and I got off with each other, two years ago, in a thrillingly sexy moment, at a work party, on a boat that was cruising up the Thames. We've hidden the relationship at work. We are more open, however, with an unofficial arrangement that we will always defend each other's section against attack from hostile forces (e.g. Mike Linson). OK, Dan can't be relied on for much, but if Mike Linson attacks, he fights like a ferret. He's sitting beside me, absent-mindedly arranging his hair. I feel a strange yearning to stroke his cheek. Despite the debacle of the weekend, I'm feeling almost affectionate towards him.

Someone arrives.

It's Jeremy, my divine new PA.

'I bought you some Dong Ding,' he says, saucily. (He's gay – as, I believe, a PA should be.)

'What's that?' I say.

'I can't *believe* you don't know!' he says, in mock horror. 'It's a Taiwanese oolong tea that costs about thirty quid a bag.'

'Why would you pay thirty quid for a bag of tea?'

'Because,' says Jeremy, pouring out some hot greenish liquid, 'it's mild. It's subtle. It's filled with antioxidants.'

I sip some. 'It tastes like hot water,' I say, 'which has been boiled with pants.'

Jeremy gives me a pert look. 'Stella McCartney swears by it.'

I sip again.

'I tell a lie,' I say, 'I absolutely adore it. Do one hundred words on it for Things We Love.'

'Will do,' says Jeremy, making his way towards the door. 'Good morning, Dan,' he says as a parting shot. 'You're looking gorgeous. Hope you had a good weekend.'

'Yes, thank you,' says Dan stiffly. Then, as soon as Jeremy's gone, he gives me a worried look.

I lean over and whisper: 'Don't worry darling, he's only being pol—'

Dan leans close. He checks no one is looking at us. Then he whispers very quietly but very urgently: 'I've *told* you not to call me that at work.'

I don't say anything to that, but I sit there quietly seething with impotent rage. (Is there any other kind?) What am I going to do about him?

I can't consider it now though.

Sarah Shelton arrives, and all relationship tensions are pushed from my head. She flashes the room a stiff smile, and then she sizes up her team coldly. She takes the Divide and Rule approach to management. As her gaze rests on me, I feel like a fly staring into the eyes of a lizard. Shelton is accompanied by a very feminine and good-looking woman whom I recognise from somewhere. She's late-forties with ginger hair, very firm, clearly fake breasts, and expensive but rather tasteless clothes. (Tassels on satin shirt. Looks like a D & G take on cowboy styling.) Breast Woman is being accompanied by Poppy Simon, my deputy editor, who glances at me sheepishly. What the hell is going on? Already my heart is beating.

'Good morning!' says Shelton in her louche Estuary voice.

Sarah Shelton comes from Penge. Indeed her whole life has been one sustained attempt to expunge the Penge from herself. She's plumped her face, she's Botoxed her lips. You could probably buy a house in Penge for the money she's spent on her outfits. But her voice is still pure Estuary.

The room stays silent as we wait for Shelton to begin. She milks the pause. Then . . . 'Before I hear your wonderful ideas,' she says, 'I want to present someone special. You probably know her as a singer, TV presenter, and contemporary female icon. Now behind the camera, she's Executive Producer of *Daybreak*, which makes her approximately the best-connected woman in London. She is, of course, the gorgeous, the talented . . . Greta Kay.'

Greta Kay! I remember her. What did she present? Hang on a second . . . Didn't Arthur shag her? MUST see Polly asap.

'Now as you know,' says Shelton, 'we've been toying with different strategies for upping the readership of *Lifestyle*.'

Excuse me????!!! EXCUSE ME??!! That one just hit me right in the stomach.

'And I'm delighted to announce that next week Greta has offered to help out *Lifestyle* as Guest Editor.'

WHAT? WHAT???!!! WHAT THE *FUCK* JUST HAPPENED??! Oh, no. My work is the *one* area of my life that's going well. I *can't* lose this.

'That's why I've invited Poppy Simon along,' Shelton continues, '*Lifestyle*'s divinely talented Deputy Ed, since I know you guys know each other from Telly-La-La Land.'

Poppy glances at me again, and I realise my mouth is hanging open. Oh, God. It's bad enough being royally shafted, worse still to act like it's a surprise. People are watching. I must act like this is all a simply wonderful idea that Sarah and I have been chatting about for months.

I smile happily. Meanwhile I'm thinking: Shelton, you bitch!

## Arthur

It's 10.35. I'm at my desk, but I've still not written a word about King Arthur.

So far I've done my e-mails, I've read today's advice on *Learn Love in a Week*. I've also done my admin. Most of it anyway. I've got a comedy gig next week so I go on Trainline to buy train tickets. I hate Trainline. It seems to be manned by a troll. Before he gives you the tickets, he sets you riddles.

He opens with a toughie: What's your special Trainline password? I take a chance on that, *and I'm right*! Turns out my Trainline password is the one I have for most things – *Excalibur*.

So then the troll tries to get me with a confusing combination of riddles: What day do you want to travel? Do you want to sit in the direction of travel? What class do you want? I deal with those. After ten minutes, I actually think I've achieved my objective – a return ticket to Birmingham.

But then I'm passed to the NatWest security troll, who wants to ask me some basic security questions. He starts off with a difficult riddle: Could you name the first, fifth and sixth letters of your online NatWest security password?'

What is my online NatWest security password? I try *Excalibur*.

It doesn't work. I try *Malory*. Doesn't work. I try *Kerouac*. I try *Bergkamp*. I try: *Fuck off you tw* . . . I run out of space.

Now I beat my computer and shout for a bit. This is unbearable. I feel stuck in a dull domestic tragedy. I need adventure. I need success. I need to rescue moist-breasted ladies from streams.

Which reminds me . . .

I open up *Looking For Lost Magic*, and I start writing at a heroic pace.

Immediately the phone rings.

Oh, for fuck's sake.

'Hello,' says a dour Midlands voice. 'It's Angela Legg.'

'Hello,' I say. I have no idea who Angela Legg is.

'I believe you're coming to our school tomorrow to talk about your book?'

Right. The school visit. 'Yes,' I say, in my professional voice. 'Indeed.'

'I'm glad you're coming,' says Angela Legg, 'we've had trouble getting the kids to read, especially the boys. Now, your first session is at nine-forty-five. But do you think you could get here for nine, so you could also improvise a story for the school assembly?'

'I'm sure I could,' I say evenly. 'How long do you want it?'

'Well,' says Angela Legg, 'for about forty-five minutes.'

*For forty-five fucking minutes??!!* 'How many children have you got?'

'There'll be 500 children,' says Angela Legg, 'if we include Reception.'

*Five hundred fucking children, including some who are four!* Jesus Christ, I want to pull out of this! Can I pull out of this? No, I can't. I really need the money. 'Sounds do-able,' I say politely. Oh, shit. I'm so nervous I feel a bit sick. 'Anything else?'

'Just tell them about the book you wrote,' says Angela Legg. 'And make sure you keep it clean. Some parents complained about the last visiting author.'

'Right,' I say.

'So the school is Thomas Cranmer School in Mitcham,' she says. 'That's spelled C R A . . .'

'I know how to spell Cranmer,' I say. 'Wasn't he the one they burned to death?'

'What?' says Angela Legg, much alarmed.

'Yes,' I say. 'He got burned in a big fire.'

'Oh,' says Angela Legg. 'Well, *don't* mention that to the kids.'

For fuck's sake, I'm thinking: the man was a Protestant martyr. I don't think his fate is a secret. And besides . . . you're a teacher. How come you've not been curious enough to learn about the fate of the man after whom your school is named?

I don't say that.

I say: 'I'll see you at nine tomorrow morning.'

As I put the phone down, I feel almost weak with worry. How the hell am I going to manage tomorrow? It's not the improvisation that scares me. My kids make up stories all the time. They do that, no trouble. But they have a *lot* of trouble keeping them clean. Children have a very Anglo-Saxon view on stories. A story isn't over till the fat lady farts.

## Em

We do *Travel* before *Lifestyle*.

*Travel*'s new editor, Gillian, says she wants to focus on the Staycation. 'Despite what the travel companies say,' she says, 'you don't *need* to go away before you do anything.' She enthuses about lidos and parks and an amazing museum in Chiswick that has stuffed animals, before Shelton interrupts.

'You don't need me to tell you that newspaper revenue is falling,' she says. 'And the stuffed animal museum sounds great, but I can't see them buying as much advertising space as . . . say . . . Thomas Cook. Would you mind terribly if this week's *Travel* looked at *Reinventing the Package Holiday*? Talk Benidorm. Talk kids' clubs. Talk Mark Warner . . . but *don't* mention Madeleine McCann.' Gillian nods like a startled rabbit and then puts a line through everything. Then Shelton turns to me, and says: 'Right! And how are *Lifestyle* going to divert us this week?'

I flash my full-beam professional smile. I need to puncture Greta Kay's tits with my sheer unadulterated brilliance.

'This week,' I say, beginning confidently, '*Lifestyle* is taking the theme: *Learn Love in a Week*, based on the new hit website.'

'I've not heard of it,' says Shelton.

'It's huge in California,' I inform her. 'Today's headline piece will be written by Alain de Botton. He's doing a piece called "Opposites Attract". He's looking at love in its classical forms: "eros" – love of a lover; "philia" – love of a friend; and "storge" – which is . . . love of storge.'

Shelton gives a mirthless smile. 'When's he promised his copy by?'

'Eleven-thirty.'

'Great. I can't wait to see it!'

She wants to see my piece! The woman is such a control freak! Dan says she sometimes rewrites pieces in *Vroom* which have already been subbed.

I continue the presentation: 'We started to trail the idea on our website,' I say. 'We've been asking the question: What do you resent about your partner? Already, *loads* of people have been tweeting in.'

That's where Greta Kay interrupts. 'And what answers have you had so far?'

'It seems that the women of this country,' I say, 'feel they're doing ninety-five per cent of the laundry, and they're not taking it well. That's a common theme. And there was one woman whose man checks the daily petrol consumption and writes down figures in a little book.'

'Can I ask,' Shelton interrupts, 'have any men been on the site?'

Of course they bloody haven't. Men go online to read about football, or to gaze at Megan Fox in her bikini. Not to talk about laundry.

'Get some more male writers, please,' says Shelton. 'As long as they don't mention football.'

I say: 'Of course!' and pretend to make a note. (*The top professional is never scared of accepting help.*) Shelton doesn't say much after that, so it's all smooth, till the end. In fact, we finish by 10.35. Perfect. It means I can slip out. I need to speak to Polly urgently.

Shelton intercepts me as I leave.

'Where are you going?' she says.

'I'm seeing someone about a story,' I say. 'We'll share an early brunch.'

'What happens if I need to talk over ideas?'

I look into her eyes. My heart is beating, but I know I must say something.

'Then I suggest,' I say, 'you speak to my "divinely talented" deputy ed. And to be absolutely honest, Sarah, it would have been polite if you'd spoken to me before you offered my job to *Loaded* magazine's chest of the year 1999.'

Shelton stares at me a moment, then she comes at me like a pterodactyl. 'Your section lacks three things,' she says coolly, 'voice, wit, and readers. You have a week to find them.'

Oh, God. I always knew she wanted to get rid of me. But that's the first time she's actually said it.

## Polly

11.12. I arrive at Leon first.

When Em shows up, I'm at our normal table on the terrace outside, with a cappuccino and half a muffin. As soon as she sits down, she eats that. That's so Em . . . If there's something she wants, she's like a dog in front of some mince: she just can't stop herself.

'So come on then,' I say. 'What happened this weekend with Dan?'

She holds her hand up. 'I'm dying to get into that,' she says. 'But something's come up.'

'What?'

'Sarah bloody Shelton has hired a Guest Editor for next week!'

'No! Who?'

'Greta Kay.'

'No!'

'Didn't Arthur once shag her?' she says.

Ugh. I really don't want to go into that again.

'He hints,' I say, 'that they had a romance unmatched since Antony and Cleopatra went bobbing down the Nile in her barge. Actually, he snogged her, once, and he mythologises her because she's the only famous person who's ever kissed him.'

'Spiritual. What dirt's he got on her?'

'Why don't you call him?' I say. 'Actually I was thinking . . .'

But I don't get to make my request. Em is already dialling. She raises a finger at me, as if to say: Don't interrupt. The call is in progress. Why is the person on the other end of the phone deemed more important than the person who's actually sitting next to you? Even if that person is Arthur?

## Arthur

It's now 11.23!

I've got four hours before I have to pick up the kids. I've got to write fast. If I can't get this book polished, and sold, quick, then I'm going to have to commit suicide, or go into teaching.

My phone is ringing again. Each ring is like a jab in the ribs.

'Hello!' I say.

'Arthur,' says a velvet, purring voice. 'It's Em.'

'Hi, Em!'

Polly must have asked her about getting me to write for *Lifestyle*.

'Got a couple of questions for you,' she says.

'Oh, yes . . .' I'll be honest with you, Em. I don't want to write for your silly rag, but I feel very flattered you're asking. 'Ask me anything.'

'Could you name three things that men do not like about women?'

'Erm . . .' I say. 'I'd go for (1) nagging, (2) watching films that star Matthew McConaughey, and (3) cushions.'

There's a small pause. She's obviously writing that down.

'You're a genius!' she says.

'Thank you. So . . . What's question two?'

'Apparently you shagged our Guest Editor.'

What?!!!! 'Who?'

'Greta Kay,' she says. Just hearing Greta's name makes me go cold inside. It feels strange: last night I was thinking about her; today she's appeared in my life.

'Erm . . .' I say. 'I did *not* shag Greta Kay.'

'What did happen? Tell me the full story.'

'The full story? I'm not sure I remember much,' I say.

That's a lie. I recall every single detail.

'Tell me what you remember.'

'Well, twelve years ago,' I tell her, 'I did a gig in the Comedy Café, and she was there because she was shooting a piece for *Greta Kay's Pop Challenge*. That was the one where she went round the world, singing duets with top musicians.'

I remember the gig itself. Greta Kay is without doubt the most charismatic and sexy singer I've ever seen. She sang the Carol Kidd song – 'But when I dream, I dream of you . . .' – so that you just knew that she was in love with this guy, but there was someone else, someone even *more* special, that she only saw when she dreamed. While she was singing that line, she looked into my eyes. It was electric.

'Anyway, after the gig, I got chatting with her. She was in London for four days, and we basically spent all of them together.'

'Doing what?'

'Talking mainly. On the last day we stayed up talking, and it was round six in the morning when she said, 'You can stay over, if you want to sleep. I do mean . . . just sleep.' Then, to make it more clear, she told me all about her boyfriend.'

'I hate it when they do that,' says Em.

'I didn't mind.' Being in bed with a sexy woman I've never

touched: that's my absolute favourite situation. I can't think of an arrangement more open to exploitation.

'So what happened?'

'We just kissed a bit,' I tell Em.

That's one way of putting it. Another is that we watched the sunrise over Kensington Gardens. Then gradually we turned our heads towards each other *so* slowly, so that first of all I could just feel her breath on my cheek, and then gradually her nose rubbed against mine, and then our lips met, and then we just touched lips for half an eternity, and *then* we had the world's longest and most succulent kiss.

'Then the next day she left for Tokyo,' I say. 'That's it.' That was my great Nearly Happened. That was the night I was nearly signed by Barcelona. 'We saw each other again after that, but . . . you know . . . just as friends.'

'Right,' says Em. 'So . . . what's she like?'

'Well, there are two views on that.'

'And the first is?'

'She is a typical Californian. She does daily meditations, in which she sees herself making money. She talks a lot about 'empowerment', but she's got staff. She talks about 'integrity', but she's got fake tits.'

'OK. And what's the other view on her?'

'That she really is the person she tries to be.'

'Meaning?'

'She's a sort of human angel. She's incredibly loving and passionate and wise. And actually she's not from California at all. She's from the mountains of Montana. She moved to Texas when she was twelve, which is what gives her the sexy accent.'

'And what's your view on her?'

'I think she's the most exciting person I've ever met.'

'Apart from me, of course.'

'Yup,' I say. 'And Polly.'

'OK. Great,' says Em. Typical journo: she seems disappointed I'm not giving her more dirt. 'Anyway . . . thanks for that. So . . . last question.'

'Yup.' Come on then, offer me a job. Offer me a job. I want to know what it feels like to be wanted.

'The question,' says Em, 'relates to today's *Learn Love* exercise.'

'Oh, right. What is the question?'

'What do you want?'

'What do I want?!'

'Yes.'

I want to be left alone so I can finish my book. I want to place my ears between Greta Kay's thighs and I want the confusion to stop. I want it to be like when I saw Polly outside Bar Italia and it felt like the sun was shining and angels were singing.

I say: 'I want success.'

'Why?'

'To get Polly off my back.'

'You want success to get Polly off your back?'

'Yes,' I say. 'I feel completely unheard and without power.'

'Ooh,' says Em. 'Sorry . . . I've gotta go.'

*You've got to go?!* I just said, I feel unheard and without power. Besides, I thought you were about to offer me a job!

''Bye,' she says, and she rings off.

I stare into space for a moment. Then I take out a piece of paper and I write . . .

*Sometimes I think my whole life went wrong because we didn't make love that night. Part of the trouble is, her body remains a mystery. I've never pulled a t-shirt over her head, and seen her naked in the half-light. That haunts me. While making love, we might have found that we just fitted each other like two long-lost soul mates who have finally come home. We might have panted into each other's mouths, and we might have felt a white-light ecstasy that spoke of God. What bothers me more is that when we talked, she seemed to open up whole universes in my head. When I talk with Polly, we discuss the schedule.*

Which reminds me: it's now 11.43. I've got three and a half hours to write, before I must pick up the kids. I hide the piece of paper underneath a pile of admin. I reopen *Looking For Lost Magic* and write furiously, for two whole minutes.

Whereupon there's a scratch at the door and Mrs Thompson appears. She obviously needs a wee.

I ignore her.

She comes forward and licks my leg.

'Mrs Thompson!' I shout. 'Just leave me alone for a few bloody minutes!'

## Polly

It's now 11.48. Em is walking away from the Leon counter. She's got her own coffee. I notice she's *not* got a muffin to replace the one she ate. As she approaches, my phone rings.

'Excuse me,' I say.

She gives me an irritated look. Even though she's just made a call, she resents me taking one.

I pick up.

'Polly,' says a deep voice. 'It's James.'

Just hearing his voice, I feel like I'm back at school and Jessica Harlow has just said: 'Mike Stevens fancies you.' I feel fluttery and excited.

'Hello, James,' I say. 'How are you?'

'Ugh,' he says. 'I'm in Luxembourg!'

'Why?'

'I'm trying to buy a mental hospital.'

'Why?'

'It's a big neo-Gothic building overlooking a lake.'

'What'll happen to the mental patients?'

'Release 'em, I imagine. It's Luxembourg! No one will notice.'

'James,' I say, and I'm aware that I'm purring like a happy cat. 'You're an extremely naughty man.'

'Say that again,' he says, 'but like you mean it.'

Already I'm blushing. I drop my voice. 'James . . .'

'Polly,' he says, 'do you still play hockey?'

'Er . . . no.' Because I'm not twenty-four. Neither do I go out to dinner with strange men, then spend the next week wondering whether to call them. 'Why?'

'Remember when I came to your flat to pick you up for our date?'

'Sort of.'

'You'd been playing hockey. In your bathroom there was a white Airtex top that was still wet with sweat. To this day, someone need only say "Airtex" and I feel a bit peculiar.'

Oooooookay. That was slightly sexy. But it was also *way* too much to volunteer this early on in our renewed relationship.

'Come on,' he says. 'Give me a thrill. Let me hear it.'

'What?'

'Polly Pankhurst saying: "My white Airtex top was wet with sweat."'

No, really, no.

'James,' I say. 'Did you call for a reason?'

'I'm sure there must have been one,' he says. 'Oh, I know. I talked to Fritzi and Yoren who are doing the design job on the new Wiltshire place. We'd love you to come on Friday so you can give us your thoughts on the meadow. If you're interested, they've actually got a grand in the budget.'

*A grand?!!! Just for a consultation?!!*

'Would you be interested?'

'Yes, I would.' To be honest, I'd come for nothing. I need to see a green hill dotted with oaks. I need to look at that, and I need to smell some jasmine, and I need to hear a blackbird singing. I need that quite urgently.

'Great,' he says. 'Have you designed many gardens yet?'

'Yes,' I say, 'I've done several!' OK, most of them were mine. And one of them was technically a roof terrace. But obviously they've all been fantastic works of art.

'Are you doing one at the moment?'

'Yeah. I'm doing a great one in London. It's a normal suburban garden. It's long and thin.' I'm aware, suddenly, that everything I'm saying is an innuendo. 'But at the bottom there's an extra section you're not expecting to find. You go through an arch, and . . .'

'Whose is this garden?'

It's mine, James. I'm describing my garden. I want you to reach my secret, extra bit. 'Ooh . . . a client,' I say.

'I'd love to see it!' he says.

'Well, you must!'

'Yeah, but . . . before Friday?'

Oh . . . God. I go quiet. In the background, I hear a woman talking.

'Wendy has just reminded me,' he says, 'we're in New York then Italy for most of the week.'

'Oh.'

'I'd like to come tonight.'

No no no no no you can't do that.

'I'm in London for a meeting this afternoon, but we're leaving Heathrow at ten . . . I can come to you from six till seven, tell me that's possible?'

'Erm . . .' I say. My heart is wildly beating, but out of terror more than attraction. 'It's possible,' I say.

'I'll pass you to Wendy for the address,' he says.

'Right.'

He passes over the phone. Feeling a bit shaky, I speak to Wendy. I give my address.

I glance at Em who's looking impressed.

**Em**

I'm giving Polly a look that clearly says: No . . . Really, Polly, you'd better come off that phone right now, or I will dunk it in your coffee.

**Polly**

I turn off the phone. I can't help it. I give Em a triumphant smile.

She gives me an arch look. 'Do I take it James Hammond is firming up his interest in having you "consult" on his garden?'

'It seems that way,' I say. I'm almost beaming. I can't believe that, of all the women in the world, he's choosing to flirt with me.

'That's great,' says Em. 'But I really do think you should have told him that the garden you're working on is yours.'

She's right. I suddenly feel a bit unwell.

'I can't believe it!' I say. 'I've invited James Hammond to my house!'

'Luckily, your garden is amazing!'

'But I implied it was a client's.'

'It could be mine,' says Em. 'I could pop by around six, bringing home a light supper and some wine.'

'You are outrageous!' I say. 'What are you after?'

Em smirks. 'I'm after Hammond.'

'You're going out with Dan!'

'And you're married!'

'Look,' I say. 'I don't want to shag James Hammond.'

'Nor do I,' says Em, grinning. 'I just want half his fortune.'

I smile. 'I just want his staff,' I say.

'Well, let's tell him that tonight!' says Em. 'We'll say: "James Hammond, we give ourselves quite freely to your staff!"'

'Yes,' I say. 'But I've got to show him the garden first.'

'Yes, and that's where we'll corner him. We'll say, "*Hammond!*"' Em growls the word 'Hammond', and then she laughs. Em always laughs at her own jokes. '"*Hammond*,"' she says again, '"*Hammond*, show us the Hammond organ: we'll show you our . . . bushes and our . . . water features . . . And then you can take us in the compost."'

I say: 'I've never heard it called "the compost" before.' And we both cackle like a couple of horny witches. I love this about Em. We're both seeing each other on a difficult morning. Somehow we're still laughing.

I quickly text Arthur. I tell him about James's visit. I ask him to make sure everything's tidy. Then I turn to Em.

Her phone is now buzzing.

## Em

A text has come in. I quickly check it.

'Oh, *shit*!' I say. 'Shit in my handbag!'

'What?!' says Polly.

'De Botton has pulled out! Fuck de Botton!'

Polly smirks at this.

'What are you smiling at?' I ask her.

'You said Fuck de Botton!'

'I sent him one e-mail this morning, and he's pulled out.'

'Well, does that mean de Botton has pulled out?' says Polly, who's refusing to see the gravity. 'Or that you've pulled out of de Botton?'

Polly is still grinning. I've completely lost my sense of humour suddenly. I've got eighty minutes before we go to press. I've just lost my star writer.

How the hell am I going to get a male writer in eighty minutes?

'Why don't you try Arthur?' says Polly.

I'm about to say: Sorry, Polly. I'm not sure Arthur is a replacement for Alain de Botton. Although . . . come to think of it, I did like his line on cushions. But maybe Arthur could be a fine columnist. He's compulsively honest. Anyway, right now I just need anyone. As long as they can do the piece in an hour, and they can spell, they've got the job.

'I'll give him a try,' I say.

I press dial straight away. Polly looks pleased.

While waiting for Arthur to pick up, I chink my spoon against my cup.

Come on, come on. It's now seventy-nine minutes till we go to press and I need a writer. But will Arthur be able to do it? If I force him to scope out the question, he should be fine.

*Come on, pick up.*

'Hello again!' he says.

He seems out of breath.

'Hello!' I say. 'What are you doing?'

'Just . . . dabbing up some wee,' he says.

'The dog's?' I ask.

'There are several suspects,' he says.

I'm suddenly unsure of the wisdom of calling him. Certainly, his professional skills need refreshing. It's basic presentation: when answering the phone, don't discuss urine.

'Listen,' I say. 'We're doing a piece on the theme of "Opposites Attract". Do you have a view on that?'

'Yup,' he says. 'It's bullshit. Opposites don't attract. Famous people go for other famous people. Welsh people go for other Welsh people, and they live in Wales. And this is as it should be. You don't fall in love with your opposite. You fall in love with someone sexy, and then you resent everything they do differently.'

OK. He certainly has a view. And he holds it passionately.

'So why do you think people fall in love?' I ask.

'For women, it seems to be based on a complicated mathematical formula: $X + Y \times Z$ – where X equals his age, and Y equals his bank balance, and Z equals his resemblance to Brad Pitt / the fact that her sister's just got knocked up / a random impulse inspired by wine.'

'Why do men fall in love?'

'Women have breasts. We want them. But after a while the women take them away.'

'And . . . why do you suppose that happens, Arthur?'

'Because – despite being told several times – we have refused to grasp the basic principle of Clean As You Go. In punishment, the breasts are taken away.'

'But there must be some way,' I suggest, 'to get them back out?'

'But,' says Arthur, 'no man has found it, or he'd have told the others. That's the thing, Em . . . falling in love is easy. You meet in the moonlight, you find her lips pressed against yours. But what happens if you're meeting in the kitchen and she's telling you how to make the tea? How do you *stay* in love: that's what you should write about. That's harder.'

'But what do you think?' I say.

'I don't know,' says Arthur.

'Well,' I prompt, and as I do, I realise I'm looking at my breasts. At least mine are real. 'So come on, Arthur,' I prompt. 'If you fall in love because you think they're sexy, then you fall out of love because you think they're different, how do you fall back in love again?'

'I don't know!' he says. 'But it must be something to do with thinking their differences are there to help.'

Perfect. That's your conclusion. Good boy. 'Right,' I say. 'Just . . . give me an example.'

'Well . . . like . . . Polly doesn't listen to my stories or jokes; I have to find another audience. She's also got better manners than me; I've had to learn some. Is that such a sacrifice?'

'And what do you think Polly gets from you?'

'Nothing,' he says. 'She makes that a matter of some pride.'

'And what is it you're offering?'

'An expert analysis of Arsenal's midfield,' he says. 'Plus I can wire up the TV. Plus I'm actually very loving.'

I laugh.

'OK, Arthur,' I say. 'That's brilliant. I need five hundred words on this subject. In the next forty minutes . . . Can you do it?'

He doesn't answer.

'Maybe you could write a piece a day, throughout the week. You'd be telling the readers how to *Learn Love in a Week*.'

'But I don't think you *can* learn Love in a Week,' says Arthur. 'And anyone who says you can is surely part of the problem, and they must be made to taste the sting of the lash on their lying deceitful shoulders.'

Right. OK. He's just attacked my basic concept, quite rudely. I'm beginning to detect why he doesn't get much work.

'Thank you for your honesty,' I say. I will never ever offer you work again. 'OK . . . 'Bye.'

I click the phone off.

Polly is giving me a hopeful look.

'Well,' she says. 'Did he have any good ideas?'

'He was original, pithy and passionate,' I say. 'I said he should write it.'

'I heard,' says Polly. 'Thank you *so* much.'

'He refused.'

'Hang on,' she says. 'I will kill him.'

She dials straight away.

As the phone rings, she gives me a businesslike look.

'What are you paying?' she says.

'Two hundred quid,' I say. Does she know that's the minimum rate for five hundred words?

'Four hundred,' she says.

'Three hundred,' I say. 'But he *must* do it in the next forty minutes.'

That way, if it's shit, I can redo it myself.

**Polly**

Arthur takes ages to pick up.

And when he does, he makes no attempt to disguise the bolshiness of his tone.

'What??!' he says crossly, which already makes me want to hit him.

I get right down to it. 'Arthur,' I say. 'Apparently Em was just offering you three hundred pounds for forty minutes' work, and you refused.'

'She didn't mention the money!' he says.

'I don't think you asked,' I say. Is it integrity that he has, or just obstinacy? 'Arthur,' I say, 'write the piece. I'm not asking – I'm telling. And if you don't do this, I won't divorce you. I will stay with you out of spite.'

'OK,' he says. 'I'll fucking do it!'

Jesus, I hate it when he swears!

I turn off the phone as quick as I can.


**Arthur**

Malcolm arrives dead on time. It's a sunny day outside, and together we stride happily down the alleyway towards the school.

'Having a good day?' he asks.

'Not really,' I say.

'What's up?'

'I've written a novel,' I begin.

'You've written a novel?' he says. He's wildly impressed.

'Sort of,' I say. 'I'm trying to polish it, but it feels like the world is no longer designed for people who enjoy calm, solitary pursuits. I feel like I'm being buzzed at every moment. The phone rings. The bell sounds. Even when I'm on my own, my computer pops up little messages to say: "Firewall settings have been set to home."'

'Well,' says Malcolm weightily, 'in my work as a Life Coach . . .' I'm thinking: You're not a Life Coach, Malcolm. You're a builder who likes giving out advice. '. . . the first question is always: '*Are you doing the work you wish to do?*''

'And the answer would be yes.'

'Can I ask you something,' says Malcolm. 'As a child, were there any things you were good at?'

'Yup: underarm farts, and swimming underwater with my eyes open. I don't think you could make money from those. I'm already doing the thing I most love, Malcolm: I'm writing a novel. The problem, is I have a wife who wishes I were writing for newspapers.'

'Does she?'

'Well, she wouldn't care if I was an assassin, so long as I earned some cash, and got home for bathtime.'

'Well, maybe it's Polly who's got the wrong job,' he says. 'And she can't change it because of yours.'

I give him a suspicious look. 'Is she paying you to say that?' I ask.

By now we've reached the playground where mothers are gathered in a hopeful ring around the door. As we arrive, the first kids are appearing – the first actors on the stage. First to emerge is Philip Edmonds – a slouchy unprepossessing boy with messy hair. Nearby Janet Edmonds waves excitedly.

Malcolm beams at this.

'It's like *March of the Penguins*,' he says.

'I'm sorry?'

'The mums return from their hundred-mile waddle,' says

Malcolm. 'And the kids arrive, and the mums give them a big delicious mouthful of sicked-up fish.'

'I suppose so,' I say. 'Except these are middle-class penguins, so they give rice cakes.'

We watch Janet Edmonds trying to embrace Philip Edmonds. Unfortunately he's already in Year 2. He doesn't let her. Boys learn fast to withhold their affection.

'Do you suppose,' ponders Malcolm, 'the mums ever think: I'll take a different one today? I mean . . . surely every mum would rather take, for example . . . him,' he says, pointing at Alfie Jones (a remarkably handsome child). 'Rather than for example . . . him,' he says, covertly pointing at Duncan Smith (a confused-looking boy with a snotty nose).

I don't say anything to this.

At that moment I see my children. All three of them are together. Robin is holding Ivy's hand. Malory is looking round for me, eager as a meerkat. She sees me, and beams. I feel an explosion of love in my chest.

'It'd never happen,' I say, as they come running over. 'Because every parent thinks their child is the best.'

I kneel down and try to hug all three of them together. I feel fantastic.

Then they all talk.

Malory tells me she must make a Tudor house. Robin tells me he must practise his dance. Ivy says she must poo. Malory says the house needs to have at least three floors. Ivy says her poo is already starting to come out. I've been with them thirty seconds, I'm already feeling bombarded by information. 'KIDS!' I shout. 'We shall make houses, *and* we shall dance, *and* we shall poo. But not at the same time. Let's get home!!'

Several mums give me uncertain looks. But the kids cheer. And we all head home.


**Em**

4.03. The whole *Lifestyle* team are gathering in the boardroom. I am leaning on the cupboard at the side of the room.

Jeremy comes and stands next to me.

'*Mein Führer*,' he says quietly.

'Puppytoes,' I reply.

'Tell me,' he whispers. 'Why do you think Greta Kay wants to be Guest Editor of our paper?'

'I was wondering that. Maybe she thinks she's going to be sacked from *Daybreak* and she fancies editing *Lifestyle*. Our job is to make sure she doesn't achieve her ambition.'

'Are we going to bring her down?'

'Don't be ridiculous,' I say quietly. 'Our job is to be as supportive as possible, while hoping she fucks up.'

Jeremy gives me a Kenneth Williams look. 'Soo . . . Matron,' he says. 'What would you have me do?'

'Stand there being beautiful and silent.'

'That what you're doing?'

'Yes.'

'Well,' he says, 'it'll be a first.'

We both go silent when Greta arrives, flanked by Sarah Shelton and Poppy Simon. Greta comes over to me and touches me on the arm.

'I've just got to say,' she says, 'I loved the piece about "Opposites Attract". *Loved* it . . .'

I give her an uncertain smile. I know your sort, I'm thinking. You're a Love Bomber. You scatter love on the land like bombs over Dresden. You don't mind who cops it.

Sarah Shelton claps her hands.

Everyone looks at her. She pauses to generate the right amount of icy power, then she gives Greta the same introduction, word for word, that she gave earlier. Uptight bitch.

Everyone claps. Whereupon Greta smiles and gushes.

'It's been *great* meeting some of you today,' she says. 'I can't wait for next week's edition, for which I've decided the theme will be . . . *Men*. What men are we meeting? Can I ask, who here is single?'

Almost everyone puts up their hand straight away. I feel a bit embarrassed actually. It looks like the team I've assembled is rather one-sided.

'So,' says Greta. 'Almost all of us.'

'It's not almost all of us!' I protest. 'Jeremy, you're not single. You said you slept with someone last night.'

'Yuh!' he says. 'But I'm gay, so that's sort of like saying hello.'

'So,' says Greta brightly, 'we're all experts on the dating scene. Let's talk about the kind of men we're meeting out there. Selina?'

Selina Gordon is a self-conscious anorexic who writes about diet. 'Erm . . .' she says. 'They're . . . great.'

I glance at Greta.

I want to tell her: These are English people, you Yank bint! They're not going to spill their guts that easily. Meanwhile, Shelton is watching the display with all the raw enthusiasm of a newt. Greta's enthusiasm is undiminished though. She turns to Holly Goldsmith. She's the daughter of two geography teachers, and compensates by dressing like a slut. I hate to think who she's letting through the cat flap.

'How about you, Holly?' asks Greta. 'What sort of men are you finding?'

'They're . . . fine.'

'OK!' says Greta. 'So that's great.'

She is utterly dying a death. Nearly time to step in.

'Let's talk about the sort of men we'd like to meet,' says Greta. 'Let's talk Hot Men, Powerful Men, *Mad Men, Mr Men*, Men we'd like to ride like they were racehorses . . .'

'Yes,' I say. 'But if we ask: "What sort of men are we *actually* finding out there?" we'd have to say the main types are . . . Dull Men, Stinky Men, Men who wear hair gel, but only on the front of their heads. Men who are scared of commitment. Men who should be committed to mental institutions. Men who collect things – DVD box sets, football programmes, restraining orders. You can go for an older man. That's like getting a rescue dog. He's got his own basket, but problems will emerge.'

Jeremy guffaws at this one. Shelton doesn't. I suddenly realise I may have pushed it too far.

'Maybe we can use some of that,' says Greta, giving me a soft feminine look. 'But generally I feel more positive about the men I meet. I'm sorry if you don't.'

Ouch! You bitch. I'm going to get you for that. You can run like a deer, but I will bring you down.

## Arthur

When dying men are asked: 'What do you regret?' the most common answer apparently is: 'I worked too much. I wish I'd spent more time with the children.' I can how this happens if the men were selling double glazing and they were never home because they were chasing a few more sales. But I'm writing a book in which I'm attempting to recover the lost paradise of an Arthurian world. It feels like important work. I absolutely love it. And I want to say to all those dying men: 'Listen. I've got three children, right here. Feel free to come over.'

But of course my kids could kill anyone who wasn't highly trained.

It's now five o'clock. I am helping Malory make a Tudor house. While helping Robin make a cake. While also trying to work out what to cook them for tea. I get out all the nourishing things I want them to eat – spinach, carrots, ham. Then I just cook pasta.

5.15 p.m. . . . I place the pasta on the table. At which point Malory tells me she'll have pesto, Robin tells me he wants tomato, and Ivy hurls her bowl off the table. It lands on top of Mrs Thompson. For a brief moment, she's wearing it like a Chinese hat.

Throughout all of this, Mrs Thompson is following me around wanting biscuits. And Malcolm is talking, almost without stopping, about barges. His barge will be ready on Saturday, he tells me. He has plans to use it as an Occasional Performance Space for Community Theatre. He's already got permission for this, he assures me, by writing a letter to British Waterways. He offers to read me the letter. He starts reading the letter. My head feels like a seagull that's trapped in the engine of a plane.

In short, the afternoon is challenging. But you must enjoy your achievements, says the wise man, as well as your plans. And, at 5.48, as I begin tidying up the tea – clearing plates, wiping pesto off walls – I briefly reflect that, miraculously, a number of achievements have occurred . . .

1) I have helped Malory make a Tudor house.

2) I have helped Robin make a cake.

3) I have persuaded everyone, finally, to eat some tea.

4) We have all helped Malcolm with his badger head. OK, we've painted it pink.

Better still, Malcolm's now mending the dishwasher. He pulls it out and he lies down behind it.

Which is the moment that Mrs Thompson starts barking, and I realise Polly's guest is at the door. And now, just briefly, I do lose my calm. I swear. I say a word that rhymes with 'duck' – fairly loud. But the kids don't hear. They're in the living room dancing to a CD of the songs from CBeebies. I pretend I haven't heard the door. And I rush round the house, tidying it more quickly than anyone has ever tidied before.

**Polly**

I'm walking down the pavement towards home.

It's 5.58. I'm supposed to be seeing James in two minutes. *At my house.* How is this happening? Maybe he won't turn up!

Oh my God.

There is a white Rolls-Royce outside my house with a chauffeur wearing a blue cap. He's here. He's getting out of the car. He's wearing a powder blue suit and he's looking intimidatingly well groomed. Lordy-Lord, I feel tense . . . I still haven't told him I have a family!! How am I supposed to slip in that information? 'Oh, by the way, James, this garden is actually mine. And those children are actually mine. I'm also not twenty-four. I'm thirty-five, I've got stubbly legs and an overdraft, but please, please, let me come and stay in your mediaeval abbey, I give myself quite freely to your staff!'

Oh, Lord, he's turning. What to say?

'Polly!' he says.

'James!' I say. 'I give myself to your staff!'

He's about to kiss me, but now he pauses. 'I'm sorry?' he says.

Did I just say what I think I said? 'I'd give anything to have your staff,' I say.

'Yes,' he says. 'They are wonderful!'

He steps forward and kisses me on the cheek. I've got to tell him.

'So,' I say. 'No daughter?'

'No. She's gone ahead to the airport.'

'Oh . . . good.' *Good?* Why is that good? 'Shall we go in?'

As I lead him towards the front door, I take his arm. God. Now I think I'm in *Downton Abbey*. That is too much, but I can't let go now. I've got the Earl by the arm. I must lead him in.

'Are they a nice family?' he says.

'Yes! Actually I . . .'

'I imagine you get to know them very well!'

'Yes!' And in this case I know them *particularly* well because . . .

The door opens. I let go of James's arm. Arthur is there. Downton's handsome head footman, holding my child. Loud music is playing. 'The NumberJacks are on their way!' someone is announcing happily. 'The NumberJacks are on their way!'

'Hi!' says Arthur, sticking out his hand. 'Come in! We're just celebrating Sum Baby's birthday. We've made him a cake, and a Tudor house.'

James steps into the hallway. He heads immediately for the back garden. I notice the evening sunshine is streaming in. Good. I dodge round Ivy (who's not supposed to be my daughter) and I go into the kitchen.

Oh, no. It's bad. Very bad. My head computes the damage like Sherlock Holmes . . .

1) The dishwasher has been pulled into the middle of the floor.
2) The stove is matted with the sort of scum that suggests a student hovel.
3) There is a paint mark on the wall.
4) There are plates on the bookshelf.
5) Outside the back door, there's what looks like a giant mutant head.
6) With every step into the kitchen, I realise I'm crunching on hundreds and thousands.
7) And that fruit bowl is still filled with crap. It's *his* mother's phone charger in there, for God's sake. *Why* should I deal with that? I cannot be looking at that fruit bowl any more. I feel a little squall of rage. I've been offered a new job, which could bring me the new direction for which I yearn. Could he not help?

Luckily, the back door is open. I glance at James. He gives a friendly wave to Robin and Malory, who are doing some kind of waltz, and he goes straight out to see the garden.

I approach Arthur.


## Arthur

Polly corners me by the bin. Already she's looking bothered.

'Darling,' she says quietly. 'I *do* wish you'd tidied up.'

*Jesus Christ.* Why can't she, just once, come home and say something nice?

I say nothing.

'That's James Hammond,' she whispers. 'He wants to see the garden.'

I say: 'I hope he likes it!'

She leans in and whispers even more quietly.

'He thinks this is a client's house.'

Right. So she's disowning our house and family. *OK.*

'Am I the client?' I say.

'Yes. You're also Em's husband. She's coming in a minute. Could you delay her and talk to her?'

'What about?'

'I don't know. Ask her about work. Just don't ask her about the weekend.'

'Do you know if she used my piece?'

'No.'

'Typical.'

'Be nice to her. She's bringing Turkish food.'

'Oh, well, that's something,' I say. 'I'll invite Malcolm.'

'I don't want Malcolm this evening.'

'It would be polite, considering Malcolm is doing our dishwasher.'

At this I point to the floor and Polly notices something she ought not to have missed: Malcolm is lying there, fiddling with the dishwasher pipes.

I think Malcolm may be mildly sociopathic though. He is *impossible* to offend.

'Hello!' he says. He gives Polly a friendly wave.

## Polly

Oh, God. *Why* is Malcolm still here?

And now James Hammond is coming over. No no no. James Hammond should NOT meet Malcolm. But I should NOT be rude. What to do?

'James,' I say, 'this is Malcolm, who's . . . Malcolm, this is James Hammond.'

Malcolm waves. 'Hello!' he shouts.

James gives him a nod. 'Nice to meet you,' he says briskly.

There's an embarrassing silence.

Then it gets worse. At that moment, a freak accident occurs. Malcolm must have disconnected a pipe or something.

And a gush of water shoots out of the wall, and it hits James right in the crotch.

*Oh, God.*

Malcolm leaps up. 'Oh, the Pope's arse!' he exclaims.

'Oh, Lord!' says James.

'James, I am SO sorry!' I say.

I immediately fumble in a drawer for a towel, then I remember this isn't supposed to be my house. Luckily James doesn't take that in. He's more bothered by Malcolm, who grabs the towel off me and makes as if to start rubbing James's trousers.

'Please,' says James, backing away.

'I am *so* sorry!' says Malcolm.

'I am fine,' says James. He takes an apron from the drawer. 'I'll wear this to cover it . . . Thank you.'

Throughout all of this I'm glaring at Arthur, willing him to take control of the situation.

Malory arrives.

'WHY is he wearing Dad's apron?' she shouts.

I make further eyes at Arthur.

'Kids,' he says. 'You need to go upstairs and have a bath. Malcolm, you should come as well.'

'I'm not going to have a bath with your kids!' says Malcolm.

'Just . . . come upstairs,' says Arthur. 'I'd like you to look at the boiler.'

At last, everyone goes.

I turn, agonised, to James. He now has the apron on.

'James,' I say. 'It looks like you're about to do a spot of baking.'

James just stares back at me. 'God, you're gorgeous,' he says.

Oh, God. I can't be flirting in my own kitchen. But he doesn't know it's my kitchen. What am I doing?

'James,' I say, 'let's go out into the garden.'

## Arthur

OK. I've now dealt with the situation.

I've got the kids in the bathroom. They're there now, having the nightly debate: can you bring Barbie dolls into the bath? Ivy is of the view you can. Malory thinks you can't. Robin thinks we should allow the Mermaid Barbies, and the two princes. '*But*,' he qualifies, sounding like a little gay murderer, 'you *must* take their clothes off first. Then afterwards you have to squeeze out their heads, and put them on the radiator.'

I go up the stairs to our bedroom where I find Malcolm with his head under the boiler.

'Malcolm,' I say, 'thanks for helping.'

'It's a pleasure.'

'So . . . Would you like to stay for dinner?'

'I'd love to.'

'Em will be here,' I tell him. 'Polly's best friend.'

'Is she a fox?' says Malcolm.

'She's more like a gerbil. She's small and rounded and unexpectedly vicious.'

'She sounds sexy.'

'Don't get ideas, Malcolm. She's not for you.'

'Why?'

'She's . . . high-maintenance.'

'I can do maintenance.'

'You can do plumbing. It's not the same thing.'

'It is,' says Malcolm, and he gives me a sweaty grin. 'It's all about applying gentle pressure with the stopcock.'

I laugh at that. I can never tell if Malcolm is an idiot or if he's very wise.

'In fact,' he says, raising a finger gnomically, 'going out with a lady is like doing the plumbing. You meet her, you discover she has some kind of problem. Then you remove her cladding, and you check out her pipes.'

I laugh at that too. At the same time I'm seeing the problem with involving Malcolm in our evening.

'Malcolm, why don't you stay up here?' I suggest. 'And before you have dinner, feel free to shower and borrow some clothes.'

'Thank you!' says Malcolm.

I turn and look out of the window. Polly is at the bottom of the garden with her visitor. She's looking into his eyes, while fondling the leaf of a sage bush. It's horribly clear. She likes him. She really likes him. It feels like a tiny rusty knife being stabbed into my heart.

## Polly

I've not had time to work on my garden for several days now but, luckily, it is looking spectacular. Bees are buzzing to the Echinacea, butterflies are fluttering to the Verbena, and the grass looks lush.

We go through the jasmine archway, and we come out in the secret bit at the bottom. We survey it together. It's actually looking great. I pull out my phone and take a few snaps. There are a few apple trees dotted around, providing shade. There's a path that goes through the trees and up to a bank of grass where I've got a little statue that Arthur inherited from a gay uncle. Down the north side of the garden, I've got a bank of Christopher Lloyd-style riotous colour. It's all exotics and hots – peaches and pinks and reds. It's a veritable orgy of floral colour.

You can tell James really likes it.

We are having the most delightful conversation I've had in ages. He's already enthused about my outrageous floral combinations. And he's not asked me once about any of the usual dreary subjects – e.g. half term, or how the children are doing at school. He's not mentioned the kids at all. OK, that is partly because he doesn't know they exist. But it's also because he's been showing me a map of the grounds of Bodsham Abbey. I haven't quite got my head round them, but they look amazing. If you go round the side of the Chapel, you come to a field that overlooks the green hillside Inshaw painted. James has been probing me as to what could grow there. He loves magnolias. He wants to know if they'll flourish in Wiltshire soil. Personally I think magnolias are the Celine Dion of the plant world: they flourish all too briefly, for which they are over-rated; the rest of the time they are an ugly, spindly waste of space. But I don't say that. I just say: 'I'm sure most things could flourish in your garden, James, given the right attention.'

As I say that, I realise my words are heavy with subtext. *I* will flourish in your garden, I'm telling him. *You* will provide the water. And for a brief moment I see myself as a luscious leafy green plant, and James is watering me with his long hose. (What is this? Some sort of weird plant-based watersports fantasy? Who cares? For once, I'm having fun.) It's all pretty much perfect. Apart from the clothes. James does look a bit weird, leaning against an apple tree, wearing an apron.

I can't help but smile at him.

'James Hammond,' I say. 'You look like you're a Calendar Boy.'

He gets the reference. 'Yes,' he says. 'I'm naked under this apron. Wanna look?'

I *do* want to see under his apron so much. So I fall to my knees and I lift it up and I take out the Hammond organ.

No, I don't. Of course I don't.

I just say: 'Well . . . maybe, if I can come on Friday.'

And as soon as I say that, it's like snakes are writhing out of the flowers hissing: '*Polly*! *What* are you doing?'

Oh, no. What have I *said*?

## Em

Arthur opens the door looking like Lady Chatterley's lover. He's wearing jeans and a black shirt. He looks stubbly and manly and slightly cross. Delicious. Better still, he's holding two glasses of wine.

'Hey, big boy,' I say. I take the wine. I neck the glass. Then I kiss him right on the lips.

He doesn't move.

'How was your weekend with Dan?' he asks as I come into the kitchen.

'Fine,' I say. I really don't want to discuss it.

'What happened?'

Bloody hell, there's no escape. I'm going to tell him.

'Dan,' I say, and just saying his name makes me get furious, 'took me to Spain.'

'For the weekend?'

'Yes. It was a five-star hotel, overlooking the Alhambra.'

Arthur smiles as he refills my glass. 'Sorry, Em,' he says. 'You seem really angry about it. Why?'

'*Because I thought he was going to propose!*' I say. 'We were in the fucking honeymoon suite, overlooking the fucking Alhambra. Drinks arrived. I thought: I better not say anything. He's about to propose. He said . . . "Have you ever had Athlete's Foot?" "Er . . . no!" I said. "It's strangely delicious," he said, "when you scratch." I was suddenly less certain I wanted to accept him. It's hard, to be honest, to accept someone's proposal, once they've said the words "Athlete's Foot". Anyway, my concerns were misplaced. Dan didn't propose, so basically we just had a normal weekend: I got pissed off, he spent the weekend apologising. I tell you, that man could be Olympic Champion at saying sorry.'

Arthur stares at me, looking all brooding and handsome.

'How long have you been together?' he asks.

'Two years!' I tell him. 'This is what happens, Arthur! I meet men, and I give them years of love, sex, and much-needed fashion advice. Then they *leave!*' Suddenly I'm boiling over with rage. 'Dan is a stupid fucking child!'

'But . . . what do you want him to do?'

I almost shout it at him. '*I want him to propose!*'

'But . . . it doesn't sound as if you even like him.'

'*I still want him to propose!* Otherwise I'll feel like I've spent two years at the birthday party of a child, and I've not even got a prize!'

Arthur grins. I don't see the joke. I can, though, see his chest hair through his opened shirt.

'You're a man,' I ask him. 'Why do you think he hasn't proposed?'

'Dunno,' says Arthur. 'But all blokes are scared of marriage.'

'But why?'

'Well,' says Arthur. 'You know what the *Learn Love* course says? Men are like snails. They are scared elusive creatures. They must be lured out, with beer and treats. Then they must be trapped.'

'But how do you trap them?' I say.

'You don't stay with them for two years, Em. Give them six months. Maximum. Enough time so they fall in love, not enough time so they take you for granted. Then you say to them: "Darling, I love you. But I've been offered a job in Berlin."'

'I don't know anyone in Berlin.'

'Invent one. Or invent one somewhere else. Somewhere overseas.'

I think it through. 'I could say I've been offered a job in New York working on American *Vogue*. I know Tiggy, the deputy ed. She's hinted they'd take me.'

'Perfect. That should be enough to get the snail's attention. **Then** you say: '*Or* I could stay, and we could marry.' And *then you must utterly ignore him, till he gives you an answer.*'

I stare into Arthur's eyes. How come Polly doesn't see this? He has authority.

### Arthur

I'm feeling a bit nervous. Em is staring at me with a mad determination. I feel as if I've woken something in her, and anything could happen.

'Give me another glass of wine,' she says.

I do. She drinks it down fast. Then she takes out her phone.

'*What are you doing*?!' I say. I'm very worried now.

## Em

'For too long,' I announce, 'I've been waiting for that man, like a dog tied up outside the bookie's. I'm going to make him propose.'

And I dial Dan's number.

'You're dialling him *now*!' says Arthur.

'Why not?' I reply.

And, actually, I feel totally confident about this. Well . . . I do till he picks up.

'Hey, Em,' says Dan.

'Hello.'

'Sorry I got cross at the airport,' he says.

'That's OK . . . Dan,' I begin, 'I need to talk to you.'

'Oh!' He sounds instantly worried. 'Why?'

'Erm . . . I've just been offered a job, to go and work on American *Vogue* in New York.'

He's silent.

'God!' he says finally.

There's another long silence.

'So,' he says tentatively. 'Do you want to go?'

'I'm certainly very tempted!'

'Oh,' he says. He sounds disappointed, but he's not saying anything. Why don't men speak? More silence.

Suddenly my mouth is dry. I am staring at Arthur. He's willing me on. I'm sensing Dan won't want to hear this, but Arthur is willing me on. I must say the words.

'Or . . .' I say '. . . I could stay, and we could marry.'

Dan is silent. Apart from the slight sound of panting.

'Hello?' I say.

Now I'm panicking.

'Erm . . .' he says. His voice has gone schoolboy high. 'Wow!

That's . . . That's such a sweet offer.'

*Sweet*. Sweet?! Nobody calls me sweet and expects to live.

'You don't need to say now,' I say. 'But I need to give them an answer this week.'

'Right,' says Dan, sounding terrified.

'Well, we're seeing each other on Friday.'

'Are we?'

'It's the launch of the new Hammond hotel.'

'Of course,' he says weakly.

Fuck him! Fuck him! I've just proposed marriage to him! He's acting like I've just told him he's got cancer. He's clearly going to say no. I suddenly realise this phone call was a terrible mistake. It must end. Now.

'Let's talk then,' I say. 'Good night.'

'OK,' he says, putting on this horrible, eager-to-please voice. He's definitely going to refuse me. 'Good night.'

I turn off the phone.

Fuck me with a big pole, what have I just done?

I'm still staring at Arthur. He has delicate lady-like eyelashes.

'He's gone!' I say. I feel desperate. 'And he didn't answer!'


## Arthur

Em is giving me that old-fashioned feminine look – the one that says: *I'm lost, I'm lost, and you've got all the answers!* It's very sexy. Polly never does that.

'*Of course* the snail didn't answer,' I say. 'He's hurried back to the shell where he feels safe. He's terrified.'

'Why?!'

'Because . . . there's only one thing a man fears more than commitment, and that's losing the woman he loves.'

Her look softens into something even sexier – admiration. 'You must write this down,' she says. '"How to Trap a Man".'

I'm not falling for that one, ever again.

'I already did one piece for you today,' I say, 'and you didn't like that.'

'I loved it!' she says. 'The editor loved it! We printed it!'

'Oh! *Really?!*' (Teacher liked my piece. Nice.)

'Yes! I want you to do a piece every day this week.'

'Oh!' I say. I'm very pleased about this, so naturally I hide it. 'OK,' I say.

'By the end of the week, you'll be a star of lifestyle journalism.'

I smile. 'And you will be engaged.'

Em smiles at me. She looks pleased and flushed and impossibly luscious. Em is the complete opposite of Polly. Polly is tall and considered. Em is short and out of control. She steps forward. She stands on tip-toes and kisses me right on the lips.

Her lips are very soft.

What the *hell* are we doing?

It's like we both snap to our senses at the same time. We both talk together.

'I'll go and write down that advice now,' I say quickly.

'I'll go and say hi to Polly,' she says overlapping.

She leaves. I go to my office and write.


## Polly

I'm going over it again and again in my head . . .

James said: 'I'm naked under this apron. Wanna look?' I said: 'Maybe, if I can come on Friday!' That was basically saying: I will have sex with you on Friday. Well . . . wasn't it? *Why* did I say that? Now I'm all flustered, and so I've been asking him questions, and he's telling me about his business, and I'm not really listening. I'm just nodding and pretending to listen.

Then he says it again: 'So can you come on Friday?'

He wants to close the deal.

Can I come on Friday?

Can I?

Can I come?

I *need* to tell him about the kids. He'll find out at some point, so why not now?

*How* do I tell him?

'James,' I begin.

But suddenly Em appears through the jasmine archway.

'James Hammond!' she says, bustling towards him, holding out her hand. 'It's so nice to see you again!'

'Your garden is beautiful,' says James gallantly. 'Almost as beautiful as your children.'

Em blushes. 'Yes! Well! You know what they say . . . children are like farts. If they're yours, they're surprisingly lovely.' She takes him by the arm, and leads him towards the house. 'Shall we go inside? I picked up some Turkish food on the way home . . . Thank you so much, by the way, for the wonderful piece you did last year.'

'Any time,' says James.

Em takes that literally. She's so grabby. 'Perhaps you could do a regular column for us. You know . . . James Hammond, the Secrets of Business.'

'I thought,' says James, 'there was only one secret of business: the customer is always right. Unless he's in LIDL.'

Em chuckles and leads James inside. Fortunately, Arthur and Malcolm are nowhere to be found. The food is on the table.

Trouble is: so is Ivy. And she's naked. And she's got her fist in the hummus. I give Em a look as if to say: Please . . . deal with that.

She doesn't know how to, though.

She picks up Ivy, but she holds her away from her body, like she's scared of touching her. It doesn't work. Ivy still splodges hummus in Em's hair. Em does a little whimper, then stands Ivy in the kitchen sink.

'Wash your hands,' she says. She turns on the tap. She turns to us. 'I'll just . . .' she says, pointing to her hair.

She leaves. With Ivy standing in the sink like a bit of meat that needs to defrost.

I turn to James.

He looks back a beat too long. Our feelings are horribly apparent. I fancy him obviously, and OK that is disturbing, I haven't fancied anyone in ages. But what's really unsettling is the way he seems to be the answer to all my dreams. He's calm. He's rich. He's actually *asking* me to design gardens. *We belong together, James! Let us run off and create a world of floral magic!!*

But I am bothered by the sight of Ivy in the sink.

'So,' says James, 'can you come?'

'I'd love to,' I say.

'Oh, great,' he says. 'Who knows? Maybe we could do loads of gardens together.'

I have to tell him. I have to tell him.

'But,' I say, 'I need to . . . make arrangements.'

'Of course.'

No, James. Not any arrangements. I *must* tell him.

'You see, James, I have children.'

I'm looking into James's eyes. For a tiny moment, he looks surprised.

In that instant, you can tell he hadn't considered I have children, which I find deliciously flattering. (I'm thirty-five, what does he expect?) I can tell he's also embarrassed he's been flirting with a mother. But then his manners kick in, and he covers it up.

'You have children?' he says smoothly. 'Where are they?'

'Erm . . . one of them is right there.'

I point at Ivy. She's still naked in the sink. She's now spraying water on to the floor. James looks discomfited. It's all going wrong. I must tell him.

'I am sorry,' I say. 'I should have told you earlier. That's my garden. This is my house. These are my children.'

There's a tiny silence, which is incredibly embarrassing. Then he collects himself.

'Nothing wrong in having a child!' he says smoothly. 'Unless you've kidnapped her . . . Have you?'

'No. If I were kidnapping a child, I probably wouldn't have kidnapped that one!'

Ivy is now squirting washing up liquid methodically into the sink.

There's another silence. I'm trying to think of more to say. But I can't think of anything that ought to be said out loud, on the subject of my willingness to kidnap a naked child. I also really want to stop Ivy before she empties the whole bottle.

Em arrives.

'Sorry about that,' she says. 'It's not really a good look: hummus in hair. So . . . James Hammond, are you staying for dinner?'

'I'd love to stay for dinner,' he says. 'But . . .' He takes off the apron. Which suddenly exposes the big wet patch on his trousers. His voice trails off.

'But you've wet yourself,' says Em.

'Yes,' he says. 'I've had such fun, I just lost all control. Erm . . . So this has been lovely, but I must go and change. Good night!'

He kisses us both on the cheek.

'I'll call you soon!' he says.

He goes.

And as I shut the door, I am hit by an avalanche of embarrassment.

'That could have been worse!' says Em.

'How?' I say. 'I suppose we could have covered him in petrol and set him alight.'

Em grins. 'It's OK,' she says.

'Em,' I say. 'I haven't been so embarrassed since I was at school, and I called the teacher Mummy.'


## Arthur

I feel so tense.

I cannot take it. Polly is flirting with that cock of a man, and meanwhile I'm looking after the kids, and Malory and Robin are, once again, refusing to get out of the bath. In fact they're hitting me with demands. Malory is saying she'll get out, but she wants a hot chocolate. I'm saying she can't have a hot chocolate, because she'll wet the bed.

'I do NOT wet the bed!' says Malory. 'And you SAID I could have a hot chocolate!'

'I did not,' I say.

'Well then, I am NOT getting out of the bath,' says Malory.

'OK FINE,' I say, slightly too loudly. 'Just stay in the bath. *I do not care.*'

They both look at me a bit surprised.

'To be honest,' I say, 'you can help me with something that I'm very worried about.'

That gets their attention. 'What?' says Malory.

'Tomorrow I have to go to a school to make up a story in their Assembly.'

Malory doesn't see the problem. 'But you are brilliant at making up stories!'

'Yeah, Dad, you're brilliant at it,' says Robin loyally.

I love them. For a moment I think everything's going to be fine. 'OK,' I say. 'So let's make up a story now, and in fact you're *not allowed* to get out of the bath till we've made one up!'

They smile at that. I put on my storytelling voice. 'This story is about a little man,' I begin, then I pause for inspiration. 'And one day the little man gets sucked down a plughole.'

Malory sticks her hand up. I love it when she does that.

'Yes!' I say.

'How,' she asks, 'does the man get sucked down a plughole?'

'Well . . .'

'Is he made of wee?'

They laugh. I laugh.

And then immediately I remember that there was only one rule for the visiting author: keep it clean. If anyone says anything like that tomorrow, I'm fucked.

Now I'm tense again.

Polly pokes her head round the door.

'Why aren't they out of the bath?' she says.

'I'm about to do it!' I say. Now I feel tenser still.

Polly comes into the room. She's holding a mug. 'Malory,' she says, 'I brought you a mug of chocolate!'

Now I do lose it very slightly. 'Polly!' I say, a bit sharply. 'I *said* she couldn't have chocolate!'

'I just thought it would be nice!'

'OK! Fine!' I say, far too loudly.

Immediately Polly looks at me, alarmed, as if to say: *What's* the matter with you?

Oh, God. And now she's going to tell me off, and we'll have a row. 'You know what . . .' I say. 'I'm done! I'm *done*! I'm DONE!' I feel absolutely furious suddenly. I wiggle past her out of the door. I need to get away. I need to calm down. I need to figure out what I'm going to do in the morning.

## Em

As soon as I hear Arthur raising his voice, I go straight upstairs. It's like at school when you heard people chanting 'Fight! Fight!' You just have to look.

Arthur is fleeing the bathroom looking flustered.

Polly pursues him. 'Is there a problem?' she says.

'Yes! There is,' he says, turning on her. He starts speaking very fast, and very precisely, like an actor who wants each word to be clear in the gallery. 'I said she could not have chocolate. You've overruled it. If ever I make a decision, you overrule it. And if ever I raise my voice, you intervene.'

'Don't shout at me,' she says.

'I am NOT shouting,' says Arthur, who is, in truth, dangerously close to shouting. 'I am also not swearing. I am also not trying to hit anybody, and *yet* you intervene. How am I supposed to have any authority when you will not let me raise my voice? You know what? I've been doing childcare all day.'

'What?' says Polly. 'I often do that.'

'Well, it's not easy, is it?' he says. 'Particularly as I've also been carrying out your instructions about starting a new career. Which is not going to be easy, given I only get eight seconds between interruptions. To be honest, it's been a stressful day.'

'Arthur!' she says. 'I've had a long day as well. I've had stress!'

'I've hosted a birthday party for Sum Baby,' says Arthur. 'I've had people shouting at me, all day, and for much of it I've also had to listen to the singing of Mr Tumble. So . . . *don't talk to me about stress.*'

As I edge carefully between them, I feel a bit like a pheasant on a shoot.

'I'm going to go,' I say.

They both look at me. There's a tense silence.

But that's interrupted by a man coming down from the second floor. He looks kind and handsome, albeit somewhat overdressed. He's wearing a tuxedo, complete with bow tie and cummerbund.

'Malcolm!' says Polly. 'You look like a mayor!'

'I like to think,' says the ginger man, in a sexy Dublin accent, 'I'm the mayor of people's hearts.' He turns to me and shakes my hand. 'I'm Malcolm,' he says. 'Did I hear you say you're going?'

'I need to get home,' I say.

'Grand,' he says. 'I'll give you a lift.'

'It's a bit of a trek.'

'I have time!'

'Do you,' I ask, 'have a mayor's carriage outside?'

'I have a van,' says the man. 'And it has plenty of room. I'll just have to move the cement mixer. Come on.'

## Polly

I am furious with Arthur. I hate him shouting at the children. I also hate him shouting at me, especially in front of the children, *especially* in front of Em. I have been working all day for this family, and every time I've seen him he has scowled or shouted. What is the matter? I really need to speak with him.

But first I must find him.

I look all around the house, and I finally find him hiding at the bottom of the garden.

'Arthur,' I say.

'*Leave me alone!*' he shouts.

*What* is the matter? He's shouting at me like a mad child.

'Arthur,' I say calmly.

'No!' he shouts. 'I mean it . . . No! Don't say one word! Not one fucking word! Leave me alone!'

*What the fuck has got into him?*

## Em

Funny how life works out . . .

You go out for an evening, expecting to have dinner with the Businessman of the Year. You end up going home in the van of a very overdressed Irish builder. Sitting in a seat which has just been vacated by a cement mixer. As I look round, I can't see a single element of this van which might be mentioned in *Lifestyle*. The dusty dream catcher dangling from the mirror? We are not recommending those this season. Nor are we suggesting that, leaning against the driver's seat, you should have scaffolding. But I feel, for once, like I've got nothing to prove, and it's all strangely relaxing. I would count the drive as this week's Guilty Pleasure.

We reach my street.

'You can pull over here,' I tell him.

He pulls over. He runs round my side and opens the door.

'Thank you,' I say. I'm not sure whether to give him a kiss or a tip.

'Which one is yours?' he asks.

'Number ninety-nine. Top flat.'

He looks up. 'You have a broken window,' he says. 'I have some glass in the van. Will I fix it now?'

I've ignored that window pane for two years. I can last a couple longer. 'That is extremely kind,' I say. 'But no, thank you.'

'Another time,' he says.

'Yes,' I say. And to bring this to an end, I reach up and kiss him on the cheek.

First he looks astonished. Then he just beams the happiest smile I've seen in a long time.

'Thank you,' he says.

Oh, dear. This is basic seduction technique. When someone kisses you, you mustn't say 'thank you'. Though it's better than 'sorry'.

There is only one thing for it: complete physical union

# Tuesday

*Learn Love in a Week* – *the online course that will change your life*

**Day Three**: I hate the pictures on romantic websites. The men are always steering yachts, and they've got sweaters tied round their shoulders and smiles on their faces, as if they're quietly happy about a business deal that went fantastically well . . . Life's not like that. No man wears a sweater on his shoulders, and if he does he needs a slap. Most men do not steer yachts, they've got yoghurt down their tops, and they're pissed off because their business has fucked up . . . In life, things go wrong, and love's biggest challenge is to cope with it. The trick is to give sympathy, and that's not easy. Upset people are a drain, and if they're your partner, you may be personally affected by their mistakes. That's why giving sympathy takes real generosity. But here's the upside . . . At some point, you'll be upset and you'll want the same in return. In love, you get back what you give out. Love is like a game of Frisbee. It's less good when you make little tight exchanges. It's better when you're standing back and you're flinging the Frisbee in the breeze, because you trust each other, you know it'll be caught, and you're having fun.

**Today's exercise**: practise seeing things from your partner's point of view by spending ten minutes writing a character portrait of them. Talk about their siblings, their obsessions, their dreams. It will make you feel warm towards them.

**Today's challenge**: try, just for one whole day, to listen to your partner totally without judgement, even if they've fucked up. *Especially* if they've fucked up. The basic rule: the person who's upset gets to do the talking. Ask open questions such as 'What happened?' and 'How did you feel?' and then listen. Do NOT say: 'Cheer up!' or 'Well . . . look at it this way!' – these are all ways of saying: 'I've had enough, will you now shut up?' Relax. They will shut up, eventually. They will be lighter for having spoken, they'll cheer up and be grateful. Then they'll get pissed off again.

## Polly

As I drift from sleep, I'm picturing myself working on James Hammond's meadow.

I imagine trees and the smell of jasmine and a blackbird singing. I imagine myself putting down my fork and James Hammond arriving with a tray of drinks and saying something complimentary with strong earthy undercurrents prior to giving me a long lusty kiss.

Then I think of James fleeing into the night. I think of Arthur shouting at me in the garden, and I feel tense and scared. I feel like Mum has said: 'just you wait till your Dad gets home!'

I open my eyes.

It's seven a.m. Arthur's not in bed with me. He must have slept on the sofa. His pillow is undented. His books are in the same position they were before: Don DeLillo's *Underworld,* and Bolaño's *The Savage Detectives.* Spine up, pages down, they're still sprawled there unread. They look like people who've fallen from a great height.

Ooh. And now he comes into the room. Dressed. He stares into my eyes a moment. He looks tired, a little blank.

'Hi,' I say, softly.

'Hi,' he says, a bit businesslike.

'Can you make me a coffee?' I say tentatively.

'I've got to go.'

'Where?'

'Thomas Cranmer School in Mitcham. So I can be burned alive.'

I have no idea what he's talking about.

He turns to go. 'I'm afraid Malory has wet her bed.'

'Can you get the sheets in the washing machine?' I say. 'Then I can dry them before I go.'

'I've got to go to work,' he says, and he tramps off down the stairs.

He seems to want a medal because, for once, he's going to work.

I give it a moment then I leap from bed.

By the time I get downstairs, he's holding his coat and his bag, and he's picking up a bin bag which I left by the front door. He carefully places the bin bag behind him. I'm trying to be conciliatory but that annoys me. ''Bye,' he says briskly, and goes out. I go into the kitchen, where his cereal bowl is standing self-righteously in the middle of the table, next to his giant, man-sized coffee mug. *He* had to go to work, they seem to announce importantly. *You* can clear us up. I feel another burst of fury. I run to the front door. I open it. He's just going out the gate. 'Why didn't you take out the bin bag?' I shout madly into the street.

He gives me another of his blank looks. 'Because I was holding my coat and bag,' he says. 'And because I'm not a bin man.' And then he just goes.

What am I going to do?

**Em**

*Lifestyle* will be brilliant today . . .

A genuine Hollywood star is in town. Yes, he's pushing a steaming cowpat of a film, but he'll look positively spiritual. Then I've got pieces about Colin Farrell who's doing theatre, a think piece about Wayne Rooney who's launching a chain of burger restaurants, and a TV chef who's keen to talk about how he's overcome his demons. I've met the said chef. I think his problem isn't demons, so much as sex addiction and cocaine abuse, but thank the lord for demons, I say. They must be constantly overcome, they must be discussed in intimate detail, next to bright glossy photographs. Without demons, *Lifestyle* would be three pages of adverts, arranged round a recipe.

It's one of those days when *Lifestyle* has more or less written itself, which is as well because I can't concentrate. Why did I propose to Dan? I've tried three times to call him since but he's turned off his phone. He's elusive at the best of times, even when he's not just been proposed to. Now he's hiding away like a scared vole. He's probably trying to work out if he can avoid me for the rest of his life.

Anyway that's why I'm hanging round by the lifts, waiting to bump into him. I've been here ten minutes now. I've deleted a hell of a lot of texts. I won't talk long. I'll just say 'hi'. I'll be sexy, I'll be brief, then I'll go.

Where the hell is he? He's probably hiding in the car park.

Oh, piss.

Now Greta Kay is coming. She's wearing a white jumper of extraordinary softness. Her breasts are two plump angora pillows.

'Em!' she says, as if just seeing me has made her morning. 'Hi!'

As she kisses me, I smell her perfume.

'How are you?' I ask.

'*Brimful* with ideas for next week.' She's being nauseatingly positive. She presses the button for the lifts.

At that moment Dan arrives, looking like an Indie guitar hero.

He's wearing sunglasses and a big belt, and his shirt is undone. He sees me and he immediately looks awkward. Bad sign.

I go over. 'Hi, Dan!' I say. I'm trying too hard to be breezy. I'm talking a bit too loud. I kiss him.

He recoils just slightly, as if I've got bad breath. That's not good. I'm aware of Greta watching.

'Hi!' he says. 'You OK?'

Wow! He really is awkward. He manages to stammer on the 'You'.

'Yip,' I say. 'You?'

He gives a brief nod, then he looks nervously at his feet. We're both awkward. I've proposed marriage to him, and suddenly we've got nothing to say to each other.

'Erm,' he says. 'I'm not seeing you this evening, am I?'

Would that be a bad thing? 'Er . . . no.'

'Good,' he says, looking around shiftily. 'Anyway let's chat at Hammond's on Friday.'

'Yes,' I say. We've already agreed that. He turns to go. 'And,' I say, 'there's also Staff Drinks tomorrow.'

'Is there?' he says.

'Yeah. We're celebrating that Sarah Shelton's been editor for ten years.'

'Oh,' he says.

I'm making a balls of this. He's trying not to see me, I've forced him into a date. This isn't good. Then it all gets worse still. Dan now sees Greta. He bolts towards her. Dan is the biggest fame-whore I've ever met. He leaps at Greta Kay like a frisky Jack Russell.

'Greta Kay!' he says, doing his sincere voice. 'Can I just say . . . I'm a big fan.'

'Thank you so much!' says Greta huskily.

'How are you finding working with Em?' he says, as I walk over.

Greta takes my arm. I like that. 'She's wonderful. I'm learning so fast.'

OK. That was bullshit, but it was flattering bullshit.

'Oh . . . nice,' says Dan. He clearly doesn't know what to say. 'So . . . Best get to the desk. Those zombies won't fight themselves.'

He heads off to his office, which is on the ground floor. He couldn't wait to get away. Bloody hell. He's clearly going to say no. The lift doors open and I see myself. I look haggard. Fuck Dan. He's taken the last of my bloom, and now he's going to chuck me.

Beside me, Greta is studying me in the mirror. 'You OK?' she says.

I turn. She looks calm and caring.

'Yeah!' I say.

'I may be out of line here,' she says. 'But I just felt there was a bit of a vibe there.'

I look into her wide face, and I make a decision.

I tell her everything.

She makes the lift go up to the fifteenth floor to buy us more time.

'The important thing,' she says, as the lift is coming down, 'is . . . do you want to marry him?'

'I don't know!' I say.

'Oh, come on,' she says. 'What do you want?'

Now I feel rattled. I hate people asking me that. *I don't know what I want*. I'm a blind person, looking down a well, in the dark. 'I'm waiting to hear what he wants first.'

'But you're in charge of your own destiny,' says Greta.

'I'm not sure I am!' I say. 'He needs to decide.'

'But also you need to decide.'

'Well . . .' I say. 'There's no one *else* out there. I feel like he's my only option.'

'Em,' she says, 'you must not take him because you think he's your only option.'

'But I'm thirty-four,' I say. 'I know what's out there. There *are* no other options.'

'Em,' she says, and she takes my arm. She looks like the cool big sister every girl wishes they had. I like her, I've decided, and I just love how she's at least ten years older than me and she still looks good. 'You'd better get one thing straight in your head before tomorrow, or you'll make the wrong decision.'

'What?'

'You are a gorgeous, witty, beautiful woman. You have options. There are loads of men out there, waiting for you.'

'Where are they?' I say. I really want to know.

The lifts open. I see Mike Linson and the boys from Sport.

'I don't know,' says Greta, smiling now. 'But I don't think they're here.'


## Polly

I've done it. I've got the kids to school.

I'm hurrying towards my car, thinking about James. It was incredibly embarrassing telling him that I have kids. Will he be over that? Will he still want me to come to Wiltshire to work on his meadow?

I'm disturbed by a cheery American voice.

'Good morning, Polly, how are you?'

I look up to see Tilly Sweeting. She's a blonde ex-lawyer who's so prissy she quite literally wears a hairband. She looks like the BBC2 testcard girl who's aged thirty years while learning way too much about catchment areas. Tilly is the most omnipresent person in our area. She's the President of the school Parent Teacher Association. She also organises the school fete. She's one of those people you really need to avoid, or you'll end up being asked to do something.

She's walking in the same direction as my car. I have no option but to walk with her.

'The teachers unions say Friday's strike *is* going ahead,' Tilly informs me.

Oh, dear. Already I don't like the way this is going.

Before I had children I naively thought that you handed them over to the school and they just got on with it. But, no . . . The schools shut all the time. They shut for strikes. They shut for holidays, bank holidays, and half terms. They shut for Inset Days, Polling Days, and if there's so much as a snowflake in the air, they shut for Health and Safety. Plus you're expected to go in. You should read to them. You should talk about your work. You should accompany them on School Trips. And there are School Trips roughly every other day, and for every one of them you sign a form, and on that form there's a box in which you tick if you are willing to accompany the School Trip, and if you put a cross on that box, a tiny accusing finger pokes out, and a hissing voice says: '**Why** *can't you accompany the School Trip?* You are a *bad* mother.' That's what it's like being a mum. The finger points. The guilt builds and builds. Until, one day, you find yourself saying: 'Yes! I *would* like to be a Class Rep!'

Actually Tilly asked me to be a Class Rep last year. I said no. The guilt's at bursting point.

'We're trying to keep the school open on Friday,' she says.

'Oh, thank God for that!'

'But we need parents who can do presentations for the school.'

'Oh.'

'Can you do something?'

'Well,' I say. 'Maybe Arthur could.'

'What could he do?'

'Well, he could do a show on improvisation and storytelling,' I suggest.

'That would be *amazing*,' says Tilly. 'They're hoping to do a day of performances. I'll definitely mention that to the PTA.'

I give a big non-committal smile. She goes.

Oh, dear. I think I just said something for which I'll suffer. Add it to the list.


## Arthur

OK . . . OK.

I'm at Thomas Cranmer School in Mitcham, and I'm at the back of the stage, watching five hundred children being herded into a hall. In a moment I must entertain them, with a forty-five-minute improvised story, which must be clean.

Fuck, I'm scared.

DO NOT SWEAR. DO NOT SWEAR.

My heart is beating.

I shut my eyes and pray to Thomas Cranmer in my head.

'Please . . . allow me to inspire these children. And if you could grant me one really funny gag, quite early on, make it clean.'

I get a sudden mental image of Cranmer – a fierce bishop from the sixteenth century: he'd probably not be an ideal source of comedy. Particularly if he were on fire.

DO NOT THINK ABOUT THE FIRE.

Damn that Legg woman! I know I'm just going to go out there and be UNABLE to think of any story that doesn't involve a burning bishop called Bishop Albus Fuckbum.

Oh, Lord.

We're about to start.

Ms Legg steps out on to the stage.

She clears her throat a couple of times and they all go quiet.

'Good morning, everybody,' she says with a brightness so fake it's almost sinister.

All five hundred children chorus as one. 'Good MORNing, Ms Legg. Good MORRRRRRRNING, friends.' Their five hundred voices have combined together to make a dirge. They sound like slaves, forced to sing as they board the boats.

Right,' says Legg. 'We are very LUCKY to have a guest in school this morning. He's written a book. So I want you to *listen.*'

Ms Legg, you really are no Fearne Cotton. You're killing this crowd.

'And if *anyone* misbehaves,' she concludes, 'I will take down their names, and send them straight to Mrs Dawkins, is that clear?'

Oh, for fuck's sake. You've just placed the thought in their head that it's all going to kick off and I won't be able to deal with it. Why don't you also tell them I'm a big gay who wears ladies' clothing?

MUSTN'T SWEAR. MUSTN'T SWEAR. MUSTN'T SWEAR.

'So,' she concludes, 'please give a WARM THOMAS CRANMER WELCOME for Adrian Midglet.'

Arthur *Midgley*, you bitch! Arthur Midgley!

I step out. As I do, I take in my crowd.

I've got to give it to them . . .

The kids do me proud. In the middle, I see a toothy girl in bunches. She's screaming with pleasure. At the front, I see a tiny Reception child. He's looking up at me with wonder, as if Batman has just walked out on the stage. At the back, I can see a row of Year 6-ers. They're cheering like they're the audience for *Oprah*. I have never seen a more warming display of generosity. It hits me like a delicious hit of skunk.

I smile.

My performing instincts kick in. I figure: I know it's nine o'clock in the morning and I'm in a school . . . I see before me a crowd. I shall work it.

'Hello!' I say.

'Hello!' they chorus back.

I dive into the storytelling.

I speak to a girl in Year 3, who says she's good at swimming. So we improvise a story in which Trisha has to swim into a murky pond, to rescue a drowning kitten. Reception all do the sound of the drowning kitten. 'Miaow miaow'. Staff do the sound of the large terrifying frogs. I mime their gigantic lashing tongues. I also mime a mad duck, who flies over Trisha's head and then does an egg on her head. That pretty much brings the house down. For them, this is about as good as it gets: seeing a grown man, laying an egg, in the middle of Assembly. At a time when they should be doing Maths. At the end of the story, Trisha reaches the kitten. She swims back. She steps through the squelchy mud. (Gleeful sound effects from Year 1!) Trisha rescues the kitten!!!

The school gives this a spontaneous round of applause!!

Wow! I think. I'm actually storming this.

I've improvised a story. It was funny. It was slightly educational. And it was as clean as a queen's bottom.

I glance at the clock.

I've done thirty-five minutes. I've got ten to go. I figure I'll tell them about my book, and then I'll get off.

I say it's about a boy called Colin Hitchin who's being bullied, and how he learns to cope. I perform the first chapter. I've done this bit before. I'm on safe ground.

'My name is Colin Hitchin,' I say, in my Colin Hitchin voice. 'The guys call me Colin Bitchin.'

Throughout the performance, I've been aware of Angela Legg eyeing me guardedly. She gets up and walks out.

Where has she gone? What's she doing?

Suddenly the fire alarm goes off.

I'm instantly chilled. Naturally I assume that the alarm has been pressed because of me. I just know something's gone wrong.

Immediately staff rise and start marshalling. In three minutes, five hundred children troop out.

I sit on the stage, wondering what I should do.

No one speaks to me. In this imaginary fire, I'm a faggot.

After five minutes Angela Legg reappears and says: 'Could you come to the headmistress's office?'

It's just like being a kid again. Immediately my heart is pounding. I follow.

What's happening?

She tip-taps her way pertly to the headmistress's office.

What does she want? Does she want to explain the fire drill and how I might fit into it? Does she want to congratulate me on an excellent opening session and offer me a permanent post?

Mrs Dawkins is in the office, sitting in an armchair. Angela Legg sits beside her. I stand in the middle of the room like a naughty schoolboy.

'We're sending you home,' says Angela Legg.

'What?!' I say. 'Why?'

'You used bad language.'

'What? What did I say?'

'You said Bitchin.'

'What?'

'And that's bad language.'

'Oh. I'm really sorry,' I say. 'I have children of my own. I'm not in the business of trying to teach them to swear. I'm just trying to teach them that their imaginations are fun.'

'Yes. Well, I warned you about this on the phone. Did I not warn you?'

'Yes,' I say. 'You're in the clear. But listen . . . I really am sorry, but I've prepared for the day, and so have you. I don't even mind about the fee, but let's carry on. And if I say anything else you're uncomfortable with, why don't you send me home then?'

'You have to go now,' she says. 'Or we'll call security.'

I want to say: For fuck's sake! The word 'bitchin' appears in the first fucking paragraph of the fucking book you fucking asked me to talk about. And it's not even a swear word, you stupid fucking cow! But suddenly I see there's no point. I'm feeling a bit winded and shaky. I just know that whatever I say they won't listen.

'OK,' I say. 'Well . . . I'm very sorry. Goodbye.'

And I walk out of the school, feeling disappointed and unpaid.

## Polly

I've been checking my phone for texts. James hasn't been in touch.

I'm just finishing a spectacularly boring meeting, run by Giles Dempsey, a vain uppity whizzkid who's the company's new

Finance Director. He's all floppy hair and brown shoes which he likes clicking together. He has been talking for an hour, during which time he says that he loves what we're doing, the work is vital to the company strategy, but our budget is being slashed.

At the end everyone's packing up when Giles says: 'Oh, I read your husband's piece.' He says it with a sort of sarcastic sneer. 'It was in a paper I picked up on the tube this morning.'

'Which piece?' I say.

He pulls out a copy of yesterday's *Lifestyle* which he's got in his bag. He flicks to the right page and I see the words '"Opposites Attract" by Arthur Midgley'. As my eyes scan through it, I am tense. I feel like Mum has just found out I've drawn on the wall.

I smile thinly for Giles Dempsey. 'May I keep this?' I say. He nods. I thank him for the excellent meeting. I say goodbye with exaggerated good cheer. Then I head fast down the street.

As soon as I reach the street I call Arthur.


**Arthur**

I'm trudging dejectedly through Mitcham when Polly calls.

'Hello,' she says.

'Hi.'

'You OK?'

'Yes,' I say. Polly is already pissed off with me. I'm really not ready to tell her I've fucked up.

'I just saw your piece in the paper,' she says.

'Yeah?' I say faintly.

'Well done,' she says.

I wait. She's just praised me: clearly damnation is about to follow.

'"You're not attracted to your opposite. You're attracted to

[111]

someone sexy, then you resent everything they do differently. What does that mean?'

Here we go. The Inquisition is about to start.

'It means,' I say, 'that I was attracted to you because you were sexy.'

'I *was* sexy?'

'You *are* sexy. But there's tension because you're tidier than me and more organised.'

She totally loses it. 'We don't have schedules because I like them!' she shouts. 'We have them because there are five people in this family who need organising!'

Oh, wow. She's totally exploded. My every instinct is to back away.

'OK!' I say mildly. 'Well, maybe that's the point. I need to organise more. You need to relax and . . .'

'When I was a child,' she says accusingly, 'I was known as messy, and impulsive. Then I found you, and that's forced me to be the sensible one. I can't bear it! You *crush* the life out of me, then you *blame* me for it.'

I don't say anything. There's no point. So far I've said she was organised: she's said I'm crushing the life out of her! Our conversations are totally one-sided. It's like she's Mike Tyson and I'm a toddler. She annihilates me.

'Listen,' I say. 'I can't talk now. I'm at Mitcham.'

To be fair she backtracks. 'Oh my God,' she says. 'I'm so sorry. I forgot. Are you about to do a session?'

'Er . . .' I say. 'I'm . . .' I can hardly bear to say this.

'I'll speak to you later,' she says.

Execution is delayed. 'Great,' I say, relieved.

## Em

I have one hundred and twenty-eight e-mails. One from Shelton says: '*Loved* the Opposites Attract piece. S.'

I can't concentrate on work.

Maybe Greta is right. Maybe I do want Dan because I think he's my only option. She's right. I'm about to accept a lifelong commitment, and I've never even tested what other options are out there. I've never even done online dating. I need to try it, before tomorrow night. I should go online, right now, and find a man. I need a perfect man, by tomorrow.

Come on! I should get the word out. I should brand myself. I should pen an advert. OK . . .

> Wanted: one Perfect Man. Must be tall, handsome, funny, and brilliant at cooking. Must have athletic body (e.g. Tom Daley). Must have first-class Oxbridge degree in Arts subject. Must have really great job, which takes him no time at all. Must be strong, powerful, decisive man, who agrees with me about everything. Cunnilingus essential.

Oh, God. That's terrible. The problem isn't just that I'm getting fat and old. I'm also getting crude and nasty. I have a cruel twisted character.

> Hello. I have a cruel twisted character, and a scared bruised heart, I want someone who'll be kind. I may not be kind back. I am like a cactus, I am prickly and cruel: I still want a kind soft man who'll be the sand in which I grow. Cunnilingus essential.

This is worse! What am I saying? *Why did Arthur persuade me to propose?*

Actually I must speak to Arthur about a piece for tomorrow.

I dial him.

He answers on the fourth ring.

'Hello,' he says.

'Arthur darling,' I say. 'Are you OK?'

'Yeah,' he says quietly. 'Sort of.'

Oh, dear. Another sulky man hinting he needs a lady to come to the rescue. Sorry, Arthur. A girl can only rescue one man at a time.

'So,' I say. 'I got your "How To Find A Man" piece. I've made a couple of tweaks . . .'

'Have you?' he says, sounding a bit offended. 'What have you taken out?'

'The reference to sodomy.'

'Which one?'

'The bit where you say: "Men colonise women's bodies the way they once colonised the world. They always want to find the part that's unexplored, even if it's the bit you poo from."'

'But that's a lovely turn of phrase. Practically Ciceronian.'

'It's about buggery. It's not very *Lifestyle*.'

'OK,' he says. 'Fair enough.'

'So can you do your next piece by eleven tomorrow?'

'No.'

'What?' I say, alarmed. 'Why?'

'Polly got angry about the last one, and I just don't want that any more.'

'Is that it?' I say. 'Do you have any other reasons for stopping?'

'No.'

'In which case,' I say, 'I can see only one way of putting this.'

'Yes?'

'Don't be a dick. If you stop writing, you won't have learned Love in a Week. You'll have learned nothing, in two days. Worse, if you stop now, you'll make *me* look like a dick. And I don't need that right now. So please, pretty please . . . do some more fucking pieces for me, make them insightful and witty and personal, or I will come round to your house and I'll set fire to your clothes!'

'OK,' he says, sounding weak and feeble.

'What's the problem?' I say.

'Nothing,' he says.

## Arthur

The problem is I can feel a huge row is about to happen.

It's been inevitable ever since I shouted at Polly last night. She takes a zero tolerance approach to tension. At this point, her head will be like a busy legal practice. The tiny lawyers will be rushing about preparing the case for the prosecution. I must be ready because at some point she will say: 'What is wrong with you?' and there's a danger I'll just blurt out something like: 'I'm pissed off you didn't look at my cartoons!' and she'll say: '*I was* BUSY!' and then my objections will crumble as the tiny lawyers overwhelm me like a well-drilled German football team. I don't even know what I'm pissed off about, and I feel too tired to marshal a defence.

Which is why I'm so glad for the kids. I'm grateful for the distraction.

Tuesday's always a complicated day anyway. Robin stays behind for Mrs Betterton's Choreography Class. Malory is walked across town for her 4 p.m. Tap-dancing Class. Ivy walks with us, on the understanding that, on arrival, she'll be awarded chocolate buttons. She's fine with that. She'll walk to Bristol for a packet of chocolate buttons.

Amazingly, it's one of those rare days where everything goes well.

I meet them at 3.30, and they lift me with their affection and cheer and eagerness to get the chocolate buttons. On the walk Ivy collects leaves, she picks bark off trees, she walks along every wall that can be walked along. We arrive in time. We buy the buttons. Quite willingly, Ivy actually offers me some of them. I'm so grateful I carry her home. On our return, a mood of laziness settles over us and we lounge like tired cattle. Robin lies on the floor and designs imaginary outfits. Malory does a wordsearch. Ivy sits on my lap and she draws a fairy, then a fairy, then a fairy, then a fairy, then 'a fat princess who is about to turn into a dog'.

There seems to be something delicate and special about the mood tonight. I feel like an interruption could come along any second and smash it, and for a second I'm so sad I'm almost tearful.

**Polly**

James still hasn't called.

I feel like I'm sixteen again. I'm sixteen and I've snogged someone and now I might die because we're at the same party and he's avoiding me. I think he's been put off by the kids. I need him to call. I'm stuck in a world of kids and Finance Directors and grumpy husbands. I need to escape.

Even if it's for one night, I need to escape.

**Em**

I spend the afternoon signing on for every relationship site I can find. I'm drawn first to E-Harmony, which boasts 1.5 million users, and promises to match you with your Perfect Partner, based on twenty-nine dimensions of compatibility. I start their questionnaire with enthusiasm.

Do I want children? Yes, provided I can leave them for holidays.

Am I religious? Yes, I worship shoes.

Sadly the questionnaire isn't programmed to allow these witticisms, so in the end I just sign on for the sites that give me instant men, e.g. Grinder, which sends you a photograph of all the people nearby who want a shag. I click on one right away. It's extraordinary. I've not met the man. Already I know he's called Derek, he's 850 yards away, and he's nine inches when aroused.

Then I suddenly feel lost and lonely in this wide world of websites and cocks, so I go on Facebook. Good old Facebook. The friendly auntie of websites. I went on last night to discuss Malcolm, the strangely attractive man who tried to seduce me by fixing my window. He seemed kind, I confessed, is that enough to recommend a man? Not one person has commented on that. Not one.

Then I wonder if Dan has sent an e-mail to say let's meet to talk things over. I check eight times but he hasn't.

### Arthur

Polly is home at 6.30.

I still feel an argument is inevitable, but for a while everything is OK.

To be honest, I'm using the children as hostages. I stick close to them. I'm so keen to prevent attack, Ivy and I read two books about Biff and Kipper and the magic key, even though I hate them. (I must have read about sixty of those books; I still don't know which one's Biff and which one's Kipper.) Polly and I exchange several innocent conversations about towels. By 9.45 I'm washing up. I'm doing my least favourite job – I'm picking dried pasta from the bottom of a saucepan – but I'm relieved. I'm starting to think this row might never happen. There are football highlights on at 10.20. Maybe I could watch them.

The trouble is, I haven't actually mentioned the Thomas Cranmer Incident.

Nor has she enquired. And I've dropped quite a few hints. I've said 'You OK?!' and even 'Did you have a good day today?' but she's not taken the bait. There's been too much else that's been worthy of comment. She's received details of an interesting house in Ramsgate. And her mum wants to know when we'll be arriving at her sister's wedding (which happens in October).

Finally I just blurt it out. I tell her the complete story.

She's flicking through a magazine. I'm not even convinced she's listening at first. Up to the point when I say: 'So they just sent me home.'

That gets her attention. 'What?!' she says, looking up sharply. 'Why?'

'Because I said "bitchin", which they claimed was bad language.'

'But that's in the first sentence of the book, which they'd asked you to talk about.'

'I know!'

'Well, didn't you say that?' she says, and her tone of voice is suggesting I'm an idiot who could have saved myself a lot of trouble.

'There was no point,' I protest. 'All they cared about was

avoiding complaints. The worst of it is that I actually did a really good session. And that teacher was too ignorant to see it.'

'How do you know she was ignorant?'

That really riles me. Polly seems to be taking Angela Legg's side.

'She was at a school called Thomas Cranmer,' I say loudly. 'She didn't even know who Thomas Cranmer was. That's how fucking ignorant she was.'

'Don't get angry with me.'

'I'm not getting angry with you,' I say, but of course I am now getting angry. I've been holding it in all day, and now it's coming out. 'I'm angry with that teacher! I wanted to say to her: "It's not surprising your kids don't read. You're throwing out a writer who's just done a good session, because of one word, which isn't even a fucking swear word."'

'Don't swear at me!'

'I'm *not* swearing at you. I'm swearing at that priggish fucking teacher! I'd like to follow her down the street with a megaphone, saying: "You are a stupid bitch!"'

Polly's looking at me, astonished, but I can't help myself. Why won't she take my side?

'So,' she says. 'Did they give you the money?'

'Of course not!' I say.

'But,' she says, 'that money was supposed to pay for the campsite!'

'I know!' I say. 'Really, I get it! I've failed! *I've failed*! I get it!'

Polly's now looking at me like a cobra about to lunge. I've got to calm down. Quick. I check the clock. The highlights are starting in six minutes. I'll get out. I'll take the dog to the corner. I'll be calm.

'Mrs Thompson!' I shout. 'Come on, quick!'

Mrs Thompson appears in a moment. She's the only being in the house who recognises my authority. In a moment, we're outside in the cool night air, and we're walking up the road. I actually start to cool off slightly.

But on returning to the house, I see the thing that ends our marriage . . .

Polly has placed a bin bag by the front door.

Now . . .

I'm not an utter idiot. I know bin bags don't transport themselves from door to bin. I know she's not trying to provoke me at the end of a trying day. But I do kick that bin bag as hard as I can.

The bag is softer than expected. I think it's been padded by Ivy's nappies. (She's four and a half; she still wears nappies at night and we let her because we don't want to hear her cry: that's how much tension is avoided in our house.) I hate those nappies. I kick that bag like it's a penalty and I'm trying to blast the keeper. I kick it several times. It feels good.

Then I open the front door and I see Polly waiting for me, like Cato about to strike.

'You have a real problem with anger,' she says.

I'm thinking: I don't have a problem with anger. You do. If any appears, you wipe it up instantly, as if it were a little dollop of cat sick.

I nod at her. Then I attempt to pass her.

'You should do some therapy,' she says. 'You really need to get to the bottom of this.'

I head for the football highlights. I slip past her into the living room.

'*Why* are you going?' she says.

'Cos you're about to attack me. I'm about to be attacked by the person who's supposed to love me and that's the loneliest feeling in the world.

'We REALLY need to talk,' she says.

I turn and look at her a second. I'm thinking: WHY do we really need to talk? Why does everyone, every book, every magazine say 'it's good to talk'. It isn't always good to talk, particularly if it's late and all you're doing is listing your partner's faults.

'Well,' I say. 'We've got a lifetime to talk. But the Football Highlights are on now. I'm going to watch them. I need a few minutes to myself.'

At this, I give her a helpful nod. Then I slip away, into the living room, and – beautifully, fantastically – she doesn't try to stop me as I shut the door.


**Polly**

I Cannot Fucking Believe this . . .

He has been angry for two fucking days! We have BIG important things to discuss. *He's watching football*!!!


**Arthur**

I sit down. I turn on the television.

Oh my God, this is wonderful!

It's just started.

It's the Rio Ferdinand Benefit Game. It's Rio's United XI v The Rest of the World.

I stare at the lush green grass. Almost instantly I start to feel calm.

Then, consoled, I start to look about at the players. Rio's team contains United players, past and present. Becks is there. *We salute you, Lovely David!* Guess who's at Number 10 for The Rest of the World?

*Dennis fucking Bergkamp!*

Dennis Bergkamp, in front of a midfield that includes Cesc Fabregas, *Lionel Messi,* and Joey Barton.

God, I love football! Just seeing it is like having my neck massaged. It presents such a simple world. It's eleven men, versus eleven men, no women. If Wayne Rooney pushes Joey Barton, this is applauded, it's punished, it's forgotten. If women ran football, they'd have to have Time Out for a chat. Rooney would have to write Barton a card, and invite him for dinner.

And . . . oh, Lord . . . Dennis Bergkamp has the ball! He's *surging* from midfield! Oh my God, he's still got it! *Dennis, I love you!*

But there's an ambush. Polly arrives. She's holding my laptop under her arm.

'Can you turn that off?' she says.

Oh, fuck. I squeak: '*Why?!*'

'We need to talk!'

'We *really* don't.'

She hasn't even noticed that Bergkamp has the ball! This would be like her seeing Monty Don, and the Clooney, stripped naked and buying houses. I wouldn't see the point in that, but I'd *notice* it was exciting for her.

'You don't think it's useful, at all, to air our feelings?'

No, I don't! 'Cos you're the only one who's allowed to air them, and you only air your disappointments, your criticisms – frankly, I'd rather you kept those to yourself!'

She walks over and turns the TV off.

Oh, Jesus.

She stands in the middle of the room with her hands on her hips.

'*What* is going on?' she says.

If I give her the correct answer, can I have the football back?

'Well,' I say, and I speak so calmly I'm like an automaton, 'it's been a long day. I had a professional mishap, and I felt a little hurt you offered no sympathy because you were concerned about the financial implications. Sorry. I then overreacted to finding a bin bag outside, because I'm feeling quite sensitive about not getting any respect. Stupid really. Sorry. I'd now dearly love to watch football, so that I can calm down and process everything you told me earlier about how I crush the life out of you because I don't earn any money, and I don't schedule.'

There. Done.

I once read that, if you want to defuse a row, you mustn't hope to resolve everything. You must, however, see the other person's point of view. I just did that. I also apologised. Twice. Surely that wins me some football.

I get up, and I head for the button.

'Don't you *dare* turn that on!' she says.

She pushes me hard in the chest and I fall on the sofa again. I feel almost pleased about this. That's violence. That's proof. She's the angry one, not me.

I look at her.

She now holds up a newspaper. It's today's *Lifestyle*.

Oh, no. The prosecution has produced some unexpected evidence.

She places the newspaper on my lap. I see my piece: 'How To Find A Man'. I scan it quickly. Someone seems to have gone through my text conscientiously removing all the jokes, but it's recognisably mine.

'You seem to be suggesting,' she says, 'that the only way to get a man is to trap him.'

'Well,' I say, 'look at Dan. Men resist marriage, like cows resist the barn. Sometimes they need a prod.'

'Are you saying that's what happened to us?'

Oh, shit. I don't think this is a good topic for now.

'No,' I say. 'Well . . . we had kids straight away.'

'And did I force you?'

'No,' I say. And there's a big pause. I'm not going to talk. I've seen the error of that before. It's like goading a dragon.

'Did I somehow rape you?' she says.

I can't help it. I'm going to put my POV. 'No,' I say. 'I was concerned I didn't have a condom, and you said: "Just come here!" And nine months later, there was Robin.'

I trail off.

I'm staring at the blank screen, wishing the football back on.

Polly is looking at me with astonishment.

'Are you *really*,' she says, '*blaming* me because we had children?'

Oh, God. I don't know!

'Are you suggesting your cock just suddenly went into me by accident?'

That's a trick question. I'm not answering it. I go quiet like a computer about to crash. I really want to avoid this row. She doesn't though. She wants to have it. She suddenly loses her cool. She plunges into the row, with her traditional opener . . .

'I'm up every morning,' she says, gathering in volume, 'to do a job which I don't enjoy, but I have to do it because you're spending all your time writing some stupid novel.' – she's just called my novel 'stupid', I've noted that – 'Someone has to bring in the fucking money, and I do it, and you're not even grateful! And today you had an opportunity to earn some money, but you *wasted* it by swearing at some children. And I'm not *complaining* about that. I'm not *complaining* about anything. The only thing I do ask is that you might be a little more cheerful.'

'Well, right now,' I say, 'I don't feel like I'm skipping through the salty foam.'

'Why?'

'It's late and you're shouting at me.'

'You're so ungrateful!' she says. 'I support you, and . . .'

I can't take it when she says that. 'But you don't!' I shout. 'Today I was kicked out of a school for saying a word that isn't a swear word: you haven't given me a shred of sympathy.'

'I *support* you!' she says again. 'You don't earn any money.'

I can't take it when she says that. 'I *do* earn money,' I say. 'Just not as much as you'd like!'

'Judge me by my actions,' she says. 'I support you!'

'But you *don't*!' I shout. 'You interrupt me! You undermine me! You tell me to do things I don't want to do then you criticise those.'

Silence.

She can't believe it. I'm attacking her back. I'm also attacking one of the sacred myths of our marriage.

Now a full argument occurs.

We attain the ecstasy of absolute wounding honesty. We behave like corrupt government departments. Sensing a Bad News day is upon us, we rush into print with all toxic material. Christmas is mentioned. She compares me to my father. We talk money,

[ 125 ]

and exact earnings. At one point I say: 'If you'd *care* to look at my accounts . . .'

She's white hot with rage.

And suddenly she says it: 'I have HAD ENOUGH of you BLAMING ME for everything that goes wrong in your life. I give you EVERYTHING and if you can't see it, just GO!'

I can't believe she's given me an out like that.

I say: 'OK, I will.'

I grab my bag, I grab a pile of laundry that has been conveniently left on the stairs, and I go.

As I shut the door, I hear a furious scratching.

I open the door again. Mrs Thompson rushes out. She thinks we're going for a walk. We are going for a walk, Mrs Thompson, but it may be quite a long one. I grab her lead. I shut the door.

I walk off into the night.

I am out of the house.

I'm out of my marriage.

I could find a sexy stranger, right now, and I could take her clothes off.

There is only One Thing for it:

Complete Physical Union

# Wednesday

*Learn Love in a Week* – *the online course that will change your life*

**Day Four:** today you'll find you're not angry with your partner. You're angry with the world. And why wouldn't you be? It's such a beautiful world, but its economy requires you to stay in a state of fear and inadequacy, so you buy things you don't need.

**Today's challenge:** recover your power, by simplifying. Buy nothing. Turn off the bleeping electronics – your computer, your TV, your phone. As a result you will have loads of time. Use it to relax, or to help someone, or to clear up something that's bothering you – e.g. your tax return. Did I really just tell you to learn love by doing your tax return? I did. This course is unlike any other. This course actually works. Alternatively, you could just go to bed early. You may find someone there waiting for you.

**Today's exercise:** write for ten minutes, as fast as you can, starting with the words: 'I am angry because . . .' After that you'll have worked out why you're angry. Now do something about it. One thing.

## Polly

I wake at six.

Immediately I'm hit by the full awfulness of last night's row. I hate tension. I hate tension.

Then I open my eyes and I reflect that my main source of tension has gone.

Arthur is gone, and I've just taken a giant step closer to the meadow, and the green bank of grass, and the smell of jasmine. I feel like I've just taken cocaine. I feel like I've gone out in public wearing no pants. I feel extraordinarily naughty, but, secretly, rather pleased. I spring from bed. I yank open the curtains. Then I bound round my house like I'm taking possession of it for the first time.

The children's doors are ajar. I hear their snuffly breath and I feel a surge of protective love towards them. I think: You are mine, my darlings, and I shall look after you. I imagine us making daisy chains, sachets out of lavender . . .

Then I think: Their doors are open. They probably heard the whole row. I remember being a child, hearing shouts coming up the stairs. Maybe we *should* split up. For their sake.

And for mine too.

Arthur has been cramping me with his mess and his moodiness and his dismal lack of prospects. And suddenly . . . he's gone! And an alternative has come my way who's so very much more attractive.

But James didn't call yesterday.

James, please, please call. I really want to see your meadow. And you.

## Arthur

I'm dreaming . . .

I'm back at the party where I first saw Polly.

She's by the bonfire, and the smoke is shimmering. She looks so beautiful, just looking at her makes me bleed inside. I love her. I can't help it. I love her.

I hear a lighter being clicked. I wake.

I'm on a futon. I'm looking at Malcolm.

Oh, piss.

I'm in Malcolm's bedroom.

I look around. Everything is completely different from the tragic beauty of the dream. There are no women for a start. In fact Malcolm's room is about as male as it's possible to be. Beside his futon, he has a soldering gun. On the pillow there's something even stranger: Mrs Thompson, my dog. It's as if, now I've left home, Mrs Thompson feels she's taken her rightful place as my wife.

I feel awful.

Suddenly my head pounds with incredible pain. I sit up. I see Malcolm.

He's sitting across the room. He's smoking weed, and dealing Tarot cards on to a little table.

'Big Man!' he says, with a delighted grin.

'Malcolm,' I whimper. 'What the hell is going on?'

'You called me up late last night, you said Polly had chucked you out, you asked me to pick you up. I came over in the van.

I found you outside Costa with Mrs Thompson, sitting on the pavement drinking whisky. You saw me, you got up and you started running. You were running like Forrest Gump, shouting: 'I'm *not* getting in the van!' And then you ran smack into a lamp post. Which resolved the matter. I then lifted you into the van, and brought you here.' He gives me a happy grin. 'I must say,' says Malcolm, 'it was all *highly* unexpected.'

I stare at him a moment. Then I sink back on to his bed. His pillow is all dank and lifeless. I don't care. I don't think I'm ever going to get up again.

'How are you feeling?' says Malcolm.

'Dead,' I say. I've got a big round bruise on the side of my head. That must have been the lamp post.

'Perhaps you could explain,' says Malcolm. '*Why* did Polly kick you out?'

'She said I'm angry and ungrateful.'

Malcolm chuckles. 'And you are! How come she's just noticed?'

The sickening truth washes over me. 'It's because of James Hammond,' I say.

'The rich fucker?' says Malcolm. 'What's he done?'

'He's given her the job she's always wanted,' I say. And he also wants her. 'I think I'm going to be sick.'

Anyone else would have leaped up at that – the possibility of having someone puke in their bed. But not Malcolm.

'Well,' he says, 'it's the First Rule of Malcolm: *Everything happens for a reason.*'

I stare at him incredulous.

'What the fuck does that mean?'

'Everything is here to teach us. You just have to work out the lesson.'

He continues beaming at me as he puffs on his joint.

'It's so ironic,' he says. 'Now you really must learn Love in a Week. And if you don't, your wife will fuck off with James Hammond.'

Thanks, Malcolm. That's great.

He looks down at the Tarot cards in front of him.

'By the way,' he says, 'your cards are amazing! By the end of today, you're going to have a kiss.'

'Who with?'

'And by the end of the week, you're going to find love.'

'Who with?'

He doesn't say.

'Who will I fall in love with?' I say. I really need to know. '*Who with?*'

'The cards don't say,' says Malcolm.

## Polly

As the morning develops, I do rather lose the newfound sense of pleasure.

Over breakfast Malory wants Red Berry Special K, but without the Red Berries.

Ivy wants me to find her purple shoes, not the pink ones, the purple ones. (In a modern family, fifty-two per cent of all leisure time is spent looking for shoes.)

It would be easier to nail jellyfish to the ceiling than it is to get three children to school. For school, Ivy must have a book bag, a phonics book, some sun cream, a form authorising her to go to the park, a water bottle, and some fruit, which must be labelled. Robin needs more things still. He has two clubs today (Le Club Français and Tap).

As we leave the house, it gets worse. I'm desperately trying to remember where I've seen Robin's tap shoes. But outside there's a whole onslaught of mums. Sue Wilkins comes at me, asking about plans for half term. Tilly Sweeting pops over to say she's got it all firmed up for Friday. I can't take more talk! I want to shout. Will everyone please shut up?

Next door have got scaffolders. One of them says: 'Cheer up, love, it might never happen!'

To which I *want* to say: It *has* happened. And don't you fucking *dare* tell me how to behave!

Then Malory's friend Sophie appears, and Malory says: 'Can you arrange a playdate with Sophie?'

I say: 'I'm not sure!'

She says: '*Why* can't you arrange a playdate with Sophie?'

'I just can't!' I say.

'But WHY?' she shouts.

And I say, somewhat too loud: '*Because your dad has gone and I don't even know who's looking after you this afternoon.*'

Which causes something of a silence.

The kids are looking at me, astonished. Worse, several mums are now looking at me too. But at least they've ceased asking me about my plans for half term.

After that I succeed in getting everyone to school without swearing, or losing something, or promising to do a stall at the school fete.

I'm just leaving to return home when my phone rings.

'Hello,' says a relaxed, warm voice. 'It's James.'

Just hearing him has an instant effect on me. I feel like I'm staring at a green hillside filled with light. Suddenly all my problems seem to shrink.

'James,' I say. 'I'm so sorry about Monday night.'

'Don't worry,' he says. 'I enjoyed it. And your garden looked gorgeous.'

He doesn't mind! He doesn't mind!

'I'm sorry I couldn't call yesterday,' he says. 'I was flying to New York.'

There's a brief pause. Should I fill it? Should I say: I'm sorry I've got children, please let me work on your meadow?

'Listen,' he says. 'You've obviously got a great eye for plants. I'd love you to give an opinion on the meadow. Can you?'

He wants me! *He still wants me*! I play it cool . . .

'James,' I say. 'You know, there's nothing I'd rather do. I've actually been thinking quite a lot about it.'

'Oh, good!' he says.

'But the trouble is,' I say, 'I just need to work out what I'm going to do with the kids.'

'Of course.'

'And . . .' I pause. Can I confide in him? I guess I can. 'And it's made more complicated,' I say, 'since I had a row with my husband last night and he left.'

'Wow!' he says. 'You're suddenly single!'

'Erm . . . yes,' I say. 'I suppose so.'

'That's amazing!' he says. 'Sorry . . . I shouldn't say that. But you know I've always fancied you. I don't think you should have anyone but me.'

Oh. My. God. I haven't been imagining it. He likes me! He likes me!

'James,' I say, trying to keep cool. 'Before last weekend, I hadn't seen you in ten years.'

'I know! It was awful. You didn't write. You didn't phone.'

I chuckle slightly.

'So,' he says suddenly, 'do you think you might split?'

'I don't know,' I say quickly. Then I add: 'But it's possible.'

'Well, my advice is, don't ask him back for Friday. If you're getting divorced, it really helps your case that he walked out. Sort of thing the lawyers take very seriously.'

'Lawyers?!' That word's like a slap round the face. How would we even afford them? 'Gosh. I don't think we'd be involving lawyers.'

'Everyone says that. At first.'

'But I'm sure we could split everything OK. All the Arsenal programmes are his. Everything nice is mine.'

'Yes, but there's also custody.'

'I'd never try to stop him seeing them. He's brilliant with the children. Far better than me.'

'For *God's sake*, don't say that again!'

James has raised his voice to me. I don't like that.

'Right,' I say guardedly. 'But I'd always be happy for them to go to him.'

'You say that now. But then . . . Say the kids don't *want* to go to his house because they've got a party. Or . . . just say he gets a horrible girlfriend, who wants to spend the weekends smoking and feeding them doughnuts. Or . . .'

'*I get the picture!*' I say. I didn't mean to shout, but he's making me panic.

'The important thing is to get in early. I use Simon Hambleton. I'll send you his number.'

I say: 'Thank you.' I'm thinking: This is too much, too soon.

'But this is too much, too soon,' says James. It's like he's inside my head. He's so commanding. 'You can find someone to look after them for Friday. And you'll come. And you'll look out at a glorious bank of green grass, and it'll all seem clearer.'

'Yes.' You're right, James. That is what I need. I need a bank of green grass and a gorgeous man by a tree.

'Just say you'll come,' he says.

'I will come.'

'Great,' he says. 'There's one other thing I'll need . . .'

'Yes?'

'You, Polly Pankhurst, saying: "My white Airtex top was hot and wet with sweat."'

I pause.

That is so . . . teenage. But I must admit . . . it's exciting being desired. I feel twenty-four. I feel I'm twenty-four and my life is open and there's everything to play for. I like that.

He's silent, expectant.

I'm outside my house, leaning against the fence. I take a deep breath. I figure . . . what's the harm?

I check no one's watching. The scaffolders have disappeared. I say: 'My white Airtex top was hot and wet with sweat.'

There's a silence.

Then he says: 'Hah! Now I can die happy. Ooh . . . I'd better go. 'Bye.'

He rings off.

I realise I'm standing outside my house, watching the other mums get into their cars. I'm so aroused, I'm actually squeezing my thighs together. Can anyone tell?

The phone rings again.

'Hello,' says a quiet, sad voice. 'It's Arthur.'

Oh, wow. That's chucking a bucket of cold water over me.

'Sorry,' I say quickly. 'I *really* can't talk to you now.'

'Polly, I'm very sorry I got cross last night.'

I don't want to think about last night. 'Well, thanks,' I say. 'But I don't need an apology right now. What I need is to get to work.'

'I'm not going to be cross any more,' he says solemnly.

'That would be amazing,' I say. I really need to wrap up this call. 'Learn some happiness.'

'I'll come home now, and I'll start learning it.'

'NO!' I say. '*Don't!*' I'm talking far too loud. Suddenly I'm terrified that he'll come back, and I'll be buried under that fruit bowl for the rest of my life, and I'll never see that meadow.

'What are you saying?' says Arthur.

'I don't want you home,' I say.

'Why?' he says.

'It's not just the happiness, Arthur,' I say. I'm fumbling with my keys. 'It's the money. It's not that I'm greedy, but it's not fair I carry all the responsibility. It means I can't even think about changing jobs. I've had enough.'

'So far this week I've done two pieces for Em,' he says. 'That's six hundred quid up to yesterday.'

'Yes,' I say. I'm back in the house now, and it suddenly occurs to me: The tap shoes are in the toy box! 'Well, earn another six hundred today. Then you can come home. We need money, Arthur. And if we're splitting up, we need twice as much.'

'Why?' says Arthur.

'Well, presumably you'll need to pay for a home of some kind,' I say. 'Unless you can find another woman to live off.'

On that, I put the phone down. I'm not trying to be abrupt. But I really need to get to work.

**Arthur**

I turn the phone off and I stare into space.

'What did she say?' says Malcolm.

'She wants me to earn six hundred quid today. Then I can come home.'

Malcolm is delighted by this turn of events. His little eyes twinkle. 'Oh, that's fantastic!' he says.

'Why is that fantastic?'

'Because your task for the day could not be more clear: you have to earn six hundred pounds.'

'How am I going to find six hundred quid?'

'I have no idea at all,' says Malcolm cheerfully. I've never seen a man more pleased about not knowing something. 'But I suggest we attempt nothing without breakfast. Let us go down and see Mrs Hennessy.'

'Who is Mrs Hennessy?' I ask.

'She's my landlady,' Malcolm confides. 'I also think she may be a witch.'

'What makes you think that?'

'Come down and you'll see.'

So I follow Malcolm downstairs, and we enter Mrs Hennessy's kitchen.

It's remarkably chaotic and unfriendly in there.

Mrs Hennessy is a thin woman, standing at the sink. She has hennaed hair which is grey at the roots, and a grey bitter face that hasn't known the benefit of too many facials. A surly teenage girl in school uniform has her feet on an armchair as she plays at a DS. She doesn't look up.

Malcolm says: 'Good morning!'

I say: 'Good morning!'

Mrs Hennessy gives Malcolm a sour look. She doesn't even look at me.

'Come and sit down,' says Malcolm warmly, directing me towards the kitchen table. I sit down, and find myself facing an opened copy of the *Radio Times* which has been liberally sprinkled with sugar.

'Now!' says Malcolm. 'Would you like some muesli and soya milk?'

Of course I wouldn't. No one actually wants muesli and soya milk, unless they're a hostage.

'And I'll make you some peppermint tea.'

Peppermint tea? Who the hell starts the day with a peppermint tea? At home I have coffee. 'Thank you,' I say.

Mrs Hennessy switches on the kettle. 'Lisa!' she says crossly. 'You are late!'

The surly girl gets up. She passes without glancing at me.

Wow. If everything is here to teach us, then the reason for this is abundantly clear: this is not my home. I couldn't feel more unwelcome if I'd entered a synagogue, naked, on the back of a big pig. There is not a shred of doubt in my mind. I need to earn £600. I need to get home.

My phone rings. It's Em.

Desperate for escape, I dodge out of the kitchen, and I answer it.

## Em

I'm in the car park outside the office. I seem to make most of my calls from out here.

'Hello,' says Arthur.

'Hi,' I say. 'Listen . . . Do you want to do some more pieces?'

[ 143 ]

'Yes,' he says. 'I really do.'

'Great,' I say. 'Actually I need your advice. I really don't know what to do. You know you told me to avoid Dan till he makes his decision?'

'Yes.'

'Tonight it's Staff Drinks,' I say. 'So I *have* to see him. I feel so nervous about it. He's got two days to decide if he wants to marry me. How the hell am I supposed to make him want me?'

'Just . . . be yourself,' he says.

I fucking hate it when people tell me that. I never know who I am.

'Will you come to the drinks with me?' I ask. 'I need a wingman.'

'OK.'

'Why don't you come in now to discuss ideas and we'll discuss ideas? Then you can stay for the drinks.'

Arthur says 'fine'. At the very same moment an incredibly hot man walks towards Reception. The day is looking up. I'm going to be OK.

## Polly

I've reached work – a huge open-plan office, with high windows and a brown carpet.

Ughhhh . . .

I feel like the Little Mermaid. I've met my prince, and he lives in the world of the beautiful people that I long to join. But meanwhile I'm stuck with the fish. OK . . . technically I'm not stuck with fish, but my desk is next to the IT department, and one of them is eating a tuna sandwich.

*How the hell am I going to escape?* That's the question.

And I'm starting to see an answer. It starts with me visiting Bodsham Abbey for a party, in which I shall see James's meadow and have one night to capture his heart.

But before I do that, I need to find childcare.

And how the hell am I going to find that, now Arthur's gone? It's horribly clear . . . If I'm ever going to get out of here, I need to see the Sea Witch: I need to see my mum. And I'm going to have to make her do the thing she'll do anything to avoid: I need to make her babysit.

## Arthur

Malcolm is driving me to my meeting. We're stuck in a traffic jam.

Above us there is a big billboard advertising holidays in Cuba. In the picture a gorgeous young woman is standing with a handsome trumpeter. She seems to be blowing in his ear. She looks happy. But why wouldn't she be happy? She's a young gorgeous model, and she's probably been paid several grand to fly to Cuba to blow in some man's ear. Let's see her in ten years' time and see how happy she is then. If that man has spent ten years playing his trumpet, she won't be blowing in his ear. She'll be blowing up his car.

Malcolm interrupts my thoughts.

'Big Man!' he says, passing over his phone. It's a surprisingly modern one, with a keyboard. 'You need to do your *Learn Love* exercise! I've opened up your account.'

'How did you do that?'

'Just 'cos I'm Irish,' he says, 'I'm not as thick as you think.'

I look at Malcolm. He gives me a warm smile.

'I don't think I can write in the van,' I say. 'What's the exercise about?'

'You're supposed to write, for ten minutes, starting with the words: "I'm angry with the world because . . ." So . . . tell me. What makes you angry?'

'I am angry,' I say, 'because, wherever you look, there are adverts for holidays, and yet the world is about to overheat. A plane flying to Miami uses as much petrol as a year's driving. Why can't we shoot them from the sky? Why shouldn't I be angry? We are the generation that finally destroyed the planet, and all we talk about is the economy.'

I trail off.

Malcolm is giving me an encouraging look. 'Keep going!' he says.

'I can't!'

'Aren't you angry with the world?'

'I'm furious!' I say. 'But I probably wouldn't be quite so angry if I was successful, and Polly loved me.'

'Ah!' he says happily. 'So maybe you're angry the world has ruined your love.'

'I am!' I say. 'But is that the world's fault? Or is it mine?'

At this, we arrive at the barrier of the massive complex where Em works, and Malcolm grins at the security guard like he's greeting an old friend. 'Hello, Big Man!' he says. (I thought I was Big Man!)

'Are you here for the shoot?' asks the security guard.

'Yes,' says Malcolm.

'Other side of the car park,' he says. The barrier goes up, and we drive in.

I look at Malcolm incredulously.

'Malcolm,' I say. 'Why did you just say yes?'

'It's the Second Rule of Malcolm: *Always say yes*. You never know where it might lead you.'

'In this case, it's led you into a car park.'

'A free car park. I think I may sit here and have a little smoke.'

He pulls the van into an empty space and he grins at me.

'Erm,' he says. 'Will I come in and say hello to Em?'

'I don't think it's the best time.'

'What do you think she'll be doing?'

'I'm sure she's working.'

## Em

It's amazing.

E-Harmony have been in touch. They're offering me seven matches.

I scroll through, rejecting them all. I reject one because he's fat. Two because they're in IT. Another because he's called Colin. Another because he clearly shaves his eyebrows. Another because he likes quad biking. And the last because he looks like someone I knew at school who, allegedly, had skiddy pants.

This is ridiculous. I'm rejecting suitors in half a second. How am I ever going to find a man with whom I can spend my life? I see what's going to happen. Dan is going to chuck me. And then my life will become a long series of empty affairs. Fuck Arthur! Why did he persuade me to propose to Dan?

Oh, Lord, Arthur's going to be here in a couple of minutes. I should get some make-up on.

## Arthur

Wow. This is like visiting the Wizard of Oz. You imagine the

*Lifestyle* offices would be big and glossy. But they just take up a bit of hallway. For our chat, Em shows me to 'the meeting room' – a large cupboard, opposite the disabled toilets. It looks like it used to be a sick room. It has no windows. It's got a lock on the door. There's an ancient computer on a desk in the corner which looks like it's there to record interrogations.

I like seeing Em at work. When I see her outside she's normally drunk and ranting about Dan. At work, she's a different beast. She seems sexy and motivated. She's wearing a classic *Mad Men* era outfit. Her skirt is tight around her curvy hips, and she's got on a white silky blouse that offers a generous glimpse of her famous cleavage.

'So,' she says. 'Brilliant feedback on your first pieces. And you want to write something new?'

'Yes,' I say. 'I *really* do.'

'Great. What ideas have you got?'

'None,' I say. 'I wish I did. I really need to earn some more money, right away. But I've got nothing.'

'Okaaay,' says Em. 'Well, when magazines give advice about love, they always say the same thing. Can't you do that, but in your own inimitable phrasing?'

'Do they always say the same thing?'

'Sure.'

'What do they say?'

Em puts on a special voice. She sounds like Audrey Hepburn, doing cabaret. 'They say: "*Talk about your feelings / Talk about your sexual fantasies / Talk about your yearnings, your dreams!/ Take a break!/ Take a mini-break . . .* "'

'That's outrageous,' I say, interrupting.

'Why?'

'If you follow this advice, you'll end up in debt, and in an airport, next to a tense person who's trained to talk about their feelings. The biggest threat to love, surely, is that we're all busy, skint, and stressed: the last thing you want to do is arrange another trip.'

'Oh, come on,' says Em, 'if you take the holiday, there will be the moment where you find yourself standing ankle deep in water, sharing a kiss.'

'There'll also be the one where you lose your passport. And the one where you're now home and nothing's changed – except you've got debts of two grand, and a big pile of sandy socks. Those moments don't help. I honestly think modern culture is destroying love.'

## Em

I *love* it when Arthur makes grand statements like that. It seems so bold and sexy. When Dan makes big statements, he's usually talking engine size.

'How is modern culture destroying love?' I ask.

'Like . . .' he says. 'On Monday I Googled the phrase "opposites attract". I immediately got shunted to FIVE websites that offered "safe uncomplicated fun for the married person".'

'Did you go on them?'

'No. But I could've, so that was unsettling.'

'But you *didn't* go on. And nor did Polly.'

'No. But she spends every night on Primelocation.'

'Does that matter?' I say.

'I've *twice* spent the weekend in Louth,' he says, with surprising bitterness. 'And I've spent weeks discussing Whitstable. And even if we moved to Whitstable, we'd still be typical modern people – restless, dissatisfied and a bit cross.'

'But why do you think people are restless and dissatisfied and a bit cross?'

'Because of magazines probably! Magazines that are passing on the advice that big businesses want them to. So they're a bit like sheep, who are getting their advice from the wolves.'

'What do you mean?'

'Because, according to you, everyone is saying . . . if you don't feel love, go somewhere, do something. And if you've got a problem, put your foot down and speak about it.'

'And what would you say?'

'I'd say: be contented . . . stay where you are . . . accept your partner, and give them love.'

'Is that what you'd like to say to the women of the world?'

'Yes,' says Arthur, who's suddenly coming across like Russell Crowe. He's big and cross and magnificent. 'Or maybe I'd also like to say: *Stop looking at fucking houses, it's time for me to have you!*'

He says this with surprising force.

Arthur, you big sexy bull, if you were in my bed, I wouldn't be online. I'd be on you.


**Arthur**

Em gives me an intense look.

'This is great!' she says, like she's making a decision. 'I've not heard this! You're an ordinary man, but you've got a great marriage, and you can write about it. You're the Wilde of the suburbs, in a suit bought from Next.'

I'm confused by that. 'But . . .' I say. 'Didn't you hear?'

'What?'

'Polly chucked me out last night.'

'*What*??!!!' says Em. 'Did she?'

'Yes. So I don't have a marriage to write about. I don't even have a room to write in.'

Em's looking at me with renewed fascination. I'm now keen to move on. I didn't mean to talk about Polly. I suddenly feel naked, and shaky, and in slight danger of crying.

'Well,' she says. 'I'm going to get you guys back together!'

'Thank you, Em,' I say. 'You're gorgeous, and I love you.'

She flushes fetchingly.

'OK,' she says, taking control like a young matron. 'You'd better sit at that desk. You can use that computer. Write a piece for me. Five hundred words on "Why I'm Angry About Love Advice". Two hundred quid.'

'You promised me three hundred for the first one,' I say.

'I was desperate,' she says. 'And I was negotiating with Polly. From now on the pieces will be two fifty.'

'Done,' I say. Two hundred and fifty found. Three hundred and fifty to go.

'Good boy,' says Em.

She steps forward and gives me a hug. I'm sitting down so, for a moment, my head is pressed against her soft scented breasts. It's a great place to be. If I turned my face I could kiss them.

## Polly

OK. This is the plan . . .

I need to call the Sea Witch (Mum) to get her to do childcare on Friday. Which will be difficult. Obviously she offered to do it on Sunday, but she didn't mean it, so she'll resent me for taking her up on her vacuous offer. She'll also ask about Arthur, and if I tell her the truth, she'll be cross.

Oh, dear.

I go to the pond in Green Park – a place I normally find calming, but still I'm nervous. Finally I count to ten and force myself to dial.

She answers.

'Hi, Mum,' I say.

'Hi, darling,' she says. 'I'm buying bridesmaids' dresses for Sophie's wedding.'

It's been two months since my sister announced she was getting married. Since then my mum has discussed the subject for about twenty-two hours a day. I listen to her for a minute, but then I cut her off.

'Mum,' I say. 'You know you offered to do childcare so I can go to James Hammond's on Friday?'

'Oh,' says Mum. 'That's the day I'm having lunch with Roger Chalmers.'

'Can you reschedule?'

She pauses as if I've insulted her. It's like I've just asked her to clean out the oven.

'He's chairman of the IFU,' she says. 'He's not the sort of person one reschedules.'

'Or maybe you could just finish lunch early, so you could get to ours by three-thirty?'

'Why can't Arthur do it?'

'Well, he's . . . we had a row and he's left.'

'*What?*' shrieks Mum. 'What do you mean, he's left?'

'He's gone.'

'For ever?'

'I don't know for the moment.'

'Well, don't you think you're being a bit hasty?'

Why does she never understand what I'm saying? 'I'm not

saying he's gone for ever,' I say. 'But he's gone *now*, and I really want to go to James's or this opportunity will go.'

There's a pause. Then I hear Mum saying: 'Can you bring us the peach?'

Whereupon I get so mad I put the phone down. I'm angry with myself mainly. Why am I trying to get Mum to help me? Why do I even talk to her? I've just talked to her for three minutes, and I feel as if I've walked face first through some brambles.

**Em**

I'm back at my desk.

E-Harmony have sent me more matches.

There's an interesting one called Ben who says he likes travel and films. He's quite handsome. *Quite* handsome. He's nothing on Arthur.

Oh, dear. It's rather exciting having him in the meeting room, beavering away. I feel like he's my private slave. I'd like to have a private slave. That's what I want. I want a man who's utterly devoted to me, a man I can beat. I'd like to beat Arthur actually. I'd put him over a table, and I'd leave red welts on his rounded beasty buttocks.

**Polly**

After speaking to Mum, I work for thirty-six minutes exactly.

To fetch the kids from school at 3.30, I need to leave work at 2.35. That's not easy. I have about twenty-five e-mails that really must be answered today. Several people call. As I walk out of the office, it's already 3.12, and I'm angry. As I pass Reception I am furious. 'Hello!' says Debra on Reception. I say: 'Hello!' She says: 'How are you?' I say: '*Fine!*' and I push open the door.

As I walk down the steps, I now start worrying about Debra on Reception. Should I have asked 'How are you?' over my shoulder? *I'd passed*: my body language wouldn't have been demonstrating the right degree of concern. I feel ashamed, but should I go back now and say 'How are you?' to Debra on Reception? *Fuck Debra on Reception!* Why are you expected to be polite, all the bloody time? What's happening? I've lost my husband, but I still feel trapped.

As I walk out of the building, I get an idea.

I call up James. Just dialling his number feels naughty. I feel like I'm stealing into someone's house. I feel like I'm running my finger down his back.

He answers straight away.

'James,' I say.

'Polly,' he says. And I can't help it. Just hearing him makes my heart flutter. I feel like . . . a moment ago, I was looking at a brick wall. Now I can see a chink.

'How are you?' I ask.

'Urh!' he says.

'*Where* are you?'

'I'm in New York. I just tried to see Ivan.'

'Who's Ivan?'

'My son with Irina.'

'Who's Irina?'

'Ex-girlfriend who lives in New York. I turned up this morning and she wouldn't let me see him.' How many bloody girlfriends does he have? This is ridiculous. I feel jealous.

'Why can't you see him?'

'It's not my day.'

'Was he there?'

'Yes! He was standing behind her, holding hands with the

nanny. I had this big bear for him. I gave him the bear. Then . . .
I had to go.'

'Poor you.'

'I wish I were with you,' he says suddenly, 'right now.'

He likes me. He likes me!

'How are you?' asks James.

And I can't help it. James sounds so understanding, I tell him
everything – about Mum, her saying 'Can you bring the peach?',
everything.

'Polly,' he says, in his most commanding voice, 'you know
what your trouble is?'

'What?'

'You're scared of tension.'

'Am I?'

'You know what I've done today?'

'What?'

'I've closed two hotels, which amounts to firing about four
hundred and fifty people.'

'God . . . and doesn't that bother you?'

'You can't make an omelette without breaking eggs.'

'You think?'

'The world of business is ruthless. Only the toughest keep
going.'

'But doesn't it upset you?' I say. I've reached the car now. I get
in.

'No,' says James. 'It's all just a game. You know what Oscar
Wilde said?'

'No.'

'"*Many things don't matter very much. And most things don't
matter at all.*"'

'Did he work for Head and Shoulders?' I say.

James laughs. (I made James Hammond laugh!)

'You're so gorgeous,' he says.

I say nothing.

'Listen . . . my meeting is about to start,' he says. 'I've gotta go. I love you.'

The phone goes dead.

Hang on a second . . . Did he just say: 'I love you'??!! I don't think he meant to say that. And . . . yes . . . I know it . . . If a man declares his love before the first date, he'll be cheating on you by the second. Still . . . *James Hammond* just said: 'I love you.' It gives me a divinely warm feeling.

Oh, Lord. It's now 3.28. I'm supposed to be at the kids' school in two minutes, and I'm six miles away.


**Arthur**

I'm just reading back 'Why I'm Angry About Bad Love Advice' when Em appears. 'Hello, handsome,' she says, coming into the room and looking at the screen. 'Do you mind if I read this now?'

'Please do.'

She stands next to me and leans over my shoulder. Her hair is tied up and I notice the nape of her neck. It's something about being newly single, I'm feeling like my libido is back. I also notice the hairs on her arms, and the shimmery tights on her legs. As she reads, she chuckles several times, which is probably the sexiest sound in the world.

'Very good,' she says, at the end.

'So do I earn the cash?'

'Well, I have to run it past my editor in the morning. But it's good.'

'I enjoyed writing it,' I tell her. 'Sometimes I went several minutes at a time, without thinking about Polly.'

Em looks into my eyes.

'How are you feeling about that?' she says.

'Empty,' I say. 'I haven't felt this bad since I was heartbroken as a teenager.'

'You were heartbroken as a teenager?'

'God, yes. When I was seventeen I was chucked by a girl called Sue Frame. After that I wanted to run away from school. I didn't want anyone who'd ever seen us to see me on my own. Nine months later I was still writing the initials SF in the margins of my books.'

'But you're an attractive guy, Arthur, I can't believe you spent your teenage years being chucked.'

'Well, you learn fast – don't you? – the first rule of teenage love.'

'Which is?'

'Dump 'em first. I used to get off with people and then I'd walk off, right there and then, just to make sure I dumped them before they dumped me.'

'Yes,' says Em. 'I remember!'

'What do you mean?'

'Well . . .' she says. 'Remember the night you met Polly?'

'Why are you asking this?'

'Do you remember when you first saw her?'

'Sure . . . I was at a May Day party in a field, a few miles out of town. I came out of the dance tent, and I saw Polly by the bonfire. And I talked to her, but it didn't go well.'

'Why?'

'She looked so beautiful I felt a bit weak. I just blurted out:

'You are without doubt the most beautiful woman I've ever seen!' and she sort of smiled and said: 'I'll see you soon.' And she just went and got in a car. And I watched her walking away and I felt crushed.'

'Yup,' says Em. 'I remember. I was in the car.'

I look at her sharply.

'What do you mean?' I say.

'Oh, Arthur, for God's sake,' says Em. ' Don't say you don't remember!'

'What?'

'I was there too!'

'Were you?!'

'Yes!' says Em. 'You and I got off with each other that night.'

I really don't know what she's talking about. '*What?!*' I say. 'What do you mean?'

'You remember! We were dancing together by the speaker stack.'

'*We were dancing together?!*' I can't access this memory. 'I don't remember . . .'

'Oh, fuck you, Arthur. Don't say you don't remember my dancing?'

'Hey, Em, your dancing is normally unforgettable.'

'Well,' says Em, 'we danced together and they played Sister Sledge singing "Thinking of You".'

Now I really am picturing it. Sister Sledge is singing: '*Only love/ and the things you do to me . . .* ' In front of me is a short, very energetic dancer, wearing a top hat and a sports bra. I haven't been too aware of her up to then, but during the song we kiss. It's a glorious kiss – sweaty and passionate. I look at Em now. For a moment I remember the exuberant dancer. She had flares and sweat glistening in the hollow of her back.

'*That was you!*' I say.

'Of course it was! Don't you remember us kissing?'

'Actually I do remember kissing, but I thought that girl was Spanish.'

'I'm not Spanish!'

'No.'

'I remember that you just walked off and you didn't come back. Why did you do that?'

'Well, I suppose I went outside, and I met Polly.'

'You met me, you walked off. You met Polly, and she looked so beautiful you felt a bit weak.'

'That's right,' I say.

I realise how much time has passed since I met Polly. All this happened fourteen years ago – almost half a *lifetime*. I realise I'm with Polly now, because of the actions and decisions of a twenty-year-old man. A twenty-year-old man who danced all night and who met women by bonfires at 6 a.m. (*6 a.m.*?! That seems the most extraordinary bit. Why wasn't I *asleep*? It seems so long ago. I'm now in my thirties. I'd still consider taking drugs, I'd consider having an affair, I'd never *dream* of missing my eight hours' sleep.)

I'm feeling old and sad and wise.

## Em

Arthur is looking young and sweet and lost.

It's obvious we're both thinking the same thing . . . we could have been together! Perhaps we *should* have been together! Sure, he chose Polly then, but the twenty-year-old Polly was an exquisitely beautiful human being. She had a lot to offer. But now,

I realise, I offer much more. I realise I've grown. I also realise I'm looking for a man, and here, in front of me, is a prize specimen. A man who could have been mine in the first place. A man who's suddenly available.

I could get off this desk now and I could sit on his lap. No one ever comes in this room. Everyone could be out there working. We'd be inside quietly making out!

'And cut to fourteen years later,' Arthur says sadly. 'Polly's just chucked me out.'

I've got to stop fantasising about Polly's husband.

'Oh, come on,' I say. 'Polly is the mother of your children. You're always going to love her.'

## Arthur

I feel really humbled by the way Em's trying to help.

'But perhaps I might never sleep with her again,' I say. 'Although, to be honest, even before this happened, we haven't done that in a while.'

'Why?'

'Oh, I don't know. We developed issues.'

'How?'

Em leans forward. It is the most attractive thing about her: she really listens. Plus . . . I can see her bra strap.

'Well, there are a lot of things,' I say, 'that Polly hasn't liked for a long time.'

'What?'

'Well, she . . . . she's really up for anything. Anything . . . Provided I touch her exactly where she likes it, and I don't take too long.'

We both smile.

'Can I ask,' asks Em. 'Normally magazines advise people to talk about what they want, sexually. Do you do that?'

'No!' I say. 'No no no no no. That'd be a terrible idea. She'd say: "What do you fantasise about?" I'd say: "Other people."'

'You think about sex with other people?'

'Actually, I don't,' I say. 'I just imagine them nude.'

'Nude,' says Em. She's now smiling. We're both enjoying this. This is nice. It's good to have a talk, sometimes, which doesn't lead anywhere.

'To be honest,' I say, 'this is my issue. I can't *take* all the talking!'

'What do you mean?'

'Like . . . I'll put my arms around her, and she'll say: "Did you lock the back door?" And I'll say: "Yes." And I'll kiss her. And she'll say: "I don't like it when you stick your tongue out." And I'll try to kiss her again, but by now I'm feeling like my sexual technique is the subject of 180-degree review. And then we'll kiss, and she'll take my hand, and put it on her nipple.'

'She's showing you what she wants. Isn't that sexy?'

'No. It's as if she's hurrying me up, like I'm a tardy pupil. Like she's saying: "*Now, nippy nippy. We haven't got all night.*" I am capable of having sex! I don't need instructions!'

'So,' says Em, 'if you could say one thing to the ladies of the world, what would it be?'

'You don't have to keep making suggestions. Act as if a suggestion has been made already. Work out what it is. Let us feel how we want to feel.'

'How do you want to feel?'

'I want . . . I want to feel masterful, and slow, and, frankly, slightly cruel.'

'Do you?' says Em. She gives a mischievous smile. For a

moment I'm ten again, and Helen Hughes and I are doing Inspections.

'Yes,' I say. 'And I don't want to *talk* about sex at all. Men don't. We want a woman who looks us in the eyes, and who *knows* what we want to do. We want a woman who is silent and reverent and slightly dangerous.'

Em is staring into my eyes. She flushes. Then she stands up. She goes to the door. And she locks it.

I stare at her with astonishment.

She doesn't move. She just stands by the door, and she looks into my eyes. She looks silent and reverent and slightly dangerous.

Oh my God. Oh, no no no no no no. I wasn't suggesting . . . She *can't* mean she wants us to . . .

*Does she?*

My mouth is dry. I swallow.

Em looks into my eyes. Then, gently, she removes her jacket.

Oh my God. I think she's taking me literally on the 'I-don't-want-sex-with-other-women-I-just-want-to-see-them-naked' thing. I know she's absurdly proud of her breasts, but she can't possibly mean to . . .

She places the jacket on the chair.

Underneath, she's wearing a silky white blouse with a frilly edge. Em is mad. She can't possibly think we're going to . . . I'm not moving. I don't move. I say nothing. I sit there.

I look into her eyes.

She seems to *want* to undress. I've always wanted to see her breasts. Actually I've imagined them, but . . . You can't just undress . . . can you?

Or can you? Perhaps nakedness isn't cheating. I'm not saying anything. I'm not doing anything.

Em sucks in her bottom lip. Then she unfastens all the buttons of her blouse. Oh, God. The tension is unbearably exciting. I've never felt more aroused in my life.

She places her blouse on the jacket.

She has a black bra. Her breasts are white and full.

What am I going to do?

I can't do nothing. That would be rejecting her. She's exposed herself. She really has.

I must do something.

And I am drawn towards her breasts like a moth to the moon. Mesmerised, like a worshipper, I kneel before her. She looks down at me. Suddenly, I uncup one breast. And, for a brief moment, I flick my tongue over it.

## Em

At that moment we both realise what's happening.

I gasp.

He stops.

He stands and moves back.

I instantly reach for my clothes and start putting them on quickly.

'We really have to stop,' I say.

'Quick,' he says. 'Talk to me about something boring.'

'What shall I talk about?'

'Talk about your desire to have a place in the country.'

'I've just found a little place in Devon.'

'Devon's too sexy!'

'I've found a place in Luton!'

'That's good. Tell me about the dry rot.'

'I have got dry rot,' I say. 'And I need to get the survey done.'

'Tell me about the building plans.'

'There's a stud wall, which I want to knock through.'

'Perfect,' he says. 'Tell me about the Ofsted reports on the local schools.'

'Listen,' I say. 'Polly is my best friend. I love her. I don't want to lose her. And I don't think you want to lose her either.'

'Really, Em,' he says. 'I've got it. We must never, *ever* mention what just happened.'

'Well . . . nothing happened,' I say. Now he's making too big a deal about this.

'You can't say that! Something happened!'

'We didn't have sex! We didn't even kiss!'

'I just licked your nipple.'

'That's not sex! That's barely even harassment!'

'It's still something!'

He's being way too serious about this, and it could get us into trouble.

'Arthur,' I say, 'there're lots of perfectly innocent reasons why someone might lick someone else's nipple.'

He stares at me. 'Give one.'

'To . . . clean it?'

'Clean it??!!' he says.

He looks anguished and upset and terribly serious. This isn't working. So I do the only thing I can.

## Arthur

*And now she just bursts into tears!!*

This is even worse than her undressing. I really don't know *what* to do. I'm so confused.

'I'm so sorry!' she says. 'I just don't know what to do! I'm about to lose my job. And Dan's telling me tomorrow if he wants to marry me. And I just don't know if he wants me.'

I look at Em who's pulling on her blouse. She looks so imploring, and so damn sexy.

'I'm sure he wants you,' I say. 'Or he could do.'

Em is doing up her buttons.

'You must *never* tell Polly what just happened,' I say.

'Well, I won't if you help me,' she says. 'Dan will be seeing me tonight. I've got to make him want me. Will you help?'

'How?' I say.

'Yesterday you told me "How To Trap A Man",' she says. 'Now I need to know "How To Be Attractive". Can you do that?'

'Yes.'

'Good,' she says. 'In fact, this is going to be the subject of your next piece. Which you're going to write now. You should be in the perfect state for it.'

'Are you really suggesting,' I ask, 'that all that was to prepare me to write a piece?'

'That's my story,' she says. 'And I'm sticking to it.'

She's fully dressed now and reaching the door.

'So get writing,' she says. 'Make the piece absolutely brilliant, or I shall spank you.'

She goes.


**Em**

Bloody hell. That was a close escape. I really need to calm myself down.

So I browse E-Harmony for a bit.

Then I click on to Alex James's Twitter feed, and I ground myself by reading about cheese.

## Polly

My life is falling to bits.

I was *forty-eight* minutes late for picking the kids up from school. I found them all in the office looking sad.

Then we came home. I think Tilly Sweeting must have told people that Arthur has gone because I started getting *bombarded* by texts. 'Are you OK?' 'Yes!' 'Are you OK?' 'Yes!' And the children started moaning and complaining. (I forgot to buy food. We missed the tap dancing.) Suddenly they were shouting, and making a mess, and demanding snacks, so I yelled at them, and then I turned on the TV, and I started cleaning the kitchen with a mad determination.

So on the downside, I've shouted, I've starved them, and I've forced them to watch TV.

On the upside, I have scraped between the kitchen tiles.

In a minute I'm going to go to the toy cupboard. I'm going to cull some Barbies. Then I'm going to make a pogrom of the Polly Pockets. And then I'm heading for Arthur's cupboard.

## Arthur

It's 6 o'clock. I'm supposed to be meeting Em outside the lobby.

I walk out. I notice the warm summer evening. Then I get a shock.

I see a red van, with canoes on top.

Malcolm's still here!!

I run over.

He's leaning back in the driving seat with the door open.

Mrs Thompson is sitting on his lap. She sees me. She springs out of the car and rushes towards me, whimpering and waving her tail like this is the happiest moment of her life.

Malcolm smiles. 'Big Man!' he says sleepily. 'Did you think more about what you're angry about?'

'Er . . . yes,' I say. 'I wrote a piece about it. I feel I should do way more.'

'You did one thing,' he says. 'The point is, you must take action to make a better world, but don't get obsessed. You wrote a piece. You did what you could.'

Malcolm is smiling at me with Jesus-like calm. I feel relaxed. But then I come to.

'Malcolm!' I say. 'What the hell are you doing here?'

He looks at me with his sleepy grin. I'd be prepared to wager that he's experimented this afternoon with more of his home-grown skunk.

'Just sitting,' he says. 'It's been amazing. There are pigeons up there that . . .'

He's about to pass on his report on the pigeons. I must stop him. 'Malcolm,' I say. '*Why* have you waited here all day?'

His eyes are happy though slightly bloodshot.

'I have to admit it,' he says, 'I really like Em. I thought I'd wait around and say hi.'

'But . . .' I'm grappling to put my finger on what's so odd about this situation. 'You waited a whole day!'

'I know. It's like a fairy tale where the soldier stands under the lady's window for forty days and forty nights. That's love.'

'No, Malcolm, that's stalking.'

'Oh come on . . . You don't need to tell her I waited all day. I might have been doing some work locally. I wasn't. I was sitting here throwing toast at squirrels.'

'Didn't you have some work to do?'

'Hey,' he says, 'I've got loads of work coming in!' He gives me a meaningful look. 'Exciting work! *Loads of it!*'

'What is it?'

'That's a secret. But the point is . . . I work for myself. If I want to spend a day in the van, I can. Besides, I just really like Em and . . .'

'Listen,' I say. 'Em is going for drinks where she's meeting Dan, so it's a bad moment to suggest.'

'OK,' says Malcolm. 'To be honest, Arthur, I was also waiting around 'cos I was worried where you were going to stay tonight, and I thought you might appreciate knowing that I can look after Mrs Thompson, and there's a place with me if you'd like it.'

'Oh,' I say. I feel moved by that. 'Thanks.'

'And you wouldn't have to bum me or anything.'

'Thank you.'

'So will you call if you need me?'

I remember the Second Rule of Malcolm.

I say: 'Yes. But you'd really better leave now.'


**Em**

Arthur and I enter the Diamond Lounge.

Dan *is* here. He's on the sofa with the boys from *Vroom*. As I come in, I give him a little wave.

No response.

OK. There are twenty people by the bar, but there's no one on the dance floor. I *know* he can see me. *Why* is he ignoring me? I've done the little wave. He should do something back. A wave. An eyebrow raise. A nod perhaps. Would a nod be too much to ask?

Has he texted?

I texted him, an hour ago, saying, 'Going to Shelton's drinks. C U there?'

Nothing.

I texted him a few minutes ago: 'Going to bar with Arthur. What do you want?'

Nothing.

Plus . . . I've not had a single Facebook comment about my most humorous anecdote about seduction by maintenance.

Plus Alex James hasn't Tweeted. Not since 3.26. What the fuck is *he* doing?

'Hey, Em.'

Arthur is finally here with the drinks.

'Thanks,' I say. I take the glass, and I take a big glug.

Nice. Vodka Red Bull. The gasoline kick of the vodka, with the caramel buzz and the fizz.

'He's not looked at me once,' I say.

'Maybe he hasn't seen you.'

'I've texted him twice. He's not replied.'

'Then he's ignoring you.'

I look down at the phone.

'You're turning into one of the mosquito people,' says Arthur.

'Who're they?'

'They're tiny creatures that buzz at lights.'

'Fuck you, Arthur.'

He smiles at me. 'I'm trying to help,' he says. 'That phone is sucking away your power.'

'People need to get in touch with me!'

'Em,' says Arthur, and he actually takes the phone, he turns it off, and he slips it into my chest pocket. 'Take control of your life.'

'OK,' I say.

'Although,' continues Arthur, 'you might want to keep your phone on for one more minute. You could read the piece I did. "How To Be Attractive". I e-mailed it to you. And I can't go home until you've decided it's good.'

'Well, why don't you give me the advice?' I say. 'And we'll say it's good enough if it succeeds in attracting Dan.'

'So I don't get my money,' says Arthur, 'unless you seduce Dan?'

'Yes,' I say.

'Wow,' says Arthur. 'Your employment criteria are bloody harsh.'

## Polly

Mum's just sent a text. 'Sorry I got cut off today,' she says. I'm tempted to write back: 'You weren't cut off. I cut you off. I just didn't want to compete with some peach bridesmaids' dresses.' But I ignore her. I still haven't got the kids to bed. And I'm already exhausted.

## Em

'So come on then, Arthur,' I say. 'There's a man over there ignoring me. He's ignoring me now. He ignored me yesterday. And suddenly it makes me think I might have a future of being ignored by that fucker. Educate me. Thrill me with your advice. Tell me "How To Be Attractive".'

He grins.

'Are you ready?' he says.

'I couldn't be readier!' I say.

'OK,' he says. 'The first thing is . . . leave him alone, but know he will come to you, when he's ready. In the meantime, assume your power.'

'How?'

'Slowww down. Know this . . . You are a queen.'

I try to imagine that. I take a deep breath.

'You are a filthy dirty queen,' he says. 'You are the centre of your world. And when you go amongst those men, know that you go like a queen amongst courtiers.'

I like the idea of this. I survey the dance floor.

'That's good,' he says. 'You have the smirk of the sexy dirty queen who's been on the gin. You're ready.'

'What do I do?'

'You walk off. You pick the most handsome courtier out of the crowd, and you look into his eyes, and you laugh. But only if he's told a joke, or the courtier will think you're a half-wit.'

I laugh. Suddenly I'm feeling OK. In fact, I'm feeling more than OK. That Red Bull is kicking in, and the music is getting louder.

'Can I make the courtier dance?' I ask.

'If it looks like he can move,' says Arthur.

'And can I dance myself?'

'You most certainly can,' he says. 'You must go with your instinct at all times. And as you dance you must think: I am attracting all the courtiers towards me, using my Lady Sex Magnet.'

'What,' I ask, 'is my Lady Sex Magnet?'

'The question you must ask yourself,' says Arthur, who's smiling like Errol Flynn, 'is . . . *where* is your Lady Sex Magnet?'

For a moment, I do ponder that. I also have a sudden flashback to this afternoon.

'You got it,' he says.

'Will you dance with me?' I ask.

'There's absolutely no way! I can't be near you. But you'll be fine dancing on your own.'

'Oh! I know I'll be fine dancing on my own,' I say. 'If I go out on that dance floor I'll be like a racehorse in with the donkeys. Will you be OK?'

'Yeah, I think I'll go and say hi to Dan actually,' says Arthur.

'Find out if he likes me!' I say.

'Stop caring,' he says. 'Remember . . . Dan, like all men, is only a courtier. You are a queen.'

'I'm a queen.'

'Be distant like a cloud, be strong like a snake.'

'I'm doing it.'

'And now,' says Arthur smiling, 'switch on your Lady Sex Magnet . . . Not quite so much pelvis.' He smiles. 'Good girl. Off you go.'

And at that point, the music is turned up. It's Lady Gaga, who I love 'ah-ah-ah!' and, I don't know, maybe it's just the Red Bull hitting me, but suddenly I do have one of those moments. I think: I'm out with my wonderful witty friend, whom I adore, and I've got a sexy man over there, and he's considering my offer of marriage, and in the meantime, Gaga is playing, and the dance floor is filling, and the first drink of the night is now quite definitely zinging through my system, and I am a queen amongst courtiers, and I've got a Lady Sex Magnet, and I am *turning it on*. And I wink at Arthur. And I dance off.

## Arthur

Now I'm on my own.

I know only one other person here: Dan. I should go and speak to him.

Or maybe I should dance with someone. I've been chucked out of my home. This is definitely the moment to do it.

Heading towards Dan, I go across the edge of the dance floor. I'm doing that thing of walking while jigging a bit. I'm technically not dancing, I'm just walking. I'm limbering up, in case the music suddenly *grabs* me. I pass a couple of women. I smile. They both turn away.

I wasn't even hitting on them! They turned away like I was a leper. Jesus. It's brutal being single. Who'd ever want to be in this position again?

Now I head over to Dan with some keenness. Does he want to marry Em? I'm suddenly desperate to find out. And if not, why not?

He's in the corner on some sofas. I'm actually not sure it's Dan at first, but I recognise the mole on his cheek. He's got one of those big ones that has long hair on it. How did Em ever kiss him?

'Hi, Dan!' I say.

'Hi . . . man!' he says, a bit too enthusiastically. It's obvious he can't place me.

'It's Arthur, Polly's husband.'

'I know that!' says Dan. He clearly didn't know that. Now he overcompensates. 'So . . . It's so good to see you! Hey . . . are you guys coming to the Hammond launch on Friday?'

'I think Polly might be going. With Em.'

'Oh,' he says.

'I came in to work with her today,' I say. 'But I haven't really spoken to her . . . How is she?'

'She's a bit intense,' he confesses. 'I think she wants to get married,' he adds, rolling his eyes.

'Oh,' I say, as casually as possible. Don't want to sound too interested. 'And is that what you want?'

He goes quiet again. It's as the Online Wizard says: men are like snails. And this one's now in full retreat, like he's just been jabbed with the spade.

'You don't need to tell me what you're thinking, by the way,' I say. I'm trying to reassure him, quick. Before he disappears completely. 'I remember having to make that decision. Nightmare.'

'Did Polly propose to you?' he says.

'Yeah. It's the modern way: the man must be prodded towards the church.'

'Yeah!' says Dan, who seems reassured by the direction the conversation is going. He's halted his retreat. In fact, he's reaching his curious snail eyes towards me. 'Why is that?'

'Well . . . I think men are gamblers,' I say. 'We're thinking: I like you, I *love* you, but . . . next time I might get Claudia Schiffer.'

'Yeah!' says Dan, with a raise of his eyebrows.

'Though we know that, even if we did get Schiffer, we'd one day come to resent her bucktoothed German face, looming, waiting for a kiss.'

'Yeah!' says Dan, more ruefully now. 'And the trouble is,' he says, 'you don't actually get Schiffer, you get some skinny bird who works in PR. You give her your body, but you don't give her your address.'

I say: 'Yeah!' I'm thinking: My God, this snail is right out of his shell. Right. Time to pull him out and cook him in garlic.

'What would you say is your biggest fear?' I ask.

Dan looks me in the eye. I've blown it. That was too big a question. He's not going to answer it. Probably he already knows I'm Em's spy.

But he does answer. 'It's the lifetime of commitment, isn't it?' he says. 'That's the biggie. I'm thinking: I will never be able even to fancy another woman. Ever again.'

'Yup!'

'I might as well cut my cock off, and give it to Em so she can wear it around her neck on a string!'

'I know what you mean!' I say.

'Do you?' says Dan, giving me a serious look. He seems quite content to have a heart-to-heart provided it's all disguised behind semi-ironic comedy. 'Do you feel Polly wears your cock like a deeply inappropriate accessory?'

'Erm,' I say. And I'm actually trying to answer Dan's question, but, considering it, I'm not sure what I feel Polly does to my cock, and I don't care. I've been trying to avoid thinking it but now I can't: I feel as if the floor to my world has been removed, and I'm about to plunge into a chasm. I just wish I were with Polly now. I hate this bar, and this conversation. I wish I were at home. And then suddenly it hits me in the stomach that I might never go home again. And for a moment, I think I might cry.

And there's no way I'm doing that next to Dan. So I make my excuses.

## Em

They're playing Lady Gaga again. I love this song. 'Ra ra oomer . . .' I must stop mouthing the words. 'Ra ra Oomerah!'

OK. Let's cast loose into the sea of dance. Let's be confident. I *should* be confident! I go three nights a week to Dennis Wonder's

Swing Beat Jazz. I'm up against two blokes from IT who are jogging from foot to foot like they need a pee. I'm a queen amongst courtiers. I'm owning my own space.

Why is everyone else dancing at the other end of the dance floor?

My Lady Sex Magnet isn't working! It looks like it's driving them off! This is bad. Come on. Someone please dance with me. Someone!

*Someone???!!!*

*And . . . yes, a man appears!*

I've attracted one in. And he's a big one as well. He's a very good dancer. Very flamboyant. Looks like he goes to the gym.

Ooh. He's turning. Come on, let's get a look at you.

And let's see what moves you've got. 'Cos I've got some like this. And I've got some like that . . .

Ooh. He's approaching. He's approached as far as he need.

He's a big one, and he's a bit sweaty and a bit close. Plus he's a bit bald.

No. No.

I'm turning. I'm turning away from you. I'm dancing away from you. Dancing *away*.

*Ooh. He's reappeared.*

No. I'm dancing away from you, you big sweaty freak. I'm dancing away. I'm a solo dancer. Finding my own space. On my own.

He's reappeared.

*May Day, I need a port!* Help! There's a stricken vessel out here lost in the sea of dance. Come on! Someone!

'Oh my goodness, Dan!'

*It's my boyfriend! He's saved me!*

He holds my hands. He must be drunk too. He never touches me in front of colleagues! 'Em!' he says. 'We need to talk. Do you want a drink?'

'Yes!' I shout. I'm possibly being a bit too eager.

He looks into my eyes. 'See you on the terrace,' he says. 'I'll get us both a drink.'

## Arthur

I'd forgotten the sheer horror of clubs.

After leaving Dan, I string things out by going for a very long wee. Then I go outside to the terrace. (If anyone looks at me, I put a little frown on my face like I'm looking for someone.) Then I return to the toilet.

While drying my hands, I drift into conversation with a man in glasses who clearly thinks I'm a bloke called Phil who works on the News Desk. I don't disabuse him. I carry on talking to him, even after he reveals he works in Accounts, and I notice he has remarkably long nasal hair. I carry on talking to him even after he leaves the bathroom. Outside it, the music is unaccountably loud, however, and I can't even hear what Accountant man is saying. In fact, we have the worst conversation in the history of conversations . . .

He says: 'Where do you live?' I shout: 'Richmond!' He nods. Then he says: 'Where do you live?' I shout: 'Richmond! In a little ghetto of posh people who are all gathered round a school.' I now nod. He gives it a moment, then he shouts again: '*Where do you live?*' And I shout: 'Richmond! RICHMOND!!' And then I have one of those troubling moments of self-consciousness. I see myself from the outside. I'm the man outside a toilet, the one shouting 'Richmond' over and over again like a balding Dorothy who wants to go home. I must get away. I give the Accountant a polite nod, and I head back up the stairs.

Where, fortunately, I'm met by Em.

Thank God for that. I need to check she's OK. I need to go.

She's swaggering a bit. I forgot this about Em: she gets pissed quick. She's also progressed, remarkably early, to the stage of the evening where you just shamelessly down abandoned drinks.

She grabs my arm. 'Oh my God!' she shouts. 'He just said he wants to talk!'

'OK. Great.'

She leads me to a quieter spot on the balcony.

'But,' she says, 'aren't I supposed to be distant like a snake?'

'That was to make him chase you. That's now worked. He wants to talk.'

'Right . . . So I must talk.'

'No. No no no *no*! You must *listen*. I think he's keen, but scared. Be soft. Let him speak.'

She gives me her imploring look.

'But what's he scared about?'

'He's scared of being stuck,' I say. 'He's scared he won't be able to fancy you for ever.'

'But . . . why don't men speak about their feelings?'

'They don't want to be killed! We've learned that, if we speak the truth, we get pummelled. Be soft, be feminine, be understanding. Let him talk. Let him talk all the way home. Keep saying: "I know! I *know*!" Then when you get home, keep repeating the magic words. Say: "Darling, I love you. I want you rich, successful and free." Then lick him on the back of his balls.'

Em looks shocked. 'Really?'

'If you want him. Obviously you'll feel like you're nosing an uncooked chicken. He'll feel like he's in heaven.'

'I thought I was being the queen, why am I being all submissive now?'

'That's what we want: a queen, who's submissive to us. Be feminine. Tend to him. Come tomorrow, he will propose.'

'And so it shall be,' she says solemnly. Then she downs someone's wine.

So I say: 'Good . . . You're OK?'

'Yes,' says Em.

'OK. I'd better get home.'

'Yup,' says Em. 'I suggest you beg Polly's forgiveness, and you crawl back on bleeding knees.'

'Give me a moment,' I say. 'I need to hear what Dan says.'

'I'll tell you. I'll tell Polly. We'll call her together. But keep out of the way for a few minutes.'

'I will!' I say. 'Where's Dan now?'

'Getting us drinks,' she says. She notices another abandoned drink and downs it. 'I can see him! I'll go and fetch him out.'

'Remember . . . be soft, let him speak.'

She waves me away impatiently. 'Yes!' she says. She's slurring a lot now.


### Em

I am actually now feeling like a Dirty Sexy Queen, who is slightly drunk. I've got whisky and ginger . . . And I've got Dan. My Dan. Dan Dan Dan. He's all that I've ever wanted, I know that now. I have my thumb hooked into the front of his jeans. I'm leading him up the stairs.

What the hell is he going to say?

We get out on the balcony, and I find a quiet spot. He gives us both a Marlboro Light – *see*, that's something else that's good about Dan: he *smokes* – and we light up, and practically the first thing he says is . . .

'So . . . New York!'

And I'm about to say: 'What?' But I don't. I'm on the ball. I just say: 'Yeah! New York!'

Then we both stare at the river, as if we're contemplating the celestial hugeness of New York.

'I can't believe you're going!' he says.

I say: 'I can hardly believe it too!' Then I get a bit scared I'm giving it away. 'Well,' I say, seriously, 'I *believe* I'm going.'

'What are you going to do there?'

'*Vanity Fair* . . . Associate editor,' I add. (I have a bit of trouble with the 'Associate Editor'.)

'What does that mean?'

'Not sure.'

'You're not sure?'

'I think Americans have lots of Associate Editors. It's like being Vice President. If you make the tea in an American firm, you're a Vice President.'

At this point there's a sudden lull in the conversation. I nod as if to say: Yup, I think I've said all I can about Vice Presidents. I check Dan. He is staring at the water, doing his trendy frown. Normally I'd butt in, but I'm trying to remember Arthur's advice: let him speak. Besides, I do really want to know . . . what's he going to say?

'Em,' he says. 'You and me have a good time together.'

'Yes.'

'Em . . .' he says, again. And now . . . he actually takes my hand, and he looks at me with intense feeling. Oh my God! It is finally happening! *He's proposing!!! Be soft, let him speak.*

'Em,' he says again, 'I'd like to come to New York with you!'

'Would you?!!' I say, a bit squeakily.

'We could be together!'

I can feel the panic bubbling in my chest. This isn't how it was supposed to go.

'We could go to restaurants, and we could . . . dig the Downtown Scene together.'

'No!' I shout.

'What?' he says.

I'm trying to be soft. But I'm afraid I shout: '*You **can't** come to New York with me!*'

He says: 'Why?!'

'Erm . . .' I say. I'm making a mess of this. I'm pissed. How did I get into this bloody conversation?

'Em!' says Dan definitely. 'I want to come to New York with you!'

And I shout at him: 'You can't come to New York unless you marry me.'

'What?!'

'You can't come to New York unless you marry me!'

Now he looks really confused. 'Why?' he says. 'Are you American?'

''Course I'm not American!'

'It sounded like it was a legal requirement.'

'No!' I say. I take a deep breath. Then . . . 'I'm not talking about legal requirements!'

'Right!' says Dan, who's suddenly looking a bit cowed. 'So . . .'

I've got to get the conversation back on track.

*Be soft, let him speak.*

I take control. I take his hand.

'Or,' I say, 'I could stay and we could marry.'

He says: 'What?'

'Or,' I squeeze his hand, 'I could stay and we could marry.'

He frowns.

'You're . . . just . . . you're confusing me now. Are you going to New York or not?'

'No, I'm not.'

'Why not?'

'I've just . . . gone off the idea.'

'You've just gone off it?'

'Listen, Dan. I can't carry on like this!'

'What?'

'You and me, like this.'

'I know!' he says. 'That's why I want to go to New York.'

I can't take this any more. I say, 'There is no New York!'

*'There's no New York!'*

'No. I just made it up.'

*'You made up New York?'*

Oh, for fuck's sake, he thinks I've invented New York!

'Obviously the place exists. I just made up going there.'

'Why??!!'

''Cos . . . 'Cos I can't carry on, just . . . going out with you. I need to get married or split up.'

He gives me a long look.

Then he says: 'Listen. I just don't understand! Why did you . . .'

And at this point, I can't take it any more. I can't take the lies and the bluffings and the tactics. So suddenly I just scream at him. 'Because I don't want to be a secret!' I shout. 'And I don't want to wait around *any more*! I am a woman, God damn it! I am a beautiful woman, you little fucker! And I want some fucking devotion! So I want you to fucking propose to me, or to *fuck right off!'*

He stares at me astonished.

Obviously I do suddenly realise I've gone way further than I meant. But I tell you one thing I'm very good at: I can change tack in a second.

And I do that now. 'But, Dan darling,' I say quietly, 'don't think about this now. You've got till Friday to make up your mind.'

And he says: 'Right.' He's confused now.

So I grab the front of his jacket, and I snog him.

OK, I must confess he stiffens slightly. Any second now he'll disengage and he'll say: 'Listen, let's get a drink.' But I don't let him. I hold him, and I snog him, and, just in case there's any danger of him running off, I put my hand on his cock. And as that hardens palpably to my touch, I think: Yup! I've still got it.

## Polly

9.45 p.m. I'm emptying the dishwasher.

It's finished. Well . . . it has licked the dirt off the plates, and it has transformed it into a paste, which it has spat into the corners of the cups. If Arthur were here, he'd probably say that lentils have blocked the dishwasher's sprayholes. He would take out the spinning bit, and he'd rattle it thoughtfully. The dishwasher is another of Arthur's Areas of Responsibility. The dog. The dishwasher. And the bikes. Those are his areas. Oh . . . And mince-making of course. That's his area. He's also in charge of anything to do with the television. He does the leads. He also orders all the movies from Love Film. I glance at them now. He's arranged the movies along the shelf, along with a few DVDs he got from a charity shop. He's got *My Life As A Dog, Paris, Texas, The Umbrellas of Cherbourg, Knocked Up* and *In The Line of Fire*. A little card says 'The Richmond Film Festival organised by Arthur Midgley (Artistic Director)'. And beside that are the books he's chosen for me. OK, I admit it. He's in charge of all entertainment in the house. Ooh, and sponges. He buys those scouring sponges – those ones that are green one side, and pink the other. He worries when we're out of them.

Oh, God. This is awful. I miss him.

I wish he were now. He could be cooking mince, while dismantling the dishwasher, while discussing sponges. I'd be happy. I tell you who I also miss – that stupid dog. I get so used to her habits – her barking when someone's at the door, her obsessive concern that there are cats in the garden – the house seems quiet without her. Her basket is standing unused. I look at the saggy cushion, and her bowl, and the squeaky hedgehog Arthur bought her for Christmas.

I feel sick with guilt. Here are Arthur and I wondering what we should do, who we should love. That silly dog does none of that. We're not even the same species as her, but she loves us. And actually I love her. I love how she patrols under the table for crumbs. I love how she comes upstairs when we're reading stories. I wish she were lying on the floor now like a big draught excluder.

What should I do? I feel like my heart has been ripped in two.

The phone rings.

*It's Arthur!*

I love it! It seems so gloriously reassuring to have a husband calling. But – oh, God – is that reason enough to accept him back?

'Hello,' I say. I lean back against the counter.

'Hello,' he says. 'Are you OK?'

'Yes.'

I can tell instantly that he's being friendly. It doesn't really matter what he says. He's being friendly. It feels like the sun is shining and we've got a fridge full of food.

'Listen,' he says. 'I'm so sorry I got angry yesterday. I love you.'

'Thank you. I'm sorry too. Bitchin isn't a swear word. I wish I'd said that.'

'Thank you,' he says. 'I feel a whole lot better just from you saying that.'

I've walked into the living room. I see myself in the mirror. I look beautiful. I look beautiful and my husband is back.

'Ooh,' he says. 'I've spent the day working for Em, and she's giving me five hundred quid.'

'Really?' I say. 'Well done.'

'Yeah, obviously that's not the six hundred you asked for.'

'Never mind.'

I can't really tell how I am supposed to be behaving. Wasn't I supposed to be being angry? I am *so* glad to hear him.

'Where are you?' I ask.

'In a bar next to Em's office.'

'It'll take you ages to come home,' I say. 'So hurry.' Did I mean to say that? I think I did.

'Oh!' he says, brightening audibly. 'I can come home?'

I chuckle. 'Arthur, it is your house.'

## Arthur

I can't say how good this makes me feel.

I don't need to move out. I don't need to live with Mrs

Hennessy, and be hated by her family, and petition solicitors for access, and ruin the children's lives. I can just go home.

'Polly?' I say.

'Yes.'

'I love you.'

There's a pause.

'I love you a lot, Polly.'

## Polly

There's a silence.

I sit on the sofa.

I realise he's left a space. It's now my turn to say 'I love you' in return. But I feel like my mum suddenly. Maybe I'm not an emotional person. I just can't say it.

'Polly,' he says again. 'I love you.'

'Do you?'

'Yes,' he says. 'I love every bone in your foot. I love every list in your head. I love you.'

He leaves another expectant pause.

I still can't say it. Actually I'm scared to. I *do* want him back. But I also really *do* want to go to James's. It's not just the job. He offers excitement and newness and everyone says it: you regret what you don't do, not what you do. And if Arthur comes home I'll be trapped in that fruit bowl for ever.

'Darling,' I say. 'Come home.'

'I will.'

'Come straight home,' I say. 'Don't buy any sponges.'

He laughs.

'I won't,' he says. 'Oh . . . Hang on . . . I think Em wants a word.'

'Oh, OK.'

Em comes on the line.

'Hello, Polly darling,' she says. She sounds remarkably drunk, even for Em.

'Hello, Em.'

'Hello, my darling.'

And she's being loud too. I hold the phone away from my ear.

'Have you had a couple of drinks?' I ask.

'Just a couple. I want to get you back together,' she announces. 'Why don't you both come on Friday?'

'What?'

'So you can be there when Dan gives his answer to my proposal.'

'Where is Dan?'

'He's . . . He's just getting us both some drinks.'

'Is he?'

'Yes. I'm trying to give him some space. Your husband explained it to me. Arthur . . . I think he's brilliant, your husband. He said: "Be soft, don't let him speak . . ." No. He said: "Be soft . . ." He said: "Be soft . . ."'

'I've got the gist of what he said, thank you. It sounds very intelligent.' Actually it sounds obscene.

'It *was* intelligent, Polly,' says Em. She's dull when she's drunk. '*Intelligent*,' she says again. ' Have you had an argument?'

'Yes, we have.'

'Is it because he licked my breast?'

'I'm sorry!'

At this point, there's an awful silence. I feel like I've been punched in the stomach.

'What did you just say?' I prompt.

'I . . . I didn't say anything.'

I suddenly feel sick.

'What did you say?' I repeat.

'I said nothing!'

'Em,' I say, very loud. 'Did Arthur lick your breast?'

'Excuse me, Polly,' she says. 'How dare you? I have *never* . . .'

'*Did* he lick your breast?'

'Yes. He did . . . A bit. But it's fine. He loves you . . .'

'*How can it ever be fine that he licked your breast?* What was the context?'

'Well . . . Polly . . . he came to visit me this afternoon . . . we were *talking* Polly. He said . . . he wanted you and . . . he was very sad, not been so sad since he was sixteen . . .'

'*How did he come to lick your breast?*'

'It wasn't the whole breast, it was just the nipple.'

'But *why?*'

'He was talking about what men want – apparently they don't like us to talk – he said I want to . . . I want . . . I want to be silent and masterful . . . And I just sort of . . . took off my . . . And for . . . about half a second . . . he licked my breast . . . But . . . the way one might lick breasts between friends.'

'*The way you might lick breasts between friends?!*' I screech. 'Friends don't lick breasts.'

'Lesbians do. And they are friends.'

There's a long silence. I hate her. I hate her. I've never felt so betrayed.

Then Em says: 'Listen, I'm really sorry, but I must say I think he's wonderful and he loves you and you must get back together.'

I don't say anything. I don't think I've ever been this angry in my life.

She doesn't seem to realise.

'I'm seeing you Friday night, Polly darling,' she says.

I just cut her off.

I say: 'Can you pass Arthur a message?'

'Of course I can, darling.'

'Tell him: "Don't even fucking think about coming home unless you want to be killed."'

And I turn off the phone.

I fling it hard at the wall.


## Arthur

Em has drifted away while she's been talking to Polly. But even from a distance I can see something's gone wrong. She's looking round for me guiltily.

I go over.

'What?'

'Hi!' says Em. She is really pissed. 'I'm sorry, Arthur,' she says. 'Polly said she doesn't want you to go home.'

'Why?!'

'I told her what happened today. Vis à vis, the nipple-lick.'

Oh my God. 'But . . . *why*?'

'I didn't mean to. I'm sorry, Arthur. I . . .'

My stomach falls away. I have a feeling I've not had since I was at school: I'm in big, *big* trouble. And like all the times I've ever been in big trouble, it seems to have come from nowhere. What the fuck did I do? And with Em of all people!

'Oh, God,' I say. I'm starting to realise how badly Polly will be taking this.

'Don't worry,' says Em. She touches my cheek for a moment. She takes my hand. 'Come on, let's go and dance some more.'

I know Em's a journalist but this is incredible. She seems to have no shame or remorse whatsoever. I pull away. She goes back into the club.

I stay outside on the terrace.

I'm in shock, but it's clear: my marriage is over.

A few minutes pass, I just stand on the terrace staring into the distance. But then I notice a couple of people looking at me as if to say: Who's the assassin?

That's the trouble with this fucking world. You've got to act like you're happy, even when your wife's just chucked you out, and you don't know where you're going to stay.

I need help.

People are staring.

I pull out my phone, and I pretend to send a text.

Next to me a woman is doing the same thing too, except she's sending out messages very quickly, and she's got a sleek i-Phone. She's a beautiful red-headed woman in her late-forties.

She glances at me.

'Arthur?' she says.

I look at her.

I realise, with a shock, it's Greta.

I'm still almost faint after the row with Polly. But still . . . It's Greta!

She no longer has long rock-star locks. Her hair is sleek and flat. She's a little heavier than she was. Before she seemed tall and athletic. Now she seems rounder, more of an Earth Mother, but the prettiest Earth Mother you've ever seen. She's wearing a cream suit which is tailored so it's tight round her waist. She looks even better than she used to.

'Greta!' I say.

'It's so great to *see* you!' she says. She kisses me, bringing a waft of expensive perfume. 'Why are you here?'

Erm. Why am I here? My arrival seems so long ago. 'I've written some pieces for *Lifestyle*. *Learn Love in a Week*.'

'Oh my God! You're Arthur *Midgley*! I've read those. I *love* them.'

'Really?'

'Do you know I'm Guest Editor next week?'

'I heard that!'

'I'm going in tomorrow to talk ideas, I'll tell them I want more Midgley.'

'Great!'

She stares at me. When English people look, our gaze is quick, furtive. We don't want to be found out. But Greta's confident. She's American. She really looks. I stare back at her. Everything happens for a reason, I think. Why the hell is she here now?

'So now I'm really looking forward to next week,' she says, 'but tomorrow I've got two problems.'

'What?' I say. I'm having trouble taking it all in. Everything seems a bit dreamlike.

'Oh, I'm working for *Daybreak* and we need a guest for 5.30 tomorrow morning.'

'You've got to find a guest who will go on TV at 5.30 in the morning?'

'Honey . . . finding a guest is nothing. Finding childcare, that is harder. But I will find something. My God, Arthur! What have you been doing for the last . . . like ten years?'

'Oh!' I say, trying to remember. 'I've had three children, and I've been looking after them.'

'No! You've been a . . . what do they call it . . . a stay-at-home dad?'

'I prefer the term trophy husband.'

Greta roars with laughter.

'So this is perfect,' she says. 'Everything connects . . . Do you know what I need for *Daybreak*? A man who looks after children. Would you please, please consider coming on, for a five-minute slot, which pays a fee of one hundred pounds.'

I'm still feeling winded, but I'm aware that I've achieved my task! I've earned six hundred quid in a day!

'Sure,' I say. 'But what would I say?'

'Just . . . keep it light. The magic of childcare. Why men love it. Why they're great at it. You'll be gorgeous.'

'Great!' I'm not sure if I'm the man for live TV, but maybe I am. 'Are you sure I have a high enough profile for you?'

'Sure! You're Arthur Midgley, writer of *Learn Love in a Week*, the new smash-hit column.'

She smiles. I can't believe it. Greta Kay is suddenly back in my life. Maybe there's hope.

'So Arthur!' she says. 'The other problem is my nanny's got a hospital appointment.' She gives me a searching look. 'I don't suppose . . .' she says. 'Could you help?'

'How?'

'Watch my son for the morning, while I do the meeting?'

I stare at her. Obviously I would do absolutely anything just for an excuse to be in her presence. It's Greta Kay, my all-time fantasy woman. At the same time, I'm aware she's asking me to be a stand-in au pair. If I offered to do that, would that be helpful or servile? I'm also aware she's suggesting me as an expert on childcare. I should demonstrate a willingness to do some.

'I'd be delighted,' I say.

'You are a star! So . . . My meeting's at eleven. I'll get the car to send you to mine as soon as you leave *Daybreak*. Then you can just look after him there for a couple of hours. Is that OK?'

'Er . . . I'd have to stay over tonight,' I say.

Those words came straight out before I considered them.

Greta gives a surprised look.

'Don't get me wrong,' I burble. 'I'm not making a pass at you. I . . . I just need a place to stay.'

Oh, no. Has that improved things? A moment ago, I was a TV expert. Now I'm homeless.

Fortunately Greta laughs.

She says: 'How come you don't have a place to stay?'

'I had an argument with my wife and she threw me out.'

'I *love* you!' she says. 'Always busy with some drama. Of course you can stay. I have plenty of rooms. In the morning, you can get the car from my place. And then you can watch Tyrone.'

I look at her. She looks into my eyes with her wise mountain gaze.

'So,' she says. 'Shall we go right away?'

I say: 'Yes.'

**Em**

Where is Dan? Where's my drink? I'm lost. I need someone to help.

**Arthur**

Greta has a Bentley waiting outside, and she's got a man called Bernard, who's waiting to drive her home. The back of the car is all white leather. I shut the door behind me and there's a sort of muffled thud. Greta climbs in to my left. Her buttocks make their way in first, but soon the whole of her is in and Greta turns to me slowly. She says: 'So?'

And it's like we've not been apart. We talk.

She's been married since I last saw her – to a Canadian cyclist who was globally famous about eight years ago. He won the Tour de France. He also wrote a bestselling book in which he ascribed his extraordinary success to God. This was then undermined when it emerged he might, just as easily, have attributed his good fortune to drugs. They're divorced now.

'I'm sorry to hear it,' I say.

'It's OK,' she says. 'I like being single.' As she says this, she looks very directly into my eyes. The incident with Em has stirred something in me. I sense the cub scout rising to attention as he senses the presence of Akela. 'For one thing,' Greta continues, 'I'm devoted to my work. You have to be, if you want to succeed. And sometimes I'll work till two in the morning.'

'But,' I stammer, 'don't you miss having a man in your life?'

'Oh,' she says, and she smiles very slowly – I think it's the key to her extraordinary charisma and power, the unhurried pace at which she moves – 'if you've got a bit of money and a lovely swelling chest, you can always get a man, though he may not be the best.' She smiles more. 'Oh my God, that rhymes! I should set it to music and become a famous singer all over again – "The Song of the Happy Cougar".'

Bloody hell, she is being brazen. Actually I'm finding her a touch too brazen. Nevertheless, I can't help but be aware of something extraordinary. Everything happens for a reason, and, remarkably, I'm in a car, with my fantasy woman, and she's single, and so am I, and she's flirting. It feels like something sexy is about to happen. It doesn't though. *It doesn't.* What happens is

Greta talks and I listen. I'm still feeling winded about Polly. At the same time I feel like a snail who's been pulled out of his shell. I feel utterly exposed. But I'm feeling everything. I'm seeing everything. And I stare into Greta's hazel eyes, and I try not to fall in love with her.

There is only one thing for it: complete physical union.

# Thursday

*Learn Love in a Week* – *the online course that will change your life.*

*Day Five:* many relationships are killed by myths. Common ones are: 'I *can't* be happy till we move to Spain!' or 'I *need* a child!' What is it you think you most want? Money, fame, a big house, a clean house, another house, kids, the return of that one special person? What is your myth? Root it out like a little worm, and examine it.

*Today's exercise*: declare your myth. See yourself getting what you say you want. Don't concentrate on the point of capture – the first sex, the reunion, the apology . . . Project yourself *five years* into the future – to the time when you're *used* to your fantasy house / your fantasy person / your fame . . . Write: 'In five years' time, I am . . .' and, for ten minutes, describe your new life as fast as you can.

*Today's challenge:* read back the list of things you want. Consider how many of them you can have *now*. Perhaps you long for Spain since you imagine yourself drinking fresh orange juice and walking through a garden of geraniums. So . . . get some geraniums and some juice right now.

Perhaps you'll realise you don't want what you thought you

wanted. (Even Spanish people can be unhappy, and many people with kids are pissed off!) But perhaps you really do want to go to Spain.

So go! Go and be happy!

**Em**

I'm on my bed.

I open my eyes. I see a clock saying 4.28 a.m.

I'm going to be sick.

I lean over the edge of the mattress. There's a washing-up bowl.

The light comes on. I turn.

It's Malcolm. That gives me a shock.

'Hey,' he says.

'What . . .' I start to ask, but I am unable to complete the sentence. I am sick.

He steps forward, he lifts the bowl, and holds my hair.

When I finish, Malcolm passes me some tissues. Then he goes out.

I wipe my face.

Then I quickly visit the bathroom. I empty the bowl. I clean myself up.

Then I visit the living room.

Malcolm is on the sofa. He's just sitting there in his jeans and his brown jacket with the furry collar. He's got a mug, a plate, and my laptop.

'Better out than in,' he says cheerfully.

'Malcolm!' I say. 'What the *hell* are you doing here?'

He smiles. 'Just checking my e-mails.'

I check the clock. It's 4.28 in the fucking morning!

I say: 'It's 4.28 in the fucking morning.'

He says: 'I know! Nobody's replying at all.'

I am so confused. Am I drunk still? I am aware that I am a little bit drunk, and that moments ago I was sleeping, before which I was very, very drunk. I can't even remember what I was doing.

I'm going to be sick again. I run into the bathroom again but it's a false alarm. I just lean down the toilet saying 'ooaaaaaaoooo' as if I'm trying to call someone at the other end of the pipes. Then I see myself in the mirror. My eyeliner has smudged everywhere and my hair has gone a bit rock 'n' roll, but, actually, I look good. I put in a scrunchie, and I brush my teeth.

Then I hurry out of the bathroom again.

'Let me ask again,' I say. 'What are you doing here?'

'I'm trying to decide about canoes for Saturday,' he begins. 'I offered them to Polly and Arthur but they haven't confirmed. So I'm wondering if I should offer *both canoes* to the Lea Valley cubs.'

Why is he talking about canoes? I have to stop him doing that.

'They have *two canoes*. They need two more.'

At this point I totally lose it. I shout at him quite loudly: 'Malcolm, stop talking about bloody canoes!'

At this Malcolm seems just slightly surprised. But he continues to look at me with his happy expression.

'*Why* are you here?' I ask.

Jesus, this better be good.

'Well,' he says, 'I was expecting Arthur to stay last night. I called in at the Diamond Lounge. I saw you outside and decided to take you home.'

I don't know where to start with that. 'You . . .' I say. 'What gave you the idea it was right to take me home?'

He isn't bothered by the question. 'Well,' he says. 'First . . . you were hanging on a lamp post. I said: 'Em!' You didn't seem to know who I was. First sign of trouble. Then you fell to your knees and started to crawl towards some bins. You looked like a little fox. I thought: Fair enough. Maybe she wants to crawl home. Then you fell asleep. So I just picked you up, and I put you in the van.'

'Right.'

'I'm afraid you were sick a couple of times.'

'Is . . . Is the van OK?'

'Oh, the van's fine!' says Malcolm contentedly. I've noticed this about him. He loves talking about the van, for any reason at all. 'I had a plastic sheet there anyway. Luckily I knew where to go. I found your keys. I carried you up here, and I put you on the bed, in the recovery position.'

'You put . . .'

'I used to be a nurse.'

'Did you?'

'Oh, I made loads of friends when I was a nurse!' says Malcolm proudly. 'I met a couple of my best friends when I put them in the recovery position.'

'But stop . . . Malcolm,' I manage. 'When did you carry me home?'

'A couple of hours ago,' he says.

My head's starting to throb. 'So . . . what the hell have you been doing here for two hours?'

'Em,' he says. 'I did quickly fix your window.'

I look. He has fixed my window.

'Malcolm,' I say. 'First of all, can I say . . . thank you so much for bringing me home. That was kind. I must admit, though, it was also a bit weird that, having done so, you *just stayed*!'

Malcolm grins. 'I suppose it does sound a little strange when you say it. The truth is, I was tipsy myself so I decided to make a coffee.'

'You made coffee!'

'And toast.'

'Malcolm!'

'And I saw your computer so I decided to check my e-mails. I've got some business on just now,' he says delightedly, 'that's going amazingly.'

I don't pursue that. 'When you found me,' I say, 'was there any sign of Dan?'

'I checked the Diamond Lounge. It was shut.'

I think about last night. I remember I got very drunk. I remember dancing. I vaguely remember shouting at Dan. After then I realise it's all a haze. But I remember enough to realise it . . . Dan must have gone home and left me. The thought hurts more than you'd expect.

'Malcolm,' I say, 'on Monday I asked Dan if he would marry me.'

'Did you?'

'And last night he left me at a club too drunk to stand up. It's not great, is it?'

'Well, it doesn't look good at this stage, but . . . Maybe he had to go to make a call or something.'

'Oh, God!' I say.

'What's wrong?'

'I'm thirty-four, Malcolm! I'm getting old! And I'm greedy and selfish and people are noticing!'

Malcolm just looks at me kindly. 'Em,' he says, 'be kind to yourself. You're lovely.'

'I've got dimply thighs!'

'For God's sake,' he says. 'Will you look at yourself? You're going to be gorgeous when you're sixty-four.'

'You think?'

'I could imagine you, aged seventy-four, and I'd still be thinking: Ooh, I wouldn't mind.'

'You're just saying that!'

'And besides, if you want to love your love, don't worry if they're sexy. Just concentrate on *knowing* them.'

'What does that mean?'

'I don't know. Well . . . It means . . . Love is not just about seeing your lover . . . The amazing thing is when you're trying to *feel* what they're feeling . . . Like . . . you're *touching* but you lose who's who and who's touching . . . It's like you're not you any more, you're them . . . You're together and it's amazing . . .'

As Malcolm has been talking, I've been on the living-room floor listening to him. But at this point, I crawl forward on my knees, and I kiss him.

## Arthur

Lordy-Lord!

I'm going on breakfast television this morning.

I don't even watch breakfast television. I have *seen* it. Not for a while, actually, though I remember what it was like. I've got a mental impression of bright studios, and men with tanned faces, talking, with restrained pleasure, about a new kind of yoghurt. It looks easy enough.

Now I'm about to do it, it seems harder.

I wake at 5 a.m. in Greta's spare room. I go almost immediately to the front door where a uniformed man is waiting with a car, like a KGB officer come to take me away. I'm then taken to the studio, whereupon I meet an extraordinary barrage of ladies who all have blonde highlights. There's a receptionist. There's another at the lift. There's a producer called Barbara who says she just wants to check I'm all right. There's another in make-up who puts thick foundation and eyeliner on my face. That bothers me. I'm going on TV to talk about my life as a stay-at-home dad, in thick make-up . . . Surely the viewers will think, Who is this poof, discussing parenting?

But I say nothing. Increasingly in my life, I don't speak up.

I've not been home for two days now, I've lost all my bearings. I don't know what's normal. I don't know if I should be nervous.

Should I be nervous?

YES! I'm about to go on national television, and I haven't a clue what I'm supposed to say. Yes. Suddenly I am nervous.

I'm shown into the Green Room. There's another lady with highlights. She offers me coffee. I take the coffee and sit. I pass an American pop star. I don't know who he is, but he's wearing sunglasses and a white tuxedo. He's either a pop star, or he's deranged and doesn't know what time of day it is. I hear him drawling out the phrase: 'When I was singing at the Emmies . . .' I try to catch more. Sadly he is drowned out by a remarkably self-confident lobbyist called Andrew Richmond. He introduces himself. Then he turns back to Rolf Harris, saying, 'There are four main objections to wind farms.' In my mind I begin rehearsing the four main objections to Andrew Richmond; at the same time, I'm trying desperately to think what it is I'm supposed to be talking about. It must be something important.

There's a screen above the American pop star, where I can see the *Daybreak* team discussing Afghanistan while interviewing a man described as the 'former commander of British Armed Forces'. Jesus. Everyone here is very highly qualified. *I don't even know what I am saying.*

Someone else comes into the room.

It's the former Deputy Prime Minister. That's strangely comforting. I like her. She's looking lovely and a bit mumsy in some flat shoes. Andrew Richmond goes quiet, as if calculating whether he should come over, right now, to start lobbying her about wind farms. I think she senses it. She avoids him. She comes over to me and sits next to me, flashing me a weary but sympathetic look.

I smile back. And before I know it, I'm talking to the former Deputy Prime Minister, and we're having the most unlikely conversation . . .

She says: 'Hello.'

I say: 'Hello.'

Then she leans forward and whispers . . .

'Sorry . . . it feels like I've got an eyelash in my left eye. Can you see one?'

I lean forward. Of course I'm deeply flattered that I'm being called in to help the former Deputy Prime Minister. At the same time, I'm terrified I'll have to help. Luckily she is blinking rapidly. She shifts the eyelash. I say: 'You just got it.' I find a tissue. I dab it out for her.

'Ooh,' she says. 'That's better!'

I look into her eye while she blinks a few times.

'Now it just looks like you've been crying,' I say. 'What are you discussing?'

'Poverty in the West Midlands.'

'That's OK, then,' I say. 'You'll look *really* concerned.'

The former Deputy Prime Minister smiles! She has a warm, confiding smile.

'What are you discussing?' she says.

'Stay-at-home dads.'

'Are you for them or against?'

'I am one. So I'm basically against.'

We both smile at each other. She has a very understanding manner.

'I feel a bit orange,' I say. 'Do I look OK?'

'You look very handsome,' she says, 'albeit slightly crumpled. I take it you were too busy to iron your shirt?'

'Yes!'

'It only takes two minutes,' she says, in a mock playful tone.

'Hey,' I say. 'Everything only takes two minutes!'

'But who has two minutes, right?'

'Exactly!'

'People say it to politicians all the time: "Minister, do you have two minutes?"'

'It's not just politicians. I got on a bus last week, the driver invited us to "take two minutes to familiarise yourselves with our basic safety procedures".'

'It's a nightmare!' she says.

'Do you floss?' I say.

'No,' she says.

'Only takes two minutes!' I say. We smile at each other. 'Do you make sure, each evening, you tell your partner you love him?'

'No!'

'Only takes two minutes! Do you make sure, each evening, you make love to your partner?'

'Well . . .' she says, grinning.

'Only takes two minutes!' I say.

At this point, she giggles. She's enjoying herself! I'm now in a sort of ecstasy. I'm making slightly saucy conversation with the former Deputy Prime Minister. I want to do it more.

But alas, the producer arrives, uttering the fatal words . . .

'Arthur! It's time for me to take you through.'

## Polly

I'm dreaming . . .

I'm at a school dance, with David Harding, my first serious boyfriend. He's saying: 'I've got a drink for you. Try it.' 'What is it?' I say. 'It's a drink!' 'But what is it?' I say. 'Just try it!' I sip the drink. It tastes like mouldy lemons. It goes into my heart and it *burns*. 'What is it?' I say. 'It's acid,' says David Harding with a horrible leer. 'The taste of *pure heartbreak*.'

I wake up in a panic.

I sit up.

I remember David Harding. I once looked for him everywhere at a party, and found him in an upstairs corridor snogging Samantha Drew.

It took me months to get over it. I used to sit at home, shaking and smoking cigarettes out of the bathroom window. My friends tried to get me out. They wanted me to meet someone new. I said: 'I don't want to have someone new. I don't want to allow that to happen again!'

I was seventeen at the time, but it feels like yesterday I was smoking cigarettes out of that window. I feel like I've let down the seventeen-year-old Polly. I've allowed it to happen again. And it's worse . . .

This was my very own husband, and he wasn't with Samantha Drew. He was with *Em*, who's supposed to be my best friend. It's the most sickening thing I've ever heard in my life. I don't feel angry. I don't feel heartbroken. I just feel dead.

## Arthur

Oh, God.

It's time for me to go on national television to talk about a subject I know nothing about.

The producer is leading me into the studio.

I'm stepping over cables and dodging past cameras.

In moments, I'm sitting on the famous sofa, next to the two presenters who look just like they normally look when you see them on TV, although they're now wearing way more make-up.

They both whisper hello. I like this. It feels like we're all in on a big secret.

The lady shakes my hand, mouthing: 'We're just coming out of the break.' She doesn't say her name. I think she assumes that, as a general rule, everyone knows who she is. I don't. I don't think she's the regular presenter.

Then, suddenly, we're off.

She turns to the camera, with a serious look. I can see words written. 'Ten years ago,' she intones, 'there were sixty thousand stay-at-home dads. In a decade that number has risen to six hundred thousand . . .'

I glance at a monitor, where you can see what's being broadcast. It's very unsettling. I'm aware that what's happening, right beside me, is going straight on to live television. And they're about to cut to me. Oh, God.

Suddenly I feel paralysed with nerves.

She continues . . .

'In the studio to talk about it is father of three, Arthur Midgley.'

She turns to me. She carries on talking. 'He's the writer of the hit new column . . .' But I'm not listening at all. I'm just thinking: I'm live on national television. I'm trying desperately to look normal, but my eye is twitching, and my heart is racing, and I realise that thoughts are hurtling through my brain faster than a bullet train through a station.

'Arthur,' she says. I glance at the monitor. I can see myself. I look a bit orange. 'Good morning.'

She pauses expectantly.

I say: 'Good morning.'

So far, so good.

She says: 'Do you call yourself a stay-at-home dad?'

'I prefer the phrase trophy husband,' I say.

It went better when I said it to Greta. The presenter gives a thin smile, like someone posing for a photograph. In that moment, I suddenly become aware what the game is: we're both desperately trying to be casual, so we look good on camera. I realise we're not doing well.

She's looking at me expectantly. Should I be talking?

'I'm a Writer/Actor/Dad,' I say. 'A WAD: one of those creative guys who does loads of childcare, not because he wanted to, but because he earns less than the wife.'

'And do you find that the other mums give you funny looks in the playground?'

'Sometimes,' I say. 'But that's usually because I'm hanging like a bat from the climbing frame.'

She doesn't laugh. She fixes me with her look of bland professional interest, and asks another question . . .

'Did you want to be the primary carer?'

'No,' I say. 'But we had the children, and suddenly she was saying: "I'm the one with the regular wage: why don't you look after them?" To be honest, we didn't even have that conversation, that's just what happened.'

'But you're obviously a very good parent,' she says. 'It must be very fulfilling to be so involved in your children's lives.'

With that, she stares at me expectantly.

I panic.

Is that a question? That was just a statement! And actually I'm not sure I agree with it.

Should I talk?

'Well,' I say. 'I do love my children very much, but . . .'

As soon as I start talking, she glances down at her pad. What is she doing? Then I realise . . . she knows the camera is on me, so she's giving herself a moment to prepare the next question. It feels very odd. Now I'm a lone man, who's on live national television, talking to himself. And I'm talking too loud, and I'm sounding a bit desperate . . .

'The thing is,' I say, '*I'm a man*! If I'm good at something, I expect awards, I expect cash. I feel like I'm running a playgroup, for no money, for people who shout at me. I'm not even in charge of the playgroup. The rules all come from the government, which is my wife.'

She's now looking at me again. There's a pause.

To anyone watching, it probably feels like a fraction of a second.

To me it feels like an hour. I realise what's happening. She's looking in my eyes, but we're not connecting at all. Then she continues talking, in the same smooth perky tone. It's horrible. I feel like I'm being smothered in blandness. I'm being suffocated in cotton wool.

'But I'm sure,' she says, 'your wife must appreciate it: having someone who's looking after the kids.'

She's done it again! That was another statement! Should I agree with it? I don't know if I do agree. *She's not asking me questions*: she's trying to force me to say that I love being a stay-at-home dad, and I love my wife and . . . I am feeling suddenly furious.

'Listen,' I say. 'If a man has just made two million by going to Cape Town to clinch a big business deal, his wife will cut him some slack. If all he's done is go to Clown Town, she expects him to have cleaned. My wife is part of the modern generation. She expects a career, she expects children, and she may not want to raise them herself but she'll want to supervise whoever's doing it. And that can be a trial.'

'Are you suggesting,' she says, 'you'd like to go back to the fifties system, where the man was in charge, and he expected to come home and find his dinner on the table?'

Oh, come on. Now she's trying to pin me down as a 1950s reactionary.

'I don't even want equality!' I say. 'I'm happy for her to be the boss. I'd just like her to be a boss who's more enlightened – e.g. if I'm occasionally a bit grumpy, she might let it go. She treats me like *she's* a fifties husband. She's saying: "I've earned the money, now put a smile on your pretty little face."'

Once again, she stares into my eyes and does a fake smile.

She's not listening to me at all. I think someone is talking in her earpiece.

'I bet, at the end of the day,' she says, ' she tells you she loves you.'

'At the end of the day, she's usually telling me to wipe the surfaces. Besides . . . I just talked to the former Deputy Prime Minister,' I say, 'and she agreed with me. We're Brits: no one says they love their partner. Nor, for that matter, do they have time to make love, even though, as I and the former Deputy Prime Minister agreed, it would only take two minutes. It's a maddening situation,' I say. I don't know what I'm talking about now, but I'm damn well going to say it. 'I'm expected to look after the children, and yet I'm not allowed to have any authority over them. I'm not even allowed to raise my voice. I'm not even allowed a moment's anger. The world is getting so uptight and controlled and prissy, it feels like you can't move. I feel like a hawk on a leash. And – possibly from media pressure, I don't know, generated by programmes like this – I'm expected to feel *full of love at all times*! I'm *told* I must feel love, all the time! Well, sometimes I *don't*!'

Throughout all this, I'm looking at her stricken face. I can tell she's desperately looking for a way to wrap this up. But I'm not giving her one. I'm not even letting her speak.

'Ah,' she says, turning for the camera. 'I bet that . . . deep down . . . she loves you.'

'If she does,' I say, 'she probably wouldn't have chucked me out on Tuesday night.'

'Did she?'

'Yes. She's taking the kids to school alone this morning. I hope she remembers their plimsolls.'

'Thank you, Arthur Midgley,' the presenter says.

She turns to the camera.

'And now let's turn to the subject of wind farms. By 2025, the government have pledged green energy will be responsible for forty per cent . . .'

I'm looking at her, confused. For a moment, I think: Am I now supposed to say something about wind farms? But suddenly someone tugs lightly at my sleeve. It's the producer.

'I'll take you out!' she says.

And before I know it, I'm stepping over the cables on my way out. I want to go and say goodbye to the former Deputy Prime Minister, but suddenly it occurs to me that I just said something I really shouldn't have. In fact, my high-speed mind is now scanning through the whole conversation, like an anti-virus software, checking for bugs. The software hasn't yet produced its report, but I have a suspicion what it will say. Of that interview, the stuff I shouldn't have said includes . . . all of it. I was not supposed to say a single word of all that. Oh, shit.

**Polly**

I've stopped feeling dead now. I'm coming out of shock. I'm starting to feel something.

I'm also having a lot of trouble getting the kids to school.

It's now 9.02. We're supposed to have been there ten minutes ago. As we hurry towards it down the alleyway – still eating toast, buttoning up shirts – most parents are coming back the other way. Several of them give me a sympathetic look, the sort you'd give someone who's been newly diagnosed with cancer. God. *Everyone* seems to know about my private life. I'm even stopped by a Year 6 mum. I don't know what her name is. She says: '*Did you remember the plimsolls?*'

I give her a confused smile. Actually I have forgotten the plimsolls. I tell Malory I'll come back later with them. I bundle them into the school Reception, and quickly sign the Bad Parents register, to explain why they were late. (At this point the Finger of Accusation is poking at me wherever I look.)

I'm hurrying up the alleyway back towards home when the phone rings. I answer before I consider what I'm doing.

'Hi, darling,' says Em.

I instantly go cold. I feel tight inside.

'Hello,' I say guardedly.

'Just wanted to check you can come tomorrow.'

'I'm sorry?' I say.

So far the entire morning has been a confusing blur, but now I know what I feel and it's rage that is roughly as strong as a nuclear bomb. If Em keeps talking, I will explode, and I will blast most of London twenty miles into the sky. Satellites above the UK will see a gigantic mushroom cloud, and their windows will be showered with strimmers, and bits of Saab, and posters advertising the school fete.

I force myself to take a deep breath.

'James Hammond's party,' she says. 'I thought perhaps we could go there together. As you know, Dan is giving me his answer, and I'd love you to be there. Possibly so you can celebrate the announcement of our forthcoming nuptials. Or more likely to console a suddenly quite upset woman. Either way, do say you're still coming?'

'Why?' I just about manage to say.

'I need you, Polly. I feel scared.'

I say: 'Em.' Then I pause. I feel like I'm hovering over the red button.

She says: 'Yes?'

Do I want to press the button?

I do. I speak very coldly and steadily: 'What makes you think I give a fuck what you feel about anything?'

Em is really not used to me talking like that. She says: 'I'm sorry?'

'I don't, Em. It's not surprising you're single.'

'I'm not single. I'm seeing Dan tomorrow night, and I'm finding out if he wants to marry me.'

'He won't,' I say. 'Because you're a selfish, venal, greedy bitch, and you deserve to die alone, in a house filled with shoes.'

'Polly!' says Em, astonished. '*What* is the matter?'

'Em, you called me last night. To be honest, I suspect you may have drunk a little. You said you'd let Arthur lick your nipple.'

'*Oh, that!*' she says. 'You're upset about *that*?!!'

'*Yes!*'

'Oh for God's sake, nothing happened!'

'*He licked your nipple!*'

'But I didn't even kiss him! There was no sex at all! He spent the evening trying to help me win Dan. It meant nothing!'

'Em . . .'

'Two days ago, I said: "Your husband is a sex god any woman would want." You said: "Right now, they can have him."'

'*It wasn't a fucking invitation!*' I say, far too loud. Two mums blatantly turn and face me. I actually don't care that the whole of Richmond is hearing this conversation. I'm finished here. The whole place is finished.

'It doesn't exactly imply,' says Em, 'that you're treasuring your husband like he's the bones of a precious saint, does it?'

'I'm allowed to hate my husband!' I shout. 'He's *my* husband.

It doesn't mean I want you to shove your tits in his mouth like he's a baby who wants a feed!'

At that the two mums turn and hurry off. Yes, run, you silly little bitches! I want to shout. Run . . . back to your pointless kitchens and your stupid lives!

'Look,' says Em. 'You'd thrown him out.'

'I only threw him out a few hours previously,' I say. 'That hardly implies it's my final word on the subject! I never thought you had much loyalty in you, Em, and I was right. If you had genuinely loved and adored my husband, I'd probably have forgiven you after you'd been together ten years, but you left it less than a day! A pig would show more restraint!'

'Polly, stop it! *Stop it.* I apologise. But you must understand, Dan is about to tell me if he's marrying me or not. I have been feeling very insecure about it . . .'

'No, Em, NO! This is not a bloody court!' I shout. Meanwhile I look around, and I realise, with some satisfaction, that I've cleared the entire alleyway. 'Don't even try to cite some ameliorating psychological insight. You shoved your tit in my husband's mouth! And I don't want to talk to you *ever again.*'

'Wait! Polly . . . You don't mean that.'

'I mean every word. This friendship is over.'

'You can't mean that!'

'*Why not?*' I say.

And I'm thinking: Come on, bitch, you'd better give me a bloody good reason.

## Em

I can't believe Polly wants me to explain this. I feel wounded.

I'm trying to walk into work, but now I stop. I'm just inside the complex. I've gone through the security barrier and I'm leaning on the crash barrier at the edge of the car park.

'Come on,' says Polly. 'Give me one reason why I should ever talk to you again.'

So I just tell her. 'Because, Polly,' I say, 'when you first slept with a man, you told me. When you were first in love with Arthur, you told me. When you first *kissed* him, you told me. When you were first pregnant with his child, you told me. And I was *happy*, Polly,' I say. Up to now, I've held it together. But now I'm starting to cry. That's good. That helps my case. 'I'm not like you, Polly,' I say. 'I don't think about what I'm doing. This time I did something very wrong, and I apologise. But I did something wrong for *one second*, you must surely forgive that.' I'm properly weeping now. I can't believe she would take this so seriously. 'I *am* selfish,' I say. 'I accept that. I am stupid. But I have *been* there for you, Polly, all along, and I have *always* loved you, Polly! I *love* you, Polly! You are loved, Polly. Don't you realise that? I could *cope* with being unmarried for the rest of my life. I could not cope without my best friend!'

I feel desperate. I'm really crying now.

But down the other end of the line, Polly says absolutely nothing.

She just turns off her phone.


## Arthur

I'm sitting in the car in a mild state of shock.

It seems so unbelievable that, moments ago, I was on national television. I'm now in a traffic jam. I heard that, when people first parachute, they are terrified beforehand, but afterwards they immediately want to do it again. I feel like that now. I feel . . . Is there some other TV show I could go on? I could go on *Vanessa*, and get some more stuff off my chest.

My phone rings.

It's my literary agent – Sally Winklehorn at RSJ. I've not talked with her in a long time. Even when I call Sally Winklehorn, I don't speak to her. I speak to an assistant called Karen who tells me the money hasn't arrived yet.

'*Darling*!' says Sally Winklehorn.

'Hello.'

'I'm in a hotel in Germany,' she says. 'And I just saw you on telly.'

'Oh.'

'Brilliant! Just brilliant. And why didn't you tell me you were writing a column for the *London Times*?'

'Well, I have been.'

'I mean, the thing about publishing these days is it's all about what kind of media splash you can make. And I think, darling, you splash.'

'Do I?'

'I'm actually at the Book Fair today,' says Sally Winklehorn. 'Why haven't you got something for me to sell?'

'I've got my novel about the teenage boy who's the reincarnation of King Arthur.'

'Sounds great.'

I'm a bit confused by that last statement.

'I sent you a first draft of my book two weeks ago,' I say. 'Karen e-mailed to say you'd read it.'

'Ah,' she says. 'But that was before you were on breakfast television, talking Man Power, and revealing intimate details of the sex lives of politicians.'

'While I was waiting on your notes,' I say, 'I've been polishing.'

'Forget that,' she says. 'I think we need to strike while the client is hot. I'll get Karen to send it straight away. I'll see what I can do. 'Bye for now. *Auf wiedersehen.*'

'But . . .' I say.

She rings off.

I may be hot, but I still can't keep my own agent on the phone.

I look up, and realise with surprise that we're outside Greta's house.

Suddenly I'm worried. I'm so used to Polly worrying about me being indiscreet, what's Greta going to say? I wonder. She put me on TV, and I didn't say a single word I was supposed to. She could be furious.

I thank the driver. I step out of the car. I'm just about to climb the steps to her house when Greta comes out. She stops outside her front door – looking fabulous in a camel-coloured work suit which contrasts magnificently with the red blouse underneath. Her jewellery is all amber, and matches the amber of her eyes. She looks fantastic. She looks at me, then smiles.

'Hey, you!' she says, leaving the door open, swooping down the steps towards me. 'That was fantastic. You're a natural.' She kisses me on my cheek. She speaks huskily into my ear. ''Course, you didn't say *remotely* what we agreed, but you got a great response.'

'What do you mean?'

'We get instant feedback on the website. Already, thirty-nine people have written in.'

'Is that a lot?'

'For a five-minute item about stay-at-home husbands, yes, that's a lot.'

'But why? What are they all saying?'

'They divide into four types.'

'Four?'

'The ones who say you're a sexist pig . . .'

'I said I didn't even expect equality!'

'I know. The second bunch have pointed that out. They're the ones who agree with you. Already they seem to be organising themselves into a group: Trophy Husbands Answer Back or THAB.'

'THAB?!'

'Yeah, honey, it's all happening,' says Greta.

'But,' I say, 'I might have . . . accidentally revealed something about the former Dep—'

'This is live TV,' she says. 'We serve a higher purpose: ratings. And that's why, Arthur, I loved you so much. You stirred things up, and you looked hot.'

'Did I?'

'My God! You looked hot as a mouse in a microwave! Several people have said that. That's the third group.'

'So what's the fourth group?'

'Oh, come on, pupkin. Don't be naïve. The fourth group are the biggest.'

'What are they interested in?'

'They ain't interested in you at all. They're just interested in the fact that the former Deputy Prime Minister doesn't have time to make love to her partner, even though, you said, it could be done in two minutes. By a distance, that's the scoop. *That's* what's put the clip on to YouTube.'

'It's on YouTube??!!'

'Sure. I just uploaded it myself. The title is *Just Takes Two*

*Minutes.* Listen, you naughty man, I love you but I gotta go.' With this Greta holds my head between both hands and kisses me again.

## Polly

I'm walking down the Embankment towards the office when Mum calls.

As her name comes up, I look at it with hatred. I'm about to turn the phone off, but then I think: Nope, just for once, I'll take her on.

'Hello,' I say flatly.

'Polly darling, I'm afraid I *still* haven't been able to reach Roger Chalmers,' says Mum. Her tone manages to imply she's been up all night trying.

I say: 'Right.'

She says: 'I had a thought about James Hammond, though. You could ask him if he wants to do Sophie's wedding at one of his hotels.'

I say: 'Right.'

'Just a thought,' she says, with a snigger, as if she's cracked a hilarious joke. 'Darling . . . has Arthur come home?'

'No.'

Pause. What is she going to say next?

'What are you going to do about the kids?'

'I don't know.'

'There are studies about this,' she says. 'Without fathers, children are far more disposed towards drugs, or promiscuity, or alcoholism.' (It's not surprising I feel constant guilt! She just implied I'm turning my kids into drunk crack whores!) 'It's very important,' she says, 'if at all possible, for children to have two parents in their lives.'

Listening to her talk, I realise I feel cowed, small. Right. I'm fighting back.

'It's a bit rich,' I say. 'Coming from you, isn't it?'

'I'm *sorry*?' says my mum. She heard me fine, she just doesn't expect me to challenge her. 'What do you mean?'

'You're lecturing me about childcare, and, on the one occasion I've asked you to do some, you've refused.'

'I have a *lunch*,' says Mum, 'with Roger Chalmers . . .'

'You'd just have to finish your lunch at two-thirty, and you could still make it. That's how much you don't want to help me.'

'*Polly*!' says Mum, outraged. How is it she manages to use my name like a slap? 'What is the *matter* with you?'

'I'll tell you,' I say. 'I've realised that all the things Arthur hates about me, I've got from you. You're intolerant. You're obsessed with money and status. You're totally lacking in sympathy.'

'I'm not lacking in sympathy!'

'My husband has left me: you don't even know why. And I've spent my whole life, filled with shame, because you won't allow me to feel any emotion that doesn't suit you.'

'Polly!' she growls. 'Take that back!'

'I take nothing back,' I say. 'In fact, I'll go further. Mum, you can fuck off out of my life. Fuck you. Fuck Roger Chalmers. And fuck your boring fucking wedding.'

After that, I turn the phone off, and I put it calmly back into my pocket.

Wow. I've said the worst things I can imagine saying, and I feel surprisingly good about it.

I turn and look at the Thames and I take a long slow breath.

I'm not a nuclear bomb now. I'm a programmed missile. And I know exactly where I'm headed. I know what I need to do.

I call up JTS, and I speak to Debra on Reception. I ask her, at some length, politely, how she is. Then I tell her she needs to tell the department I'm sick and won't be in for a few days.

Then I take another deep breath, and I collect myself. So far this morning, I've blown away my best friend, my mum, and my job . . . and, in a strange way, I'm enjoying it. I think: What else could I lose?

And then it hits me.

## Arthur

OK. I know this is something you really, really shouldn't say about any child, but I must . . .

Greta's son is a twat.

When I first see him, Tyrone is sitting in front of *Ben Ten*. He has his massive trainers up on the coffee table. He has a baseball cap. He has a sweatshirt emblazoned with the words 'Mr Big'. I say to him: 'Hey, Mr Big! I'm Arthur. We're going to hang out for an hour while Mum goes to a meeting. Anything you'd like to play?' He says: 'I'm watching *Ben Ten*, you dork!'

After that, I figure: I'll let him watch *Ben Ten*. I'll find Greta's computer and go online.

I go upstairs to Greta's office. It's a fantastic office. It has a view over the back garden. On the walls, it has a Bafta *and* an Emmy. It has pictures of Greta with Bill Clinton, Bob Dylan, and the Dalai Lama. It has a Jeff Koons on the wall, showing brightly coloured crotches in bikinis. There's a picture of Greta which dates from the exact time I met her, and nearly slept with her. She's sitting on a sofa with Michael Stipe. They're both turned round and facing the camera with identical expressions on their faces. They look in tune, they look creative, they look deeply happy.

I stare at them for slightly too long, then I fire up Greta's computer and I go online.

First I read up about James Hammond's new Wiltshire hotel. Then I go on to the *Lifestyle* website. Then I go on *Learn Love in a Week* and I read today's exercise: 'Declare your myth'. I know the answer to that . . . For the last few years I have – not all the time, but sometimes – wanted Greta Kay. That's what, I believe, could change my life. I want to take holidays with her. I want to be in kitchens with her, sharing our private jokes. It's not just that she's sexy. She believes in me. And she has contacts. And she's got advice. And wisdom. She's like a human One Stop Shop that could change my life in every aspect.

I'm distracted from such thoughts by a weird animal scream outside.

I stand up and look out of the window. Greta has a large beautiful garden with a lawn and a willow tree. Tyrone has trapped a cat in the corner of it. He is holding a bamboo pole, and he's poking it at the cornered animal in an effort to turn the cat into a big furry kebab.

I get the window open in a hurry.

'Tyrone!' I shout. '*No!*'

He stops and turns to me with a pissed-off, whingey look on his face. As far as he's concerned, the cat's in his garden. He's well within his rights to hunt it, if he wants. That's the least he can expect from his morning.

'Don't touch that cat!' I shout. 'Throw down the pole!'

He drops the pole, but his manner suggests he's about to pick it up again.

I run for the stairs. When I'm halfway down, my phone rings. I check the phone. It's Polly.

Just seeing her name, my stomach lurches like I've just leaped off a cliff.

**Polly**

I'm at Bar Italia – the very place where my relationship with Arthur started, although I was sitting outside on that sunny day, ten years ago, when he sat down beside me and we started talking. Today I'm inside. I'm lurking at the back, feeling like a Mafia godfather doing a purge. This is my last, most important call.

Arthur picks up.

'Hello,' he says. He's panting in a macabre way.

'Hello,' I say, feeling like an executioner.

Silence.

'Where are you?' I ask.

'I'm at Greta Kay's house,' he says quickly.

I say: '*At Greta Kay's house!*' and I immediately lose my composure. In my heart of hearts, I know Arthur has no interest in Em. But Greta Kay is another matter. When we were first going out, I once saw him talk to her on the phone. His face lit up like a lovesick teenager.

'What are you doing at Greta Kay's house?' I ask a little petulantly. Already I'm feeling threatened.

'I met her at the *Lifestyle* drinks last night,' he says. 'She asked me to look after her son for the morning.'

'Right.'

I leave a silence. There's so much I could ask, but I don't want to. I need to keep control. I need to sort things out.

'So,' I say. 'How do you propose we look after our kids?'

'I don't know,' he says impatiently. Jesus! Is this not important?

Does it not *matter* to him? 'Maybe you should have thought of that before you threw me out.'

'I did not throw you out!'

'You said: "I give you everything, and if you can't see that, just go!"'

'You didn't have to do it.'

'Well . . .'

'Just as you didn't have to lick Em's breast.'

I wait. He leaves a long guilty silence. Then . . . 'I'm sorry about that,' he says. 'But, *really*, I'm not interested in Em. It . . .'

'Arthur,' I say quickly. 'I don't care! I want a divorce.'

Oh, God. I didn't mean to say that. Did I? Well . . . what's he going to say?

'OK,' he says quickly. 'Let's divorce!'

There's a long silence. I think we're both realising what we've just said. I'm testing myself to see what I feel. But actually I don't feel sad. I just feel totally cold. I feel cold as a dead fish on a slab.

Then I immediately think of the children, and the guilt hits me like a heart attack.

'Arthur,' I say. 'I don't want the children to suffer.'

'Yes,' he says immediately. 'I agree.'

There's a silence.

'Let's keep everything just the same for them,' I say.

'Yes,' he says. 'I agree.' For some reason we're both talking in stiff, polite voices. We're being very adult about this. 'Listen,' he says, very hurriedly, 'I really can't talk now.'

WHAT? What is more important than our marriage? Does he not WANT to fight for it at all?

'I'll be home to pick up the kids from school,' he says.

'I'm off work today,' I say. 'I'm getting them home at lunchtime . . .'

'So I'll see you,' he says hurriedly. 'We'll talk then.'

And the phone goes quiet.

He's gone.

Oh my God. We've agreed to divorce. And he's gone.

I let out a breath very slowly.

I put the phone down on the counter.

I'm trying not to cry.

I look towards the tables outside. I remember so clearly how, ten years ago, he sat down and talked to me there. In my mind, I can actually see us – the people we used to be. We look fresh and hopeful and young and so happy. We look like a couple who've just won the Mixed Doubles at Wimbledon. I glance in the mirror and see myself. I look tense and middle-aged. I look like someone who was in the Singles, long ago, and who lost.

## Arthur

Mr Big is back inside watching more *Ben Ten*.

I'm staring into the garden, thinking about Polly. All I can think of is her saying: 'Let's divorce', and her horrible brisk tone, and I feel paralysed. I feel like I'm holding a big tray of grief inside me, and if I move it'll spill everywhere, and it'll burn.

But then I hear Greta arriving home, and I walk towards the front door.

Greta bursts through it full of life. She's holding a brown bag packed with food.

She sees me. 'How'd you guys get on?'

'Fine.'

'Well done, soldier!' she barks. 'Drop and give me head!'

I say: 'What?'

'I'd like to be the parade sergeant in one of those war films. I'd be like . . . the sergeant in *The Love Army*. I'd be like . . . "*Soldiers, first of all I'm gonna be training you in oral sex. I'm gonna show you how to bring your opponent to pleasure, without (1) you getting a sore neck, or (2) her complaining her legs are cold. We're gonna look at positions . . .*"' At this point Greta pretends to point at a board. '"*We call that The Ice Cream Cone. Only for the highly trained.*"'

Amused by her own joke, Greta opens the kitchen door. Now she realises I'm really not laughing.

'What's the matter?' she says.

'Polly and I just agreed to divorce,' I say.

'Oh my God!' says Greta, instantly taking this very seriously indeed.

'Yup.'

I shouldn't have talked. Now I think I'm going to cry. I hold it together. Greta holds my hand. We sit together on her bottom stair. She stares into my eyes. I stare into hers.

'Tell me everything,' she says. 'What's happened?'

I look at her. Shall I tell her about Em? But that's not what happened.

'Well,' I begin. 'Polly . . . threw me out because she said I was angry.'

Greta says nothing. She just stares and waits for me to carry on.

'But actually,' I say, 'maybe it's her who's making me angry.'

'How?'

'I don't know,' I say, in a tiny voice. I'm in danger of crying. It's so humiliating.

She looks at me. 'Well,' says Greta, 'what does she *say* that makes you most angry?'

'She says . . . "I support you!" By which she means: I support you emotionally, and financially, 'cos *I* earn all the money.'

'And . . . what's wrong with that?'

''Cos she *doesn't* earn *all* the money,' I say. Even discussing this is making me angry. 'And it's humiliating to be told, all the time, that you don't earn anything. And if she was at all supportive she would know that.'

Greta says 'OK!', very lightly.

'I *do* earn money, Greta! I'm writing this book, which is the best thing I've ever done. I could earn us loads of money. But I can't. 'Cos she keeps interrupting and undermining.'

'Speak your truth quietly and clearly,' says Greta, 'Do you say to her: "Please leave me alone. I'm doing something important"?'

'No,' I say quietly. 'I don't feel I have the right to do that!'

'Why?'

''Cos I don't have any money!'

Greta smiles. 'OK.'

'Well . . . I have *some* money. I just don't have any confidence! Which is partly because of her.'

Greta looks doubtful.

'You've read *Men Are From Mars* . . . ?' I say.

'Sure.'

'John Gray's most basic point is that men need to feel they're experts. Daily, she's criticising the centre of my working life. She's saying my work will fail.'

This is better. I'm back on firm ground. I'm deconstructing texts of pop psychology, while complaining about my wife.

Sadly Greta's not buying it. 'So,' she says. 'You think John Gray's saying to the women of the world: 'Women, butt out . . . don't criticise our expertise!'?'

'Yeah!'

'Well, I'd say a different thing to the men of the world. I'd say: 'Men . . . we *are* criticising your expertise. Try listening.''

Shit. I thought Greta was going to give me sympathy on this.

'OK!' I say, a little testily. 'And I'd say to the women of the world: "We'd listen . . . if you *once in a while* said something positive.''

'You think the women of the world need to learn that?'

'Yeah! It's the most common bit of love advice, in the world: "Give ten compliments for every negative.''

'I'd give completely different advice,' says Greta. 'I'd say . . . Don't depend on your partner to boost your fragile self-esteem. I'd say: Get by on what everyone gets by on – a mixture of passive aggression, and the odd mumbled thanks. The Low Barb diet.'

I laugh at that. It's confusing laughing, when you're trying not to cry.

Greta gives me a wise look. 'That's what I've learned,' she says. 'You can't change your partner. You can only change yourself. If there's a gulf between you, all you can do is build a bridge, and then you'll see if she comes across.'

I don't know what to say to that. I become suddenly aware of the weird situation. I'm in Greta Kay's house, and I'm staring into her eyes, and we're actually holding hands. She's been drinking mango juice. I can smell it on her breath.

'What's the most annoying thing about her?' she asks.

'She's impatient,' I say. 'Like when she's throwing things away – which is pretty much her favourite pastime – she doesn't look at what she's chucking. In the last few months, she's thrown away the backs to two remotes, a credit card, and the implements I got for changing bike tyres.' Towards the end of this list, I get a bit loud. When I think of those bike tyre thingies I go tense inside.

'And have you told her to be more careful?'

'Only once.'

'What happened?'

'If I criticise her she goes all silent, then she'll wait a couple of days till I'm doing something wrong, then she comes at me like a Ninja.'

'So she won't be criticised?'

'Under no circumstances.'

'That's annoying!'

'Thank you!'

'But it still doesn't seem worth getting divorced over.'

'You divorced!'

'Yeah,' she says, ''cos my husband was hitting me, he was banging at least three of my friends and, despite this, he was going on chatshows talking about his love of God.'

'I'm sorry.'

'Soldier,' she says. 'I cope.'

'Yeah.'

''I'm sure you do too. What do you do when she throws your stuff away.'

'I cope with flexibility and manly intelligence,' I say. 'I make new backs for the remotes using card and Sellotape!'

Greta does a chuckle which is throaty and quite astonishingly sexy.

'You struggle on?' she says.

'I struggle on,' I say, glancing at the freckle on her cheek.

From nowhere I have a weird thought: I could just kiss her.

'On a more positive note,' says Greta, smiling, 'your *Daybreak* appearance was a total game-changer! Next week *Lifestyle* is all about men. We want you to headline. Guess what your new column's called?'

'What?'

'*Trophy Husband.*'

I say: 'Really?! *Lifestyle* want more?'

'Oh, yeah,' she says. 'They want to give you a year's contract, to make sure they get you before someone else does. You're having a good day, my darling. It's not even lunchtime. You've had nationwide TV coverage. You're looking at a contract in London's biggest paper.'

Objectively, I can see this is good news. But I don't immediately change moods. I'm like a dinosaur. Once I'm lumbering in one direction, it takes me a couple of days to turn round.

'Your problem ain't nothing to do with your wife,' says Greta. 'Your problem is you don't believe in yourself. And you should. You're hot, soldier! Everyone wants you!'

I say: 'Yeah?' I'm looking at the pupils of Greta's hazel eyes. I swear they're dilated.

'Hell, yeah!' she says huskily. 'You have the soul of an angel, in the body of a big gorgeous man.'

'Yeah?' I say again. I can't stop myself from glancing at her mouth. She notices.

'Yeah,' says Greta, distractedly.

Her lips open slightly.

I slightly lean towards her.

Then, slowly, she reaches forward, and I get a tiny jolt of electricity as her nose touches mine. Then our lips meet, and I shut my eyes for a moment during which time slows down and love floods my system.

Oh my God!

*We're kissing!* Greta Kay and I are kissing!

Her hand lightly touches my ear. It's delicious. She wants me.

Then . . . She makes a brief mouth movement, and, for a moment, her tongue flutters against mine, quick as a fish tail in a stream.

Oh my God! We're . . .

Dazed, I pull away. I say: 'I'd better go.'

'You better,' she says, and her eyes look drunk. 'Or I'll rip your clothes off like I'm tearing fur off a rabbit.'

Then she smiles sleepily and says: 'Wait, let me kiss you again.'

And she does.

## Polly

I leave Bar Italia. I'm about to head for the tube. I think: No . . .

I've got no job to do. I'll walk home.

And I do. I walk across Piccadilly. I walk across St James's Park. I walk across Hyde Park, and the walking does something to me.

My feet are pounding the path. They're making a beat. I feel like Gloria Gaynor. I grow strong. I learn how to carry on. I feel like I'm stripping down my life to the core essentials. So far today, I've pushed away my job, my mum, my best friend and my husband.

Although . . . it must be conceded that, of the four, one is making way more effort to be let back. Throughout my epic walk, Em texts constantly.

Text one says: 'Polly, I am *so* sorry.'

Text two says: 'Please please come tomorrow.'

Text three says: 'I've cut the offending breast off, and have given it to a priest to be burned.'

Text four says: 'I love you. Please come tomorrow.'

Text five says: 'Priest has taken breast.'

Text six says: 'He has exorcised it. He has burned it. Please forgive me.'

Text seven says: 'I'm happy to cut the other one off too. If you'd like.'

Text eight says: 'Should I accept Dan? *I don't know.* I'm lost without you.'

Text nine says: 'I think James Hammond really likes you. He was just asking about you.'

This one arrives as I'm reaching Ravenscourt Park. I stop. I lean on a beech. I take a deep breath. Then I call her.

'*Polly!*' says Em, clearly delighted to hear me. Her voice is full of sunshine. For a moment we are two girls reunited, and I must admit . . . it feels good.

I say: 'How come you spoke to James Hammond?'

'Yes,' she says friskily. 'I thought that was the bit that got you. You've no integrity.'

I let that go. I feel so happy to have her back on my side. I feel like I'm unfreezing.

'How did you even speak to James Hammond?' I say.

'I am extraordinarily well connected,' she says. 'I had his number from when we interviewed him.'

'Is he in the country?'

'Listen to you, you're so in love with him!'

'No, I'm not!'

'You're desperate to hear anything about him!'

'How co— Did he . . .'

'Did he ask after you? Of course he did. I said: "Just to confirm, I'm coming tomorrow." He said: "Great. But is Polly coming?" I said: "Yes!" and he said: "Good." So please come, or you'll make me look like a liar.'

'I'm coming,' I say. 'I'll just have to tell Arthur to babysit.'

'Good.'

At this point there's a long silence.

Then she says: 'Polly, I'm so glad we're talking again, because there's one thing I really have to tell you.'

Now I'm worried again. I say: 'What have you done now?!!'

'I . . . had sex with Malcolm.'

'*You had sex with Malcolm*?!' I say. I'm relieved that the news is nothing to do with me. I'm still astonished.

'Yes.'

'How . . . Was it . . . OK?'

'Actually it was . . . divine.'

'*Divine?*'

'Yes. He did a massage and then he did a sort of . . . Guided Meditation.'

'This sounds less like sex, and more like a workshop.'

'Polly,' says Em. 'That man went down on me for half an hour during which time I hallucinated I was in some kind of heaven. And prior to that, he took me home, he helped me be sick, *and* he repaired my window. He offers quite a service.'

'So are you . . . are you seeing him again?'

'Not sure . . . I'm seeing Dan tomorrow and he's telling me if he wants to marry me.'

'But . . . do you still want to marry him?'

'Why shouldn't I?'

'You shagged Malcolm. At the very least that implies you've got doubts.'

'I do have doubts. I am also thirty-four, Polly. I might want children.'

'*Do* you want children?'

'No. But I *might* one day. And Dan has his faults. But the most unlovable people are those who most need love. Dan deserves someone to love him, and I think that person could be me.'

'You want to marry Dan?!'

'OK, I know he's vain, silly and superficial, but so am I, Polly!'

'No, you are not!'

'I am.'

'OK, you are. But you're not as bad as Dan. He's a talking hairstyle. He's a *Big Brother* contestant. He's a fool in good clothes.'

'Polly!'

'Hey, I'm not really judging him, because, you know what, Em, I've barely met him. Do you know why? 'Cos he doesn't see you very often.'

'Oh, come on.'

'He avoids you, Em.'

'Well, he often goes to events in the evening.'

'Yes, because he's scared to go home. Do you know why? That man hasn't a clue who he is. He doesn't say anything that isn't ironic. Em, you know it yourself . . . He's the sort of man who'll stay for a few years – he'll hang around apologising and making a mess – then one day you'll find out he's shagging some girl in his office.'

'Yes, darling!' she says. 'There is always that chance. There's also a chance that we might have a lifelong love, and that's what I'm hoping for.'

At this point, there's a long silence.

'So if he proposes,' I say quietly, 'are you planning to accept?'

'Yes. I love him.'

'In which case,' I say, 'could you forget everything I just said?'

A silence. Then . . .

'Provided you can forget this nipple business.'

Another silence. I guess if she's so desperate she's shagging Malcolm, it's not that surprising she had a crack at Arthur. Besides, it's Em. It's not like I ever loved her for her integrity. I love her because she's passionate, and surprising, and utterly ridiculous.

I say: 'It's a deal.'

There's silence. I can tell we're both smiling down the line, and it feels good. I feel like . . . men will drift in and out of our lives, but through it all, the girls are together.

'Well,' says Em. 'Let's see what he says, shall we?'

'Yup.'

'OK. I'm sorry again. I love you. 'Bye.'

I say: ''Bye!' and I turn off my phone.

And it's only then that I think: Hang on, how does she do that? She drags me into her world and I forget mine. Em is so totally self-centred, I realise I just went through a whole conversation with her without telling her Arthur and I are divorcing.

I also realise that the prospect of the night at Bodsham Abbey is getting more and more interesting. I wouldn't miss it for the world.

## Arthur

Greta's kiss has changed me.

I feel like a giant. I feel extraordinarily emotional. I feel like I've just come back from the war and everything is sad and beautiful but unbelievably precious. I walk out of the tube. The station looks beautiful. I suddenly feel terribly sad I might be leaving it. I pass a school where parents are waiting to pick up their kids. They look beautiful. The men have got big shorts, and bad sandals, and little paunches. They look lovable. The mums have all got nice hair, and sunnies, and they're all holding coffees in front of them, like they're compasses. They look beautiful. I love them all.

Then I just feel very guilty.

Then, as I bound towards home, I think of the kiss with Greta, and suddenly I am horny, I am dizzy, I am slightly in love. I haven't felt like this since I fell in love with Polly. I used to put my arms around her in bed, and I used to feel this burst of happiness in my breast. I loved the slenderness of her shoulders. I loved the way she twitched when she slept. When we were first going out, I once drove a removals van to her mother's house, and I felt proud just to be with her.

I suddenly think: Why am I thinking about Polly?

I suddenly think: Jesus . . . you are starved of affection! Someone gives you one kiss and you get a crush on them! STOP BEING SO SELF-INDULGENT! PULL YOURSELF TOGETHER.

I reach my street. I see two mums peering at me anxiously from across the road. I suddenly realise they know I've left. And now I feel the first prickles of discomfort. The mums at our school *talk*. If one of them has got some good gossip, it's like the Twilight Bark in *101 Dalmatians*. If one knows that I've gone, *everyone* will know, won't they?

Oh balls . . . Did I not just announce it myself on national television this morning?

I did. Oh, no. Does Polly know about *Daybreak*? What is she going to say?

Will she know about Greta?

Will she be cross?

I don't like being in love, my emotions feel out of control. I can't take it.

As I turn round the hedge to approach our house, I'm being bombarded with impressions and emotions. I see the funny sign that Robin and I stuck to the door. (It says: BEWARE OF THE DUCK, and it has a picture of a duck.) The sign is three years old now. Seeing it gives me a pang of nostalgia.

Then I look through the kitchen window, and something awful happens . . .

I see my children, and I feel so much love for them, it makes me feel sick. Ivy is painting. Malory is drawing. Robin is neatly cutting toast into soldiers. Oh my God. I don't want to hurt their precious little lives.

Robin sees me first.

He looks so pleased to see me, his face lights up in a smile that is spoddy but nakedly loving.

He's at the front door in less than two seconds. They all are. I'm hit by a broadside of child. Ivy hugs me first. She's shouting: '*Daddy*!!!' And she's thrusting her arms round me. Robin says: 'Good news! We've got the class list for next year. I'll read it to you.'

'Kids!' I say. 'It is bloomin' lovely to see you. I *need* to see the class list. But first I need ten minutes with Mum.'

They don't listen, of course. They love me. They don't listen to a word I say.

Malory says: 'Daddy, what are these?' She's got my Gustav Klimt pictures all over the table. 'Who is this?'

'That's Gustav Klimt,' I say.

'Why have you drawn him over and over and over again?'

Good question. Why have I?

'Was it to do with work?' says Robin helpfully.

'No,' I say. 'It's important to do some things just for the fun of it. And I really like drawing pictures of Gustav Klimt. You can draw him *any* way you like.'

Malory gives me a sneaky look. 'I am going to draw him as a beetle!' she says.

'Good idea!' I say.

'And I will draw him as a fairy!' says Ivy.

'Do I *have* to do him silly?' says Robin.

I say: 'No. You can draw Gustav Klimt any way you want. That's the point. Surprise me.'

And they like that. I leave them at the table, all eager about drawing pictures of Gustav Klimt.

'Where's Mum?' I ask.

'She's upstairs in the bedroom,' says Robin.

'You guys do some drawings,' I say. 'I just need to go and speak to her.'

## Polly

Arthur's here. I can hear him downstairs.

I don't know what to do. I've got a terrible pain in my shoulders and neck. I've had a very emotional day already, I need to keep things calm. I need him to agree he's still doing childcare tomorrow. And then I need to get him to move out, probably to Malcolm's.

## Arthur

Our bedroom is on the second floor.

I stop for a moment on the landing below. From here I can see into Malory's room, and suddenly I have a flashback of Polly and me sitting on the bed, watching Malory and Robin perform a series of mad dances. On the stairway there are some figures of Flynn and Rapunzel which Ivy and I made, last week, out of the cardboard from a Weetabix box. Rapunzel's long hair is approximated with a big yellow ribbon, which is attached to her hair using a hairclip. Ivy and I had an incredibly involving game. Rapunzel was letting down her hair, over the bannister, and Flynn was trying to climb up. Rapunzel's face, drawn with felt tip, has got smudged with water. It seems unbearably poignant. It occurs to me that next time I see Ivy, we'll be at the zoo, or in a McDonald's. We won't be playing Rapunzel up the stairs. Am I getting it all wrong? Suddenly our long playful afternoons seem like an Eden, and I don't know why I'm leaving.

What am I doing? What am I going to say to Polly? I'm not ready for her. I sneak up the stairs as quietly as I can. I reach the top. I look quietly into our bedroom.

I see her.

It's the strangest thing – looking at someone who doesn't know you can see them. I continue as long as I can.

Polly hasn't heard me. She has her back to me. She's got the duvet on the floor. She's organising the books on my bedside table. She picks up *The Savage Detectives* and reads a bit.

Oh my God.

It's the first time I've seen her since we said the words 'Let's divorce'. She's no longer mine. I look at her like she's a stranger I don't know.

I see a thirty-five-year-old woman in blue jeans and white t-shirt. Her hair is tied back showing her exquisite cheekbones. Loose strands have escaped the hair tie and they dangle down her lovely neck. She looks so beautiful – this woman who I'm due to divorce. Now I feel more emotional still. I feel like I've had two layers of skin removed. I feel like I'm listening to Nick Drake singing 'Northern Sky' – that moment when the piano comes in and it's like sunshine after rain, it's like tears after rage.

Oh, no. I still love her.

## Polly

I'm only pretending to read.

I know he's looking at me. I can hear him panting away like a love-sick scout master.

## Arthur

'Darling!' I say.

She turns.

We look, agonised, into each other's eyes.

Neither of us knows how to behave, but she puts down the book.

I step forward.

How do you greet someone when you've just agreed to divorce them? We share a fumbling hug. Briefly I hold her back. I catch her scent. (She smells of apples and jasmine and freshly washed denim. I love it!) As I pull away, I see she's wearing make-up. (For me??!)

'How come you're home?' I ask.

'I decided not to go to work,' she says.

I say: 'Why?'

'I figured I had more important things to do than work,' she says, giving me a meaningful look. 'I don't even know if I want to do that job any more.'

'Really?'

'Yeah. I should do what I've longed to do for ages: I should give it all up. I should design gardens.'

'Good idea,' I say. Wow. Things are changing fast. Already she seems totally different. She seems vulnerable. It's fantastically endearing.

'So,' she says. 'Was it nice to see Greta again?'

'Er . . . yes!' I say. She kissed me, Polly, and I felt love. It was like you and me all over again.

'Good,' says Polly. 'Right. There're a couple of things we must discuss . . . Friday.'

Yes, Friday. Apparently it was my refusal to schedule which squeezed the life out of you. Let's schedule! Let's schedule like it's the last day on earth!

'I am going to James Hammond's. Are you still OK to look after the kids?'

'Well,' I say. ' Just tell me this first . . . Do you like him?'

Polly blushes slightly. The trouble is, I find that rather fetching.

'Erm,' she says. 'That's a ridiculous question. I'm going there to attend a party and to consult on his garden. That doesn't mean I need to mate with him, like I'm a little puppy.'

'Polly,' I say evenly. 'He's a very rich man who could invite anyone. He's clearly asked you along because he likes you. Do you like him?'

She looks into my eyes for two whole seconds.

'Yes,' she says. 'I do.'

Oh, Lord.

'Well, go,' I say. 'I'll look after the kids.'

'Thanks,' says Polly, and she touches my arm.

This is weird. It's like our relationship has leaped on to a new phase when we're friends and can tell each other about our crushes.

'Why do you like him?' I say suddenly.

'Well, Arthur,' she says, 'for a long time I've felt squashed by you.'

'Why?'

'You don't do laundry. You don't Hoover.'

'Do you think James Hammond Hoovers?'

'James Hammond doesn't need to,' she says. 'He has staff. In all his five houses. And all sixty-eight hotels.'

'Sounds like a great guy,' I say. 'But how would he manage, if he was in a quiz, and he was asked to name Arsenal's defensive cover in the 1998 season?'

Give her credit – Polly does smirk. 'In those circumstances,' she concedes, 'he'd be hopeless.'

'*Thank you*,' I say.

'But I could tell him it was Martin Keown.'

'I love you,' I say. Then, hurriedly, 'And I mean that in a let's-get-divorced sort of way.'

'Thank you,' she says, after a little pause.

'By the way, I can't help noticing I asked you why you liked James Hammond, and all your reasons were to do with me.'

'Because you're annoying,' she says. 'You don't clean the bath. You break drawers and you expect me to mend them.'

Normally I'd say something like: 'So?? You throw away the lids of the milk cartons while we're still using them!' But she can't hurt me now. I'm a giant. It occurs to me maybe I should run off and have an affair with Greta. Polly's justifying it with every word she says. I say something I've never said on the subject of housework. I say: 'Tell me more!'

'OK,' she says. She's a bit taken aback. Housework is normally a key area for wife vs husband combat; she's surprised I'm giving her a free shot. 'Even quite manly things, you don't do. You don't change light bulbs. You never order food. You can't drill a hole . . .'

At this, she peters off. She's punched herself out! Why didn't I discover this before? Women love to criticise their men. You must say nothing in your own defence. After a while they stop.

I say: 'Is there anything I do actually do?'

'You're better than me at driving long distances,' she says. 'And you know how to turn the boiler on when the pressure goes.'

'If you want to,' I say, 'you can also give some praise.'

'That last bit was the praise section,' she says.

I actually laugh at that one. It's not surprising I get down. Why did I ever base my fragile self-esteem on her opinion? She's completely unreasonable. She's hardly mentioned a single thing I do well.

'Of course, we could get a cleaner,' I say.

'What?!' she says, surprised to see me coming at her.

'That would seem to answer most of your problems.'

'We can't afford a cleaner!' she says. 'That's why I want *you* to clean!'

'Well, there we have it,' I say. 'You want me to be the cleaner. That's why you refuse to give me any sympathy. Cleaners should be seen and not heard. That's basically the trouble. You insist on having higher status than me, then you get annoyed when I try to assert my rights.'

'What?!' she says. She thought this fight was over. As far as she's concerned, the bell has gone. I've now risen from the canvas, and have got her in a headlock.

'That's why we rowed on Tuesday,' I say. 'I'm sure, if James Hammond had had a professional setback, you'd've given sympathy. If you gave me more respect, you'd give me more licence, and you wouldn't resent everything I do that doesn't suit you.'

'What?!' she says. 'Are you now *blaming* me for why you left? Is that what you're doing?'

That's exactly what I'm doing, and I'm delighted she's finally seeing it.

'Is that it?' she says. 'As far as you're concerned, it's completely my fault? I'm an unreasonable bitch who wants to turn her husband into a cleaner?!'

'Ugh!' I say. 'Now you're upgrading my criticism.'

'What are you talking about?'

'If I say something slightly wounding, you plunge the knife in yourself. You make the wound three times bigger, then you cut a couple of limbs off, and then you fall writhing to the floor. It's unfair!'

'Why is it unfair if you hurt me?' she says. She's getting riled now. She turns away from me, and starts wrestling with the bedclothes.

'Because it's a way of shaming me into silence,' I say. 'Which means I'm not being heard.'

'That's just your perception!' she says.

She picks the duvet off the floor. She hurls it over the bed. But she doesn't get it to land quite right. So she does it again.

Then she suddenly breaks off.

'Ah!' she says, wincing with pain.

'What is it?' I say.

## Polly

I've got *searing* pains up my back.

'Ow!' I say. 'I've tweaked something in my back!'

'Shall I massage you?' he says.

Can I let him do that? It seems wrong, but bloody hell it's hurting. 'Thanks,' I say. I lie down on the bed.

'But I don't like it when you ask me to massage you,' he says, 'and then you refuse to take your top off so I'm prodding you through some wool. So take your top off, please.'

He's being all commanding suddenly. Normally I'd say something sarcastic about that, but now I do something uncharacteristic. I just take my top off, I lie down, and I wait for him to help.

## Arthur

When I return from the bathroom, Polly is lying on the bed on her front.

I look at her naked back. Then, before I start, I warm the oil in my hands, and I do the trick of holding my hands just above her back so she can feel the warmth. Then I start very smoothly, working with my thumbs gently up the twin valleys between her shoulder blades. She's got a knot of tension in the usual place, under the right shoulder blade, and also tightness to the ligaments of her neck. I smoothe it away. She moans. I work steadily, in even circles.

As I work, I look at her back. I realise I know every freckle.

I know the sexy dimples she has above her buttocks. I

remember the first time I saw them. I felt weak with desire and I licked them.

I look at them now. I realise I know the shape of her buttocks, and I push the duvet down a little to reveal them. I rub oil smoothly round the small of her back and I stare at her buttocks.

I'd like to press my hips against them.

I'd like to . . .

'*Why* did we stop having sex?' she says suddenly.

God. That's caught me out.

'Tiredness,' I say.

'Yes,' she agrees.

'And sex got replaced with property searches.'

She says nothing. She knows I'm accusing her. Plus I'm now squeezing her shoulders. She loves that.

'Did you . . .' I ask tentatively '. . . like it?'

'Sure,' she says. 'As a lover, you're . . . like a Volvo. You're large and reliable. You could be depended on to get me . . . into the garage. And . . . a lot of people like Volvos.'

'And do you?' I prompt.

'Well, I'm expected,' she says, 'to let the Volvo sleep in every morning, or he wakes and starts swearing.'

I sort of laugh at that one.

'Did you like it?' she says.

'What?' I say.

'Sex.'

'Er . . . sure.'

Pause.

'But . . . what?' she says.

'There's no "but",' I say.

'I can tell you've got a but.'

'Who says?'

'Oh, come on,' she says, with an awful frankness. 'We're splitting up. We might as well become friends. I'm happy to admit it. Our sex life probably did get a bit stale.'

'We did it less than once a month,' I say. 'Even Mighty White doesn't stay fresh that long. And you sometimes eat Mighty White.'

'Are you talking about . . . fellatio?' she says.

'Yes,' I say, 'I am talking fellatio.'

'I do that.'

'You do it about once every five years. And when you do it, you immediately run from the room with bulging cheeks.'

'I don't.'

'You look like a hamster running off to feed her young. It spoils the moment somewhat. That stuff isn't poisonous, you know. Actually, it's nutritious. Lots of Vitamin C. Really they should be selling it at Planet Organic.'

'Perhaps,' says Polly. 'You could offer to deliver it fresh. Just hide behind a shelf and wait for someone with a cold to come by.'

I laugh. I love it when she's funny.

'So,' she says, 'you wanted me to go down on you?'

'A few times a year maybe. I'd've been happy to return the favour, twice as often. I like it.'

'Do you?'

'Yes. It's exciting. Albeit difficult. 'Cos you won't let me lift your legs up.'

'That makes me feel like I'm having my nappy changed.'

'You are a bit inflexible, do you know that? You would have so much more fun if you loosened up and let a few things happen to you.'

'Sorry,' she says.

I've hurt her now.

'The massage was lovely,' she says. 'I feel better already.'

She moves out from under me. She sits up and pulls her t-shirt on over her head, which gives me a second to look at her breasts. They are small but they're perfectly formed. Now she leans against the pillow and looks at me.

It occurs to me this could be the last time we're in bed with each other, and I've just let her get away from me.

'I didn't mean it like that,' I say. 'You know . . . there's a lot of talk about Great Sex. I think the secret of love is to have Bad Sex, often.'

She smiles. 'You think that's the secret of love?' she says. 'Have Bad Sex, often?'

'I do.'

'Some woman is in for a treat. Arthur Midgley, offering bad sex, often.'

We both smile. There's also a loaded moment when we're still looking into each other's eyes but we're not smiling any more.

## Polly

I'm thinking we could have bad sex, now. He does seem way more attractive all of a sudden. Maybe the Volvo could back me into the garage one last time.

Then I think: *What* are we doing?

I quickly get off the bed, and I pick the remaining pillows off the floor.

'I just want to keep things even for the kids,' I say. 'That's why I took them out of school at lunchtime. I don't want to take them back.'

'OK!' he says.

'Let's do something special for them,' I say.

'OK!'

'Let's take them to Longleat Safari Park to see the lions!'

'What?' he says. 'I really don't want to do that. Why do we always have to make a plan?'

'*Lifestyle* magazine voted it as Best Family Day out,' I say.

'Of course,' he says. '*Lifestyle* magazine is written by workaholics in their late-twenties. They know nothing about families. And not much about lifestyle.'

'Arthur,' I say. 'The kids know something's up. Please, just . . . be calm and sweet for one day.'

'OK,' he says.

'So let's do as *Lifestyle* recommends,' I say. 'Let's just jump in the car, and we'll pop there in an hour.'

## Arthur

See . . .

This is how *Lifestyle* magazine screws up your life.

*Lifestyle* magazine doesn't know it takes twenty minutes to get Ivy out of the house during which time she shouts continuously. *Lifestyle* doesn't know about the traffic jams on the M25. Or the incident near Heathrow involving the Chechen woman who tries to clean the windows, leading to a tense altercation. *Lifestyle* doesn't know about the vast queue to get into Longleat. Or that, during the long ordeal of the journey, the entire car will be forced to listen to the CDs of the Rainbow Fairies. (I'm so over my excitement that Kirsty and Rachel are friends with the fairies!)

This is not popping.

When I came home, I felt tender and sad. I'm now in a car, and I feel cross and unable to speak.

## Polly

It's extraordinary.

Earlier, I truly believed my marriage was over. Now the entire family are in the car, in a safari park. Are we doing the right thing? What are we doing? I don't want to think about it for a while. I just want to look at lions. Sadly we can't really see any though. We're in a tightly packed row of cars, which are forty yards from some lions, who are all lying down asleep. The family in front are trying to do something about that. They're beeping.

'Dad,' says Ivy. 'Why are the lions sleeping?'

'You're quite right,' says Arthur. 'Those lions should get up. Haven't they got jobs to do, or Pilates or something?'

I turn to him.

'Are you hinting?' I ask lightly.

'Well,' he says, looking back. 'I do think animals are wiser than us. Lions are not bothered about Ofsted, or moving to the country. They think . . . have I eaten anything? Yes. Am I safe from attack? Yes. In which case I'll just sleep.'

What's he implying? 'Are you hinting that I am too driven?' I say.

'Do you know the biggest difference between men and women?' he says. 'When men speak we are not, always, trying to teach a lesson. Sometimes we're just telling a funny story about lions.'

As he says that, it's like an alarm going off in my head.

'Oh my God!' I say.

'What?'

'There's something I completely forgot to tell you about!'

'What?'

'You're supposed to do a story-telling session, for the kids' school, at ten-thirty tomorrow morning.'

He stares at me. He seems to be going white.

'I arranged it with Tilly Sweeting on Tuesday,' I say.

At this news he goes completely quiet, like a computer about to crash.

'Sorry,' I say.

## Arthur

Got to admit, I am immediately *panicking*.

She wants me to do a show, in front of the kids' school!

I am, let's be honest, really pissed off that Polly volunteered me to do something, without consulting me. But mainly I'm just terrified at the prospect of doing a show in a school. Last time I visited one I was chucked out for swearing. If I visit another one they'll probably put me in a cage and set me on fire.

'Well, let's just send Tilly a message,' I say, 'and tell her we can't do it.'

'It's a teachers' strike!' she says.

'So why are the parents forced to break the strike?' I say.

'Because some parents work,' she says. 'And they need to leave the kids in school.'

'But why do I have to teach instead?'

'You're not teaching! You're just helping out with a day of Talent Shows and Fun.'

'I don't want to have anything to do with Talent Shows or Fun,' I say. 'I suggest we keep well away!'

'What?!' says Robin, whose ears are batlike whenever there's anything of relevance to him. 'But I'm supposed to be doing my dance! I've had to get the whole class to practise at lunchtime. We're not missing that, are we?'

'Of course we're not missing that!' says Polly soothingly.

'You can take them in to school,' I say. 'But say I couldn't come in.'

'Tilly's arranged a whole day,' says Polly. 'You're doing an hour. They're counting on you.'

With every word I feel more and more trapped.

On a whim, I switch on the radio. It comes on, very loud. It's actually one of my favourite songs – The Killers singing 'All These Things That I've Done'. The chorus is just starting: 'I got soul, but I'm not a soldier'.

Polly turns the music right down, so I can barely hear it. I *hate* it when she does that.

'"I got soul"?!!' says Ivy. 'What is a soul?'

'Oh,' says Robin. 'It's on the bottom of your foot.'

'That is not a soul,' says Malory. She went to a religious school for a year, so this is one of her areas of expertise. 'I will tell you what is a soul. You know you have a body, what can eat, and what can pinch? You have *another* body and that is the soul and it is joined to everybody else in the world and it can walk through walls and it can live *for ever*.'

There's a loud beep from behind.

I suddenly lose it. 'Fucking come past, you cock!' I snarl, very quietly, but with some venom.

Polly turns to me straight away.

'I am sorry,' she announces, 'I don't care what's going on. I am not going to let that go.'

I say nothing.

'I can't believe it!' she whispers. 'I asked you to be calm, for one day. And you just swore in front of the children!'

I glance at the kids in the mirror. They're not paying any attention to us. They're not paying any attention to the lions either. Malory is singing: '"I got soul, but I'm not a soldier!"' Ivy is playing with her Barbies. Robin is inspecting the Longleat leaflet.

'Why are you so bad-tempered?' says Polly. 'You're just like your dad!'

That's the very worst thing she can say. I can't take it. I must escape. No! NO!! *Speak your truth quietly and clearly.* I must communicate.

'Can you just give me two minutes?' I say.

She says: '*Why?*'

'I'm feeling tense.'

'*Why* are you feeling tense?'

'I am feeling tense,' I whisper as quietly as I can, 'because we're divorcing. And because you have signed me up for a show I don't want to do. And I'm on a trip I didn't want to do. And it cost us fifty-eight quid and three hours to get in here, and we're now surrounded by man-eating animals, and we're *stuck in a fucking traffic jam.*'

OK, I realise I just swore again. But I did it quietly. And I couldn't help it. The man behind beeped again.

'But I was *not* swearing at you,' I say, whispering furiously, 'I was swearing at the man in the big Jeep behind us. The one with the shaved head who looks exactly like a big cock.'

I check. In the back they're still singing: '"I got soul, but I'm not a soldier!"' They didn't hear.

Polly looks at me astonished.

She says: 'Look, I have already said I'm sorry. Don't make me beat myself up about this.'

That's her joker, that comment. That gets her out of every situation. 'I'm not asking you to beat yourself up,' I say. 'You have however just given me some very bad news, and that has given me a little tiny spark of rage. However, you tried to smother that spark, which has the effect of turning it into a fucking fire.'

Yes! *Yes! I know*! I swore again, but the cock just beeped twice more.

'Stop, right away,' says Polly. She jabs a finger at me.

I check the mirror. The kids have stopped singing. They're all now listening to us. Their faces are scared. Now I feel like a murderer. We're arguing in front of the children. We need to drop this row, right now. She doesn't though.

'Take a grip of yourself, right now,' she warns.

'Listen,' I say. 'If you left things alone, they'd be fine. But you can't. It's like Iraq. You move in, and it causes chaos.'

'Are you trying to compare this,' she scoffs, 'with the invasion of Iraq?!'

I check the mirror. The kids are giving us agonised looks. I'm a self-indulgent shit. I can't take it. I get out of the car.

'What are you doing?' says Polly.

'I'm going!'

'You can't!' says Polly.

'Why?'

'You are surrounded by lions!' she says.

'As long as they don't try to micromanage me,' I say, 'I'll be fine.'

'Where are you going to go?' she shrieks.

'I don't know!' I shout. 'To my parents'!'

'Good,' she shouts. 'Work out what your problem is!'

I'm so angry, I'm hardly looking at her. I'm just striding manfully away.

But then I hear a bark. And I turn and see Mrs Thompson. She's barking at the window of the car. She wants to join me. I run back for her. I let her out.

At this point, I notice movement. Some of the lions are watching me. Not the males obviously. They're just lying around looking at clouds. But three females get up.

I break into a run.

The three lions start to approach.

At which point, I start to sprint, faster than I've ever sprinted before.

## Polly

I can't believe it.

I asked Arthur to keep things calm and normal. He's just run off, pursued by lions.

I watch him sprinting madly for the gate.

'Where is Daddy going?' says Ivy.

'Daddy just got out for a walk,' I say.

'Is he having a race with the lions?' says Ivy.

'Yes,' I say. 'He's having a race with the lions.'

'Is Daddy racing the lions?' Ivy asks me.

'Yes,' I say. 'He's racing the lions.' Then I put on the Rainbow Fairies CD. If I talk any more, I'm going to cry.

## Arthur

I feel so depressed.

I've now, definitely, left my marriage. And I'm now walking up my parents' street towards their house. Is there anything more depressing than being a thirty-six-year-old man who's returning to his parents because he's got nowhere else to go?

I pass the second-hand bookshop which banned my dad after he called the shopkeeper a cunt.

As I reach my parents' house, I stop feeling sad and just feel tense. Standing at the door, holding their door knocker in my hand, I realise I'm bracing myself. Everything happens for a reason, I think to myself. Everything is here to teach us. I knock.

There's no answer.

I wait a minute. I knock again.

Still no response.

*Perhaps they've died,* I think to myself. (The idea seems strangely reassuring.)

I knock again.

Suddenly my mum is at the door. 'SORRY-I-didn't-hear-the-door!' she bellows.

My mum is a bit deaf. She's called Cynthia. She's a scatty, jumpy, kind-hearted sort of mum.

'I-wish-I'd-KNOWN-you-were-bringing-Mrs-Thompson!' she shouts, from the doorway. 'Only-I'm-looking-after-this-one-for-Barbara.' (She's holding a dachshund under her left arm.) 'And-if-you'd-*called-yesterday*-I'd've-got-you-a-STEAK-for-tea-and-probably-you-know-some-of-those-nice-DAUPHINOISE-they-do-at-Marks-EXCUSE-ME-there-IS-food-we've-got-EGGS-we've-got-QUICHE-we've-got-hummus-we've-got-PLENTY-of-milk.'

I say: 'Right. Thanks.' I give her a brave smile. Whenever I see my mum I'm determined to be nice to her. In fact I step forward and I kiss her on the cheek. Well . . . I try. At the last minute she

turns her mouth and I get the kiss slightly wetly on the edge of
the mouth. Then, while hugging me, she pats me on the top of
the bum, twice – pat pat – like I'm a big racehorse. That's *really
annoying*. Then she breaks the hug and bends down to stroke my
dog.

'Hello-MRS-THOMPSON,' she bellows.

Mrs Thompson is as confused by my mum as I am. On the
one hand, she's happy because she likes my mum who smells of
cooking. On the other hand, she's a bit freaked out, and she really
doesn't like the look of that dachshund. Like me, my dog doesn't
know how to cope. She compromises by doing everything. She
whimpers a bit. She wags her tail with excited affection. Then she
leaps for that dachshund and bites its ear. For a brief moment, my
dog is clinging to the dachshund like a cartoon piranha clinging
to a rod. But my mum cuffs her smartly on the head. 'Oh-Mrs-
Thompson,' she says – *smack* – 'don't-be-SILLY.' Then my mum
waves airily to the hallway. 'SORRY-about-the-mess,' she says.
'I-have-ASKED-Dad-to-clear-it.' At this point my mum spies an
old gent passing up the road. 'Ooh!-There's-Roy,' she says, and
she hurries out.

I take a deep breath and turn.

Why do I find my parents *so* upsetting? Is it that I'm autistic?

Certainly, confronted with their house, I suffer an overload of
my senses that makes me feel desperate. My parents' hallway is so
full of stuff you have to forge a pathway through the debris. There
are wardrobes, coatstands, armchairs, coats, wellies, bags, boxes,
boots, and a teddy bear with a t-shirt reading 'I love Cork'. The
whole display has then been liberally covered with magazines,
jigsaws, and plastic bags which fall to the floor as I pass.

Having traversed the hall, I reach the staircase which is more perilous still. You have to step gingerly between piles of books. Then you reach a mezzanine, where you are greeted with a huge glass table that's covered with bills, old keys and cactuses.

I can't believe I was brought up in these conditions.

'Dad's-upstairs!' shouts Mum, who's now jogging after me up the stairs. 'SORRY-about-the-table.' Up to this point, she's been uniquely jagged and confusing but now she raises her game further. She hits me with a fast combination punch of seemingly disconnected information: 'He's-COMPLAINING-about-his-TIBIA-again-but-he's-SEEING-Dr-Demadis-tomorrow-the-problem-really-is-he's-SO-FAT-just-go-in-say-hello-but-for-God's-sake-DON'T-ask-him-about-his-*TOE*.'

I say: 'What's happened to Dad's toe?'

'Well-he's-LOST-half-of-it,' says Mum.

'How come?'

'Gout.'

I nod to my mum as if this explained everything. I can hear my dad in the living room. I pause a moment, then I push open the door.

**Polly**

I've got a text from Tilly Sweeting.

'Is Arthur still on for tomorrow?'

I ignore it.

It took us ages to get out of Longleat, I need to drive for a while without stopping.

**Arthur**

In their living room, my parents have two distinct styles of furniture. They have some fine antiques my dad inherited – e.g.

there is a nineteenth-century cabinet made from delicate walnut and thin glass. But there's also loads of modern shit – e.g. a gigantic suite of black leather chairs and sofa. It looks like an aristocratic house which has been squatted by two mentalists who are fatally addicted to buying stuff from Amazon. And there in the middle of it – looking huge, befuddled and a bit cross – is my dad.

'Hello!' he says grimly.

Dad is sitting on a chair which has an adjustable foot rest that's controlled by some buttons on the arm. He looks like Captain Kirk after being stranded on the bridge of the *Starship Enterprise* for thirty years, during which time he's eaten a hell of a lot of curry, and watched several series of *Spooks*. His chair is surrounded by several piles of books, on top of which he's placed his ash tray and his fags.

He leans forward as if he's threatening to get up. I save him the trouble. I lean over and he gives me quite an affectionate hug.

'Goodness,' I say. 'You've a lot of stuff in here.'

'Most of it's your mother's,' he says.

I glance at the books. A history of Norse travel. An encyclopaedia of medical terminology. A biography of Rommel. I don't think this stuff is Mum's.

'Did you finish the Cumming?' he asks. We're both fans of the thrillers of Charles Cumming. Dad recently sent me *Typhoon*.

'Yes,' I say. 'It was brilliant.'

There's a pause in the conversation. Dad and I usually communicate by writing. Latterly, we've e-mailed, but before then it was letters. When I was nine, my dad walked out on the family and I was sent away to a boarding school where I was beaten almost every day. (It's not surprising I'm scared of schools!) Dad kept in touch though. My mum would send him my school reports, and, after reading them each term, Dad would always send me a letter in which he'd offer an in-depth critique of my personality. He'd use bullet points, and capital letters, so he could emphasise key words, such as 'DISCIPLINE' or 'SELF-INDULGENCE'. He stopped sending the letters when I was eighteen, but he didn't need to. Criticise a child enough, and they'll hear your voice in their head for the rest of their life.

'How come you're here now?' asks Dad.

'I've had a row with Polly and I've left,' I say.

'Oh,' he says, and rolls his eyes as if to say: Well, what do you expect?

Mum, however, is considerably less mellow on hearing the news. I hadn't even realised she was listening. But suddenly she hurls the door open with a bang like she's a detective bursting into the nest of villains and says: '*WHAT???!!!*'

'We've rowed,' I say. 'And I'm not sure what to do.'

'But,' says Mum, 'if you go, who's taking the kids to school?'

'I don't know!' I say.

'But shouldn't you have thought of that before you went?'

'Well . . . yes!'

'Hang on!' says Mum, getting more hysterical. 'Don't they have school on a Thursday?'

'Yes,' I say.

'And don't you normally pick them up?' she says.

'Er . . . yes!'

'Well,' shouts Mum. 'then-surely-the-children-are-still-WAITING-at-school!'

'Mum,' I say. 'They weren't at school today.'

'*They-WEREN'T-AT-SCHOOL-TODAY!*' shrieks my mum,

who's clearly glimpsing some kind of abduction scenario.

'*Mum!!*' I say, slightly too loud. For the first time in this visit I do actually begin to lose my cool. She does this, my mum. She sucks you, remorselessly, into her own panic. 'The kids are with Polly, they are *fine!*' I say, in a clearly cross tone.

Mum looks at me, hurt. I immediately feel guilty.

'But,' says Mum. 'But . . . but . . .' For a brief moment she's almost clucking like a big chicken.

'They're being looked after,' I say. 'But I don't *know* who'll look after them in future!'

'Well . . . well . . .' says Mum. She's still utterly confused as to how to act. But suddenly she sees a solution. 'Well,' she says. 'SIT THERE. I'll GET you some PÂTÉ.'

Mum, I want to say, I don't think this is a problem which can be cured by pâté. But I don't.

Suddenly I feel very sad again. I actually think I might cry. On a deep level, I haven't a fucking clue what I'm doing with my life and I think I might actually have just pushed Polly away and the worst thing is it was entirely my fault and I just want her love and I just want to give her love . . . why does it have to be so hard?

On a more immediate level, though, I would like some pâté.

**Em**

I'm trying to concentrate on Sarah Shelton who's outlining nine things she wants done by the morning. But I keep thinking of Malcolm. He is so sensitive. I have never in my life so enjoyed having someone touch my back. God. Why am I thinking about Malcolm? I'm embarrassed to be thinking about him, even within the privacy of my own head.

## Arthur

I glance up at Dad. He's looking at me guardedly. He's also clearly wondering how to proceed. Since I've been in this room, there have been two main topics of conversation. The second-discussed the fact I've walked out on my family. The first-discussed *Typhoon* by Charles Cumming. As far as my dad is concerned, this was the better topic.

'Well, *I* thought,' he announces, 'it was Absolutely *Fucking Brilliant* – though I did have a few questions about the history in it. I'd question, for example, that the CIA would intervene in Chinese affairs to the extent Cumming suggests. And . . .?' continues Dad, leaning forward conspiratorially. 'I don't know that they'd have had *access* to that sort of weaponry.'

I look at my dad.

And at this point, I make a terrible mistake.

I say: 'Really?'

Whereupon he launches into a half-hour monologue. He opens on Cumming. He takes in Malta, 1942, where he spent the war. He goes into some length about his research into the history of our family. Occasionally I do try and participate in the conversation. 'So this was in 1941?' I say at one point. But my dad gets louder and he keeps going, like a tank advancing across rubble. Everything is here to teach us, I tell myself. And, after a brief digression on the Luftwaffe's superior firepower in the Arnhem campaign, my dad pauses to light another Silk Cut.

I grab the opportunity to say something. 'Dad,' I ask. 'Would you say that you absorbed any negativity from your father?'

He reflects for a moment, then launches into a very long anecdote which involves him and his dad during World War 2. 'He got me up in the night,' he says. 'He was shouting: "*Court

*Martial! Court Martial!*" and he dragged me out into the hallway and beat me with a cane.'

See . . . This is why I hate therapy: the myth that you might describe some trauma and then it will vanish. Listening to this story, I don't think: '*Of course!* Dad was beaten by his own dad! I'm part of a whole cycle of angry dads! I shall break it and be free!' I think: I've heard this story twenty times before. I've had enough of it. And, to be absolutely honest, I've had enough of my dad. He doesn't need therapy. The last thing he needs is an excuse to review his personal history. He needs a bit of exercise, and a change of pyjamas.

I'm desperate for him to stop talking. At one point, I get up, I leave the room, I go to the kitchen and get a drink, but my dad *keeps on* with an explanation about the structure of the Mosquito bomber. My father is a steadfast man. Once he's begun a lecture about the structure of the Mosquito bomber, he completes it. I give up trying to escape. I return for another bout. Punch drunk, I sit staring at my dad. And meanwhile my mum comes in and out of the room, bringing pâté, and wine, and hummus, and carrots, and peppers arranged in the shape of a face. Not knowing what else to do, I drink and eat and drink. Dad does the same. Without trying to, we neck a whole bottle of wine.

How can I escape? I realise Mum has given me a clue . . .

'Dad,' I say. 'What happened to your toe?'

He looks at me with absolute fury for a second. Then he launches into it.

'The NHS,' he announces, 'is completely *fucked*. I blame that cunt Blair.'

And suddenly I can't take this any longer.

'Dad,' I say. 'I'm going to have to stop you there.'

'Why?'

'I'm just going to have to stop you.'

Dad looks at me all crumpled and hurt. For a moment I can see the scared boy who was beaten by his dad. I don't care. I flee from the room.

But unfortunately I'm stopped by Mum in the corridor.

'I'm going upstairs,' I say. 'I need an early night.'

'Well, I've *done* the sheets,' says Mum, with an absurdly powerful note of defensiveness in her voice. It's as if she's just endured an interrogation in which she was berated about her slackness in dealing with sheets. 'But you can *get more* out of the linen cupboard, if you need.'

'Right,' I say.

And then I stand there, while my mum speaks for several minutes about linen, and then she touches on my dad's toe, and then she mentions the cold that my dog had when Mum last visited.

Suddenly I shout: 'Mum! You must be quiet. I've got to go! I need to write something.'

'Right,' she says.

I step forward and I kiss her. She's so taken aback, she forgets to pat my bum. I break away and see she looks hurt. As I make for the sanctuary of the bedroom, I feel guilty, I feel unheard, I feel furious. Just like I feel with Polly, only worse.

Which brings me smack in the face with the most basic psychological truth . . .

I act as if I think Polly is my mum.

It's a hideous thought.

This is actually one of my favourite Klimts . . .

This is one of Robin's (Klimt in gorilla suit) . . .

This is one of Ivy's . . . .

This is one of Malory's (Klimt as beetle) . . .

# Friday

*Learn Love in a Week.* – the online course that will change your life.

**Day Six:** OK. Here's the good news . . . When you think you're angry with your partner, you're actually angry with your parents. If, for example, you're trying to go out, and your partner says: 'How long are you going to be?' and you get tense, this is because, in your mind, you're hearing your mum saying: 'For GOD's SAKE, will you HURRY UP? We are LATE!' And that is why you want to shout: 'Just give me FIVE MINUTES, I am doing my BEST!' but you know this sort of fighting talk will lead to frostiness in the car. It's so easy to get trapped in a cycle of tension and blame and counter-attacks. How do you escape? Therapy? Do therapy if you must. Perhaps you wish to be more boring at parties. But I can tell you what you'll find: your parents messed you up. But of course! That was their job.

**Today's exercise:** for ten minutes summarise *how* your parents messed you up and how they *made you feel* – e.g. 'They only gave me attention when I did well at school so I became a tense workaholic who toils all the time like a hamster on a wheel.' Write the words 'I am angry at my parents because . . .' then write for ten minutes.

**Today's challenge:** reverse this with an affirmation that makes you feel good – e.g. 'I am loved, I get attention: I work with peace and pleasure!' And each day meditate and repeat your phrase till you believe it. And when you believe it, it will become true.

And by the way, when your partner is angry, it's because they too are angry with their mum. So don't take it personally. Anger comes from fear. Be kind.

**Arthur**

Everyone else adores my mum.

She's the sort of mum who will drive to Bristol to bring her son a bag of laundry, a Breville sandwich-maker, and some pâté. She's a tireless maker of pâtés. She's a helper of neighbours. She's also a World Champion hunter of bargains. The words 'fifty per cent off' do something inside her. She's like a monkey before some ice cream. She doesn't think; she grabs. Then she gives the item to a child as a gift, in a plastic bag. Nothing wrong with that, as such. But I don't want a shirt that was reduced to £12.99 at River Island. What I want is that my mum might calm the fuck down, and occasionally let me talk. And I'd also like her, just once in a while, once a month maybe, to say something positive. It's like a point of principle, with both parents, that they never give a compliment.

Example . . . My parents are sent the *London Times* every day (along with three other broadsheets, and usually a couple of books from Amazon). When I get up in the morning, I find Thursday's *Lifestyle* on the kitchen table, and it's opened on the page of my article: 'How To Be Attractive'. I deduce that my parents have seen the piece, and must therefore be up-to-date with my new career. But, if so, they are determined not to mention it. When my mum arrives in the kitchen, she gives me ten minutes' material on why she hasn't emptied the dishwasher yet. She also mentions my dog's cold, her thoughts about Christmas, and her suspicion that my father has what she calls 'an anal cyst'. Not wishing to encourage her on this subject, I interject.

'Did you see my piece in the paper?' I ask.

'Yes,' she says. 'We always get that paper. Well, you know we do. It's delivered. Every day except Saturday.'

'Right,' I say. 'I've been doing them all week.'

'Are they paying you?' she says.

'Yes.'

'Have they paid you yet?'

'No. But I'm sure they will.'

'Aren't you supposed to send an invoice?'

'Yes. I suppose so.'

'Well, don't you think you'd better send one?'

She's done it. It took her about thirty seconds, and she's found several things I haven't done.

At this point Dad appears and mumbles about tea. He sees the piece in the paper, and reads it, over my shoulder. Then he sort of grunts – 'hmmm'. Honestly, it's like I'm in the paper for indecent assault.

'I've got a new career as a columnist,' I inform him.

'Yup,' he says. 'I saw that one yesterday.' His tone implies that he's got several things to say about the article, but he'll need to read it a few more times, before he gives his final report. I'm wondering . . . should I say something? Is it absurd to be thirty-six and still waiting on a crumb of parental approval?

I'm saved from the dilemma by the phone ringing. It's Em. While taking it, I manoeuvre back to the bedroom.

'Arthur!' she says.

'Hi, Em!' I say. 'Did you get the piece I sent you this morning?'

'Oh,' she says. 'Yes, I did. I've not read it yet. What's the theme?'

'Enjoy your love,' I say. 'It may not last.'

'I'm sure it's brilliant,' she says, a bit offhand. She's clearly not bothered by the piece. So why's she calling?

'Listen,' she says. 'Are you happy to talk to Radio 5 Live?'

'About what?'

'They want to discuss WADs.'

'A WAD?'

'You know . . . a useless creative dad – a Writer / Actor / Dad.'

Didn't I make that phrase up? Em is using it like it's common parlance.

'Er . . . sure,' I say.

'Great!' she says. 'They'll call you in a moment.'

What?! They're calling me *now*?!

'Will you do it?' she says.

'OK. Fine.'

'Good,' says Em. 'Plug the column. Plug, plug, plug. And maybe you could mention that your editor has been taking your advice, and is finding out tonight if her proposal will be accepted.'

'Yes,' I say. 'Good luck with that.'

'Ooh, Shelton is lurking,' says Em. 'Better go.'

The phone goes silent. I look round at my old bedroom. I cannot believe I'm about to be called by Radio 5 Live.

My phone rings.

But it's not Radio 5 Live.

'Hi,' says Polly.

Her voice freezes me like a tranquilliser dart.

## Polly

'Hi,' he says. He sounds spooked. I take a sip of coffee to gather myself. 'Where are you?'

'Home,' I say. 'I've taken the day off work. Where are you?'

'At my parents'.'

'Oh,' I say. I realise I've been half expecting to find he's at Greta's again. 'How is it?'

'Well, they're both insane of course. She thinks everyone in the world is her mum, so her constant concern is to get her apology in first, before she can be attacked.'

'And what about your dad?'

'Well, his mum was an Oxford don. She's been dead thirty years, but he's still trying to prove he's done his reading.'

'So,' I say, 'you think people reckon that everyone else in the world is their mum?'

'Yip,' he says. 'That's the tragedy of it.'

'So,' I say. 'You think that I am your mum?'

'It's funny you should say that,' he says. 'You're raising a stupefyingly horrid notion, but there's something in it.'

'You think I'm your mum?' I say.

'NO!' he protests. 'No no no no no! I *know* you're not my mum. But I realise that I've projected the world of my childhood on to the rest of my life.'

'What do you mean?'

'Because my parents are such mad Baby Boomers – i.e. selfish credit-card junkies who don't listen to a word anyone says – that's why I get cross. I feel like I'm not in control of my own fate. I don't matter.'

'Well,' I say. 'You do matter.' Suddenly I think I'm going to cry. I need to change the subject. 'Arthur,' I say. 'I'm sorry I arranged for you to do a show in front of the kids.'

'I *could* do a show for them!' he says. 'But I need more notice. And it's not a very tempting prospect, given that the last one fucked up.'

'It didn't fuck up,' I say. 'You just said one word that wasn't a swear word. I'm sure it was still a great show. I'm also sure you'd do a fantastic one this time.'

'You think that?' he says.

'Of course!' I say. 'I believe in you.'

'That's not what you said at the time,' he says. 'Had you, I'd've been consoled. To be honest, I probably wouldn't have left the house.'

'Well,' I say. 'Judge me by my actions. I arranged for you to do another show. I arranged for you to write in the paper. I believe absolutely in you.'

Silence.

## Arthur

She's saying something I've never considered during our entire marriage. I've always assumed that, in her mind, the relationship between us was like the relationship the Empress Cleopatra would have had with the slave who cleaned her toilet. I've assumed her intention has always been to make sure I continued cleaning her toilet, and that I did it well and silently. But I realise there's another interpretation. She's not Cleopatra. She's actually an angel who's trying to help. She's right. She did arrange that column for me, and that's proved a hit, which has transformed my fortunes.

Then I think . . . hang on, she's still trying to get me to do that bloody show!

'Jesus!' I say. 'You really don't give up!'

'You need to keep trying,' she says. 'You need to practise your school show. It could be a source of income for you.'

'Polly!' I say. 'It's quarter-past nine. The show is scheduled to happen in about seventy-five minutes' time. I'm at my parents'. I'd never make it home on public transport.'

'No,' she says. 'But you could in a car.'

'Where am I supposed to get a car?'

'Malcolm is turning up, any second, in his van.'

Oh, fuck. She's got me.

'I can't speak to you now!' I gabble. 'Someone else is calling!' That's not even a lie!

I ring off from Polly. A Manchester number is trying to reach me. I press the green button.

'Hello,' says a cheery voice. 'This is Hannah at Radio 5 Live.'

'Hello,' I say. How do I tell her I've changed my mind? I really don't want to go on the radio.

'I'll put you through now,' says Hannah, 'and you'll be on the air.'

*She's putting me through now!* I'm not ready!

Oh my God, I am on the air. I can hear a remarkably slick voice with an Ulster accent.

Oh, fuckety-shit-fuck! I need to stay and talk.

The remarkably slick voice is saying: 'But do you think that's true of David Haye? Because in his fight with Chopra . . .'

What? I'm thinking . . . They're talking about *boxing*. How can Radio 5 Live possibly link that to parenting? Maybe this is a mistake. Maybe I can just go. But then, suddenly, a link is made.

'Hello, I'm Stephen Nolan,' says Stephen Nolan. 'Ten years ago there were sixty thousand. Now there are six hundred thousand men who are "primary carers", or, as some men like to put it, "*trophy husbands*". We're going to speak now to the writer Arthur Midgley, who's a father of three. Arthur, do you think this change is *good* for society?'

Ooh. That's a big question.

At this point Stephen Nolan goes silent, and I leave – what feels like – an agonisingly long stretch of radio silence, during which time I imagine everyone who's ever hated me saying: 'Well, come on . . . *Say* something!'

Then I say: 'I . . .' which seems a good start. 'I . . .' I say it again. I seem to have developed a stutter. 'I *don't know*.' For some reason, I make the '*don't know*' sound remarkably camp. 'But it's where society is.'

'And why is that?' says Nolan.

'I don't know,' I tell Stephen Nolan. And I want to say to him: Listen, if you want someone who has actual views, I'll get my dad. 'But it's usually,' I say, 'because the woman earns more than the man, and she wants to return to work.'

'I was interested to hear what you said on the *Daybreak* show,' says Nolan. 'Do you think it's now got to the stage where women expect a career, they expect a baby, and they expect the man to look after it?'

What??!! He seems to think I'm part of a movement of women-hating angry men.

'I saw figures about this the other day,' I say. 'Only fourteen per cent of British CEOs are women. And there're still six million female carers.'

'Well, women don't run companies, they don't run the government, but it feels like most of them run the home,' says Nolan. 'And since your interview on *Daybreak*, I believe a new

Facebook group has been launched – Trophy Husbands Fight Back. Would you consider yourself the leader of the group?'

For a moment I can imagine all the potential members of Trophy Husbands Fight Back – all the bitter angry dads.

'That's not a group I want to be part of,' I say.

'Oh,' says Nolan. 'Why not?'

'Because I don't want to be fighting anyone. I also think that parenting is really important.'

'Do you?'

'I do!' I say. 'I really do.'

'And what,' says Nolan, 'do you think is the most important thing about parenting?'

'You have to make time for your children,' I say, with surprising vehemence. 'The currency of love is attention. You must listen to them, and *enjoy* them, and tell them they're wonderful. And you can't do that if you're living in a bedsit, writing e-mails about custody.'

'You think that's the secret of parenting,' says Nolan, 'praise?'

'I do. It's the secret of love, I think. Find one thing they do well, and thank them for it. Expect nothing, be grateful for everything.'

'That's good advice,' says Stephen Nolan.

'Thank you.'

'Well, let's hear what *you* think,' says Nolan. 'And, Arthur, can you hang on so we can hear your response?'

'Actually,' I say, 'I *really* can't.'

'Oh . . . Why?'

'I have a date at my kids' school,' I say. 'I don't want to let them down.'

'Good for you,' says Stephen Nolan.

And I'm about to turn off the phone when another voice comes on.

'Hello, I'm Sarah,' says a friendly voice. 'Stephen's producer. That was great! You've got such a wonderful radio presence. I wanted to talk to you actually.'

'What about?'

'I've been loving your columns, by the way. And of course your notorious *Daybreak* appearance.'

'Thank you.'

'We're doing a new show on Radio 5 Live called *The Family Hour*. Going to be daily at eleven. I think you'd be just perfect for it. It's so hard to find articulate men who understand family issues. Would you consider presenting it?'

'Oh,' I say. She's offering me a job! It gives me a delicious floaty feeling.

'It'll only be an hour each weekday, so you don't stand to earn a fortune, I should say that right now. Probably only a couple of hundred a show.'

'Wow,' I say. I realise something's happened . . . Suddenly I'm in demand: everyone wants to give me work. 'That could be great,' I say. 'But I can't talk now. I've really got to go.'

And I gather my things, and I go.

## Em

Ooh, I've got an e-mail from Shelton.

She wants to convene a meeting, this afternoon, to go through the layout for next week's editions. She wants me to come up with some alternative ideas. Hmmm . . . It seems that even though I've got a Guest Editor (Greta) and a Supervising Editor (Shelton), *I* still need to do all the work.

Actually I have got an idea, and I act on it right away. I e-mail Tiggy at American *Vogue*, and I ask if they can give me a job.

## Arthur

By the time I reach the front door, Malcolm is already there.

He's already had an effect on my parents. He's extraordinarily likeable. As I come down the stairs, I'm preceded by my mum, who's smiling and holding a glass of elderflower cordial. My dad is at the front door, beaming at Malcolm. He's excitedly telling him a story about a barman he met while on a teenage cycling tour of Limerick. Malcolm looks *delighted*.

Seeing me, he turns.

'*Big Man!*' he says. 'Oh my God, your dad is a nutter! But *brilliant!*'

At this point my mum reaches Malcolm, holding out the glass. 'SO sorry,' she's saying. 'I don't have any lemon . . . Would elderflower do?'

'Cynthia,' says Malcolm, 'I would *love* some elderflower.' And my mum is so relieved she beams. To indicate his keenness on the elderflower, perhaps, Malcolm tips back his head and downs the drink. He passes the glass back to Mum with a smile. 'That,' he declares, 'was delicious.' My mum looks inordinately pleased.

I push past my parents, and now it's my turn to contemplate them from the step. But luckily – thanks to Malcolm's magical presence – they are both looking so happy that we all seem to have lost the frostiness of earlier.

'Malcolm explained everything,' says Mum. 'While you were on the phone. Good luck with the show.'

I give her a hug. She doesn't kiss my mouth or pat my bum. In fact, the whole hug passes without incident.

'I'm sorry I can't stay longer,' I say.

'Next time,' she says. 'But anyway . . . it was lovely to see you.'

'And don't worry,' says Dad. 'In every good marriage, I've learned, you really should get kicked out a few times.'

'Do you think?' says Mum.

'Well, you kicked me out a few times,' he says.

'Yes!' she says. 'Because of the drinking.'

'I know!' he says. 'Because of the drinking. And because of the Guildford Incident.'

'Oh, don't go on about that!' says Mum.

Dad turns back to me. His eyes are sparkling. 'I have also learned that if they let you back, *don't* talk about it.'

'You think marriage is like poker,' I say. 'The best tactic is to say nothing?'

'No,' says Dad, 'I think it's more like the Battle of Verdun: both sides get tragically entrenched in their positions, and there's a lot of unnecessary bloodshed. But . . .' he says, now putting on a mock-pompous voice '. . . there are also *opportunities*, my boy, *opportunities* for extraordinary tales of sacrifice and valour. So stick in there and fight, I say. Life can be hard, but what's the alternative? Mind you, I would say that. I know that if your children disappeared from Cynthia's life it would be like cutting her arm off. But you must do what's best all round.'

'I can come and help out, *any time*,' says Mum. 'I can bring food. Well, you know, I can get my meats from my little man at the market.'

'Mum,' I say. 'Thanks.'

'And by the way . . .' says Dad, and shyly presents me with a package. 'Got this for you,' he says, passing over a book in a plastic bag.

'Something good?' I ask.

'Oh, yes,' says Dad confidently. '*Spanish Game*, signed, first edition, hardback. It's a bit scuffed, but the contents are still great.'

I feel inordinately touched. My parents are both insane, of course. But my mum has just offered to visit, any time, bringing meat from her little man. My dad has given me a second-hand book. As I pull it out of the bag, I feel like I'm uncovering my heart. It's a bit scuffed, but the contents are still great.

'Dad,' I say. 'Thank you.'

Malcolm says: 'Big Man, we must hurry.'

Mrs Thompson and I trot out obediently after him.


**Em**

What?!

I've got an e-mail from Dan.

> Hi, babe,
>
> I'm so sorry about this. I've just realised I've forgotten the Aston Martin launch tonight at the Grosvenor Hotel, and I need to go because we're doing a piece on it next week. So sorry. I'm not going to be able to go down to Wiltshire with you this afternoon. Why don't you go down, and then I'll try to get away as soon as possible?
>
> D x

Reading this through, I feel a bit numb. There's nothing that surprising about it – Dan dropping out of something, Dan scattering apologies, the use of the classic Dan phrase 'try to get away'. For the first time I realise for sure that he's going to say no. It's so humiliating, I want to die.

## Arthur

In the van Malcolm turns to me and grins.

'I heard you were chased by lions,' he says.

'Yes.'

'Man!' he says. 'I *wish* I had seen that!'

I smile.

Malcolm looks at me seriously a moment. 'Are you OK?'

'I'm *shitting* myself,' I say, 'about the idea of doing a show for the kids' school.'

'Well,' he says, 'I did say, when I became your Life Coach, you have to say yes to everything.'

'Malcolm,' I say, 'you're not my Life Coach.'

'Oh,' he says, 'I'm your Life Coach!'

'OK, you're my Life Coach,' I say. He gives me his Stan Laurel smile. 'But *listen* . . . I can't do this show.'

'But have you not done shows like this before?'

'I did one only on Tuesday.'

'Was it good?'

'Yes.'

'So what's the problem?'

'Well, the problem,' I say, 'is what I've found to be the eternal problem.'

'Which is?'

'At moments of stress, we hear our parents' voices in our heads, and they tell us we're shit.'

'Ah!' says Malcolm, giving me a surprisingly sarcastic look. 'Is that what you think?'

'Yes. I went on the radio just now, and it was like everyone who ever hated me was going: "Speak, you little *shit!*" How do you stop that?'

Malcolm is driving, but he looks me in the eye and gives me a delighted smile.

'I think the *Learn Love* course is covering this today.'

'But it's not solving the problem!' I protest. 'The *Learn Love* course has made me realise that I'm fucking angry because my parents have made me confused, unworthy and unheard. But now you're driving me to a fucking school where I've got to improvise a sixty-minute show in front of three hundred kids and I'm shitting myself!'

'Big Man,' says Malcolm, 'relax. Polly has asked me to *bring* you in. So I will. And I will give you a trick that will make you feel fine. And if it doesn't, you don't have to do the show.'

'What is the trick?'

Malcolm beams with pleasure.

'You want to know the trick that will turn scary experiences into good ones, so that you're only seeing good experiences, and you're only attracting good into your life, meaning you become happy and successful and rich?'

'Yes, Malcolm!' I say. I'm shouting now. 'That is what I need to know.'

'Well, that,' says Malcolm happily, 'is sort of like . . . the Secret of Life.'

'And,' I say, 'can you tell me it?'

'I can,' says Malcolm proudly. 'But not in the van.'

I smile guardedly. I feel warm towards my mad friend, but I'm still tense. I'm also suspicious.

'Malcolm,' I say. 'This Secret of Life business . . . is God involved?'

'Ah,' says Malcolm. 'He could be.'

Oh, shit. I know Malcolm's a bit stinky and a bit weird. He's also indisputably one of the world's happiest people. I would like to know his secret.

'But I'm not religious,' I say.

'Why?'

'Well . . . there's the carnage in His name. Plus it's unproven. Plus if you're Christian, people always hold it against you. "And he's supposed to be a *Christian*," they say, "but he never paid for those crisps!"'

'Listen,' says Malcolm. 'I am not asking you to start a crusade against the Turk. But I will ask that, for just ten minutes, you imagine He's there.'

'But, Malcolm,' I say, 'I just need love. I don't need a fucking religion.'

'Ah!' says Malcolm. 'But you can't give love until you feel love yourself, and you don't feel loved because your parents are unloving. That's what religion is: it's imagining the parent who loves you. Interesting fact,' he continues, warming to his theme, 'most religions were founded by parentless people. The Buddha's mother died in childbirth. Muhammad was an orphan. Moses was sent away in a basket. Jesus *had* parents, but he disowned them more like an angry stepchild – "You're not even my dad!"'

'So you want me to imagine a religion,' I say, 'before performing this show?'

'Yes,' says Malcolm, giving his Stan Laurel grin. 'And if that doesn't work, you don't have to do it.'

That slightly relaxes me. 'OK,' I say. 'So let's try and get there on time.'

'I'll get you there,' says Malcolm. 'You just sit there and relax.'

## Em

I'm at my desk looking at Arthur's latest piece. I'm trying to edit it. Normally one can find a loose sentence and the whole thing falls apart like a piece of bad sewing, but Arthur is deceptively professional. Ugh. I've read it through twice, I still can't see what to change. It's the death of the editor. My career is going to end. *And* I am never going to marry Dan. *Fuck* Dan. Why couldn't he have been more amorous? Because of that insipid, insubstantial little shit, I'm going to die alone. I'd like to die right now. I really would. I mean, of course it's terribly tragic and all that when people die in their thirties, but an early death really does fill a church. And I know it's superficial, but that's something I want. I don't want to be one of those old ladies whose funeral is at some wet crematorium in Enfield, attended by a dull nephew and some neighbours. I want the funeral rammed, I want them fucking well dressed, and I want them weeping like they are all, en masse, reliving the first great heartache of their teenage years. Is that superficial? I don't think it is. If you're going to live on this earth, you might as well make an impact. Fuck Dan. Because of him, I want to die.

## Arthur

Actually I do relax.

But that's mainly because I've got Mrs Thompson on my lap. I scratch her neck, and I sniff the delicious biscuity smell of the top of her head. But then I can't help it.

I blurt it out: 'I just don't believe in God, Malcolm. So your trick's not going to work.'

'I didn't tell you to believe in God,' he says, lighting another spliff. 'I told you to *imagine* you believe in God. Act AS IF God existed.'

'But,' I say, 'an imaginary God can't help me.'

'Ah, but He can,' says Malcolm. 'Because the imagination works. Don't you think?'

'No.'

'Think about it,' he says. 'If you think about food, you feel hungry. If you think about a nude lady, you get excited. So a thing doesn't have to be real for you to change. The point is . . . there's no right, and there's no wrong. There's just what you choose to believe, what you choose to imagine. You imagine the world is filled with people who make you feel confused and unheard and unloved. But I'm asking you to spend ten minutes imagining that you're clear, and you're heard, and you're loved . . . and if you do that it will totally shift your outlook and expectations, which means you'll become calm and confident and gradually your entire life will be transformed – starting with the show. This will work. And if it doesn't, you don't have to perform. OK?'

I stare into Malcolm's stoned eyes.

I nod. 'OK.' I feel reassured suddenly. It's partly because he has promised to tell me the Secret of Life. It's partly because, with the amount of home-grown he's getting through, I'm getting high on the smoke. By the time I reach that school, I'll be grinning like Jack Nicholson.

But suddenly Malcolm changes the subject. 'I tell you,' he says, 'I have never been in love like this before.'

'*Really*?!!' I say. 'Who with?'

'With Em!' he says, as if that were obvious.

'Why didn't you mention that before?'

'I try not to think about it too much.'

'Why?'

'Because it's like a beautiful dream,' he says. 'And I know if I try too hard to think about it, it'll go.'

I stare at him, astonished. He has fallen completely in love. *With Em!!!*

And, looking at Malcolm now, I realise that maybe it could work. He may not have a mansion in Wiltshire. Nor any cash. But he has a van. And he's also, allegedly, got the Secret of Life.

He hasn't, unfortunately, though, got a van that can fly, and that's what I need now. We're only a mile from the kids' school, but we've still got to drive round the corner of the park, and we've reached a massive traffic jam.

I look at my watch. It's 10.09. We're not going to make it.

Shit.

I see it.

The entire school will sit in that hall, and I won't be there, and Polly will say I let the kids down, and I won't be able to see them any more. In years to come Robin will sob to his therapist about this. 'And he never saw me dance . . . And I never saw him again!'

Malcolm pulls into a parking bay. We all get out of the van.

'This is perfect,' he says. 'You'll have to run.'

'But,' I say, 'you said you'd explain the Secret of Life!'

'Indeed,' says Malcolm. 'You'll have to run. That is the first part.'

'Right,' I say. 'So I have to run?'

'Yes,' says Malcolm, 'you must run to the other side of the woods. And then you must stop in a quiet place, under a tree.'

'Yes?' I say.

'By then the blood will be pounding, and the serotonin will be gushing, and you'll be feeling energised and good. You have to do this *every day*, mind, if you want to feel love. Love is a deflating tyre, my friend. You have to keep filling it yourself. You need discipline. You must exercise. You must eat in moderation. Most important, you must sleep eight hours a night, and spend at least an hour a day doing absolutely feck all.'

'Yes!' I say. But what I want is the Secret of Life. Not a basic lecture in diet and work-life balance. 'And then, when I reach the tree, what do I do?'

'You have to *stand* there for ten minutes. And you have to imagine you're a tree yourself.'

'Right,' I say. 'And?'

'And that's it,' says Malcolm.

'*That's it*??!!' I say. I feel so disappointed.

'Hey!' says Malcolm. 'Don't judge it until you've tried.'

'But . . .'

'You haven't even done the running.'

'Right.'

'I tell you what,' says Malcolm. 'I'll do the running bit with you.'

'I don't need you running with me. Besides I'll probably be a faster runner.'

'Fuck you!' he says, grinning. 'I am an excellent runner. If I race you, you don't stand a chance.'

So I sort of snort. And then I run past him, and I jog, quite fast, into the woods. Mrs Thompson runs after me. So does Malcolm. He catches me up after about thirty yards, and we run side by side.

'You'll never win,' he says. 'I do this every day.'

Yes, I think, but you also smoke a lot of weed every day. Plus you're not running very fast.

## Polly

Where is Arthur?

He texted at 10, to say he was a mile away. It's now 10.11.

Quite a few mums are turning up for his show. They keep coming past me saying: 'This should be fun!' and giving me the same look of enthusiasm and suspicion.

Tilly Sweeting turns up.

'Are you sure he's coming?' she says.

'Yes,' I say. 'He's coming.'

Where the hell is he? And is he in any state to do a show?

## Arthur

At this slow easy jog, it takes about five minutes to jog through the woods that lie between us and my kids' school. About a hundred yards short of the gate there's a thick copse of trees. 'We'll go in here,' says Malcolm. 'And find a place.'

I'm not really sure if we're racing any more, but I speed up for the last bit. I find a place under the trees. He joins me.

'OK,' says Malcolm. 'It's sixteen minutes past. That means you can stand here for ten minutes, and you'll still have time to reach the school.'

I feel very cynical about this. 'If I don't feel ready,' I say, 'I'm not going to go.'

'You'll be fine,' says Malcolm. 'Ten minutes.'

I look at my watch.

'Malcolm,' I say, 'I don't believe the Secret of Life is spending ten minutes a day pretending to be a tree.'

Malcolm smiles. 'That's because you haven't shut your eyes.'

I shut my eyes.

'You shut your eyes,' he says. 'And, as you take a very slow breath, you enjoy the feeling of your roots reaching into the earth. And through the roots the earth sends up power, and it's cleaning you like water.'

Maybe I'm stoned from inhaling so much weed in the van. But as Malcolm speaks, I do picture what he's saying. I see water crashing through my system like the sea exploding off rocks.

'You are a tree,' he says, 'you've been here for ever, and you're huge and slow and safe and you're fertile and you're powerful and you're loving. Do you feel that? And now imagine your body is just a trunk. Above your head there are branches and leaves. Feel that! And now . . . slowly breathe in through your leaves, and you feel timeless and inspired and loved. You're breathing in air, you're breathing in love, and it's like anyone who's ever loved you is saying: "Good man, good man yourself!" Do that for ten minutes,' says Malcolm, 'you'll be fine.'

I open my eyes. 'Are you going?!'

'I have to fix some pipes,' says my guru.

'But,' I say, 'you won't be here when I finish the ten minutes so how will you know I'll be ready to do the show?'

'Oh,' says Malcolm, 'if you can just think about your breath for ten minutes, you'll see God. If you like, you can also think: "By giving, I receive. 'By forgiving, I am forgiven. I say *yes* to everything!" Do that for ten minutes, you'll do an amazing show.'

'Right,' I say.

'Ooh,' says Malcolm. 'And I'll give you just one tip.'

'Yes?'

'Try to keep them off the subject of poo. Once they get started on that, they can't stop.' He gives me a quick hug. 'Good man,' he says. 'I'll text you in ten minutes, so you know it's time.'

'But, Malcolm,' I say. 'Are you sure I have to do the show?'

'It's like you said,' says Malcolm. 'It's all about the voices. You go and tell those kids: "Well done! *This is brilliant!*" and after a while you'll start to believe it yourself.'

With that, he grins and walks off.

And that's the last I see of him.

## Em

My family have got such an annoying attitude to funerals.

Whenever my mum sees a hearse going slowly down the street, she says: 'I think this is so stupid, don't you? The person is dead. Why must they hold up the traffic?' Then usually she also proffers this opinion: 'Don't you think a memorial service is much better than a funeral? What's the point being sad? Much better to get together a few months later, so you can *celebrate the life!*'

And I want to be absolutely clear about this . . .

When I die – which I intend to, soon – I don't want a memorial service. I want a funeral. I want my body to be dragged, agonisingly slowly, to the service. I want to be taken to the church, on a wagon, pulled by giant tortoises. I want to cause a three-mile tailback of traffic. I want those tortoises stopping outside shops, to nibble lettuce. And when my body arrives at the church, I want fucking sad music, I want Michael Gambon reciting 'And we'll go no more a-roving!', and I want everyone to bawl their fucking eyes out.

If I can't have love, that's what I want.

## Arthur

Hey. I *want* Malcolm's mad exercise to work.

When I meet people who say: 'I was in a garden, and I opened my eyes, and, there was the Lord,' I always think: You may be insane, but I envy you . . . When I'm in the garden, I see the lawn-mower.

I'm thinking: Maybe Malcolm is right. Maybe I *will* shut my eyes, and God will appear. It's definitely the right fucking moment. I shut my eyes. 'Dear Blessed Lord,' I say. (*Blessed Lord?*) 'Please help me do a good show for those children. Please let me win back my wife. And, please, if you're there, show me a sign.'

I take a few slow breaths. I imagine I'm loved. I open my eyes.

I do see a sign. It reads, NO DOG WASTE.

I shut my eyes again.

But is God there? I think. Is there anything in the heavens? I *need* to know. For a brief moment, my thoughts travel up far into the sky. I imagine the cold expanse of space. I imagine meteorites and freezing winds.

Then I open my eyes.

I see the sun shining through leaves. I see a caterpillar dangling on a thread. I see my dog waiting patiently by my feet.

Suddenly I smile.

I think: There may not be a God. But it's still amazing that there's anything at all. That's the miracle. There is a whole world. There is a whole world, and it's full of leaves, and caterpillars, and dogs, and trees, and children, and signs, and Malcolm, and Polly, when by rights there should be nothing at all. Expect nothing, be grateful for everything. And I shut my eyes, and, for a moment, I am overwhelmed with a blissful sense of gratitude.

Then Malcolm's text comes in.

'The trick to improvisation,' it says, 'is . . . say yes to everything. It's also the Secret of Life.'

I laugh, and head off towards my kids' school.

I still feel a bit sad that I haven't seen God in our local woods. But, for a moment, I do feel light. And, with Mrs Thompson following behind me, I break into a run.

## Polly

Why did I depend on Arthur?

It's 10.28. He's not here. He's not coming. There's an entire school of children in there who are hoping to have a session of improvised stories. And Arthur's not here.

I'm outside the school looking desperately for him. *Please turn up.* It's now 10.29.

I hear someone behind me. It's a Year 2 mum called Caroline.

'Hi, Polly,' says Caroline. 'Is Arthur about to do his story show?'

'Er . . . yes!' I say with a stupid smile. 'Well . . . if he turns up!'

'I must say,' says Caroline, 'I heard Arthur had . . . gone!'

'Oh!' I say. 'No! No! No! I'm sure he'll be here. You go in!'

This is agonising. Everyone knows about our split. It's like they think I'm deluding myself about his return. I look through the playground towards the assembly hall. Oh, dear. Tilly Sweeting is coming out, looking worried.

'Hi, love!' says a voice.

I turn. Arthur's walking casually towards me with Mrs Thompson. What's happening? He seems unnaturally calm.

I say: 'Hi.'

Tilly Sweeting runs forward. 'Oh, great,' she says, 'you made it! Let's start then.'

Arthur smiles. And we all follow Sweeting up the corridor past Reception.

Arthur walks ahead of me. I glance at him. Incredibly, he seems relaxed and, indeed, confident. We reach the back of the school hall where about twenty kids are waiting. Through the glass door I can see three hundred more, and about forty parents standing along the back. Amongst the waiting crowd, there are ten Year 1 children in home-made bumble bee costumes.

'Who are you?' says Arthur warmly.

'We're the Year 1 Dance Team,' they say. They seem wildly excited.

There are Year 2 kids too. They have tin cans hanging off them, on strips of Sellotape.

'And WE,' say the Year 2 kids, 'are The Coolbusters!'

And then I notice another dance troupe, which comprises just one member.

'Hi, Mum!' says Robin. He's wearing thick eyeliner, a black skirt, and a black wig, in bunches.

Oh, Lord.

How did I let this happen? Can I stop him before everyone sees?

'Robin!!' I say. 'When did you get dressed up like that?'

'Just now,' he says. 'I had my costume at school. I've been preparing it all week.'

'But . . .' I falter. 'What . . . *Who* are you?'

'I'm Chiquitita,' he says, happily.

'Who is Chiquitita?!' I say.

'She's a little Spanish girl,' says Robin.

Oh, shit.

Arthur is smiling. He doesn't realise how dangerous this is.

'Are you on your own?' says Arthur.

'Well,' says Robin proudly, 'the others join later. You'll see.'

'I can't wait!' says Arthur. 'What music are you dancing to?'

'"Chiquitita",' says Robin, 'by ABBA.' He smiles proudly at his dad. 'I know it's one of your favourites.'

## Arthur

I look at Robin.

I'm thinking: He's about to dance, in front of his school, to ABBA. I'm thinking . . . I have taught this child things which will hurt him. And I look at his big happy smile, and I think: And he doesn't know it.

I beam at him, and I do all that I can. 'Robin, it is a brilliant song,' I say. 'And I'm sure you'll dance very well.'

'I don't just dance,' he says. 'I sing.'

Oh dear Lord, please help.

'Well,' he explains, 'before a performance, Mrs Betterton says it's very important to make sure you feel loose.' And he descends into a power lunge. 'Also . . .' he continues '. . . I'm going to get a sip of water.'

With this, Chiquitita disappears into the toilets. I notice he's gone into the Boys. That's something at least. Polly grabs my arm.

'Arthur!' she says, agonised. 'Robin is about to appear, in front of the school, dressed in drag. We have to stop this!'

'Why?' I say.

'He looks like a tiny Latin prostitute!' she whispers. 'We have to stop him!'

'We can't!' I say. 'We can only encourage him, so he'll grow strong.'

'He's about to commit social suicide,' she says. 'It'll be the end of him!'

It must be admitted, I do see Polly's point of view. But I also saw the pride on Chiquitita's face.

'You're too scared of tension,' I say. 'You're not in control of this. Relax, and let it happen.'

## Polly

At this point Robin comes out of the toilets, beaming happily.

'So, Mum,' he announces, 'you're the only one – out of the three older members of the family (that's you, me and Dad) – who's not doing something in this show.'

'Yes,' I say. 'Well, that is a shame.'

'You can do something if you like,' says Tilly Sweeting.

Look here, Sweeting, don't dump me in it.

But then Robin says: 'Oh, Mum, you *could* do my intro.'

'*What?*' I shriek.

'You know . . . Like on *Friday Night Is Music Night*,' he says. (How come we have a son who knows the Radio 2 schedules?) 'There's someone who says: "This music was composed in . . ." blah-blah. You could do that.'

I really don't want to do that.

'Sorry, Robin,' I say. 'I don't know who wrote "Chiquitita" and when.'

'It was Bjorn Ulvaeus,' Arthur and Robin say, in exact time. 'And it was 1979,' finishes Arthur.

Right.

Arthur is grinning at me.

'Polly darling,' he says. 'I know how important you think it is to support school functions.'

I don't know how to bloody perform. What words are you supposed to use?

**Arthur**

I don't know what it is. Is it because of Malcolm's magical ritual? Is it just because I'm delighted to be home? I'm loving being back at the school.

I watch the Year 1 Dance Troop do a song called 'Buzzin' Around'.

Then I see The Coolbusters do one called 'Get Them Diddling Cans', which is all about the excitement of recycling.

Then Tilly Sweeting, who's compering, says: 'Mrs Midgley is going to introduce the next act.'

She leaves the stage.

Polly now totters onstage. She looks nervous. She doesn't seem to know what to do with her hands. She puts them in her pockets. She takes them out.

'Hello,' she says. 'The next piece is the Year Four Dance Troupe who will be dancing to "Chiquitita", which was composed in 1979 by Bjorn Ulvaeus of ABBA. It's . . .' she says. 'It's a slightly strange song . . . but lovely.'

Where is she going with this?!!

'And it's the favourite song of Robin's dad,' she says. She glances at me quickly. 'He also is strange, but lovely . . .' No, Polly! This is no time for a public display of affection. I may cry. 'And he's going to do a show for you in a moment. But now, boys and girls, please welcome Robin Midgley as . . . Chiquitita!!!'

At this . . .

Polly scuttles to the side of the stage and she sits on a plastic chair.

An audience of adults probably would have clapped at this point, but this crowd are mainly schoolchildren. They've not been told to clap, so they haven't. Instead there's just a tense silence.

*But then . . .*

At this moment, Robin stands up smartly.

And, like the great choreographer he is, begins to conduct his troupe with brevity and command.

He nods at Year 4. Instantly, they all stand to their feet. Robin then nods again. Now Year 4 split into two choirs, and they run – they actually *run*, they have been quite extraordinarily well drilled – to the sides of the stage, where they kneel down. Then there's a last nod and the music comes on. It's the first jangly guitar chords of 'Chiquitita'.

Which is the cue for the movement of the last section of the cast.

And that is our son, Robin Midgley. He sprints from the wings on to the stage. He stops still in the middle. Then he hurls himself to the floor, with his sobbing head resting on his arm.

Seeing this, the first choir stand. They sing. They entreat Chiquitita to explain her trouble. For a moment, she shows her sad Spanish eyes to the crowd, but then, overcome, she collapses like a dying swan.

Determined she should be galvanised, the other choir start up. They implore Chiquitita to make a full breast of her troubles. They assure her that she can rely on them. For a moment Chiquitita rises up. She's going to struggle on to face a new day. But the pain is too much. She falls, once more, to the floor.

*But now the chorus starts.*

The cheery oompah music kicks in, and Chiquitita *rises* to her feet, and she starts dancing a high-kicking march round the stage as both choirs now sing triumphantly. They sing of the transience of heartaches. They entreat Chiquitita to dance on into a new dawn. Now Chiquitita isn't to be stopped. As the oompah chorus kicks in again, both choirs now march, high-kicking onto the stage. And electrified by their support, Chiquitita starts leaping about in an explosion of kicks, leaps and sensational choreography.

**Polly**

OK. I admit it. Arthur's right. James is right. I *am* scared of tension.

And right now I'm tense. I'm very tense. As I watch Robin's cavorting, I'm practically frozen with tension.

*BUT*, glancing round, I notice that the children of St Mary's School seem to be enjoying themselves.

And, tentatively, I start to think that Robin is getting away with this.

**Arthur**

I have never felt so proud in my life.

I cannot keep my eyes off my son's performance. It's gawky. I'd say the whole project is misconceived. But I can also see that he is performing a strikingly original piece of choreography, and he's performing it with conviction, and energy, and – dare I say it – *professionalism*.

OK. I am aware that in another school, a child could be killed for doing choreography like this. And, in truth, even in this one there are a few kids who are clearly of the opinion that all this prancing is a bit gay. But these kids have seen *X-Factor*. They've seen *Strictly*. They know that some of Robin's moves are a bit weird. They can also, however, see that he's *going for it*, and they like that. And as the song reaches its end, Robin leaps into the air – he leaps into legend! He leaps into folklore! – and he's caught by the four strongest boys in Year 4. They lift him still higher. As the last bars of the song play out, Robin is held at shoulder-height, frozen in arabesque.

And now the entire school stumble to their feet, and they all scream.

Robin's dance has been a tremendous hit.

The left chorus bow. Everyone claps. The right chorus bow. Everyone cheers. Only now is Robin lifted down. And as he jogs forward smartly to take his bow – he does it with consummate professionalism – the entire crowd scream their approbation and respect.

And my little gay son plays it beautifully. He takes the applause. Of course he does. He deserves all the applause he can get. He flings his wig into the crowd, and, to roars, cheers and stamping of feet, he bows deeply, twice.

But then – just as the applause has peaked – he holds up his little gay arm. He even does that beautifully. He looks like Grace Kelly waving from a sports car.

'And now . . .' he says. He's keeping the energy going like a mini Graham Norton. 'Please keep your applause going as he comes out to make up a story – he's my dad – he's brilliant – but he's also a bit of a *fool!* Mr *Arthur Midgley*!!'

Oh my goodness, I think from the wings. Robin, that was a brilliant introduction. I love you. I absolutely fucking love and adore you and I would do anything to support you in anything you do.

Then I feel a moment's tension again.

Up to now, I've been so preoccupied by the drama of coming

home – seeing Polly, my nerves at doing this show – that I haven't focused on the essential fact that I have a performance to do. The first one since I was chucked out of Thomas Cranmer School in Mitcham. And, I realise now, if I'm going to do justice to the warm-up act – I'd better raise my game, right away.

So I take a long deep breath, during which I imagine that I'm calm, I'm deeply loved, and that the scars have gone and I'm ready to sing a new song, Chiquitita. Then I jog out on to the stage. I look out at the crowd, who have been so expertly warmed up. I see hundreds of grinning, eager faces, and I love every single one of them.

## Polly

Arthur comes springing on to the stage like a big camp kangaroo. A gigantic kangaroo, wearing a pink scarf and a trilby hat.

Immediately the kids are electrified.

How does he do it? He comes out, and everyone's excited.

'Hello!' he shouts. 'All the boys, say "*Hey, Arthur*!" like you're Buzz Lightyear from *Toy Story*. "*Hey, Arthur*!"'

He points the mic at them.

'*Hey, Arthur*!' chorus a hundred and fifty Buzz Lightyears. 'And now all the girls,' he says, looking into the faces of a hundred and fifty girls. 'You are a crowd of very funky witches. You say: "*Hello ha ha ha ha*!!"'

'*Hello ha ha ha ha*,' say a hundred and fifty cackling witches.

'And now,' he says, 'we are going to make up a story together, and you guys are going to help. When you get an idea, put your hand up. And, remember, you can say anything. OK . . . So . . . *This is a story*,' begins Arthur, putting on his best storytelling voice, 'about a little man. A tiny little man.' He shows them how big with his hands. 'About this big.'

A boy in Year 1 puts his hand up.

Arthur says: 'Yes?'

The boy says: 'Is he made of poo?'

Oh, Lord.

## Arthur

I look at the boy. He is grinning with pride at me. He knows that (1) he just got away with saying 'poo' in public, and (2) he just made the entire school laugh. Is that something I want to discourage?

'The little man *is* made of poo!' I confirm, to the satisfaction of the entire crowd. The boy himself especially. He couldn't be more pleased with his contribution. Even so, I glance at Tilly Sweeting. She's suddenly looking very witchy herself, and I'm very keen to establish an identity for this unfortunate man that doesn't rely on his faecal composition. 'But what,' I ask the crowd, 'is the man's name?'

Ten hands now shoot up.

I choose Imogen Levy – a shy bookish girl in Year 5. Should be safe enough.

'Yes!'

'Is he called,' she asks, ' Mr John Henry Poo?'

## Polly

I must admit that, again, this gets an absolutely massive laugh.

But I glance at Tilly Sweeting, who's looking very tense.

## Arthur

I look at Imogen Levy who has a little twinkle in her eye. Is that something I want to put out? 'Imogen,' I say, 'he is!'

More laughter.

As far as the kids are concerned, this is the best beginning to any story that there's ever been. Everyone wants to be part of it. One of the Reception boys is so excited he gets to his feet, holding his hand up. He doesn't even know what I'm going to ask. Already he knows he's got the answer.

'And,' I say, looking the boy in the eye, 'every morning the little man goes for a walk, and as he does he sings a song.' The boy's hand goes up further. He *knows* he can improvise a song in public. I can't stop that kind of confidence. 'How does the song go?' I ask him.

The boy jiggles his hands in the air as he sings:

'I'm Misssster Poo/ And I live down the loo/ And I'm very scared of brushes.'

The crowd love this. Whoops from Year 6.

Okaaaay. 'That's great,' I enthuse. 'But, in stories, the scariest things happen. We need something bad to happen. (That's why you should welcome bad things happening: if there are no bad things there is no story.) So what happens to Mr John Henry Poo?'

Twenty hands are up.

I point to someone in Year 6.

'Yes!'

'One day he gets flushed down the toilet and he gets lost.'

'Very good,' I say. Plus I feel relieved we've moved the story on. Now it's time to hear about John Henry's adventures in the sewage system – the rats that he meets, his great quests. 'But what does he *want*, Mr John Henry Poo?' I ask the school. 'What is his dream? Everyone has to have a dream!'

The first boy is on his feet again.

'Yes!' I say.

'He wants,' shouts the boy, 'to go back to the bottom what he came from.'

In the huge laugh that follows, I stare at the boy astonished. That is brilliant. This is a coprophilic creation myth. It has echoes of Graham Greene. It could be called *The Turd Man*.

Then I look at Tilly Sweeting.

She looks tense, and angry, and I get a waft of witchy fear.

But then I think . . . fuck her. I'm going to concentrate on the hundred and fifty witches, who actually like me. I look out at them. I look at the hundred and fifty Buzz Lightyears too. They are all, I realise, having a lovely time. As far as they're concerned, a miracle has occurred: a grown man is onstage at their school, talking about poo. This is about as good as it gets. I also realise I have a responsibility to carry on, and, damn it, I shall. I shall not stop unless Tilly Sweeting flies on to the stage on a broomstick. And if she does, I shall fight her. I shall fight her with Buzz Lightyears, I shall fight her with witches, I shall fight her with my wild untamed glee!

**Polly**

So . . .

The rest of the show went well. The beginning was obviously awkward, but Arthur dealt with it deftly, and moved things on well to safer subjects – e.g. vampires, blood-sucking spiders, and bogey-shooting guns.

After the show we find Mrs Thompson tied up outside. (She's really excited to see the kids again.) And then the entire family walk up the alley together. Robin is talking excitedly about his dance. Malory is pushing Ivy on a scooter. The sun is shining through the leaves of the conker tree, and there's that happy end-of-school sense of release, and Arthur is home. He is chatting to Bridget Harding, one of the mums in Year 5.

I still can't quite get used to the feeling that the family is back together. Are we? So much has happened in the last few days, I don't yet feel safe. As we enter our front gate, I stop Arthur and I squeeze his hand.

'Darling,' I say. 'Your show was fantastic.'

'Well,' he says, 'it's just a matter of saying yes. It galvanises everyone.'

'I've got to admit, I was very nervous beforehand.'

'So was I,' he says. 'It's useful to remember, isn't it?'

'What?'

'You can be that nervous, but afterwards all the tension just dissolves away like sugar in tea.'

'Yes,' I say. He's right. All nerves have gone, and in their place, there's something else. I look, agonised, into his eyes. If I say I love him, does that mean I'll be buried for ever? 'I'm glad you're back,' I say. 'Just one thing. Now you're back, do you think you might, please, finally clear up that fruit bowl?'

Arthur smiles. 'Yup. Of course,' he says.

And I open the front door.

Malory hurls to the floor her coat, her book bag, and her lunch box. Robin goes into the living room and begins what he calls 'a gentle warm down'. Ivy finds the Gruffalo toy in the hallway and takes him to Arthur.

I pick up the bags and books. I go to hang everything up on the pegs outside Arthur's office. And that's when I see the piece of paper lying on the floor.

As I read it, my blood runs cold.

## Arthur

As soon as we arrive home Ivy capitalises on it straight away. She makes damn sure I'm playing with her. I don't even get in the front door before she comes towards me with Gruffalo, saying: 'Dad, Guffalo wants to talk to you!' Meaning: she wants me to make Gruffalo talk.

I oblige.

I adore the Gruffalo toy. He has mad orange eyes and a fat belly. I do him with a growly voice, a bit like Cookie Monster in *Sesame Street*. I hold him, and he just seems to come alive. He loves leaping on the back of Mrs Thompson and riding her round the garden. Mrs Thompson doesn't mind too much. (Mrs Thompson is the most patient member of our family. She's doggedly loyal. She sleeps with Gruffalo sometimes.)

'Dad!' says Ivy, pointing at the bottom of the bush next to the front door. 'There's a snail!'

This is another of Gruffalo's enthusiasms: he loves snails. He thinks they're his eggs.

I sit on the tiny wall. I sit Gruffalo on the snail and he coos happily: 'Oooooh,' he says. 'This is my *egg*.'

Ivy laughs, and I have a moment of pure happiness. The family is a theatre, I think, in which you can play every part. That's my mistake: I wanted Polly to be my wife, my playmate, my guard . . . She is my wife. Ivy is my playmate. Mrs Thompson is my guard. I see it now. I have everything! I am sitting on my blessings and I'm cooing like a happy monster!

Then Polly comes out.

She looks white.

'Ivy,' she says. 'I need to talk to Dad.'

Ivy says: 'But I am talking to Dad!'

'Ivy, you can go and turn on CBeebies.'

Bloody hell. I'm instantly concerned. What can be so bad she's *volunteering* TV?

I look at Polly with curiosity. Mrs Thompson comes out and looks at Polly too.

She squats down on the doorstep and looks at me very seriously. 'We need to talk!' she says.

Oh, shit. That always means: We need to talk about all the things you're doing wrong. Well . . . I'm not doing that any more. Let's focus on a few things I'm doing well!

'Did you hear what Bridget Harding wanted?' I ask.

Polly says: 'No.'

'She runs a school visits agency apparently. She said she'd really like to take me on.'

Polly looks surprised. 'Did she think the show was good?'

'She really did. She said I could easily be one of her best acts. And the best ones do a couple of school visits a day, so she arranges little tours for them, and they do ten a week for two or three weeks at a time.'

'Can they earn any money?'

'Yeah! They get about three hundred pounds a visit, so if you do ten in a week, that's three grand. So if you do three weeks a term, three terms a year, that'd be twenty-seven grand.'

'That's amazing,' says Polly. But her tone is weirdly flat. What's the matter?

'Also,' I say, 'I didn't tell you. I went on Radio 5 Live earlier.'

'Did you?'

'And the producer there wanted to know if I'd be interested in presenting a show for them. She was talking about a grand a week.'

Polly is looking at me blankly. Why isn't she responding?

'And *Lifestyle* are talking about a year's contract. Sally Winklehorn seems certain she could sell my book. Suddenly it looks like I could easily earn a hundred grand next year.'

'Well, I'm sure you will,' says Polly. 'Well done. It looks like you've turned a corner.'

I take a deep breath. This feels like an important moment. For years she's said I don't earn enough. Suddenly it looks like I'm about to. And there is something I must say.

'Polly,' I say, as kindly as I can. 'It's easy to give someone faith when things are going well. If you'd given me some faith when things were going badly, they might have picked up quicker. It's tough being self-employed because you can't tell anyone how lonely and worthless you sometimes feel.'

She looks down at the floor.

'What's the matter?' I ask.

To my shock, when she looks up, she's crying.

'What?' I say.

'Arthur,' she says, and her voice sounds all small and wobbly.

'What?'

**Polly**

I look into his eyes, and, as I talk, I swear all trace of anger is gone. I just feel very sad.

'What's bothering you?' he says.

'That fruit bowl,' I say. 'You fill it with all the things you want me to deal with. I asked if you would deal with it, and you ignored me.'

Arthur offers an excuse that's probably been offered by no man. 'Well, Gruffalo had found an egg,' he says.

'Yes,' I say. 'But I've asked you about twenty times. And I'm

[ 313 ]

so pleased, honestly, your creative life is picking up. I'd love to be doing creative things too. But if you make me do all the boring tasks, it makes me a drudge. I do so much, and yet still you blame me for everything that's wrong in your life.'

'I don't blame you for anything!'

'You, *just now*, blamed me for causing your misfortunes by not giving you faith. You blame me for getting you to do childcare.'

'I do not blame you!' he says. 'I thank you! You've earned more of the money, which means I've been able to be with them, and I've worked when I can. I'm grateful for everything you've done.'

'Arthur,' I say. 'There is a YouTube clip of you on national television, blaming me for forcing you to do childcare! How much more evidence do I need? And you seem to blame me because I made you have children, as if the decision to have Robin was somehow forced upon you!'

'Well,' he says. 'I wouldn't say we discussed it at enormous length.'

I need to do this.

'Maybe you're right,' I say. 'Maybe we've held each other back. There are things you want to do. There are things I want to do. I'd like to go to James Hammond's launch tonight. I'd like to go to that party. I'd like to see a mediaeval monastery that's been converted into a place where people go to be happy.'

'So?' says Arthur. 'Go! Just don't fuck James Hammond.'

At this, I look at him guiltily.

'You know what your trouble is?' says Arthur. 'You're only seeing negatives. You do it all the time with me.'

'Actually,' I say, 'this week I've seen loads of positives about you.'

'Great,' he says. 'But you do it with yourself. Like . . . look at your garden. Look at your wonderful plants. Look how exquisitely they're arranged. You're a brilliant garden designer. But, in your heart of hearts, you think James Hammond is only employing you because he wants to shag you.'

No. I know he's only employing me because he wants to shag me. Still, that could lead to other things.

'But,' I say, 'it's not just about sex, is it? I like James. He has vision, and energy, and he is offering me a new start. A new job. A new life. And you regret the things you don't do in this life, not the things you do. So I should go, and you should go. Go with my love, and my blessing. Because it's more important to me that you become the person you could be than that you remain my husband.'

He looks at me astonished.

'Where do you think I should go?' he says.

'I don't know,' I say. 'Go anywhere. Go to Greta . . . You also seem to blame me for keeping you from her.'

'I don't!'

So I pass him the piece of paper.

## Arthur

I read it quickly.

Right away, I see it's bad. It starts: '*Sometimes I think my whole life went wrong because we didn't make love that night.*' It includes ickily pornographic stuff: '*We might have panted into each other's mouths . . .*' It finishes with a direct insult: '*When I talk with Polly, we discuss the schedule.*'

I immediately feel sick.

I'm thinking: I guess that does need explaining. But . . . what the hell is the explanation?

'If you'd just discussed the schedule with me,' Polly says, 'we'd have got through it!'

'I know that!' I say.

'Arthur,' says Polly. 'What do you suggest we do about this?'

'We don't need to *do* anything!' I say. 'This is what I'm saying! Not everything can be resolved.'

'I don't know what to say to you,' she says. 'But it sounds, in the first instance, like you really need to fuck that woman.'

I say: 'Listen . . . I wrote that piece on Monday. I've changed since then.'

'Oh, how nice. What changed?'

'Only a bit of me wanted her then.'

'A bit?'

'Oh, come on, we're complicated people in a busy world filled with adverts and porn: at some point you're going to get a crush. You told me to explore my feelings.'

'I didn't tell you to write semi-pornographic love letters to past loves. You obviously really like that woman.'

'I do. She's fantastic. She's my second-best woman in the world. You're my Number One. That's why we're together. But she's my fantasy woman. We're always going to have our fantasies because we're imaginative, optimistic people. And besides, she is so lovely, and I consider the moments we've been together as some of the most precious of my life. But I know that, if I had Greta, I'd also have a new fantasy woman.'

'How do you know that?'

'Because, over the course of my life, my Number One Fantasy Woman has been you, Polly Pankhurst, the girl I met at college and didn't see for four years till one fateful day when I was walking through Soho. Then this week we split and I longed for you again.'

'So that's the trick, is it,' she says, 'to prodding your flagging libido into life? I've just got to chuck you once in a while. Well, I'm not doing it! And actually . . . maybe you're right. Maybe we just stayed together out of some banal need to compromise. I'm going, Arthur. I'm going to go to Wiltshire. I'm going to design a garden for James Hammond. And . . . who knows? Perhaps this is the moment that I walk out and I change my life, so . . . thank you.'

This is horrible. Each word is like eating glass.

'Oh, for God's sake,' I say. 'I'm sure James Hammond will fuck you. But it's highly unlikely you'll change your life.'

'Well, I choose to believe I might,' she says. 'There is a difference between us. I believe in love.'

'No,' I say. 'I do.'

'I don't care what you believe, Porn Man,' she says. 'Just go. And we'll talk through lawyers about when you'll next see the kids.'

Astonished, I stand up.

'What?' I say. ' I thought you wanted me to do childcare today?'

'I'll find someone else!' she shouts.

'Who?' I say.

'Someone . . . I don't know . . . Doesn't matter . . . just GO!!'

So I do it. I go.

And as I walk away from my home I call Greta. Polly practically told me to do it.

She tells me to meet her at a hotel in West London where she's having a meeting. She knows what I want. I immediately feel very nervous and very aroused.

**Em**
After three delays, the meeting with Shelton is finally happening.

It's happening in a boardroom that's near the *Lifestyle* offices.

So far her PA has visited it three times to prepare. I don't know what the fuck her amphibian boss is making her do. Heating it up to blood temperature, probably. Checking there's a fresh supply of flies.

Greta isn't even here. We're supposed to be going through the rough layouts for Monday's edition, which Greta is Guest Editing. She's not even fucking here.

Suddenly Shelton arrives.

The rough layouts are spread all over the table.

Shelton doesn't even say hello. She just goes over and looks at them. She puts her skinny hand to her face, and she looks at them like a big scrawny flamingo who's contemplating a fish.

Then she says: 'These are no good.'

To which I say: 'Well, you should be saying that to Greta. She's Guest Editor.'

To which she says: 'Why don't you get it into your head? Guest Editor is just an honorary position.'

To which I say: 'You seem to be having it both ways. You're taking away my power, but making sure I can still be blamed. Do you think that's good management?'

Shelton turns to me and gives me one of her dead looks. She doesn't want to be drawn into a discussion of her management style.

She just says: 'What do you suggest we do with these layouts?'

To which I say: 'I suggest you shove them up your arse, you cruel, joyless bitch.'

At this, Shelton says nothing. And I have nothing to add. So I go.

## Arthur

Actually Greta and I leave the Notting Hill Hotel as soon as her meeting finishes.

We barely talk. It's an incredibly hot day in London. It's one of those bright airless days which make you want to sit in the shade panting slightly. Luckily Bernard is waiting faithfully outside with his green Bentley. We both climb in the back. Greta closes the partition to give us privacy. Then she turns the air conditioner right up.

As the car drives off, we sit side by side, staring dumbly forward. It suits me. I don't want to talk. I just want to place my ears between her thighs and I want the confusion to stop.

'What would you like to do?' she says.

I don't give an answer. I have a strange fear that she's about to suggest some must-see cultural phenomenon. A wrong word now and I could end up under Battersea arches, watching a man who bleeds.

She says: 'What do you *want* to do?' The emphasis is on the want. It's like she's challenging me to absolute honesty.

'All I want,' I say quietly, 'is to go home with you. So we can go to bed.'

She doesn't turn. But I sense a quickening of her attention. 'Yeah,' she says. 'Why?'

God. What's the answer to that? Does she want me to declare my love? Or does she want the exact opposite?

'Because,' I say, 'we nearly did that once before, and you regret the things you don't do, not the things you do. Don't you agree?'

'I think that's a piece of arch capitalist horseshit,' she says, 'which has been placed in our heads, like a virus, to make sure we keep spending.'

I'm thinking she's way too rich to be talking about capitalist horseshit. I also find it horny she's talking like a Marxist terrorist.

'OK,' I say. 'I want to be with you 'cos I think that, together, we're strong. We'll achieve mighty things. Plus, I can't imagine anything I'd rather do.'

Now she turns slowly to me. She looks me in the eye.

'OK, soldier,' she says. 'But first we need to go somewhere.'

'Where?'

She's wearing a hint of a smile.

'James Hammond's hotel. He's having a party.'

'What?!' I say. 'I'm not invited.'

'I am,' she says. 'You can be my Plus One. I got a double room.'

I look into her eyes. Oh my God. I've thought about this for years, and now it's definitely happening.

'But,' I say, 'Polly will be there and I think she's hoping to sleep with her lover.'

Greta keeps staring. Her smile is fading.

'Sounds like you're hoping to do the same,' she says.

'Yeah.'

'So,' she says. She's still looking challengingly into my eyes. 'Do you want to come?'

I look at her beautiful freckly face.

I say: 'Yes.'

'Bernard,' she says, pressing a button, 'let's go to Wiltshire!'

And then she pauses a moment before she slides up the seat towards me, steadily as an octopus moving across the sea bed. She's wearing white linen trousers. Her thigh is now touching mine.

'What are you thinking?' she says.

'I want to kiss you,' I say.

'Well,' she says, not moving, 'you know what I always say?'

'What?'

'Enjoy the wanting.'

She doesn't move closer towards me.

'Greta,' I say.

'Yes.'

'What's the secret of happiness?'

Now she swivels her body towards mine. Her right breast is touching my arm.

'Connect,' she says. 'When people come to you, they come like bees to a flower. You must give them pollen. Then you must let them go.'

She stares sleepily into my eyes.

You can come in, she's saying. But afterwards, you must go. It's one of the sexiest things I've ever heard. It's also one of the most sad. It's also a fucking pretentious way of saying: I'll shag you once, but don't count on seconds.

'You are a beautiful man,' she says.

And then it's all reminiscent of what happened in that hotel, twelve years ago . . .

It takes us a whole minute to bring our heads together.

There's a whole minute in which our noses are just touching. And then several more minutes during which our lips meet, and we start to kiss. It is a wonderful kiss. Except this time everything feels different. Thoughts are racing through my head . . . I'm thinking: Am I allowed to do this? Is this what Polly meant me to do? I'm thinking: What's Polly doing right now?

**Polly**

So glad Em is with me. She's keeping my mind off things.

On the train we discover you can buy a surprisingly good white wine. We have a glass each to celebrate her escape from the evil witch Shelton. We have another to celebrate our friendship, the only unchanging thing in this world of fickle men. Then we have another 'cos it tastes nice.

We leave the train at Salisbury.

At 6 p.m. we're riding in a cab towards Bodsham Abbey. As we drive there, I'm scanning the scenery for the Inshaw hillside. To the right there is a hill, but it's dotted with ugly bungalows. There's also a large pub of the wrong sort. It has a sign outside which assures the public that they're offering Sunday Roast 'with all the trimmings'. I like trimmings as much as the next person, but something about that sign deflates the spirit.

And then I turn to the left and I see Bodsham Abbey.

Wow.

There's a long wall. It's broken by a magnificent archway which is guarded by four security guards in black suits. Behind it there's a huge mediaeval building. It has scores of windows. It has a tower. The whole thing is built in beautiful yellow limestone. It's sublime. I want to explore every passage. I want to touch every wall. If Bodsham Abbey were a person I would take them to my bed, I wouldn't leave for several weeks, and when I did, I'd be walking a bit funny.

**Em**

Golly.

We walk through a magnificent vaulted hallway. On the lawn, there are two lines of staff in white jackets, proffering drinks.

Beyond them is a huge grassy garden. It's at least a hundred yards across. I can see to the far side where there's another limestone wall and a long swimming pool which has chairs and tables arranged next to it. Before that, there's a gathering of a couple of hundred people – the great and the good of British society.

We set off into it.

Almost immediately I'm stopped by a celebrity chef who used to do our recipes. So I get separated from Polly, but I watch her as she has her first encounter with James Hammond. He watches her approaching as if he were a hungry wolf and she a fat partridge walking towards him covered in gravy. She is looking fairly sensational, it must be admitted. She's in a backless black dress. As he kisses her he places his hand on the flesh of her back, and he doesn't remove it.

His eager lusty manner reminds me of the way Dan used to treat me, and suddenly I feel sad and unready to hobnob. So I slip away to find my room.

## Arthur

Greta and I enter her room.

I must confess, it's fantastic. On the bed there is fresh white linen and pillows that seem bulging with goodness and give. But the walls are of mediaeval limestone, and there are leaded windows looking out over the hillside.

'Wow,' I say.

'Yeah,' says Greta. 'It's a good room. I suggest we don't leave it quite yet.'

At which point I drop my bag on to the floor, and she pushes me against the wall and she gives me a kiss of quiet extraordinary dirtiness.

Then she says: 'Why don't you go and freshen up? I want to send a couple of e-mails.'

So I go into the bathroom, where I start worrying.

I'm so out of practice at sex. Is it normal, for example, to send a few e-mails beforehand? And how long exactly does it take to send a couple of e-mails?

I reckon it's five minutes.

Should I shower?

Does that seem, at best, over-confident, or, at worst, a bit medical?

I shower.

In the shower, more dilemmas present themselves. Which products should I use? How clean should I be?

I shampoo my hair. I shampoo everything. I get cleaner than any man has ever been.

Leaving the shower, I wipe the mirror with my hand. I survey my body like someone surveying it for the first time . . .

I have a six pack, if I stand under the overhead light and really clench. It's a decent enough body, but is it ready for public display? This is the thing about sex. Yes. A stranger gets to unwrap your body like it's a precious parcel. But what happens if the parcel isn't what they want? What happens if their parcel isn't what you want? For all I know, Greta's naked body may be covered in a deep reddish fur. Can you break off sex to say: 'So this has been lovely, but I should head off'?

I really should get out of this bathroom.

But what do I wear? There's a white dressing gown on the door. Should I put that on? I don't want to. I'll look like I'm in a Dutch porn film.

I put my trousers and shirt back on. I leave the socks. I leave the bathroom.

Greta is standing by the bed. She's drinking some water and she's looking intently at me.

There's an awkward silence. Greta fills it.

'I just got an e-mail from Sarah Shelton,' she says. 'Apparently Em has just resigned.'

'Really?!'

'Yeah. So Shelton wants to get rid of all her stuff for next week. She doesn't want me to use your column.'

'Oh,' I say, trying to sound casual. On Monday I didn't even want to have a column. I still feel upset to lose it. I also feel really irked to be discussing it now.

'She was probably looking for an excuse to lose you anyway,' says Greta.

I say: 'Why?' I'm thinking: Can we stop talking?

''Cos you were basically saying simplify your life; don't travel, don't buy, love will blossom.'

'Can't you say that?' I say. I'm starting to sound a bit prickly now.

'Of course you can say that,' she says. 'But it sure doesn't delight the advertisers.'

'Can't a writer go against advertisers?'

'Sure,' she says. 'If he's Bill Hicks or Charlie Brooker. So that the revenue of the paper will go up, more than it will go down, because of the loss of advertisers. You're not Bill Hicks or Charlie Brooker.'

'OK.'

'Not yet anyway.'

'OK.'

I feel like walls are being built in front of my face. She's not just saying why I've failed; she's saying why I can never succeed.

'But don't worry,' she says. '*Daybreak* will have you back. So long as you promise not to shout at the host. Don't worry. We're going to make you *soooooo* hot.'

'Thank you,' I say. I'm not worrying about that. I'm thinking: Can we stop fucking talking about work? It seems so irrelevant.

Greta now turns away. She pulls the curtains shut. It doesn't really darken the room though. The evening is too young. Light is still spilling in. I can see plenty.

I see Greta as she walks slowly towards me, and we kiss.

Her kiss is slow and gentle and it calms me like liquid balm.

She's a very good lover. She takes off my shirt, kissing each shoulder as it appears. She folds my shirt in her hands, and she turns, slowly, and places it on a chair.

I don't know how to interpret that. Is she saying: I treat everything of yours with respect, even your shirt? Or is she saying: I don't like mess? Either way, my concentration is broken for a moment, and I think of Polly. Where is she right now? She might be next door. How am I going to tell her I'm here? Or should I just hide out the whole night in this room?

Greta kisses me again.

There's a funky garlicky taste to her mouth. Greta is here! Kissing me. For ten years she's been a fantasy woman; she's about to become familiar.

Then I stop thinking because Greta kneels reverently before me. Her hands gently tickle round my back. She kisses my stomach. She starts to unbutton my belt.

Ah.

I feel uncomfortable about . . . that part of me. It's of a decent size. I have no shame on that score. What gets me is the sheer ugliness of the thing. It looks so very organic. It looks like a big mushroom you'd see growing from the side of a tree in the woods.

Very slowly, Greta pulls my belt through the loops on my jeans. This isn't right! *I'm not ready!*

To be honest, I am still a little thrown by the conversation we just had. I'm trying to get it straight in my head . . . It's not – it's really *not* – that I wanted to sleep with Greta because I wanted a column in the paper. I didn't. *Really*, I didn't. But I thought that sex with her would change everything. I thought that I'd enter her magic vagina, and I'd come out into a world where I'd be instantly connected and inspired and opportunities would come, easy as balloons in the breeze. But I see that nothing's changed. I'm still me . . . I'm still confused. I'm still powerless. I get jobs, and I lose them, through factors that have nothing to do with me. I'm about to become the lover of Greta Kay. But I'm still the same person. I'm a thirty-six-year-old man. And I've got three children. And I'm married to Polly Midgley.

'Greta,' I say. I look down at her. I am going to remember this for the rest of my life. Her beautiful face kissing the fly of my trousers.

She says: 'What?'

I stroke some hair behind her ear. 'I'm nervous,' I say.

Greta kisses the front of my jeans. 'It's just sex,' she says. 'Don't be nervous.'

She begins to undo my buttons.

I shut my eyes. In my mind I'm back in my flat in New Malden and Polly is undressing me for the first time. I remember it so clearly – that moment when she pulled me towards her and I wanted to enter her. But it wasn't just sex. It's never just sex. I didn't just want to feel her softly gripping me in my most private place. In that moment I wanted everything about her. I wanted her hopes. I wanted her fears. I wanted her past. I wanted her future. I wanted her babies. I wanted her – my love, Polly Pankhurst.

'Greta,' I say.

'What?'

'I need to stop.'

She looks up at me.

'Why?' she says.

'Because,' I say, 'I'm married. And because I've realised that I've spent the last ten years yearning for you and blaming my wife for something that was not her fault.'

'It's OK,' she says, standing. 'You lost me on "married".'

**Polly**

How do you make yourself enjoy something?

Be in the moment, Arthur always says. (Where else could I be? 1922?) I've spent the whole week imagining what might happen at this party. But now I'm here, I'm not connecting with anyone I meet.

I meet Hugo, James's son. Maybe one day he'll have his father's confidence but now he's a teenager. He has a mumbling drawling voice, and hides his hands in his sleeves, and there's something about the slow way he moves that's reminiscent of one of those aged wasps that you sometimes see in winter-time, squatting on some bread. He's also quite remarkably posh. He tells me he's 'geng into falm'. I say: 'Sorry?' He says he's 'geng into falm'. I realise he's saying he's *going into film*. Great! I'm thinking, it's just what the world needs – another arty man who feels he's too precious to work.

Annabel appears – James's teenage daughter. She's buzzing

around like a hornet, looking sickeningly good in Gucci. She stops by her brother to say: 'I don't know *why* Dad said Gervaise couldn't come! There's, like, two hundred people here, and I don't know a single one of them!' Whereupon I introduce myself. 'I saw you at my mum's party on Sunday,' I say, sticking out my hand. She glances at my palm a moment, like that's yet another problem she has to deal with, then she buzzes off. Bitch.

I feel taken aback by her rudeness. If Arthur were here, I'd tell him I want to go.

Where the fuck is Arthur? I know I told him to go, but there was something so infuriating about how he trotted eagerly away to find Greta. Is he with her now? What is he doing?

I don't want to think about him.

I'm also thinking about the kids. Arthur's mum is with them. There's a text from her saying everyone's OK. But that doesn't seem to be enough. I'd like to speak to her.

Then I suddenly get furious . . . Come on, I say to myself. You've finally made it here. Stop standing around texting about childcare like you're some downtrodden suburban frump. Turn your phone off, get yourself a drink, and work a bit of magic.

I walk over to the drinks table which is standing beside a large yew hedge. Standing next to it are two extraordinary women. From behind they look like teenagers – blonde hair, skinny legs. But as they turn I see they're sixty at least . Well . . . parts of them are. I've rarely seen so much cosmetic surgery.

They catch my eye.

'Hi, I'm Polly,' I say.

They both look at me. I'm guessing they've both had Botox injections this morning. It's given them a placid, surprised look, which is strangely charming.

'I'm Frizi,' says Frizi.

'And I'm Yoren,' says Yoren.

Their accents are impossible to locate. German, mixed with American, mixed with Dutch? I realise I've heard their names before.

'Oh!' I say. 'James told me about you! He says you guys are in charge of all the interior design here.'

'Well!' says Yoren. 'I am just in charge of textiles. Frizi is queen of everything else.'

At this Frizi smiles proudly, as far as she is able. Her pleasure is endearing. At the same time, I'm thinking, I hope your interior design holds together better than your face; you've ripped out all your original features.

'I understand there's a meadow,' I say, 'that still needs to be worked on.'

'Oh, yes,' says Frizi. 'You should talk to James about it. He wants to show you round. James!'

She calls to him.

About ten feet away, he's listening to someone who's clearly telling a long anecdote. He's nodding at them, politely, but his attention turns to me. He's wearing a white suit and red tie. He looks great, although of course it's not his looks that make him so attractive, it's his energy. He seems so certain. He looks at me again with a twinkle in his eye. He thirstily drains a glass of champagne. He places the glass on a tray. He makes his excuses to his interlocutor. He approaches me like a battleship cutting through water. Once more his hand is on my back.

'James,' I say. 'Are you enjoying your party?'

'I'm loving it,' he says. 'I read an internet survey this week. Happiest professions, apparently, are hairdressers and masseurs.

Humans like making each other happy.'

'Who are the least happy?' I ask.

'Architects,' he says. 'Poor buggers train for seven years so they can design new palaces in Abu Dhabi. End up doing side extensions in Ashford.'

A waiter's coming by. James grabs another drink and drains it like a thirsty dog.

'Come on,' he says, in his calm, deep voice. 'I'll show you the grounds.'

'Great,' I say.

As he places his hand on the small of my back again, his fingertips are cold from the glass.

## Arthur

Greta has gone into the party.

I've seen Em. She's got a room a few doors away. She's about to have a bath. She says Polly's at the party. I'm going to go down and find her in a minute. I need to speak to her before anything happens between her and James. I need to tell her we're in danger of making a terrible mistake. I need to tell her I have blamed her for things, but I want never, ever to do it again. I want to tell her I love her. But will she listen? I'm going to have to make the greatest love speech since Will Shakespeare told the Dark Lady to shag him. I don't feel ready for it yet though. I need confidence. I need inspiration.

Luckily Malcolm gave me some weed.

I go out the front of the hotel, looking for a quiet place to smoke it.

That's where I see Dan.

He's just got out of a cab. He's crashing about on the gravel with his big mole. Even from twenty feet away, I can see he's pissed. He takes some money out of his pocket, he hands it to the cabbie, and then he heads towards the hotel, calling over his shoulder: 'Thank you *so* much!'

Behind him the cabbie says: 'Actually . . . that ain't the right amount!'

Dan has seen me, and he's giving me a cheerful wave.

'Actually that ain't the right amount!' says the cabbie again.

Now Dan turns and looks at him with confusion. Then back to me. Then he says: 'Maaaaaate, don't suppose you can lend me a tenner?'

I can. I step forward and pay the cabbie off. I rejoin Dan. He fumbles in his pocket. He pulls out some battered cigarettes. He holds the packet in front of his face and nods at it. I offer him a light. He turns to me.

'Maaaaaaaaaaaaate,' he says again.

Wow. He's really drunk.

He frowns. 'Where is everyone?' he asks.

'Most of them are out the back,' I say. 'But Em is upstairs in the bath.'

'Is she?' says Dan. He seems delighted by that. 'I need to talk to her.'

'Yes,' I say. 'Do you know what you want to say to her?'

'Yes,' he says, happily. 'I want to ask her to marry me.'

Goodness! I never expected that. He's now trying to get a cigarette out of his packet. The first one he finds is broken so he drops it on the ground.

'Where have you been?' I ask.

'Launch party for Aston Martin.'

'What was it like?'

'Brilliant car.'

'No . . . What was the party like?'

'Great. There was free champagne and . . . what do you call those things in pastry?'

'Vol au vents?'

'Vol au vents,' he says. He has trouble saying that, but he goes for it again. 'Vol au vents,' he says, 'being served by really hot Eastern European catering staff who were dressed like Bond girls.' He grins. 'One of them gave me her number.'

'Right,' I say. 'Why did you take someone's number?'

He realises he's made an error.

'Well, I might want . . . catering,' he says. Then he realises he's gone too far. 'Hey, listen . . . mate . . . I more asked just . . . out of habit . . . You know what I mean?'

'Not really,' I say.

'Em *knows* this,' he says. 'It used to be the . . . moment of victory used to be the moment you slipped their pants off. That little moment when they lifted their hips off the bed. That moment when you think, Wehay! Bets are off, I'm coming in. But then I thought . . . no . . . once you've got their number that's gonna happen, so it's getting the number. That's enough.'

'How many numbers do you get?'

'Just . . . one or two a week.'

I am staring at Dan.

My head is whirring furiously. Everything he's saying is making me think: Nooooooo, there is no way on earth Em should marry you. You're a human cockroach. But I'm also thinking: What right do I have to interfere? But then I think that maybe I don't need to help Em make up her mind. But I could at least warn her what he's going to say.

Dan's managed to get a cigarette out and he's managed not to break it. The trouble is, he's holding the wrong end. He's now trying to work out how to get it into his mouth.

'Here,' I say. I give him my lighter. 'You can have that. I'll tell Em you're here.'

'Mate,' he says. 'Don't . . . *Don't!*' he says again.

I want to say to him: Listen, I'm a changed man. These days I'm not taking orders off anyone. Particularly if they're drunk fucks like you. I don't though. I just go into the hotel. I run up the stairs. I want to get to Em before Dan does. Also before she gets in the bath.

## Polly

James has led me to a wooden door in the limestone wall.

'What's behind here?' I say.

He lifts one eyebrow as if to say wouldn't-you-like-to-know, and then he opens it.

'These used to be the cloisters,' he says, as we step into them.

'Wow,' I say, as I see them. The arched walkway is smallish, only about thirty yards long to each side of the courtyard, but exceptionally beautiful despite the crumbling stone. At one side of the court there's a single apple tree – it looks more random than planned so probably self-seeded. James shuts the door. We're alone.

'The main hotel building was the Abbot's House,' he says.

'Big house for an Abbot,' I say.

'Well, I expect he liked to have room to entertain his friends and a few dozen choirboys. And as he walked out into his grounds, the Abbot would come here.'

'What are cloisters actually for?' I ask.

'Prayer, I think. Reflection,' says James, with a naughty twinkle in his eye. 'But we've given them a slightly different use.' At this point, I realise there are doors in the cloister walls. 'Round here you've got every kind of treatment you could wish for – massage, mud treatments, pedicure.'

James tries to open a treatment room. It's locked. I stalk on like a cross peacock, giving him a bit of a look.

'What?' he says.

'Well,' I say, 'really I'm no prude, but I'm not sure you're preserving the sanctity of the place.'

'Well, you could say treatments are the modern form of prayer,' says James. 'Ultimately it's all about trying to feel good, trying to feel calm.'

'Though in a traditional cloister,' I say, 'you're communicating with God. Here you're communicating with a Filipino lady who's rubbing your feet with a loofah.'

James smiles admiringly at me.

'Do you like being rude?' he says.

'Yes,' I say, looking into his brown eyes. 'I suppose I do.' We're now walking side by side. I look again at the apple tree. The actual apples are only small, part-formed and at the stage where a bird or a chance breeze can ruin their promise. Even though I'm now turned away from James, I'm still intensely aware of him. I feel like I'm being sucked towards him. I've never met a man with such naked and powerful appetites.

'Polly,' he says. 'I've thought about you every minute since we met on Sunday.'

I glance back at him quickly. How does he do it? Instantly my heart is beating hard. At the same time I'm wary. I don't know if I'm ready for this.

'And to be honest', he says, 'I've thought about you ever since you were twenty-four.'

'What?' I say. 'But that was ten years ago!'

'Well,' he says, grinning more, 'not all the time. But . . . whenever I was single, you were certainly on The List.'

'Was I?' I say.

'Oh, yeah,' he says. He's giving a schoolboy grin. He's clearly very excited by The List.

'What happens to people on The List?'

'In my mind, I summon you,' he says, 'like I'm a famous film director. "Polly Pankhurst," I say, "come in, in your hockey outfit . . . And if you could take it off . . . And stand there next to Julie Seagrove . . . "'

Right. 'Who was Julie Seagrove?' I say. 'Dare I ask?'

'Oh . . . my first girlfriend.'

'Oh, right. What happened to her?'

'She got off with me, let me feel her minge, then she chucked me.'

To be honest, James, that's way too much information.

'Oh,' I say. How does he want me to respond to that? 'Poor you.'

'Well,' he says breezily, 'I got her back in the end. Took a few years but I did it.'

'What did you do?'

'I fucked her sister,' he says cheekily. 'And her mum.'

'I'm sorry!???' I say. That one caught me unawares. 'James,' I say levelly. 'To be honest, what you just said . . . didn't sound good.'

'Well,' he says, 'it's all about how you present it, isn't it? You could also say: her mum had split from her dad, and I was a confidence-boosting first shag. And I had an affair with Lucy

Seagrove years later. And she did all right out of it.'

'Did she?'

'I gave her a Merc convertible.'

'Did you?'

'And crabs,' says Hammond. 'If I remember rightly.'

He seems to be under the impression he's being funny.

'James,' I say. 'That also wasn't good.'

'I'm sorry,' he says, and looks at me with such sincerity. 'This is why I need you,' he says. 'You can save me from myself.'

We've walked round the cloisters now, reaching another wooden door. He takes hold of the handle, then he faces me. I stand expectantly. I really want to get through that door. I'm suddenly feeling too old for this semi-saucy flirtation. I just want to see the bloody meadow. All week I've been imagining what it'll be like. I just want to see it.

'So,' says James, 'what do you think of the cloisters?'

'I like the apple tree,' I say.

'Do you?' he says.

'Look at it,' I say, turning back. 'I love an apple tree. I love the blossom of course. And the symbolism is exciting.'

'Symbolism?'

'Well . . .' I say. 'Garden of Eden. The apple tree is the first tree. And the apple is the fruit that's so delicious you'd sacrifice innocence to eat it. I like all that. But mainly I love their jagged shape. And the way they get covered with that blue-green moss that looks like it belongs in the sea.'

'Oh,' says James. 'Well, I wish you'd said that before.' And at this point he opens the wooden door. 'This is the meadow I've been telling you about. There used to be a whole orchard of apple trees through here.'

We step through.

To the right is the car park. It's massive. A plain expanse of tarmac with the tiniest amount of shade provided by a few slightly pubic pine trees.

To the left is where the orchard obviously was. It's an area about the size of a football field. All around it there are big tractor trails which expose the orange clay. And there are line upon line of tree stumps. You can still see the apple trees themselves. They're over to the right, in a big pile.

I've always said I love gardens, but I've never felt it so strongly as at this moment.

The orchard has been ruined. It's been massacred like a village in wartime. Its houses have been burned and its women have been raped. I feel weak.

'James,' I say. 'Why did you take out all the apple trees?'

'To make room for your magnolias,' he says.

'They're not my magnolias!' I protest. 'I hate magnolias!'

'On Monday I asked you if you liked them,' he says. 'You said yes.'

'That was entirely theoretical!' I say. I'm really angry with him now.

'Well, I like to work quickly and instinctively,' he says.

'You need to look at a place,' I say, 'before you change it. You need to feel what's there! What's working!'

'The orchard was never going to stay anyway!' says James. 'This is basically the only place you can land a chopper.'

'Land a chopper?!' I say.

'This is a gridlocked country,' says James. 'Soon everyone rich will be flying. And there's no point in having a high-end eco resort if people can't get there.'

'James,' I say. 'You're a fucking yob!'

'Yeah,' he says. 'But I'm a yob with money and taste.'

'Not much taste,' I say.

At this, James's face has got that smirky look boys get when they're told off by their teacher.

He says: 'You're really sexy when you're cross!'

I say: 'Fuck off!'

I square up to him like I'm about to slap him. If he were Arthur, he'd scurry off at this point like a cat who's just spotted the dog. But James isn't scared of me. He holds my right hand.

'Polly,' he says. 'Why don't you come on the payroll? At this point I've got six properties being developed. I've got twenty more that are under consideration. We need to get you in early. You can save me from my mistakes.'

I look at him astonished.

'Are you offering me a job?' I say.

'Yeah!' he says. 'Why not?'

He's still holding my right hand. I look, amazed, at his swarthy brown face. The trouble is, I'm starting to find him attractive again. In his eyes he's got that Hammond twinkle. He's also got a naked desire I've not seen in anyone's face in a long time. He tilts his head slightly to the right and his lips open.

Oh, Lord!

I suddenly realise it . . . He's about to kiss me! I'm standing beside some trees he's massacred, and some cloisters he's turned into a treatment centre, and he wants to kiss me.

*Can I kiss him?*

I think it through . . . This is James Hammond! He is my Road Not Travelled, and he is handsome, and he is right here, and he is NOT my husband . . . *that treacherous, indecisive, tit-licking fucker.*

*Where is Arthur? Why did he go?!!* I realise I cannot kiss James. I must not kiss him. Not now. Not here.

But sometimes it's not all about thinking.

And in fact I make no resistance as he pulls me towards him and presses his manly lips to mine.

Bloody hell, it's quite a kiss.

It's more like an assault than a kiss. His lips press against mine, and he thrusts his tongue into my mouth. I feel like a house being hit by a tsunami. I feel swept away by something dirty but irresistibly powerful. Gates and doors are being blasted open. I feel I should take control, but for a few seconds I . . . relax and let him ravish me. For several seconds, my body is filled with a wild pleasure which feels so intense it can't possibly be wrong. His hands reach for my breasts.

'No,' I say. I push him away.

'What's the matter?' he says, looking thwarted.

'I'm just . . .' I say. 'I'm just . . . not that happy about this.'

'Oh,' says James, failing to hide a slight note of petulance in his voice. 'Only . . .'

'What?'

'Well, I've spent a lot of money on tonight, I want you to enjoy yourself.'

He appears to be saying: I've spent a lot of money, you should put out. Is he saying that? *Is he?* Either way, I'm feeling bothered. And confused. This was supposed to be the moment I saw my dream – the bank of green grass and the jasmine and the blackbird and the man who loves me. If it's not here, where is it? *Where?!*

James comes at me again.

Luckily there's a distraction.

Someone else comes through the cloister door. It's James's

son, holding a joint, followed by Annabel, the human hornet.

She looks at her dad. She looks at me. She can instantly see what's going on, and she isn't surprised. She's just angry.

But James isn't bothered at all.

'Hello, you guys!' he calls cheerily. 'I'll have that,' he says, removing the joint. 'Polly, we should get back to the party.'

And he springs back towards the cloisters, leaving me with Annabel.

She grabs my arm in a gesture which is horribly reminiscent of her father. Meanwhile she whispers furiously in my ear: 'Are you trying to fuck my dad?'

'I don't know,' I say. 'But I'm not sure he'd put up much resistance.'

**Em**

So here's an interesting situation . . .

I am in a towel. My body is wet from the bath. There is a tall handsome man at my bedroom door . . . I like this.

I say: 'Hello, big boy.'

Arthur says: 'Dan's here.'

I say: 'Oh.' Right. He's here.

'He's very drunk,' says Arthur.

'Oh,' I say again. 'Come in quickly.'

'But . . .'

'It's draughty in this hallway,' I say, and pull him into the room. Whereupon something goes wrong, and my towel falls off.

I hurriedly put my towel back on.

The news Dan's really pissed makes me feel strangely thrown. Actually I feel angry. Why doesn't anyone want to propose to me? What is *wrong* with me?

'And I thought I should warn you,' Arthur says, 'he wants to propose to you.'

'Really?'

I'm just thinking I'm not sure how I feel about this news, when we hear Dan in the stairway.

'Em!'

Arthur and I look into each other's eyes.

'Oh, fuck!' he whispers.

'What?'

'Dan told me twice not to speak to you,' whispers Arthur. 'What shall I do?'

'Just . . . go in the bathroom,' I whisper.

He heads to the bathroom, but then stops.

'Em!' he says. 'What are you going to say?'

'I don't know.'

### Arthur

Of course I immediately think: Why am I in the bathroom? Why did I do that?

If Dan finds me in here, should I say I came in to wash? Should I have a bath?

### Em

Dan comes into the room.

'Hey, babe,' he says.

He looks moderately handsome, and very drunk. He's wearing a grey suit he wears for work sometimes. It's not freshly pressed.

'Hello, Dan,' I reply.

He walks forward. He kisses me on the lips.

'You look gorgeous,' he says.

'Thank you.'

He tries to slip his hands inside the towel. I back away.

'No,' I say. 'We can't . . . We need to talk first.'

'What about?'

'You have to give me your answer.'

He looks at me. Then he gets down on one knee. 'Em, would you do me the honour,' he slurs, 'of becoming my husband?'

'What?!'

'I mean! Em . . .' Another pause. 'Would you . . . Would you do me the honour of becoming my wife?'

I pull him up.

I say: 'Yes.'

Arthur appears in the bathroom doorway. He mouths frantically: 'Are you sure?'

I wave him out impatiently.

Dan turns round.

'What was that?' he says.

'Nothing.'

He smiles.

'Really?' he says. 'Would you like to be my wife?'

And I say: 'Yes.'

Arthur comes out again. He's mouthing: 'Why?'

And this time I just shout at him: 'Arthur, for God's sake, what are you trying to say?'

Dan turns too. 'What *are* you trying to say?' he says.

And Arthur says: 'Do you know that, this very evening, he took another woman's phone number?'

Dan says: 'What did you tell her that for?'

I say to Dan: '*Why* did you take another woman's phone number?'

'Just . . .' says Dan. 'That's all I do. I just . . .'

'You take their numbers??!!' I say, astonished.

'Yeah!' he pleads. 'But . . . that's all I do. I just . . . *Nothing happens*! And . . . Em, that's the sort of thing I want to stop. I want to stop it all.'

'All of what?'

'You know . . . drink, coke, parties, clubs. All that standing in petrol stations at two a.m. eating Ginsters. All of it. I don't want it. I want you.'

'You want me,' I say, 'as an alternative to standing in a petrol station eating a Ginsters?'

He smiles, and says: 'Yeah.'

I say: 'It's not exactly "Shall I compare thee to a summer's day?", is it?'

'*I'm sorry*!' he says. 'For you, Em, I will clean myself up. I'm gonna really *try* to . . . .'

I look at him a long time. He does look handsome. He's got an imploring look in his eye like a lost Labrador.

I say: 'No.'

'What?' says Dan.

'I've changed my mind.'

'Why?!' he says furiously.

'I don't want you because you want a change,' I say. 'I want devotion. I want commitment. I want someone who'll throw themselves out of a plane for me.'

## Arthur

Dan stares at her with his mouth open.

Then he turns to me.

He says: 'She was going to marry me till you butted in. You twat.'

I say: 'Dan, don't call me a twat.'

'You're a fucking . . .' he walks towards me '. . . tit.' He pushes me in the chest.

'Don't,' I say. I'm keeping calm. 'I don't want to fight you, Dan.'

'Oh, yeah!' he says, pushing me in the chest again. 'Are you scared?'

'I am twice your size!' I say. 'And I'm trained in karate!'

'So am I!' he says, and he knuckles me really hard on the shoulder.

Oh, Lord. I back away from him, while running it through in my mind . . .

I'm aware he's behaving badly. I'm also aware he's just had his offer of marriage refused. It would seem harsh to follow that through with punching him in the face. But I'm sorely tempted.

Luckily, we're all diverted by a knock on the door.

Em goes and answers it. Whereupon her towel falls off again.

I edge to the door where I see the receptionist looking extremely pink-faced.

'Dinner will be served in two minutes,' he says. 'You should come down.'


**Polly**

Dinner is by the pool.

Two hundred guests, seated at twenty tables. The *placement* reveals much, I realise, about where I would rank in James's world were I to continue my relationship with him. He's on the next table, with his back to me.

I'm aware of what makes him so successful. He's totally,

[ 345 ]

psychopathically direct. He wants something, he gets it. And now he's turned his attention to the guests on his table. Doubtless they are people he wants to woo. Curiously enough, he's got Dan on his table. They have some connection, I don't know what exactly but doubtless it involves cars. Dan seems to hero-worship him. I can hear James behind me, laughing, flirting. He pays no attention to me at all. There are other people to pursue. He's finished with me for the moment.

I'm sitting next to a sixty-year-old Hungarian businessman who is called something hard-to-catch. Was it Ieer . . . Pier? I ask him twice, I still don't catch it. Pier's lips are fleshy and damp – they look like slugs – they're also set in a sneer of permanent disappointment. He seems disappointed by the wine. He seems offended by some issue connected to the glass. He starts dinner by sitting down in his place before everyone else. He picks tomatoes out of the salad. He then sucks them and spits them on to his side plate. I'm out of touch, but I don't think that's good manners. I don't really have a problem with 'Ieer', however, until he reaches over, and – while discoursing on the shortcomings of Latin labour ('I work with Portuguese, I work with Spanish, but they have no education') – brushes the back of his hand, quite deliberately, over my tit.

I get up.

Actually several people are getting up. Dinner is finished. James is standing on a little platform beside the pool. He seems poised to make a speech. The guests fall silent.

'Welcome to Bodsham Abbey,' he says. 'They say you should always start a speech with a joke. So here goes . . . Where do you find a dog with no legs?' Hammond pauses for effect. 'Where you left him,' he says.

There's sycophantic laughter round the tables.

James then launches into a surprisingly boring speech. He says things like: 'So by September we had the whole site stripped down to the shell . . .' People are listening patiently. They know where they are with a bit of property talk. I'm grateful myself. My head is bulging with information. I need to unpackage it. I need to make a list. I mentally start one.

1. My dream was a mirage – the peaceful orchard where I would hear blackbirds and find love. And . . .

2. A Hungarian just touched my tit.

3. James did slightly treat me like a whore by expecting me to put out because he'd 'spent a lot of money on tonight'. I feel very different about that one grand consultancy fee now. I've been bought apparently. Bought for one grand. I am disgusted with myself.

4. His daughter is an evil teenage hornet. She saw me kissing her dad. And more pertinently . . .

5. His daughter is right next to me now. She's hovering close, keen on administering her lethal sting.

On the stage, James wraps up his speech.

'Enjoy tonight,' he says. 'In particular, enjoy the entertainment.' He leaves the stage to an obsequious round of applause.

Whereupon the entertainment starts. Well . . .

Loud music comes on – Jean Michel Jarre-type music, the sort of stuff you'd expect to see at a magic show – and a big-breasted woman walks on to the stage, naked but for a thong and a nine-foot python.

Now . . .

All credit to the girl, she does, I must confess, make an entrance. Some men are drooling. Personally I'm thinking: Oh, great, a display of semi-ironic porn. This isn't an act chosen with women in mind, but I don't want to look like a prude. I glance round and I do what I notice most of the other women are doing: I plaster a smile on my face and I watch politely.

And the girl does, undeniably, hold our attention, as she invites the snake to move, very slowly, down her arms and towards her breasts. The trouble is, the snake is in no hurry to reach them. Perhaps he'd be more stimulated if there were a couple of nice juicy mice taped to her tits. There's nothing *wrong* with the snake. He just doesn't do anything *fast*, and, after a couple of minutes, you do feel you've got the gist of his act. You feel that unless he can tell a few jokes, the snake's going to lose the crowd.

And indeed that starts to happen.

James himself – now standing a few feet in front of me – leads the disquiet. At first he enthuses about the snake to his companion – 'beautiful animal, the snake, so intelligent' – but then he's joined by an obscenely young woman with whom he starts whispering and laughing and touching. And in no time there's still a half-naked woman with a big snake round her neck, but people are now discussing dinner, and holidays, and business.

I feel extremely uncomfortable. I want to get far, far away from this place. I want to be home. I'd actually like to be at home, listening to Arthur tell me about Arsenal. I can't believe I told him to go. Why did I do that? I'd like to be in our messy kitchen, at home, with pants on the radiator and Arthur rhapsodising about Martin Keown. I feel desperate to leave.

At the same time I feel lonely and middle-aged. I don't want to be like some priggish old maid who leaves the party at 9.30. I've sacrificed so much to be here tonight. I should enjoy myself. I should chat.

To my left is a man who looks like Leonard Cohen – long nose, hooded eyes – except he's got long greying hair in a ponytail. He gives me a friendly smile.

I say: 'How much do you think the snake gets paid for this?'

'He don't get paid,' says the man, in a Wiltshire accent. 'He gets a rabbit once a month.'

I say: 'He needs a better agent.'

At this point, the man says: 'I'm his agent. He's my snake.'

And then the music changes, and the snake man becomes far more interested in the act. 'They ain't done this bit before,' he says.

I find that astounding. 'This is the first time they've done this act?!!'

'They have danced together twice before,' he says. 'This is the first time they've swum.'

'And . . .' I say. 'Do snakes like swimming?'

At this point, the snake man's expertise seems to crumble somewhat. 'Well,' he says. 'That depends really . . . .'

I now look aghast as the woman climbs into the pool.

As soon as the snake hits the water, he freaks out. He waves his head around furiously. Strangely he doesn't look scary. He looks like a cross boy. 'Owwww!!!' he seems to be saying. 'I've got really *stingy eyes*!!!'

Throughout her entire act, the dancer has had the strained, frozen smile of the magician's assistant. Now her smile becomes unusually desperate, and I'm actually worried for her. How is she going to resolve her act? I'm also – let's be honest – alarmed at the possibility that the python might get genuinely out of control. The snake has only got to swim a couple of yards and he could be running amok amongst the crowd. At the very least that could cause an ugly stampede. At the worst he could, shortly, be throttling his first victim.

No one else seems worried. They're not watching. They're not just ignorant, they're incurious. To my right, Yoren starts discussing something which sounds like Die Forge Diet. 'Carla Bruni is on this diet,' she informs the person beside her.

I'm so tense.

So it's unfortunate that this is the moment I become aware again of the human hornet. She's hovering next to me, preparing to sting. Her skinny elbow is brushing against mine. I sense her quivering rage. And I make the mistake of looking her in the eye.

Whereupon she says: 'You won't last.' I don't say anything to that. I can't see much will be gained from a conversation with her. 'Because you've got tiny tits,' she says, 'and a big arse.'

'That's undeniable,' I say. 'But what I have got is a family that love me.'

'So . . .' she says '. . . what are you doing here?'

Oh, God. I feel such intense hatred for the girl, I must get away. I put my hand on her shoulder and I move her slightly to one side as I prepare to get away from her. 'Hey!!' she says. 'Do not push me!'

Oh, really, I didn't push her. But I also didn't want to cause a scene.

I head towards James who's now deep in conversation with his under-age suitor. I need protection. I can't believe Annabel would do anything in front of her dad.

He sees me coming.

'Are you OK?' he says, a bit offhand.

I really want to keep his attention. I'm terrified Annabel's about to cause a scene.

'Er, yes,' I say. 'Though I just feel . . . there's a woman in the pool with a snake. We should at least watch.'

'It's a beautiful animal,' James informs me. 'So intelligent.'

Fuck James Hammond. He's wandering round the party saying the same thing to everyone, but – it annoys me – he still doesn't actually *look* at the snake. I'd like to smack his face. The planet is being destroyed by the greed of people like the Hammonds, and they don't even enjoy it.

Annabel has followed me.

'You pushed me,' she says.

She's about to attack me in front of a large crowd of strangers. It doesn't get much worse than this.

'Annabel,' I say, 'I did not push you.' I hold up my hands to placate her.

She walks into them. 'Don't fucking push me,' she says, and pushes me back, quite hard. She doesn't *care* about making a scene. I'm actually stumbling towards the pool. 'Don't you *dare* push me!' she says. She's seeing the opportunity, and she's justifying it: she wants to push me into the pool. I don't have any other option.

I move fast. I grab her. I make sure I push her in first.

She falls towards the water with an extraordinary shriek of outrage. You can tell that, as she goes, she's already planning the lawsuit.

We've really caused a scene now.

Everyone's watching.

James steps forward and grips my upper arm.

'Polly,' he says. 'There's a snake in that water.'

'I know,' I say. 'Beautiful animal, so intelligent. Like your daughter, in fact. They should get together and have green-skinned babies who gobble up rabbits and cash.'

Now, for a second, Hammond loses his temper. 'Polly,' he says. 'You've got no class.'

'Don't talk to me about class,' I say. 'You found an ancient orchard; you made a car park.'

'Polly,' he commands. 'Control yourself.'

Of course my head is bulging with a hundred things to say on the subject of control. But actually I say nothing. I just jab his hip with the tip of my toe. And Hammond totters and falls back into the pool. And as he goes there's a look of horror on his face, and he lands six feet away from the snake.

There's a stunned silence all around, during which I walk away as quickly as I can. I reach the edge of the crowd, desperate to escape.

But then someone grabs me.

It's Dan. 'Polly!' he says, gripping my arm so tight it hurts. 'What the *fuck* are you doing?'

Oh, no. I want to get away. I need to get away.

And then something even more surprising happens . . .

*Arthur appears!*

'Arthur!' I say. 'What are you doing here?'

He doesn't answer though.

Dan wrenches me to him. 'Polly,' he says. 'That was completely out of order.'

I've never been more grateful for my big, bad-tempered husband.

Arthur steps forward, and he punches Dan in the face. Hard.

'Polly!' he shouts. 'Run!'

And I kick off my shoes, and I run.

## Arthur

Right away, I'm feeling like Jason Bourne.

It was a beautiful punch. Dan's down. He's clinging to the floor like a Dover sole.

I glance back at the gathering. Most of the guests are just staring at us aghast. But I see the head waiter talking to his assistants. Oh, dear. We seem to have the makings of a vigilante force.

And meanwhile James Hammond is clambering from the pool.

I turn. Polly is running for the exit. Good.

I sprint after her.

We dash across the garden and into the lobby of the hotel.

Where she stops.

'Hang on!' she says. 'I just want to get my bag!'

'What??!!' I shout.

I shouldn't be surprised! Polly is absolutely incapable of leaving a place! Of course she wants to get her bag! Before leaving, she'll probably want to change her top!

'It's the red leather one!' she says to Reception.

'Why do you need your fucking bag?!' I shout.

'For a start,' she says, 'it's got my things.'

'Right,' I pant. I see she's got some logic on her side. As usual she has thought this through. But I have logic on my side too. And indeed, just as the receptionist hands over Polly's bag, James Hammond arrives.

He's angry and wet and escorted by two security guards. OK. They're Wiltshire security guards. One of them looks about eighteen and he's got jug ears. I know a man doesn't fight with his ears, but the impression he gives is poor.

'Polly!' shouts James. 'What the fuck did you do that for?'

'Because,' shouts Polly, 'you treated me like a fucking whore!'

She steps forward and slaps him.

'And you enjoyed every minute of it,' says Hammond. 'You stupid bitch.'

Polly slaps him again.

Whereupon he slaps her back.

Up to now, I've tried to remain calm. I've tried to remain gallant and impartial. But I'm very worked up. Plus I've actually trained for this moment. I was in the Dulwich College karate team. I was a green belt. And actually I seem to have been better trained than the two security guards. They blunder towards Polly, too slow for a warrior like me. We didn't just stand around at Dulwich College. We learned to act.

I jump-kick one in the face.

He falls.

I land.

Then, getting a nice swivel from the hips, just as we practised so many times, I punch the other one on the side of the face.

James Hammond now turns his attention to me.

Too late. I'm a large dangerous man. I've got hate in my heart, and I've got right on my side.

'Just calm down!' shouts Hammond. 'We can work this out!'

And maybe he's right. Maybe there is a diplomatic solution to be found.

But in the meantime I do just kick him very hard in the balls.

## Polly

At that moment I see through the window four more security guards outside on the drive, running towards Reception.

'Arthur!' I shout. 'Run!'

And we sprint back into the garden.

We don't go near the party though.

We run for the door in the wall, and we run into the cloisters. I'm terrified security men will enter them from the other side. But we reach the door unchallenged. There's no one else there.

We sprint across the meadow past the pile of felled apple trees.

We run over to the big wall.

## Arthur

I turn.

It's almost dark where we are.

No one seems to be following us yet.

But I'm sure they will.

How the fuck are we going to get over this bloody great wall?

It's about nine foot high, and the bricks look quite crumbly but they don't give handholds.

We run beside it till we find a tree.

'Polly,' I say, panting, 'use the tree to climb up.'

'What?' she says. 'I can't see how to.'

'OK,' I say. 'Step on to my shoulders and climb up.'

I crouch down. She steps on to my shoulders. I straighten. Now she's holding the top of the wall. I push her feet and she clambers up.

I cling on to a branch of the tree and manoeuvre myself up on to the wall.

We look over and down. It's dark. It's hard to see how high we are. But it looks to be at least ten foot down.

I look back into the car park.

A whole crowd of security men have appeared. They have torches.

'Polly!' I say. 'We need to jump now!'

'I can't!' she says. 'It's too far.'

'So just lower yourself off,' I say. 'And then drop the last bit.'

'I can't . . .' she says. 'I could break my leg.'

I look back. Some of the security guards are coming this way.

'Hurry!' I say.

Polly lowers herself off the wall. Soon she's dangling off it, still holding on with her hands.

'Go on then,' I say.

She looks up at me, terrified.

'I can't!' she says. 'It's too far!'

I quickly lie on my stomach on the wall, and cling to it with my left arm.

'If you hold on to my hand,' I say, 'I can lower you another couple of feet.'

She takes one hand off the wall, and holds my hand. And then the other one.

I see right away this was a terrible plan. I try to lower her, but my arm isn't strong enough. She's dangling off the end of it and it fucking hurts. I think I'm about to dislocate my elbow. And my hands are sweaty. My grip isn't strong enough to hold her. She's still clinging on though.

'Polly,' I say, 'you've *got* to let go.'

'I'm scared!' she says.

'Let go!' I whisper furiously. 'Just fucking let go! Let go!'

My arm is killing me.

And there's another problem.

I'm lying on top of the wall, clinging on to it with my left hand.

And the stone crumbles

And there's an awful moment when I fall, after Polly, off the wall.

I seem to be falling for far, far too long.

## Polly

I actually land safely.

I think it must have only been another couple of feet down.

I land on some grass.

But Arthur fares less well.

He falls down beside me. There's a hideous muffled thump as he hits the ground.

I go straight over to him. He's lying very still in the moonlight. He's on his back.

I touch his face. 'Arthur!' I whisper. 'Are you OK?'

But he doesn't move!

And at that point I realise he's bleeding heavily from a wound on the back of his head.

It's very strange. I've spent the whole week panicking about things that were unimportant. Now something truly awful has happened, I'm calm. Still, I'm running it through in my head, very fast.

I think: Head wound . . . must bind tight . . . I use a blouse from my bag.

I think: Thank God I've got my fucking bag! I pull out my phone to dial 999.

I think: Please God. Please please please. I would do absolutely anything to save him.

## Em

You've got to hand it to Polly. She's made quite an impact on this party.

She and Arthur have removed several of the leading players from the scene. James Hammond was last observed, in Reception, being kicked in the balls. He's not been back since. Nor has Dan. I'm quite glad about that. It's saved me the trouble of talking to him again.

Everyone else is discussing the incident.

'Who was the guy who kicked James?' asks the former celebrity chef.

'That was Arthur Midgley,' I inform him.

'Why did he do it?' he asks.

'There are several reasons for that,' I say.

'What are they?' says the former celebrity chef.

I begin to tell the whole story. I quickly gather quite an audience.

'Hang on,' says a PR person who once handled Martine McCutcheon, 'isn't Arthur Midgley the guy who writes *Learn Love in a Week*?'

'Yes,' I affirm.

'How is punching people consistent with his theories?' she asks.

'It's something, I imagine, to do with fighting for the person you love.'

**Polly**

Yes. Obviously I am aware of all the First Aid courses I've done.

I know there's one thing you must not do when there's the possibility of a back injury: you mustn't move the victim. But I saw Arthur fall. I think he hit the soft grass and his back was flat. I'm more bothered by the way he's bleeding profusely from the back of his skull. I think his head hit a stone.

I'm just dialling 999 when I see a passing taxi. I wave it down.

The taxi driver is a little unsure of the wisdom of having a bleeding man in his cab. But I persuade him by screaming: 'PLEASE-help-me-or-he's-going-to-fucking-DIE!!'

After that we both lift Arthur into the cab, and we speed to Salisbury General Hospital and we drag Arthur's bleeding lifeless body into Reception.

I'm happy to say that gets their instant attention.

In moments a team of people in green outfits have descended on Arthur like a flock of seagulls on some chips. He's lifted on to a trolley. He's wheeled fast down brightly-lit corridors. As we go, a middle-aged doctor asks me for the facts of the case. I try to explain.

Arthur's rushed through A & E.

He's wheeled straight on to a ward.

I'm told to sit outside in the corridor.

I sit down outside the ward on a red plastic chair. There is a nurse guarding the swing doors. To my left there's an old man. All of us are totally silent.

I sit there, saying in my head again and again and again: Oh, please, God, don't let him die.

I don't know what else to do.

I pull out my phone and I fiddle with it.

Whereupon something awful happens . . .

I click on to my photos. I see something that looks like it's my vision, the thing I've been wanting all week – the bank of grass and the apple trees all bathed in light. I'm confused. How can I have a picture of something that was in my head? It takes me a moment to realise this is a picture of my own garden. It's the one I took when I was showing it to James. So of course I'm now seeing something crushingly obvious: I was looking for something I had all along. And now I'm about to lose it. I am such an idiot.

'You must turn off your phone,' says the nurse.

I look round.

'Sorry,' I say.

I put the phone away.

Now I just sit.

I wonder what the hell they're doing in there. I wonder how much blood he lost. I wonder what the hell I'm going to tell the children.

And if he dies, I wonder how the hell I'm going to cope.

I'm hardly breathing, I'm so tense.

I sit for ten minutes. After that, I can't bear it any more. I ignore the nurse and poke my head into the ward. There are about eight people in there. They've got Arthur on his front, and they're looking at the back of his head.

A nursing sister sees me, and waves frantically. 'You MUST get out,' she instructs.

I go back. I sit down again on the red plastic chair.

Shortly afterwards a nurse comes running out of the ward. She's got an ashen face. She ignores me. She runs round the corner and disappears through some swing doors. Moments later she reappears. Now she has an older man with her who looks like a senior doctor. She also has a cylinder of oxygen on a wheeled stand.

It's at this point that it hits me with a mystic certainty . . .

I see that Arthur is about to die.

It's supposed to be that, before you die, you see your life flashing before you. But now it's Arthur about to die, and it's his life that I see. And it's awful. I shut my eyes and I see it all.

I see him on top of the wall, saying: 'Let go! You've got to let go!'

I see him standing outside the church, smiling and looking so happy because we were about to get married.

I see him holding my hand as I give birth to Robin.

I see him beside the stage at the children's school, grinning with pride because Robin is dancing.

I see him walking away from Bar Italia looking big and lovely.

I see him cycling past a library in the sunshine looking handsome.

And then, for a moment, I'm seeing the man he could be, if only he could survive tonight.

I see him taking the children to school.

I see him being attentive to them in kitchens.

I see him cooking them mince.

I see him making speeches at their weddings.

I see him at New Year's parties and he's dancing very badly and very happily.

I see him as an old man and he's sitting in a garden and he's being funny.

I also see that, in all these versions of Arthur, I absolutely love him, and I'd do anything to keep him alive.

And then I see that he's not going to make it, and I burst into tears. The grief just erupts out of my stomach and the tears run down my cheeks and I'm screaming silently. It's most odd. I feel that Arthur's soul is leaving his body. I feel he's right in front of me, saying goodbye. I feel like I want to hold his head. I want to make him stay. In my mind I'm saying, 'Arthur, you stupid, messy, bastard, I *love you*! I love you so much! You cannot leave me! Please stay!' But I know it's not enough.

And I'm just thinking this when the doctor appears. He has blood on his green smock.

'You're the wife?' he says.

'Yes!' I say.

'I'm so sorry,' he begins.

## Arthur

During the night, I am actually conscious of what's happening.

I'm vaguely aware of it as I'm lifted on to the trolley and wheeled through the hospital.

I know what's happening as they turn me onto my front and start to examine my head.

I can feel it.

I know that something terribly serious is happening.

But the strange thing is . . . it doesn't seem to matter at all.

I feel calm. I feel that all this is just a moment in time and in fact I can float away from it.

I have a strange memory of being bathed as a baby. I remember that well. I'd lean back with my head in my mother's hand, and I'd kick my legs, and she'd trickle water on my head, and we'd both feel so happy. I feel like that now. I feel calm.

And then I'm aware again of being in the ward, lying on my front. But I feel that I'm floating back, and upwards. I feel like I'm floating on the ceiling of the ward, looking down at the team of doctors as they toil diligently to save me. I feel very loving towards them, but at the same time I slip away.

I float out of the room. Outside I see Polly sitting on a red chair looking extraordinarily beautiful and extraordinarily sad. So I drift down and I try to kiss her, but it's like she knows I'm going. She's gripping her head, and she's saying: 'Arthur, you bastard, I love you! I love you!'

But I can't stay.

I'm drifting away.

The next thing I know I feel like I'm at the bottom of a pool of dark brown water. It's warm. Around me I sense slimy pond weed and scuttling creatures. And I'm going away from them. I'm swimming up up upwards. I know that at any moment I will break the surface of the water, and I will see the light. I'm about to see eternal life . . .

But then suddenly I realise I don't need eternal life, I need my home. I need Robin and Malory and Ivy. I need Polly. I'm not scared of dying, but I would miss them so much.

And it's like I'm being dragged downwards again.

I feel like I'm now going backwards.

I'm passing over Polly on the red chair.

I'm back in the ward.

I'm hearing the beeping of machines. I'm feeling bandages clamping down hard on my head.

And then, it's fucking awful – because my head really fucking hurts – I'm completely back in my body and I'm waking up.

## Polly

'I'm sorry,' says the doctor, 'that I wasn't able to come and speak to you before. And that we had to keep you out. We were very worried for a while.'

'Right,' I say. 'So . . . is he . . . OK?'

'Well,' says the doctor, 'he's fractured his skull, but we're now confident of his recovery.'

'Right,' I say. I don't think I've breathed since the doctor appeared. 'So . . . is he alive?'

'Very much so,' says the doctor. 'He just burped. Come and see him.'

And I do.

I walk through the door and into the ward where I see Arthur. He's sitting up in bed, and he's got bandages round his head. It's as if he's expecting to see me.

I'm stunned to see him alive.

I sit, very gently, beside him on the bed, and I just look at him. I don't care that there are nurses and doctors present. I touch his cheek with my hand, and I look at him, and I whisper in his ear.

'Arthur,' I say. 'I'm so sorry that I ever got angry with you. I'm sorry that I haven't appreciated you enough. I think that sometimes I was scared and I got distracted from what really matters. But listen, I love you.'

'I'm sorry I didn't appreciate you,' he says. 'You've given me everything, Polly. Everything.'

'I love you,' I say.

'I love you,' he says.

'I love you so much,' I whisper to him. 'I love absolutely everything about you. I love your face. I love your big body. I love your mess. I love your shoes. I love your big pants. I love your love for Arsenal. You are my man, I absolutely love you, and I always will.'

## Arthur

'I know,' I say. 'And I love you.'

## Polly

After that, they wheel Arthur into a general ward.

Apparently he's fine. It doesn't even matter if he lies on his back. He's completely out of danger.

Still, they want to keep him overnight.

Which, actually, I love.

There are a couple of other people in the ward, but they're quiet. And anyway I'm able to screen them out. Actually I shut them out by closing the blue curtains round the bed.

I'm allowed to stay with him. I'm not supposed to get into the bed, obviously, I'm supposed to sit beside him on a chair. But after a while I do think: Fucked if I'm spending the night on a chair. I'm getting in.

So, gently, I climb in beside Arthur in his hospital bed.

He's lying on his side, facing me, and I'm holding him. I'm touching his big muscular back, and I'm smelling the smell of his neck – his normal smell but mixed with the scent of bandages and antiseptic, which, to be honest, I find powerfully arousing.

I feel extraordinarily happy lying there holding him. I feel like . . . one day Arthur and I will grow old and ugly and infirm, but we'll always have this: the comfort of lying in bed, softly touching. It seems enough. It seems so much more than enough.

But after a while it doesn't seem *quite* enough.

Arthur and I have been in a life-or-death situation tonight. That has a powerfully bonding effect on a girl. It must be confessed, I'm acutely aware of every cell of his big body.

And I find I'm tempted to lift up the green hospital smock. I find myself with a powerful desire to kiss his slightly paunchy stomach. In fact I make my way down further. I find I'm kissing his muscular hip. I'm kissing the little line of hair that starts at his navel and makes a pathway downwards. I'm feeling a powerful yearning to continue down that path so I can perform the task that he so urgently desires. I kiss the soft bit of skin at the top of his thigh.

Whereupon, his big hand grips my shoulder.

And he's powerful and manly and very insistent. He pulls me up towards him. And we exchange a kiss in which we both express quite extraordinary depths of love and tenderness and passion.

Then he starts clutching at my clothes.

**Arthur**

I pull her dress above her head. I push down her pants. But then I think I hear the nurse coming, so I pause.

**Polly**

I don't give a fuck about the nurse.

'You OK?' I whisper in his ear.

He says: 'Yes.'

'In which case,' I whisper, 'would you like to make love to me, repeatedly, throughout the night?'

'I always want to make love to you repeatedly throughout the night,' he says. 'But that's before I do it the first time.'

'Well, let's do it the first time,' I whisper. 'And once that's done, do you think you'll be able to do it again?'

'Absolutely,' he says. 'But first I will need eight hours' sleep and some Weetabix.'

'OK,' I say. 'We'll try to arrange that. Let's get the first one under our belt.'

And so it begins.

**Arthur**

I'd love to say that we enjoy epic magazine-style sex, in which we both declare our love, and we both come to the boil many, many times. Although, in my experience, once a lady has managed that once, she doesn't say: '*Yes! Yes! More! Yes!*' She says: 'Sorry . . . don't touch me there!'

Our love-making is not expert. It's not graceful. There are no scented candles. Outside the window there are no violinists softly playing. There are just beeps, and the sound of two men snoring. But for several minutes at least we do press against each other, and we drift into a world of hair and breath and delicious intimacy.

**Em**

The evening at Bodsham is bad enough. The next twelve hours are the most traumatic of my life.

# Saturday

*Learn Love in a Week* – *the online course that will change your life*

**Day Seven:** these days, everyone talks in superlatives – 'It was amazing!' 'It changed my life!' – and this rouses false expectations and makes everything feel fake. Be aware that you can't feel love all the time. You can't feel happy all day. But you may for a few moments. And if you do, the trick is to *notice*, and be thankful. The trouble with most relationships is that there's one person who does some of the jobs, and there's another who does *everything else*, and they're furious. But in most relationships both partners work for the same length of time. And you can't feel love till you stop keeping score. Give your love, I say! Give it blindly: you'll be surprised how much you get in return. But don't *expect* anything. Especially, don't expect your lover to be a soul mate who'll change your life and make you complete. Expect them to be a housemate, who'll occasionally let you fuck them. And if they do, be grateful. You're alive. Be grateful for everything!

**Today's exercise:** at the end of the day write down three moments in which you felt happy or loving. You might like to include things people said or pictures.

**Today's challenge:** keep this going, every day, for the rest of your life. You'll start to notice the moments of happiness, you'll start to have more of them. You might have a notebook and you might fill in one page a day. When you're very, very old, this will be the thing that you most treasure. Along with your love, of course, which will have continued to grow, like a big old tree.

**Em**

First of all, I am left at James Hammond's party on my own.

Yes. Fine. At first I am able to entertain the crowd with an inside exclusive as to why Hammond's balls got kicked. But I'm only able to sustain that for a couple of hours.

By which time my audience has thinned out.

Polly has not reappeared. Dan has disappeared, probably for ever. Greta was here for a while, but even she's fucked off.

Come 2 a.m. I discover that I'm alone. Worse . . . I find that I'm drunk, I'm alone, and I'm in charge of a phone.

I try to call Polly.

Her phone is switched off.

I try to call Arthur.

No bloody answer.

I call Malcolm. Fortunately he picks up.

'Em!' he says. 'It's so good to hear your voice What's going on?

So I treat him to a very comprehensive account. I tell him about the kicking. I tell him about the disappearance of Arthur and Polly. I tell him how I refused Dan, saying: 'I want someone who'll throw himself out of a plane for me.'

Which has a fatal result.

**Polly**

In the morning, Arthur and I return home on the train.

I love a train ride anyway, and this one is spectacular. We see passing hillsides. We see canals. Throughout we hold hands like young lovers who can't believe they've got each other.

## Arthur

I get good news on the train.

I turn on my phone and see I was sent three texts yesterday evening. They're all from Sally Winklehorn at RSJ.

The first says: 'I've so far had THREE offers on the book. The highest . . .'

I show it to Polly. She says: 'Oh my God! How much do you think they're offering?'

I think about that. My good fortune seems to be rising and rising like a balloon on a hot day. 'I think the highest is going to be pretty high,' I say. 'Six figures maybe.'

'Six figures?' says Polly.

'More than a hundred grand.'

'Well, let's see, shall we?' says Polly, who's never one to savour anticipation.

I click on to the next text. 'Sorry. Got cut off,' it says. 'Highest offer is 5K.'

We both laugh.

The third text says: 'I'm pushing for two-book deal. Key question . . . Are you planning a sequel to *Looking For Lost Magic*?'

I chuckle at that. I love the idea of telling Polly I'm going to write a sequel to *Looking For Lost Magic*. I'd rather like to write an Arthurian trilogy. But suddenly all that historical romance seems a bit cerebral and a bit obvious. Anyone can see the magic of a big-breasted damsel who's rising from a stream in a wet dress. Capturing the magic in one who's standing by the dishwasher

– that seems a bit harder. But actually I'm starting to see how it could be done. That's my challenge, I think. I shall write about knights no more. My ambition, now, is to become one. I shall be Sir Arthur, Knight of Suburbia.

## Em

It's 9.30 in the morning when I get the first call.

It interrupts me at a bad moment actually. I'm in the dining room of Bodsham Abbey. (Pretty outrageous. It's in the converted chapel.) I'm eating fruit salad and talking to Lydia Boulter who's the editor of the *Telegraph* magazine (the mag I'd most like to work for). I've just told her I'm newly on the market, and I'm waiting for her to rise to the bait.

When Malcolm calls.

Despite myself, my heart flutters somewhat to see his name. I can't help it.

'I can't really speak now,' I say. I'm speaking quietly while walking away from the table. 'I need to work.'

'They'll put that on your tombstone,' he says. 'Here lies Em. She could have had a life, but she had to work . . . Listen, I believe your phone does video.'

'Er . . . yes,' I say.

'Well, you need to swap to video function,' he says. 'So you can see where I am.'

'Why?' I ask. 'Where are you?'

He says: 'Swindon Aerodrome.'

I say: 'Why?'

He says: 'I'm about to throw myself out of a plane for you.'

Oh, fuck.

The news makes me feel a bit breathless and faint.

'Er . . .' I say. 'Gosh! Erm . . .' I swallow. Should I say something? 'I know I said I wanted a man who'll throw himself out of a plane for me,' I say. 'I didn't mean it literally.'

'I know that!' he says. 'But listen, I just think you've been undervalued by that commitment-phobic bastard of a man, and you need to know that you deserve to have someone throw himself out of a plane, on your behalf.'

'Er . . . thank you,' I squeak. I'm feeling a bit panicky. 'But listen . . .' How do I put this? 'Malcolm, I know we spent a night together, and it was actually very nice. But . . . I'm not sure that I'm ready to . . . accept your hand in marriage.'

'Oh!' says Malcolm. 'I know that! I'm not saying that I'll be the only man to throw himself out of a plane for you. We could talk about this online, and we could probably get thousands of men who'll throw themselves out of a plane for you. It could be a movement. "Em," they'll say, "I love you!" And they'll leap like penguins off a cliff. I know I won't be the only one to do it. But I want to be the first. Because I feckin' love you. You are beautiful, you are funny, you are sexy, you are magical, you are interesting, you are passionate. I would give a year of my life to spend the night with you again!'

I say nothing. A waiter is looking at me with a disapproving expression.

'Listen,' says Malcom. 'Will you swap to video phone, so I can show you what's going on?'

'Yes,' I say.

And I try to, but I lose the connection.

## Arthur

Something significant occurs as we arrive home.

As I'm rummaging in my pockets for the front-door keys, Polly points at a black bin bag by the door. She says: 'Can you quickly chuck that in the bin?'

And – I must confess – I bridle slightly. I realise I could obediently put the bag in the bin. But I'd feel like a pussy. This is the trouble, I realise, for the man trying to be loving: there are no role models. Cowboys don't take out bins. You only see a bin in a cop film if a car is smashing into it. Detectives never have women in their lives at all, to avoid situations like this.

But, it occurs to me, knights do.

Knights take the whole business of serving their ladies very seriously.

'Could you quickly sort that out?' says Polly again.

And I do as any knight would, in the circumstances. I move with the speed of a fencer. Quickly, silently, and with a certain grace, I sort out the bin.

By which point Polly has now found her keys and we go in.

## Em

It's all unbelievably unlucky.

An hour passes, during which time I try to call Malcolm several times. No answer.

By the time he calls again, I'm on the train. I'm heading for Polly and Arthur's house, which is, of course, not far from Malcolm's.

Suddenly his name appears, and the little Video Phone icon is buzzing.

I take the phone out into the passageway. I press the button, and immediately I see him.

I can see a little shaving cut on his neck. But his face still looks lovely. He's also dressed in strange sky-diving clothes – a shiny suit and a sort of helmet.

'Em!' he bellows. He's shouting over the sound of an engine. 'We're in the plane!'

'Show me the plane,' I say.

Malcolm wields the camera. It doesn't look like a proper plane.

'That is the plane,' he announces. 'And now I'll show you the man to whom I will be attached. He's called Bryan Daniel.'

Malcolm turns the phone on a man sitting next to him. He has a shaved head and a sunburned face. He's wearing a sky-diving suit but he still looks like the sort of man you'd see down the pub selling pirate DVDs. He doesn't look trustworthy.

'Hello,' says Bryan Daniel.

'Hello,' I shriek. 'I feel very nervous about this.'

Malcolm puts himself on camera again.

'You're nervous!' he says. 'I'm shitting myself. I'm about to throw myself out of a plane at ten thousand feet.'

I imagine what that would be like, falling from ten thousand feet. I feel sick.

'You OK?' yells Malcolm.

'Yes. It's just . . . the thought of falling from that height . . . I get vertigo looking out of a window.'

'I get vertigo standing on a stool.'

'What?!' I say. 'But . . . you're about to throw yourself out of a plane!'

'I know!' says Malcolm. 'But I think you get out of life what you put in!'

'But . . .' I just can't quite see how to put this. 'Malcolm,' I say. 'What happens if you die?'

Malcolm grins.

'Then . . . you must tell Polly she's lovely. Tell Arthur he's in charge of the waterborne procession. And I want you to know, I died happy 'cos I died for you.'

That'd be my luck. To find a man who proves himself capable of commitment just moments before killing himself.

'And . . .' Malcolm continues '. . . I bequeath to you the *Learn Love in a Week* online course, which, I'm happy to say – as a result of the publicity you have given it – has just reached one hundred thousand subscribers.'

'What?' I say. I'm completely confused by that. '*Learn Love* is yours?!'

'Of course it is!' says Malcolm. 'Surely you knew!'

'But . . .' I say. 'If you've had one hundred thousand subscribers in just a few weeks, it . . . it could be worth a fortune!'

'I make nothing from it!' says Malcolm cheerfully.

'But you could!' I say. 'You could have adverts. You could be minted from this!'

'I know!' says Malcolm. 'But I've already paid for my barge!'

'Yes . . . But you could get things that are more valuable than a barge!'

'How could *anything* be more valuable than my barge?' says Malcolm. 'And anyway . . . the Secret of Life is gratitude, and it's easier to be grateful if you're poor.'

Someone is talking offscreen.

'Oh,' says Malcolm. 'Bryan is here. He says it's time for us to put on the harness.'

'WAIT!!!' I shout. Malcolm is a freak, certainly. But he's a very sweet one. He's also potentially a very rich one. I DON'T want to lose him. 'Put Bryan back on,' I shout.

Malcolm turns the phone round.

'Bryan!!' I shout. 'Is this safe?'

'Well, Malcolm will be tied to my front with this harness,' says Bryan. 'On my back is this parachute. There's a one in a million chance that it will fail to open.'

'And if it doesn't?' I say.

'Then we have two minutes before we hit the ground at terminal velocity. Plenty of time for us to make use of . . .' and now he pats another package on his shoulders '. . . the second parachute.'

'And what if *that* doesn't open?' I say.

'Then we're fucked,' says Bryan. 'Although there is still a chance we can be saved by Speedo here.'

'Who's Speedo?'

The camera turns to a third man. He is a skinny lunatic with mad dark hair and glasses.

'Speedo will be falling beside us,' says Bryan. 'Filming the whole thing.'

And at that moment I lose the connection.

## Polly

The strange thing is . . . though we've arrived home, it takes us a while to find the kids.

They're not downstairs. They're not upstairs in the bedroom.

Finally we find them out in the garden. They're all sitting in the shed with Cynthia. *And my mum!* They all seem happy. They seem to be having a picnic.

'So,' Cynthia is saying, 'when-you-COME-at-half-term-I-thought-we-could-ALL-go-to-Alton-Towers.'

'But what rides do they have?' Malory is asking.

At this point, Cynthia notices us. 'Hello!' she shouts. 'We're-having-our-breakfast-out-here. We're-having-bacon-sandwiches-EXCUSE-ME-I'm-NOT-saying-that's-ALL-they've-had-We've-PANCAKES-We've-had-YOGHURTS . . .'

Malory and Robin turn to us. 'Hi!' says Robin.

Then they turn back. 'But, Gran,' Malory is saying, 'what rides do they have?'

The kids are basically paying us no attention. It's extraordinary. Recently I've been suffering more and more guilt as to whether we're good parents. And in the last twenty-four hours, we've been about as unreliable as it's possible to be. Arthur has had a near-death experience, and now has a bandage round his head. We've both committed a form of adultery.

*The kids seem fine!!*

I'm not saying this is a model of how I intend to parent from now on. But it's good to know that, even if everything goes completely wrong, they'll manage.

**Em**

I'm feverishly redialling, trying to get Malcolm back.

After a few minutes, he suddenly answers.

His face fills the screen.

He's strapped to the front of Bryan Daniel.

'We're now at ten thousand feet,' he announces.

I feel dizzy.

Malcolm holds the phone to the window. I can see a patchwork of fields which then disappear underneath a thin veneer of cloud.

'Gentlemen!' says the speccy freak, Speedo. Malcolm turns the phone on him. 'It is time for us to get out of here.'

Speedo opens the door of the plane. It makes a worrying clank as it opens, and after that it's hard to hear much because the wind is roaring in.

Malcolm turns the camera to the open side of the plane. Now we're not looking through the window. We're just looking at a ten-thousand-foot-drop.

It's ten times more terrifying. The roaring of the wind is deafening.

The phone turns back to Malcolm's face.

'OK,' he informs me, shouting into the camera, 'I'm passing this to Speedo. From now on he's going to be filming.'

Bryan takes charge. 'Right, Malcolm,' he says, 'it's time for us to make sure that our harnesses are properly linked.' He still looks like a bloke down the pub, but there's an air of authority about him now. I can see he's done this hundreds of times before. He goes through a system of patting down all the straps and the parachute. Linked together, the two men shuffle towards the hideous gaping hole of the open door. Progress is awkward since they're tied facing each other. They are moving with their legs wide apart like two frogs. Malcolm has lost his normal grin. He looks pale. Terrified.

I'm scared just watching.

'Are you ready?' says Bryan.

Malcolm doesn't answer. He just nods. Suddenly he turns into the lens of the camera Speedo is holding. 'Em,' he shouts, 'I love you.'

In frame, Malcolm and Bryan shuffle towards the yawning void. Then there's a really sickening moment. The wind becomes deafening as the phone is held outside the plane directed on Malcolm's face.

He looks pale. He looks terrified. He mouths: 'I love you.'

Then suddenly Bryan and he seem both to stumble, and they *fall out*.

At this point Speedo shouts something that doesn't sound at all professional. He shouts: 'Banzaiiiiiiii!!'

And he jumps.

It feels like he's lost control for a moment. There's the awful rushing sound of the wind, and then Speedo seems to remember his job. He points the camera back at the plane which suddenly *retreats* into the sky at an alarming pace.

The camera is shaking ferociously. It's like Speedo's forgotten what he's doing in his panic/excitement. Then he gets the camera under control. It's still shaking, but Speedo now trains the lens on to Malcolm and Bryan, who are tiny figures shooting through the terrifying cloud layer.

Then the camera is back on Speedo for a moment. Who's freefalling. He manages to do the thumbs-up sign which is so loved by mentalists all the world over.

Then he's through the cloud layer himself. Then he turns the camera again and reveals that, amazingly, he's managed to *get close* to the others. How do you catch up with someone in mid-air? That's what he's done. The shot is extremely shaky, but it's clear . . .

There, plunging through space, are Malcolm and Bryan. Their clothes are being lashed by the wind and their features are flattened by the blast. Speedo goes right in for a close up. Malcolm is clearly absolutely terrified, but he manages to do a mad grin to the camera. The effect is made very odd because he's wearing goggles and his face is being pummelled by the wind.

Then . . . close up on Bryan, who also does the mad thumbs up. Then he indicates 1 2 3 with his fingers to Speedo. And both of them pull their parachute cords. Bryan Daniel seems to open his parachute fractionally earlier. Suddenly he and Malcolm are yanked out of the top of the frame. Then the roaring of the wind disappears, as if it's been silenced by a giant door. Speedo's parachute now appears to be open.

Which is why I can hear it, really clearly, as Speedo suddenly shouts something that sounds even less professional. He shouts: '*Fucking shitting hell!*'

The agonising thing is, I can't see what the hell is going on.

I hear Speedo shouting: '*Don't worry! Don't worry! I'm here!*'

At this point, the camera is clearly dropped. It seems to be spinning through the air. I see ground then sky then ground then sky then ground . . .

Tantalisingly, there is a brief moment when it settles and you can just see two parachutes in the sky but it happens so fast and you can't see if there are figures attached to the parachutes, and what's happening to them.

About ten seconds after that, the phone smashes into the field. Where the filming stops.

**Arthur**

We're all now in the kitchen. Everyone except Polly and her mum. They're out in the garden having some kind of reunion. I've noticed a few hugs.

Finally Malory says: 'By the way, Dad. Why have you got a bandage round your head?'

To which I say: 'Thank you for asking, Malory. Let me tell you.'

At which point Mrs Thompson starts barking, and we realise someone's at the door.

Robin answers it.

Em bursts through the door in floods of tears.

'Oh my God!' she announces. 'Malcolm has just thrown himself out of a plane for me! And I think he might have *died*!'

Now my falling off a wall doesn't seem such a cracking anecdote. I've lost the floor.

'What?!' says everyone.

Even Polly and her mum come in from the garden. 'What happened?' says Polly.

Em tells the whole story.

At the end, Malory says: 'But WAIT!! I don't understand. Does Malcolm love you?'

'Yes,' says Em. 'I think he does.'

'But,' says Robin, 'do you love him?'

'I'm not sure,' says Em. 'But he's certainly got my attention.'

At which point there's silence.

Then Em bursts into tears.

'But the trouble is, I feel sure he's dead,' she sobs. 'You could hear them falling from that plane, and something had gone very, very wrong. They were shouting. OK, I understand that they lost the phone, but why didn't they try to call it and pick it up? And why didn't Malcolm call me? Ever since I've been trying to call the Skydiving School. That's shut! I called the hospital. I called the police. I even called an aunt who lives near Mill Hill. She says she did see an ambulance.'

Now Em just stands in the middle of the living room, weeping. Polly hugs her.

'Where do you think he is?' she whimpers.

Whereupon Malory says: 'Hang on a second! What day is it today?'

'It's Saturday,' says Cynthia.

'But,' says Malory. 'Saturday is the day that Malcolm has invited everyone to go to the Springfield Park Community Fun Day where he's in charge of the waterborne procession. Don't you grown-ups listen to ANYTHING?'

'But don't you see,' says Em, 'he's not going to be there, if he's dead.'

'What is dead?' says Ivy.

'It's when you fall from a plane,' says Malory, 'and you fall a long, long, long, long way. And you get squashed.'

'We don't know that's happened!' says Polly.

'We don't know anything!' I say.

'But how are we going to find out?' says Em.

'Well, it all comes to the same thing,' says Robin, taking charge importantly like he's a detective who's just solved the case. 'We *have* to go to the Springfield Park Community Fun Day.'

'Well, obviously we're going to do that,' says Polly, who seems to resent the junior detective taking control.

'I shan't go,' says her mum. 'Cynthia and I are going to have lunch so we can talk weddings.'

'But the rest of us need to go to Springfield Park,' says Polly.

'How are we going to get there?' says Malory.

'I suggest,' pronounces Robin, 'we take bikes.'

Polly hates bikes.

'I say bikes as well,' says Malory.

'And so do I,' says Ivy. She can't even cycle. But she's swept along by the little Arab Spring that's occurring as everyone rises up against Polly's rule.

'But Daddy's hurt his head,' says Polly, beginning the fight back.

'I can cycle fine,' I say.

'I don't want to go on bikes,' says Polly.

At which point Malory has one of her fierce outbursts of temper. 'Mum,' she pronounces, 'you are *not* in control of us all the time and we're going to do what we want.'

## Polly

I look at Malory, who's standing up to me like a little Che Guevara. Normally I'd chase her into the jungle and order her execution. But I'm noticing that everyone is basically saying the same thing to me over and over again – relax, let go – and I feel so extraordinarily loving to my little family, I'm happy to do what they want.

So in the end Arthur goes on his bike. He's got Ivy on the child seat.

Malory goes on her bike.

Robin goes on his bike.

## Em

And Polly and I take the car.

## Arthur

The atmosphere is very strange. Everyone is cheerful, but secretly I'm feeling a bit teary.

The day before, I had a near-death experience. Yes. I know I survived. But I feel that the good luck is about to run out. I'm hoping it doesn't. Obviously we're all hoping that we're going to get to the Springfield Park Community Fun Day, and see Malcolm.

But I have a strong feeling Malcolm's dead.

As far as I'm concerned, we're going to the Community Fun

Day as a sort of homage. I'm still reeling from the news that *Learn Love in a Week* was his. How come I never suspected? How come I never treated Malcolm with the respect he so clearly deserves?

Anyway, I'm acutely aware that my strange mad friend has profoundly shifted the way I think and feel. And I'm intensely aware of his final tip: You can't feel happy all the time, but if you are for a few moments, the trick is to notice.

And actually, at the fete, that's what happens.

## Polly
Initially we're looking for Malcolm. We're worrying about him, of course we are. But there are moments when we're just having fun.

I love a fete anyway, and at this one there's everything you'd want to see.

There are children with their faces painted.

There's a bouncy castle.

There's cake, there's coffee, there's cider.

There's a madman who shouldn't have a microphone, but he does.

There are books piled high, for sale at twenty pence each.

There's a donkey.

There's a steam-powered carousel, and people on swings are screaming with excitement as they fly right out over the canal.

But the best moment of the Fun Day is the arrival of Malcolm.

## Em
The first craft visible, in the Springfield Park Community Fun Day waterborne procession, is a Dutch barge. It's one of those

flat ones. On it, there's a platform. An informal space, if you will, for a moment of community theatre. In fact, there's a team of drummers.

Now, yes, it later emerges that most of those drummers are on parole. (The drumming workshop is part of some scheme.) But they're not committing any crimes now, and they're making a tremendous sound that gets everyone's attention.

Then there are four kayaks.

And behind the kayaks, standing at the prow of his rather beautiful new barge, is Malcolm.

**Arthur**

Malcolm is beaming at the world with this extraordinary, simple-minded pride. He looks like a farmer who's just won first prize for growing the biggest marrow.

**Em**

I suddenly feel furious. I say: 'Malcolm!? Where the hell have you been?'

He's totally unfazed. He says, 'I've been on the barge! I told you I was getting it today.'

He doesn't seem to realise what he's done.

'Malcolm!' I say. 'I last spoke to you on the phone, and you were plunging towards the earth, apparently about to die. Your phone kept communicating with me until it hit the ground.'

'That's amazing!' he says.

'Well,' I'm actually spluttering, 'what the hell happened?'

'Oh,' says Malcolm evenly, 'the first parachute didn't open properly.'

'What?!' I shout.

'The straps were all twisted,' says Malcolm. 'So we had to get it out of the way before we could open the second one.'

'What?!' I shout. My whole reality seems to be fracturing. 'So what happened?'

'Oh!' he says. 'Speedo had to help us out, and it was fine.'

While he's saying this, Malcolm continues to float very, very slowly up the canal. He seems to have no idea how disorientating it might be to have a phone call with a person who declares their love, before getting lost several thousand feet above the earth.

'But . . .' I say. 'Why didn't you find your phone? Why did you just leave it in a field?'

'Well,' says Malcolm, 'afterwards I didn't fuck about looking for a phone. I landed. I thanked the Lord. Then I drank about half a gallon of cider. And then I came here to do my maiden voyage.'

Malcolm stares at Em with love.

'But it's amazing that you've come,' he says. 'If I stop, would you like to come aboard?'

'You'll lose touch with the others,' I say.

'But it's not a race,' says Malcolm, 'it's a procession. And I think you should join.'

## Polly

Malcolm pulls over, and we climb aboard, and we all ride up the canal on his new barge. I feel incredibly happy. I look at Robin who's proudly taking a turn on the wheel. I look at Ivy and Malory, who are deep in conversation with their dad. They're all smiling. I look at my kind, warm, handsome husband, and I know that I love him. And I look at the fete. I look at all the boats on the water, and I think how right Malcolm is. It's not a race. It's a procession. And it's a privilege. It's a big heartbreaking joy just to be here.

There is only One Thing for it:

Complete Physical Union!

# Acknowledgements

I do actually think you can learn love in a week. You could probably learn it, in an instant, if the circumstances are right. But writing a book on the subject – that'll take considerably longer. During the writing of this one, I've been through three agents – four if you include Simon Trewin, who gave me an hour and a half, and two great notes. Thank you to him. Thank you Tiff Loehnis. Thank you Will Francis. But thank you, especially, to Lizzy Kremer at David Higham, who's been wise and personal, and superbly passionate about this book. You're a force of nature, Lizzy, and I thank you. It was Juliet Annan who introduced me to Lizzy. Thank you Dame Annan! It was Lizzy who introduced me to my much-adored editor, Gillian Holmes. Gillian has brought many things to the project – lunch, some marvellously indiscreet gossip – but above all she's brought an injection of fun that infused the final drafts. Thank you Gillian! Thanks to all at Arrow, especially Laurence, Najma, Selina. In fact it's extraordinary how many people have helped along the way. Piers and Becky leant me their flat. Thank you, darlings! I'm indebted to my first readers: the ladies of The Film Club. Ella, Hannah, Jo, I kiss your shapely feet! I also thank your children – George, Dexter, Merle, Artie, Theo, Raffi, Saul – who contributed to a *hilarious* day of Klimt-drawing. My only sadness is we couldn't get them all in. (Who did the Klimt as a cupboard?) I'm indebted to Tony Grounds ('the best

TV writer of his generation') for so many things, but particularly the archetypal Tony piece of advice: 'Andrew, keep calm, and make sure everyone loves you'. I'm always grateful to Gary Reich, who bought an option on this – beware: it's about to expire! – and who introduced me to Arabella McGuigan, who expertly developed a TV script. Thank you Arabella, thank you Lord Reich! Thank you to the ladies at *Sunday Times Style* who looked after me magnificently when I was their columnist, especially Queen of Style Tiffanie Darke, and the various Deputy Queens, Camilla Long , Laurel Ives, and Kathy Brewis. Some of the material started as columns, which keen *Style* readers might spot. Thank you Eleanor Mills! Thank you to the ladies from *Red, Glamour, Elle, Fabulous, Brides, You, Times 2, Telegraph Magazine, Guardian Weekend*, you e-mail me such brilliant questions: eg 'What did you want before you fell in love? What did you get?' Please e-mail more. About time I wrote some new features. Thank you to the various kind people who've had me on their TV and radio shows, but especially Jenni Murray, Jane Garvey, Fred MacAulay, Kay Adams, Stephen Nolan and Vanessa Feltz. Several friends have particularly inspired or encouraged my writing. Thank you especially Tom Guard, Glasgow Jimmy, Juliet Cowan, Nick Rowe, Tree Sheriff, Sophie Stewart, David Walliams, and James Dreyfus. Thanks to Tim and Trisha. Thanks to my mum. Thank you to Livy, who's offered so many intangible things that have affected the writing – marriage, love – plus some excellent notes. Thank you to my girls, Grace, Cassady, and Iris. It was Cassady who made up the story about the faecal gentleman, whose ambition was 'to go back to the bottom what he came from.' That still makes me chuckle. But I thank all three girls, for saying so many funny things, but also for keeping my spirits up, by laughing, dancing, and by summoning me to so many many games of Barbies. Thank you to the people who helped the *Love Rules* comedy show – particularly Richard Bucknall and Pete Graham

– and all the ones who came, especially Morag in the second row: 'How long have you been with your husband?' '48 years.' 'Tell us one thing he does that's good.' 'He always makes me tea every morning.' 'Tell us one thing that's a bit annoying.' 'He *never* puts sugar in.' And thank you to you, for reading. If you've enjoyed the book, do tell someone else. We could start a love movement, one reader at a time!

# Only One Thing For It: Complete Physical Union